NEW ALCATRAZ

VOLUME III

LOSS PARADOX

WRITTEN BY
GRANT PIES

This book is a work of fiction. Names, characters, businesses, organizations, places, events, and incidents either are of the product of the author's imagination or are used fictitiously. Any resemblance to actual persons, living or dead, events, or locales is entirely coincidental.

"There can never be a man so lost as one who is lost in the vast and intricate corridors of his own lonely mind, where none may reach him and none may save."

Isaac Asimov

CHAPTER 1

Vesa hadn't turned away from Powell's body since he placed his hand on the mind transfer device. His body kept breathing, his chest heaving sporadically up and down. His eyelids rapidly squeezed shut and then relaxed, almost pulsing. Aside from these slight signs of life, he seemed dead. Slumped against the wall, his head toppled into his chest.

Where did you go? Vesa wondered. The agents on the other side of the door still screamed for their surrender, ordering her to open the door to the armory. For a brief moment, Vesa thought Powell's plan might work. She let a ray of hope seep into her brain and thought maybe the Ministry of Science would accept Powell's mindless body as a fair trade for her brother. Maybe they wouldn't require her to turn over the mind transfer device after all. Maybe things would work out. *Maybe I will see Cooper again,* she thought.

Then, just as the first optimistic thought in a long time formed in Vesa's mind, Powell's eyes jolted open, like a man who had overslept and missed an important appointment. His wide eyes darted around the room, and now Vesa reconsidered turning in Powell, the device, or both.

Sighing, Vesa said, "It didn't work." She kneeled down to look into Powell's eyes. "I'm sorry, but the machine didn't work." Holding her black pistol in one hand, she placed her other hand on Powell's shoulder.

Powell jerked his body away from Vesa. "My son?" he said. "Where is my son?" His head swiveled around to take in his surroundings, of which there were very few. The walls, floor, and ceiling were all the same gray cement. A single red light on the ceiling spun around, casting its light on the weaponry that hung on the walls. The floor had a thin layer of dust and grit covering it. "Who are *you*?" he asked. "Where did you come from?"

"It's me, Vesa." She lifted her hand from his shoulder to brush his hair from his forehead, but he jerked back and gripped Vesa's wrist. Not too tightly, just tight enough to let her know he didn't want to be touched. He pressed his back against the hard cement wall, like he wanted to sink into the surface and escape.

"I don't know you," Powell said with conviction, contorting his face at the sound of his voice. He rubbed his throat as if he could adjust the way his voice sounded. He pushed his hand on the cement floor and rose to his feet, and, for the first time, he noticed that his leg had a bullet lodged in it. He winced at the sudden realization of pain.

"I have to leave. I have to get back to my son." He shook his head and his eyes finally came into focus. "My son … I have to be there before he … before…" He let out a deep sigh from far down in his lungs and clenched his eyelids closed. He placed a hand on his lower stomach, feeling for a wound that wasn't there, then checked to see if his hand was covered in blood. It wasn't. "What is going on?" he asked and patted his stomach again. "I'm healed."

"The device, it didn't work." Vesa shook her head. "I have to turn you in. I wish there was another way, but Cooper … he's my brother. I have to get him back. I'm afraid your plan didn't work, Powell."

"Powell? Who's Powell?" the man in front of her said, twisting his face into a confused expression that Vesa had never seen Powell make before.

"You," Vesa said. "You're Powell!" Now Vesa felt her own face twisting and squinting into her own confused expression.

Shaking his head, the man said, "I'm Ransom. And I need to get the hell out of here." He wrapped his hands around his head, massaging his scalp and immediately tugging at his hair. "My hair?" he mumbled to himself. "Who cut my hair?"

Vesa cocked her head to the side. She looked at the person in front of her, and then she looked down at the device that sat on the floor. The bars were still illuminated, indicating a full charge.

"You're not Powell?" she asked to confirm her suspicions. "You're not Powell."

"No, goddammit! Now get out of my way!"

Vesa still held onto the gun. She gripped it tightly and walked backwards towards the door. Keeping her eyes on this new person who stood in front of her, she pounded the thick metal barrier with her fist. The booming sound of her banging was barely noticeable over the sounds of the alarms and shouting agents on the other side of the door.

"We're coming out!" she shouted to whoever was outside the armory. "We're unarmed. We will fully surrender."

The banging and threatening orders on the other side of the door subsided into muffled whispers and chatter on their radios. Moving swiftly, Vesa grabbed the device from the ground. It emanated a small amount of heat from whatever chips and processors moved and vibrated inside.

She wrapped it in cloth, stuffed it in the messenger bag they'd brought it in, and slid the bag deep into the air vent. She placed the cover back on the vent, and turned the screws back in with her fingers, her hands shaking the entire time. She kept one hand gripped around the pistol, and one eye focused on this person who was trapped inside Powell's body.

It worked! she thought. *I don't know how but it worked!* For a brief moment, she felt bad for Powell's body, and whoever's mind inhabited it. She knew what she was turning him over to. She knew what would happen. Her plan didn't extend beyond this, but she hoped that she would see Powell, the *real* Powell, again. Quickly, she shut that thought out of her mind. She knew it wasn't a possibility.

Once the metal grate was back on the vent, she stood to face the man in Powell's body.

"What'd you say your name was?" she asked.

"I told you, I'm Ransom," the man said, finally realizing that he was not in his own body. He looked down at the knife wound that ran across his chest.

"Ransom?" Vesa repeated to make sure she heard the man correctly. *What kind of name is Ransom?* The man in Powell's body nodded. "Well, *Ransom*, I don't know how you got yourself into this, but I am sorry for what I am about to do."

"I don't understand," Ransom said and shook his head. His voice was thick and his jaw clenched tight. "Gray. Aurora."

"I don't have time to explain. Just remember, I am sorry."

With her final words Vesa raised her pistol up in the air and brought it down hard on Ransom's head. He collapsed into a limp pile on the floor, a small gash opening up on his forehead. She turned and placed her hand on the armory door.

"I'm coming out!" she yelled. "Don't shoot!"

Vesa pulled the thick metal door open to reveal a line of agents in armored suits, holding high-powered rifles all trained on her. The red laser pointers attached to the rifles dotted Vesa's body, like some sort of electronic disease.

Standing as still as possible, she held her hands over her head. "The man in there is unconscious," she said.

By now, the alarms had stopped screaming and the red emergency lights had faded, replaced by the soft white glow of the LED lights overhead. Under the flashing red lights, Vesa felt more concealed, but now she stood exposed and illuminated.

"I need to speak to whoever is in charge."

CHAPTER 2

5280
NEW ALCATRAZ

This New Alcatraz, at whatever point in time *this* was, was different than the one I remembered. Different than the New Alcatraz in the year 5065, though it still retained some sense of familiarity. The white sun still hung in the sky. Vultures still circled overhead. There was snow on the ground, and where the old gusts of wind used to bring a welcomed breeze that cooled me down, now they only brought frigid air that drilled into my bones.

I lay on the ground, the cold snow numbing my bleeding body. After only a few minutes, I could no longer feel the stab wound in my stomach, my dislocated knee, beaten face, and cracked ribs. Or should I say Ransom's stabbed stomach. Ransom's damaged knee and beaten face.

The pain from my wounds slowly faded away, along with the rest of the feeling in my body. I welcomed the numbness, and I only wished that it could extend to my brain, and that for just a moment I could go back to the present. Back to my body.

Or maybe I could even go to a time before I got pulled into this mess. Before the Golden Dawn and the mind transfer device. Even before New Alcatraz or my life as an ARC attorney. Before all of that. Before my adult life even. Before St. Anthony's Orphanage. Before my father died. I wished I could go back to a time before things changed forever. Just reset. Like pressing a button and giving me a new life. But for now, without such a reset button, I would just settle for going back to my cramped underground apartment back in Phoenix. Anything was better than a bleeding stomach in New Alcatraz.

Eventually, behind my closed eyelids, I sensed the sky grow darker and the air grow colder. Perhaps a cloud drifted in front of the sun for a brief moment. I pulled my eyelids back until they were barely squinting open to find a cloudless sky. My supposed friend loomed over me, blocking out the sun's warming rays. My body sat in a dark, hulking, person-sized shadow. I could only see a silhouette of his shoulders and arms bulging out from his body.

"You're blocking the sun," I mumbled. He knelt down and pulled my clothing up to examine the stab wound. "Who are you?" I asked. My voice was still foreign to me, but even without being familiar with the voice, I knew it was the voice of a dying man. Weak and fading.

"Ash," the man answered. "What happened to you, Ransom? You're pale."

"Ash," I said. "I don't know who Ransom is … or was, but I'm not him. And I'm pale because all of my blood is spilling out of my stomach." I cringed and winced each time Ash moved my clothing around to check for more injuries. Ash's large hands did not have the benefit of being gentle.

"Not him?" Ash said, moving his body so he no longer blocked the warm sun. I basked in its warmth for a moment before answering and letting the coldness seep back into my body.

"Look, I don't expect you to understand … hell, I don't really understand all of this, but just trust me when I say I am not the person you call Ransom. My name is Powell." I tried to sit up, but the numbness from the cold ground fell away, and it felt as if someone was ripping my stomach opened. Clawing and gnashing at my bare skin.

I slammed back down to the hard ground, cracking the back of my head against the frozen earth. The snow around me had already become pink with my blood, crawling and seeping through it.

"It doesn't matter much, Ash, cuz both Ransom and I are dying out here. *My* mind. *His* body. We are both pretty much goners." The sky overhead was clear and blue. It was probably one of the nicest days that ever existed in New Alcatraz. The noises from the birds overhead were soothing, even though they circled and waited to pick at my bones, or Ransom's bones, when I was gone.

"I have medicines," Ash blurted out and held out the bag he had slung over his body. "I got 'em for Gray. After you and Merit got separated from me, I broke free from those monsters down there. I was lost, but I found the blue line again. It led to medicine ... at least I think it did." Ash dropped the bag into the pink snow next to me.

Rolling over onto my side and pulling the bag open, I said, "Well, why didn't you say so earlier?" Inside were rolls of gauze, bandages, vials, syringes, pills, and small sheets of medicine designed to dissolve on the tongue.

"I just don't know what any of these things are, Ransom."

"Powell," I corrected Ash. "I might know what they are."

The first thing I grabbed was a kit containing gauze and powder that coagulated blood. I pulled my shirt up to assess the wound, and revealed the red, dirty skin with blood washing across my stomach at a steady pace. Ripping the package of clotting powder open with my teeth, I dumped the entire packet onto the wound. On contact, it bubbled and turned white, letting out a low, hissing sound as the powder worked its way deep into my wound. It burned and tickled at the same time. Ash cringed in sympathy and settled into the snow beside me. I pressed a strip of gauze over my stomach and held it there for several minutes.

"Are they coming up here?" I asked through clenched teeth. Now that I realized I might not die immediately, my thoughts turned back to the hyenas, or cannibals, or whatever those things were that chased after us under Buckley Air Force Base.

"I don't know," Ash said and turned to look at the door that led into the underground area. "They haven't come up yet. Those guys were pretty frail. I threw a huge rock on top of the door."

I wrapped medical tape around my body to hold the gauze in place, then dug around in Ash's medical bag some more. Most of the stuff wasn't labeled, or whatever labels the medicines did have were simply strings of numbers, letters, or random barcodes. Serial numbers used to identify whatever concoctions Wayfield and the Ministry had cooked up underground.

I assumed most of the medicines used in these underground bases the Ministry had scattered over the country were only in their trial phase. They were experimental, or at least not available to the general public. But I had to take the risk.

"So, do you have a home or something around here? Does Ransom live around here? Are you guys prisoners or something?"

"Prisoners? Why would we be prisoners?"

"What year is it?" I asked and ignored his confusion.

"Year?"

"Dammit, Ash, this is gonna take a long fucking time if you just repeat my questions back to me. Yes, year! What year is it?"

"I — I don't know what that means." Ash was hesitant to answer incorrectly again. My vision blurred for a brief moment. Inside the medical bag, I found a bottle of painkillers. I popped two in my mouth and swallowed deep. The pills crawled down my dry throat, leaving a bitter remnant on my tongue. I picked up a handful of snow and tossed it into my mouth. It tasted only slightly better than the metallic water I had dug out of the earth some years ago in New Alcatraz with Red.

"What are you ... like, thirty?" I said as I looked Ash's beaten face over like some quack psychic at a carnival trying to guess a person's birth year. Aside from the bruises and scrapes on his face, there was a long, thick beard that stretched down to his chest. Ash's green eyes were shiny with concern for the man who looked to be his injured comrade speaking in riddles, but something in the unwavering set of his jaw, the stillness with which he held himself, suggested he was someone who wasn't ruled by mercy. "Where are your parents? Where were they born?" I said, digging through the bag like a child inventorying his candy after a night of trick or treating, I tossed pill bottles aside.

"They were born back at the village," Ash answered with a touch of pride in his voice. "My mother was a seamstress, and my father was—"

"And their parents? Your grandparents?" I interrupted as I pulled a vial of nanobots out of the bag.

"The village also," Ash answered.

"Great-grandparents?" I asked. I found a syringe and stabbed it deep into the rubber stopper on the top of the vial and pulled back the plunger.

"I suppose the village as well," Ash said. The pride of coming from a long line of New Alcatraz inhabitants faded and confusion took over his voice, like he had never considered things that far back before. That kind of thinking, the thinking of the distant past or distant future, was only prevalent in societies where survival was not the sole concern. Ash had never had time to simply ponder his existence.

"Okay, so like three or four generations ... so that's a hundred years..." I crunched the numbers in my head and tried to think of the average age of the original prisoners that were sent to New Alcatraz. "That would make it sometime in ... the year 5200, I suppose."

The thick metallic nanobot liquid filled the syringe. I knew what this was, and I was overjoyed to see that Ash had grabbed it from the medical center. They were the same type of nanobots that I injected in my own body years ago. Not the exact ones, of course—those were retrieved from what I could only assume was Whitman's disassembled body. The ones that contained Wayfield's DNA and the cure for Dark Time. But these were nanobots nonetheless.

Robots smaller than a molecule that would seek out my internal injuries and repair them. They would hopefully fight off any infection and stop my bleeding more permanently than the coagulant could. I jabbed the syringe deep into my shoulder. Ash's face winced at the sight. Pushing the plunger down, I felt the familiar warm, crawling sensation of the tiny robots entering my body. I put the vial back into the bag and handed the bag back to Ash.

Holding a painkiller in my hand and reaching out to Ash, I said, "Take this. It will help with the pain." I circled my finger around my own face to indicate his facial wounds. "If this one doesn't knock you out, you can take another. I don't think I'm making any bold predictions if I say you have never had any sort of pill before." Ash shook his head, held the pill in his hand, and stared for a long time before he threw it into his mouth. He chewed the pill into chalky bits.

Handing him one of the rifles from the armory, I clutched the bag that contained the mind transfer device, the pistols, and ammunition, and slung the other rifle over my shoulder. Ash didn't know both guns weren't loaded, and I wouldn't give him ammo until I knew for sure I could trust him.

I pushed my bloody hand deep into the snow and stood, rocking back and forth as the cold wind blew around us, whipping long dark hair against my face. Ash held onto the rifle in an unnatural way. He reached a meaty hand out for me to hold onto as I braced myself.

We stood in the middle of a pinkish red puddle of slushy blood and snow. I took two deep breaths and stared back at the entrance to Buckley Air Force Base. *Vesa*, I thought to myself. *I hope this works*.

"This village you live in," I asked Ash, and Ash nodded, "how far away is it?"

"Three or so days' walk if we rest each night."

"What if we don't rest?"

CHAPTER 3

Vesa's kneecaps crashed into the cement as the agent pushed her down, sending jagged waves of pain up through her legs. Dust and ash clung to her cheek pressed against the floor. She didn't resist, there was no point. This was it. This was the plan, and there was no going back.

The only option was to trust that whatever Powell had in him, in his body, would be worth something to the Ministry of Science or Wayfield Industries. Proof that someone could escape from the inescapable New Alcatraz? James Wayfield's DNA? Or the cure for Dark Time?

Dark Time was the time a person aged while in the past or future. If a person travelled to the past and spent six months there, they would return to their present time six months older than they should have been. It was proof to the Ministry of Science that a person spent time in another year. And if a person could not account for their Dark Time, then it was a sure death sentence. But not before the person was tortured and their reasons for illegal time travel was explained.

Vesa's rebel group had worked for years to develop a cure for Dark Time. A way to erase the missing time in a person's body. They had been successful. With the research her brother started, Finn and Whitman were able to create a cure. They isolated the genetic marker that indicated the existence of Dark Time, and they synthesized a protein that replaced the genetic marker. Eliminating this unaccounted-for time resting inside the body. With it, her group would have been able to travel through time, and the Ministry would have never known. If only their time movement device in Ashton hadn't been dismantled by the Technology Development Agency before they developed the cure. One was useless without the other.

But now, that cure rested inside Whitman's lifeless android shell just down the corridor. Her rebel group had injected it inside of the robot for safekeeping. Now, just a few meters away, the Ministry was disassembling Whitman's body and prepping it for cold storage deep below the earth under the Denver Airport.

According to Powell, that was where they stored all decommissioned androids. And, according to Powell, he would find Whitman's remains down there in a thousand years or more when he escaped New Alcatraz. To protect himself from the radiation incurred when travelling from the future prison back to his present, Powell would inject himself with the nanobots that rested inside of Whitman, and along with them he would unknowingly inject himself with James Wayfield's DNA *and* the cure for Dark Time. According to Powell, he had already done all of this. In his past; in their future. He had said it like this was a sure thing. Inevitable. All that had to be done now was for the Ministry to collect Whitman's body and store it underneath the Denver Airport. All of this was according to Powell. It all still seemed like a long shot to Vesa.

Maybe just having the only person to escape from New Alcatraz in custody will be enough, she thought as the agent cinched plastic ties around her wrists. Already doubting Powell's theories of how time travel worked, Vesa thought, *maybe tying up that loose end will make up for not handing over the mind transfer device.*

One agent drove his knee deep into her back until all the air was pushed out of her lungs. Through blurred vision, she made out more agents handling Powell's limp body, dragging him towards a stretcher. From Vesa's single blow to his head, a small line of blood trickled out of his hair and dripped down his forehead.

After her hands were secured, the agents jerked her off the floor and hauled her down the twisted tunnels. One agent at each side of her. Their gloved hands wrapped tightly around her biceps. She looked down every tunnel that branched off the main thoroughfare, twisting her neck and pushing her eyes as far to the right or left as they would go. She saw no sign of Doc.

The two of them, Doc and Vesa, had grown close over the last few years. His sister was lost to the cult of the Golden Dawn. Her brother taken by the Ministry of Science. They both suffered the same loss. Both siblings taken, probably better off dead.

The agents dragged Vesa past the spot where Whitman had plugged himself into the main security system. Just moments before, Whitman's mind had zipped through the conduits that lined the tunnels, clearing a path for Vesa and Powell. Raising alarms where they weren't and silencing ones where they were.

His vacant android body was slumped on the floor against the wall, the wires from the wall that he plugged into his wrist still dangling next to his body. Two men in white Wayfield Industry lab coats poked and prodded at the android shell.

The sight of Whitman's empty shell made Vesa wonder. *Maybe Powell was right. Maybe the Ministry of Science will store Whitman underneath the Denver Airport. Maybe one thousand years in the future, during his time in New Alcatraz, Powell will, or did, inject himself with whatever is inside Whitman's body. But if not, Powell's body is worth next to nothing to them.*

Further down the hall, Vesa past the small room where the two men had confronted Powell moments ago. The room with antiquated corded telephones lining the wall. Each phone was a direct line to another underground base built deep underground. The military man, who had introduced himself as General Moore to Vesa and her group, was slumped on the ground with his back to the wall. A medic shone a small light into his eyeballs. He looked disoriented. He sat slack—jawed, rubbing the back of his head. Vesa smirked at the thought of Powell putting up a fight when they tried to arrest him. The other man, Sheldon, whom Vesa had never heard speak, came out of the small room, a medic chasing close behind him.

"That fucking asshole cut my finger off," he shrieked, pointing at Powell's unconscious body on the stretcher.

The agents rolled Powell just behind Vesa.

"I want him locked down and transported to Denver immediately! I am going to personally oversee his transport and questioning!" The man's hand was wrapped in gauze, but the blood had already soaked through and was running down his arm.

Vesa's smirk grew into a full smile. She missed Powell already.

"And you," Sheldon said, pointing at Vesa. "You better start talking right now!" The man's face was bright red. A thick vein traced up his forehead.

"This one asked to speak to someone in charge, sir," the agent on Vesa's right said through his armored mask. "She says she has information about the man on the stretcher."

"I bet she fucking does!" Sheldon said to the agent. He reached his one good hand out and wrapped it around Vesa's throat. She felt the blood hot and throbbing in her face. Growling through clenched teeth, the crazed man said, "You guys picked the wrong fucking time to break in here. Any other day and you may have just accomplished whatever the fuck it was you came here to do."

Vesa's vision blurred and she felt her trachea may crumble any moment. Her arms struggled, but they were tied tightly behind her back.

"But today, General Moore and myself were conducting a training exercise. There was twice the amount of security here than normal." Sheldon reached up with his bloody gauze-wrapped hand and brushed Vesa's face, leaving a trail of blood on her cheek. Her arms jerked apart until the plastic around her wrists cut into her skin. "Lucky for you, I was here. Maybe we were meant to meet."

He let go of her throat, and Vesa gasped for air, as her vision returned to normal and the throbbing blood trapped in her face drained to the rest of her body. Sheldon started to walk away.

Through halted coughs, Vesa said, "I brought him here to you! I am working *with* you!" She hated the way those words made her feel. She hated that this was the plan, and that this was the only thing that would keep her brother alive.

Sheldon turned to face her again. She stared at him, and could see the large vein in his forehead pounding with each rapid beat of his heart.

"Contact Denver," she said. "They enlisted me for a covert op."

The agents who stood around looked at each other and waited for Sheldon's response.

"And your mission, it was this man?" Sheldon asked and nodded at Powell's body. Vesa shook her head.

"But he is better. Better than my mission," Vesa said and tried not to sound like she was pleading with him. Negotiating. She tried to sound honest. "He is more important."

Taking two short steps towards Vesa, Sheldon asked in quieter tone, "What was your mission?"

"My brother," was all Vesa said.

The look on Sheldon's face when he'd choked Vesa returned.

"Load them both on a transport vehicle," he said to one of the agents. "And you, get on the phone with Denver. I want a complete operational report on her before we leave."

Sheldon turned and stomped away from Vesa. He balled his one good hand into a fist at his side. His other hand just hung and dripped blood onto the floor.

"And tell me when you find the other person who was with them. He has to be here somewhere!"

CHAPTER 4

2075
DENVER, COLORADO

Vesa sat in the back of a large transport vehicle, her wrists bound by plastic restraints. Powell's unconscious body lay flat on a metal bench that ran the length of the vehicle, almost bouncing onto the floor with each pothole and bump the car hit. Two TDA agents clutching long automatic rifles sat with Vesa and the sleeping body. Blood leaking from Powell's gunshot wound soaked through the layers of bandages the agents had carelessly placed around his thigh and pooled around his body.

"He's going to bleed to death," Vesa said, motioning towards Powell with her bound hands.

"You're not permitted to speak," one of the agents said. His facial armor and helmet made him look more like some sort of faceless action figure instead of a law enforcement agent. It seemed to Vesa that every cop or federal agent she saw these days wore full tactical armor. Gone were the days of police in blue uniforms with badges pinned to their chests. Gone were the days of clearly defined authority figures who identified themselves as police. Now it was all black masks and riot gear. It was undercover and entrapment.

Outside the windowless metal compartment, Vesa heard sirens coming from the long string of agency vehicles that drove like a funeral procession towards Denver, Colorado. Undoubtedly, one of the cars carried Whitman's metal body. She pictured Wayfield scientists in lab coats disassembling Whitman in the back of the vehicle. Poking and prodding at his internal components. Boxing and labeling each tiny part. She prayed Doc wasn't in one of the cars.

He escaped, she thought. *I know he did. He wouldn't have let them catch him alive, and I didn't see his body next to Whitman's.*

Vesa's own body leaned as the car twisted and turned in circles. She felt the car driving gradually downwards, like the cars were going down some sort of spiral driveway. The temperature inside the vehicle dropped, so, even without windows, Vesa knew the sun no longer shone against the metal box she sat in. Eventually, she heard the tires of the other vehicles screech to a halt, and then her own transport vehicle slammed to a stop. Powell's body slid off the bench and fell onto the floor of the car. Vesa winced for him, whoever he was.

"Take the android to get dismantled," Vesa heard Sheldon growl from outside the van. She wondered if his voice was always so earsplitting, or if these events stressed him out more than usual. "I want his parts stored underground by the end of the day," he yelled. Boots shuffled on the ground outside, and car doors opened and closed.

Outside Vesa's car, the doors rattled and swung open. She squinted her eyes in anticipation of some sort of light filling the back of the car, but there was nothing, only faint artificial lights in the distance. Her vehicle was precisely parked among lines of hundreds of other TDA cars. All of them lined up perfectly and stretching on forever. Like two mirrors facing each other, replicating the same black car with tinted windows. Sheldon stood at the back of the car.

"Take her to holding, and take him to interrogation level five," he said, sneering at Vesa.

"Where's my brother?" Vesa demanded as the guards wrapped their gloved fingers around her arms and pushed her out of the car. Sheldon ignored her question, as Powell's limp body was thrown onto a stretcher. A Wayfield employee approached the stretcher with a first aid kit slung over his shoulder.

Waving his bloodied hand in the air, Sheldon shouted at the man with the first aid kit. "What are you doing? He can wait."

"Sorry, sir," the medic said and stopped to examine Sheldon's hand.

"We don't need him healthy anyways," Sheldon said as the medic unwrapped the bandages. He winced and looked away from the bloody mess that was his hand. "We just need him alive enough to talk."

CHAPTER 5

5280
NEW ALCATRAZ

Our feet sank deep into the snow. At first, our pace was slow, with Ash helping me as much as he could. But even he grew tired. Eventually, the nanobots had swarmed around my dislocated joint and repaired the cartilage, bone, and tendons that were stretched beyond their limits, and I was able to walk more on my own.

Although the top priority, my stomach wound was not so quick to heal. The nanobots worked diligently, but that type of wound would take more time. I checked the stab site every few hours. Each time the gauze was soaked with thick blood. I dropped the blood-soaked rags in the snow, and replaced them with fresh gauze. The flow of the blood had slowed, and Ash told me my skin was not as pale anymore. But my body was still weak.

Pain from the more minor wounds on Ransom's body still lingered. My ear felt like it had been torn from my face. My fingers were swollen, and my tongue let out a slow drip of metallic blood into my mouth.

As the sun began to fall, at the threat of night, we picked up our pace. But it was for nothing. We would not reach shelter tonight. And likely not the next, regardless of our pace.

Aside from the snow and the presence of more cacti, the landscape of New Alcatraz looked mostly the same. I could make out the mountains in the distance, and, if I squinted through the snowy wind, I could see the faint image of tall, gray trees without any leaves on them. When I first arrived in New Alcatraz, it was trees like these that provided the only shelter from the sun. Perhaps it was that exact forest where I spent my first night in this prison hundreds of years ago.

Once we started walking to Ash's village, I tried to have him start from the beginning, to explain what was going on. But it proved difficult to find where the "beginning" actually was. He told me about Ransom's son, Gray, and his illness. He told me that another man in their group, Tannyn, had died from the illness on their way to Buckley, and that Merit was somehow separated from them in the underground vault.

Except for a few times when Ash referred to me as Ransom, he seemed to handle the transition well, especially for someone who had grown up in New Alcatraz his entire life. He told me of the stories passed down through the generations about the underground vaults, time machines, and the robotic limbs. He told me how they were all descendants of great people from my time.

"Is it all real?" he asked. "Were the stories true?"

I hesitated. I didn't know how to answer him.

"Most of them," I said. "I am here, in Ransom's body, because of some of the advanced technology from my time."

"And the people who came here from your time," Ash asked with pride. "They were great men? They were the scientists that invented this technology?"

I trudged through the snow, and winced in pain. My body was getting used to the feeling of the stab wound, but I winced just to buy myself time before answering. Ash looked at me. The innocent look in his eyes was a contrast to his hulking frame.

"I can't speak for everyone sent here, but I can say that some of the best men from my time were sent here. They were great men," I told him. "They were the best of the best." It wasn't a lie.

"I knew it!" Ash exclaimed. "You — I mean Ransom — always said those stories were made up, but I knew they were true. The underground vaults are one thing, but the technology, and our ancestors … that's something else. Boy, if he were here right now, he would be steaming mad that he was wrong all this time. I can't wait to tell him!" Ash chuckled, but his smile gradually faded.

"Where *is* Ransom?" Ash asked me after a period of silence and reflection. His voice had quieted, and his body pulled somewhat inwards, like he was afraid to ask.

"I don't know, Ash. I can only assume he is in my body, since I am in his."

"You mean … he travelled through time?"

"Something like that." I couldn't even begin to explain to him what actual time travel was like or what it involved. "It's the year 2075." As the words left my mouth, I realized that meant absolutely nothing to him. "You know how there are seasons here?" I asked and Ash nodded. "Each time winter comes around, like it is now, that is one year." I never thought I would have to explain the concept of time to another person, but here I was. Ash nodded again. "Us"—I pointed to myself and Ash— "we are about three thousand winters apart from Ransom … *if* he is in my body."

"Woah…" Ash's mouth hung open and he stared into the sky.

For a while all I could hear was our feet crunching in the snow. The vultures had long since flown away and given up their pursuit of us. Every once in a while, I turned back to see if the crazed cannibals had emerged from their covered home and come after us, but there was nothing but white wind between us and Buckley. If they did crawl out of their home, they were far behind us. I knew that it wasn't good for me, but I periodically scooped snow into my mouth. My body would burn more calories just to keep myself warm from the snow, but I needed the taste of water on my tongue.

"So, if you're right," Ash said, "and Ransom is in your body ... what do you think he is doing right now?"

CHAPTER 6

2075
DENVER, COLORADO

"Get him up!" a thin man screeched to no one in particular, blood dripping from his fingers, holding a weapon that looked similar to those the cannibals Ransom encountered had used. Without question, a large man dressed in all black backhanded Ransom's face, and a trickle of blood dripped out of his lip. Blood still oozed out of the gunshot wound in his thigh. Ransom pried his eyes open.

What happened to me? Ransom wondered. *These wounds ... my body? Have I died?* Ransom tried to move, but winced and grabbed his leg. "Ahhhh," he said and threw his head back. *Too much pain to be dead.*

"Hurts, doesn't it?" the thin man said with a smile. "Remember me?" the man gritted through his teeth. Ransom shook his head. "He's playing dumb already!" the man said to the other person, the man who had just hit Ransom in the face. The man had the letters TDA branded across his chest. Ransom had never heard of that word. *Perhaps it is his name*, Ransom thought. "Sheldon," the man said, snapping his fingers in Ransom's face.

Ransom looked around and saw nothing but white. The walls, ceiling, and floors were white-stained concrete. Overhead, bright white lights, much brighter than the bulbs Ransom had seen in his village, beamed down on him. There was no furniture in the room. Ransom couldn't even tell where the door was. It was like they'd built the entire room around them.

"Why were you in Buckley?" the man, Sheldon, asked. "What were you trying to do?"

"Medicine," Ransom grunted, his voice different than he was used to.

"Medicine," Sheldon laughed. "You think I'm gonna give you medicine without you giving me any information? You are going to suffer here until you tell us *exactly* what it was you wanted down there."

"Medicine," Ransom said again, squeezing his eyes shut with each movement. "I was there for medicine." Ransom held his hand flat over his eyes to block the bright light, but it only reflected off the floor and bounced up into his eyes. Sheldon looked at the man next to him, TDA, and squinted his eyes.

"You went down there for *medicine*," Sheldon repeated. Ransom forced himself to nod. "You broke into a secure government facility, with fake IDs and uniforms ... for medicine?" Sheldon paused, awaiting an answer. Ransom simply grunted and nodded again. "What the fuck kind of story is this?" Sheldon asked.

"My son ... he needs medicine."

Sheldon approached Ransom and knelt on the ground so their faces were level. He reached his hand out and gripped the blood-soaked gauze wrapped around Ransom's thigh. Ransom jerked his body away, screaming, but Sheldon held on as blood oozed through his fingers.

"This bullshit story is not going to fly here." He gripped Ransom's thigh tighter and tighter. Ransom tried to focus on something else to take his mind away from this place, but there was nothing in the room to focus on. He was forced to face this man and accept the pain.

"We already took your DNA. The agents are running it now. Soon we will know exactly who you are." More blood seeped out of the gauze on Ransom's thigh, and pooled on the bright white floor. Ransom winced and gritted his teeth. "I don't need you to tell me *who* you are—I'll know that soon enough—but you will tell me *why* you went to Buckley. The sooner you tell me, the sooner this can all be over. If you don't tell me what you were doing down there, then this is as good as it's gonna get for you."

Sheldon unwrapped his own bandaged hand, slowly spinning the gauze around and around until his mangled fingers were exposed. He clenched his jaw and gasped as the gauze brushed against his open wound. The skin around his fingers was blue and pale. His pinky finger was gone, only a stump of white bone protruding from his hand. His ring finger was barely attached, swinging in the air by a thin strip of skin.

Sheldon's bloody stump reminded Ransom of the cannibals he encountered under Buckley. He thought back to how the group had cut off and eaten the arm of one of their own men. They left him with only part of his arm still attached to his body, bleeding and waiting for them to eat the rest of him. *It seems I can never escape these types of people*, he thought.

"He did this to me." Sheldon nodded at his hand. "Do this to him first. I don't care if he talks. I want his fingers gone." Sheldon wrapped the bloody gauze back over his hand. "After that, I don't care what you do to him. Just get him to talk, and make sure not to kill him until we know everything he knows. We can't trust that bitch down the hall. We need to compare their stories. If they don't both say the same thing, then they're both dead."

Sheldon walked to the far wall and a door appeared out of nowhere, sliding and exposing a dark hallway outside. Sheldon left and the door slid closed, enveloping the room in only white once again. Ransom was left alone with the man in black. The man reached down to his thigh, unsheathing a knife with a matte black blade, twirled the knife in his hand, and approached Ransom.

CHAPTER 7

Ash and I had walked for a day. The sun came and went. Ignoring the short amount of time we'd known each other, Ash and I huddled together at night to share our warmth. In the morning, I prompted Ash to take two more painkillers. He hesitantly threw the pills into his mouth and crunched down on them.

"Are you sure you're not him?" Ash asked again for what seemed like the one hundredth time. "Maybe you just hit your head too hard." Even though he seemed to be taking this transition well, I expected some bit of denial to creep in his mind. It's a protection mechanism when your mind can't handle the truth.

"It's not that. I know it's hard for someone like you to understand, but I am not Ransom."

"What do you mean? Someone like me?"

"From this time. This place. You aren't used to technology."

"So, this is normal for you, where you're from?" Ash asked. I shook my head and tried to think of a way to make this make sense to him.

"It isn't *normal* for me, but it isn't as crazy either. Where I am from

… it's just different. I need you to understand this, because I will need you to help the people at your home to understand as well. They need to know I am not who they think I am."

"Is Ransom gone for good?" Ash asked.

"God, I hope not," I mumbled. I tried to think through what could have happened, or what could have been happening right now in my own time. Whether Ransom inhabited my body or not, I hoped that Vesa would carry out my plan, that she'd handed my body over to the Ministry of Science. The realization I might be trapped in this body, this time, forever, gnawed at me. Even if I knew how, there probably would never be a time when it would be safe to transfer back to my own body.

As the sun dropped below the horizon for the second time since I had returned to New Alcatraz, the temperature dropped with it. Ash spread a large fur pelt out on the ground and we settled onto it. I pulled the shoulder bag over my head, and placed the mind transfer device on the ground. I opened the flap and peeked inside.

It still hummed, and the charge indicator showed it still held a full charge. The device had sat in that vault for thousands of years, soaking up the wireless power that coursed through the air in and around Buckley Air Force Base. I wasn't surprised that it was still charged even after Ransom had placed his hand on it. Even now, the wireless power from the base was probably reaching out across the desert.

"We should be home by tomorrow," Ash said in a grumbling voice. Over the two days we'd spent together so far, his wounds had gotten worse before they got any better. His face had swelled and then shrunk to a somewhat normal size. His bruises had been bright blue and purple, but now they were a brownish tan.

"Do you think Ransom's son is alive?" I asked.

Ash just shrugged.

"Why Ransom?" I asked.

"What do you mean?"

"Before, you told me people wouldn't go out here unless Ransom went. Why Ransom? Is he some sort of leader where you're from?"

"Ha! Ransom would never tell you he is a leader." Ash chuckled.

"Most good leaders wouldn't." I said.

"Ransom had gone out farther than anyone else. After that, he got a reputation for being brave, but really he was just going out to find his dad."

"His dad?" I asked.

"Yeah, Ransom and Merit's dad left them when they were young. Wandered out to try and find this underground place himself." Ash shook his head. "The morning he left, Ransom tracked his dad's footprints in the snow. Eventually, Ransom turned back, but his dad … he never returned. He was only a young boy. Just a bit older than Gray is now." Ash looked away and stared out into the black sky. Wind whipped his long beard around his face.

"So the rest of the village figured if he was brave enough to go out there when he was just a kid, he must be one of the bravest or toughest people in our village once he grew up. It was like a legend that got built up over the years. Each time someone retold the story, Ransom seemed to have walked farther out. Some people think he walked for a day or more. But Ransom told me the truth."

Ash picked up a small rock and threw it into the black distance.

"He told me he stayed close to the village. 'It's not my fault if people want to lie to themselves about how far I walked,' he would say." Ash smiled at the thought of his friend. "That's how he is. He never cared what people thought about him. Good or bad. He would say, 'If they think bad of me, talking to them will only make it worse. And if they think good of me, who am I to change their minds?'"

Chuckling, Ash said, "Anyways, they wouldn't go if he didn't go. And he had no interest in leaving the village. Figured his dad died out there and never came back, so why bother?"

Even in the distant future, children were growing up without both parents. One leaving and causing a cycle of abandonment. Father leaves son, son grows up and leaves his child. Forever and ever.

"Ransom had me convinced his dad was wrong. That he was selfish for leaving just to satisfy his curiosity. But now … after finding that place … maybe his dad was right. Now it seems he left his family out of love. He left to make things better for them. Make things better for all of us. Maybe he thought it was necessary."

I thought back to my mom leaving my father and me in Buford when I was just a baby. How she left so the Ministry of Science couldn't track her back to Buford and capture my dad, kill me. I wondered if Ransom would one day realize that his father left for Ransom's own good. But most people live their entire lives without understanding why their parents did what they did. I was just fortunate enough to go back in time and actually meet my absent parent.

The sky was pitch black now, and the stars sparkled over our heads. Unlike the other nights, there wasn't a strong wind. The desert was calm. In the distance, I heard some animal howl. I never thought I would hear such a thing in New Alcatraz, but I suppose given enough time everything would cycle back around, and animals would repopulate. Plants will grow and flowers will one day bloom. If the timeline is stretched out far enough everything gets a second chance. Things can always reset. Or at least I hoped so.

But just like the animals and plants, humans will cycle back around and settle into a life that resembles what our civilizations used to be like. Whatever type of life Ash and his people have created will morph into the type of life I knew. Given enough time humans would fight. It has already started here. They will devise ways to murder and imprison other humans. They will go to war over resources.

For the first time, I saw New Alcatraz as something beautiful. It was a time before all of that, and after. It was a place that showed what came before there were different groups and factions. It was a time before our timeline circled back around and ended up in endless wars and fighting. But I saw how it would end.

Just as the animal in the distance had an instinct to howl and hunt, the fighting would start again. The group of people, if you could call them that, living inside Buckley Air Force Base were the beginning of such a time. They were the first faction with the drive to kill and imprison. Even thousands of years separated from human civilization was not enough to keep the desire to fight at bay. I just hoped they stayed where they were. I hoped they weren't coming after us. I hoped our society's cycle didn't start over again just yet.

"You know, I've never told Ransom this," Ash said, snapping me out of my own head, "but I think it was braver for Ransom to turn around. He realized that his father was gone. He knew he had to go home and tell his mom and brother what happened. He knew that he had to live life without his father. And instead of denying that and continuing in the deep snow, he turned around to face life as it was. Not life as he wished it to be. I think that is far braver than running after his dad. Chasing a ghost."

CHAPTER 8

5280
NEW ALCATRAZ

By the third day of our journey, we had eaten enough snow to stay hydrated, but we needed food. My stomach pulled away from my ribs, and at night, when we huddled together for warmth, I could hear Ash's stomach growl over the gusty winds. Our bodies could only heal so much without nourishment. I pulled the gauze away from my stab wound to reveal dried blood cracking away over a pink cut. The skin was almost healed completely. Ash's face was not healing as quickly without the help of the nanobots. He still took the painkillers in his medicine bag, actually swallowing them whole eventually.

In the distance, I saw structures jutting out of the horizon. They were unnatural shapes. Straight lines that didn't occur in nature on their own. I held my open hand over my eyes to block the bright white sun.

"Is that it?" I asked.

Ash grunted. He had stayed quiet for the majority of the day. I figured he was concerned about how our reunion would play out. Maybe he was worried about Ransom's son.

"Is that the village?"

Again, Ash nodded and grunted. The village consisted of thirty or so huts built of clay and dirt, with roofs made of the thin gray trees that grew in New Alcatraz. More clay was wedged between the logs on the roof.

Men and women milled about the village, carrying firewood or digging up dirt. Sheep and pigs circled inside a corral. Separate from the village was a forest of fragile-looking gray trees that reminded me of my first night in New Alcatraz. Perhaps this was the same forest I slept in. But what had once been a thick, almost impenetrable, forest was now thinned out. All that remained were stumps poking through the desert snow.

"That's Ransom's forest," Ash said. He must have noticed my eyes lingering on the remains of the ash-gray trees. "That's his job. To chop wood for our village. He delivers firewood to the homes, and he brings full-length logs to his brother for the roofs of the huts. That's what Merit does. Build houses." Ash pointed over to the village. "Merit is always trying to find a way to build a house that is two levels. Each of us has a job. Ransom's grandfather and dad chopped those trees down before him. Soon Gray will…" Ash trailed off and sped his pace up.

As we closed in on the village people began to notice us. Crowding around the two of us, a handful of villagers shouted, "They're back! They made it back!" The children were the first to reach us. One boy grabbed my leg and simply smiled up at me. His eyes were filled with amazement and disbelief that we actually made it back.

It was the same way I remembered watching the first crew that visited Mars return safely to Earth when I was thirteen. In that moment, I thought anything was possible. I watched the TV screen wide eyed and smiling. Now this boy looked at me in the same way, and I realized what this trip away from the village meant to them.

Tensing my lips together to mask the fact that I was speaking, I whispered "Is this him? Is this Gray?" Ash shook his head and looked around to see if anyone else heard my question.

Even though I didn't know any of these people I felt welcomed. *Is this what it's like to be a part of something? Is this what it's like to truly belong to a community?* In my time, people merely coexisted. We didn't thrive together. At best, we tolerated each other, and at worst we actively tried to harm each other.

Everything was automatic. Information and items were delivered in a moment. Whatever interactions weren't already replaced by automation were replaced by androids. Fellow humans were only an impediment to whatever instant gratification we awaited at the time.

By now adults and children alike swarmed around me. They were happy. Waving and shouting our names. The ones that got close enough patted Ash and me on our backs. We were soldiers coming home from a war. This was their version of a parade. They were excited. Excited to see me, or Ransom, and relieved that I was alive and well. I couldn't help but smile back at them and accept their greetings. *This is what Ransom was fighting for underneath Buckley Air Force Base. Home. Family.*

"Ransom!" a woman yelled from across the village, and ran towards me. She stumbled as if she was moving faster than her feet could carry her. She kicked up clouds of red desert dust and snow behind her, and her feet smacked against the hard ground of New Alcatraz. I glanced towards Ash, who nodded at me and then at the woman running towards me. He widened his eyes so that I would know this woman was important.

"Aurora?" I whispered to Ash. He had told me about Ransom's wife during our journey home. How they had been together since they were young. Ash nodded at me again. My heart pounded inside my chest, echoing down through my empty stomach. Clearing a path for Aurora, all of the other villagers moved away.

Aurora collided into me with the force of a hurricane wind. If she had made contact with my own body, I would have toppled over into the cold snow. But Ransom was strong. Aurora squeezed my body until I felt the pain of my stab wound rip through my body. I winced and cried out.

"What's wrong?" Aurora asked and let go of my body. She looked down and saw that my makeshift clothes were stained with blood. "Oh my gods! What happened?"

"It's okay," I said. I already felt like an imposter with just those two words. The first lie in what would likely be a long string of them. I tried to think of what Ransom would do, how he might act. How a husband and a father might act.

"Gray? How is he?" I asked. Aurora's face was coated with a thin layer of dust, except for two long streaks where tears had run down her face. Her eyes were swollen and bloodshot. I assumed that, at the very best, Gray had not improved. At the worst, he had died a day or two ago.

Aurora swallowed and blinked her eyes slowly. I looked over at Ash. His mouth was tense and straight.

"He is alive, Ransom," she said, but she didn't smile. "He is alive, but he isn't good. Please tell me you found something. Please tell me he will be alright." With that Aurora started crying again.

"We found something," I said. Ransom's voice sounded strong, was almost reassuring even to me. "I don't know if it will work, but we found medicine."

CHAPTER 9

Aurora pulled me by the hand towards a round orange hut. Worn pathways traced through the snowy ground, and connected the handful of small huts dotting the landscape. Even more pathways led to a field of crops and a pen off in the distance that housed several small animals. Bulbs without any wires attached to them, like those I saw underground at the Golden Dawn's base, hung on ropes that zigzagged between the orange huts. Over the centuries or millennia, tungsten from the filaments had boiled off and condensed onto the once-clear glass, leaving them coated in dark soot from the inside. The light that escaped the bulbs was dim.

A crowd of villagers followed behind us, mumbling and whispering to each other. Some gasped at the sight of me and Ash. They were either shocked anyone returned or shocked that two of us didn't. Others yelled for more people to come. I looked back to make sure Ash was still with us. He was the only person who knew my secret, and he was the only person who could help explain what had happened before I jumped into Ransom's body.

Aurora dragged me without any regard for how long I had walked to get there. Without regard for any injuries I may have had. My feet shuffled as I tried to keep up with her. Aurora's hand was soft and warm in the cold air. She glanced back every few steps as if to make sure I was still there.

We approached one of the small huts made of dirt and hay. *How many generations of prisoners did it take to start rebuilding something that resembled a society?* I wondered.

Aurora flung the door to the hut open. A rush of warm air burst out, and swirled through the snow outside. A small boy lay on a bed near the fireplace inside the hut. A thick fur blanket covered his body, but sweat ran down his face. A single pale arm covered in a red rash hung out of the blanket, dangling just above the floor. The boy shivered as the flames from the fire leapt just centimeters from his bed.

"Gray?" I asked, and quickly realized I might have given myself away. My heart fell inside my body at the sight of the suffering boy. I questioned my own feeling as genuine or perhaps a leftover feeling from within Ransom's body.

"I pray there's still time," Aurora said. She squeezed my hand with all of her strength, which wasn't much. I guessed Gray's mother had stayed up with him for the entire time Ransom was out looking for medicine. I knew the feeling of exhaustion she felt right now. It's an exhaustion that's like falling in an endless dark shaft for so long that you would rather just hit the ground instead of spend any more time falling.

I took two steps toward Gray, and dropped my bag on the floor. His skin was worse up close. Blue veins traced under his translucent skin, and some sort of mucus dribbled out of the corner of his mouth. His lips were chapped and cracked to the point that they bled and scabbed. His chest rose and fell erratically, like a child who was sobbing and couldn't control his breathing. I knelt near the bed, but kept my distance. I knew I had the nanobots in my own body, or Ransom's body, but I didn't know if this was some sort of futuristic virus that could be impervious to the nanobots.

Maybe you are why I am here, I thought. *Maybe I am to help your father and mother through this.* I shook my head and realized the absurdity of there being any real plan or reason behind any of this. *I hope you get to see your father again … your real father.* Ash stood cautiously just inside the door to the hut.

"Ash, the medicine," I said, motioning for him to step closer. He gripped the bag containing all of the medicines. Ash moved around Aurora, knelt next to me, and dumped the bag upside down. A pile of pills, syringes, and other medical supplies spilled onto the floor. He looked at it all with amazement and confusion.

"How do we know what to give him?" Ash picked up a pill bottle that contained familiar, large, green pills. The pills that I knew firsthand could dissolve a person from the inside out.

"Not that," I told him and took the bottle. "Never take that. Hand me a syringe." Ash rummaged through the pile of medicine.

"Syringe?" he asked.

"Move," I said and pushed Ash away from the medicine. Aurora was crying again. If anything would help this boy, it would be the same nanobots that now crawled through Ransom's body. I grabbed one of the syringes and a vial of the nanobots. The large needle drew the viscous liquid out of the vial. Aurora looked on in shock and horror. Such a sight was unimaginable to her.

"Wait!" Aurora snapped. She jumped forwards and grabbed my wrist. "What are you doing? How do you know this won't make him worse? How do you know what this stuff is?"

"It's fine," Ash said and then quickly stopped talking. He glanced at me. He waited to see what I would say, if I would tell her.

"I'm sure," I told her, and nodded my head at Ash. It felt good to have someone here that I could count on in this. "I can't promise this will fix your son." Aurora wrinkled her brow at my phrasing. "Our son. I don't know if it will make him better, but I know it will not make him any worse. It's our only hope."

Aurora let go of my hand and offered a slight nod. With her blessing, I slid the needle into Gray's arm. His paper-thin skin offered little resistance to the oversized needle. I sat back and collapsed onto the floor as the long walk over the last three days, and whatever else had happened to Ransom before I moved into his body, caught up to me. I had done all I could for Ransom's son. Time would tell if the nanobots would help at all.

Outside, the wind whistled and battered against the primitive hut. I stared up at the roof until my vision blurred. For a moment, I thought maybe I would jump back to my own body, just like I'd jumped out of my body at the Golden Dawn headquarters. Maybe I'd done what I came here to do. I felt Aurora cradle my head in her lap, and brush the hair from my face. She leaned down and kissed me on the lips. That was the last thing I remembered before my mind went blank.

CHAPTER 10

2075
DENVER, COLORADO

Vesa fell into the flat mattress and stared at the ceiling of her cell. Her eyelids pulled closed, and her breathing slowed. For a moment, her mind traveled away from Denver. Away from Buckley. It traveled back to the motel at Gray Mountain. For the first time in days she had time to sleep.

The plan to break into Buckley Air Force Base was done. Ruined, and now everyone she cared for was either captured, unaccounted for, powered down and being prepped for disassembly, or their mind was stuck in a device that was hidden in the air vent back in the armory of Buckley. Things were not going well.

Now, she found herself underground in a cell with a single glass wall, looking out at a seemingly never-ending hallway and a screen broadcasting scenic pictures. Mountains surrounded by blue skies stretched on for what seemed like forever.

In the moment before sleep overtook her, and just before her body truly relaxed, a rapid knocking rang inside her cell. Her eyes jolted open, and she sat up. A man, young, maybe mid-twenties, wearing Wayfield Industries clothing banged his fist against the glass wall. Vesa puffed out a breath in annoyance, realizing how much her body really longed for rest.

The young man kept banging his fist long after Vesa was awake and sitting up.

"What?" she yelled and held her hands out to her sides. The Wayfield employee pressed his finger on a seemingly random place on the glass wall, and a circle lit up inside the glass. An intercom clicked on, and his voice entered the cell.

"Stand against the back wall please." The boy's voice made him seem even younger than he looked. He motioned with his other hand as if to shoo her away. She walked backwards, keeping her eyes on the man until her heel touched the back wall. She pressed her back against the cold cement, and pushed her shoulders back.

"Now stay there," he begged, as if he didn't know what he would have to do if she refused to obey his request. He released the button to the intercom and swiped his hand over a different part of the glass wall. He zigzagged his finger across the glass in some random pattern, and the wall slid open with a loud suction noise. The air from the hallway was cooler somehow, and it floated into Vesa's cell.

"Slowly," the young man said, stepping aside and motioning with his hand for Vesa to leave the cell. She took several hesitant steps towards the hall. "That way," he said and nodded his head.

"Where are you taking me?" she asked.

"I was told to retrieve you from your cell and escort you to another holding area," he said. He hung one arm straight down his body and nervously squeezed his bicep with the other hand, halfway hugging himself. "I don't know anything else."

Vesa crossed the threshold of the cell.

"This way," the Wayfield employee said again and motioned to Vesa's right. She pivoted on her heel and turned, leaving the young man behind her. She knew she could overtake this kid. She could likely take him out with only a few punches, or at least she could tackle him and slam his skull against the hard ground. *But then what?* She walked ahead, passing cell after cell like the one she had just left. All of them were empty.

"Do you have a name?" Vesa asked.

"I'm not supposed to speak to prisoners," he said. Even without looking at him, Vesa could tell his body tensed at the thought of breaking protocol.

"My name is Vesa," she replied, turning to glance over her shoulder to make the briefest eye contact with the young Wayfield employee.

"Keep walking, please," he said, glancing down at the floor.

After they passed the line of glass cells, the hall became just another cement hallway, same as the ones she saw in Buckley.

"Where is my friend?" she asked, knowing there would be no answer.

"I am not supposed to speak to prisoners," he repeated, this time a bit more annoyed than before.

"Is he at least alive?"

"I am not supposed—"

"To speak to prisoners," Vesa interrupted. "I know. You probably wouldn't know the answer even if you could speak to me." Up ahead was an armored TDA agent and another Wayfield employee standing next to a metal door carved into the cement wall. Vesa and her escort approached the men.

"That will be all," the Wayfield employee said to the young man behind Vesa. "You can report back to the deployment center for your next assignment." The young man kept walking down the hall, and Vesa stopped in front of the two men. The agent held an automatic rifle in his hands, and stood with his shoulders straight back and feet together.

"What is going on?" Vesa demanded. "I need to speak to someone in charge. I have information for the Ministry of Science. I have been—"

"We know, Vesa," the Wayfield employee said. This was the first time anyone had referred to her by name. "Someone will be here shortly to debrief you. In the meantime, you both can wait here together," the man motioned to the agent, who stepped forward to unlock the metal door.

"Both?" Vesa said. The agent swung the heavy door open to reveal a small holding cell.

"Yeah, both. You and your brother, Cooper."

There he was, sitting in one of the two chairs in the middle of the room. She gasped at the sight of him, running into the small cell. She wrapped her arms around Cooper's thin body, squeezing him until she knew she must have been hurting him. Vesa pressed her cheek against his and refused to let go. Behind her, Vesa heard the sound of the heavy metal door shutting and locking them both inside.

CHAPTER 11

5280
NEW ALCATRAZ

"Ransom ... Ransom?" My vision was blurred and hazy. My eyelids stuck together for a brief moment before they peeled apart to reveal the cross-hatched hay roof above me. New Alcatraz. I was still here. Still in this hut. The same fire still rested in the fireplace, only now it was a pile of embers and smoke. I let out a sigh, maybe out of frustration, maybe out of relief. I didn't know.

"Hey," Aurora whispered as I woke up. She ran her hand over my forehead, and traced her fingers through my hair. "You feeling alright?"

Alright? You mean physically? My wounds were no longer life threatening, but my stomach is still healing, my knee throbs, my fingers hurt, my head aches, and my ear feels like someone's ripped it from my head. My muscles are cramped and sore, my mouth is dry, and my stomach is growling with hunger. Or does she mean am I okay mentally? Ha! She couldn't possibly be asking about my brain. My mind that's somehow trapped in her husband's body. In the future. She couldn't possibly know that my mind, self, id, consciousness, being, spirit, soul, or whatever the fuck she would call it has somehow jumped around in both time and place. That it somehow rested in an electronic box for thousands of years until her unfortunate husband decided to boot up the same device and stick his hand on it. No, she couldn't possibly be asking about that.

"I'm fine," I said in her husband's gruff voice.

She offered a slight smile. Her fingers felt nice running through my hair. Against my better judgment, I tried to sit up. Every muscle in my body fought against me. I winced and collapsed back into Aurora's lap.

"Take it easy," she said. "You're back now. Rest." I closed my eyes and laid back in her lap. I didn't have the energy for anything else.

"Ash. Where is he?" I asked.

"Ash?" My eyes were closed, so I couldn't see Aurora's face, but I could tell she didn't understand why Ash was the first person I asked about. "He is home with Alys and Zeke. Why?"

"Right..." I said. "No reason. What time is it?"

"Time? What do you mean?"

"Is it morning? Night?"

"It is almost sun up."

"Ugh," I grunted. *This was going to be more difficult than I expected.*

"He stopped shivering," Aurora said. She shifted her body to lay next to me on the floor of the hut. A thick fur blanket wrapped around our bodies.

"Who? Gray?" I asked.

"Yes, of course Gray. You must have hit your head." She rubbed my forehead. "Shortly after you fell asleep, he stopped. That must be a good thing, right?" Her voice had a faint echo of hope, just enough to be dangerous in a situation such as this.

"I don't know. You shouldn't get your hopes up. I still don't know if this will work."

"Well I think one of us should hope for the best. I know you've never been so great at that, so that leaves me." Aurora pressed her body against me, and moved her face close to mine. For the first time, I realized I was naked under the fur blanket. My body jolted as Aurora ran her hand down my chest and stomach.

"Wait!" I blurted out. I thought I would have a chance to tell her the truth before anything like this happened. I had underestimated Aurora's vigor. I rolled away from her, but her hands stayed on my body. They continued their journey down my stomach.

"What is it?" she said and giggled as if I were simply playing hard to get. She pulled her hands away, but only to pull her dress down. She sat up with the blanket around her waist.

"What about Gray?" I asked. Ransom's son slept soundly only a meter away from the two of us. He looked much more peaceful than he did before.

"He's asleep. But it's never stopped us before," Aurora said. I could tell her patience was fading, and soon she would become either angry or hurt.

Her light skin glowed in the firelight. Her hair draped over her shoulders and brushed against her breasts. I couldn't help but think Ransom was a lucky man. Aurora moved back towards me and gripped her hand around my bicep. She brought my hand up to her body and pressed it against her breast, while her other hand drifted up my thigh. I hesitated for a brief moment before pulling away.

"It's just ... I don't feel like myself right now, Aurora." I pulled her dress up from her waist to cover the rest of her body. "I'm exhausted, and I just don't think I would be any good to you right now." Aurora smiled. She reached out and squeezed my shoulder.

"I understand," she said. She pulled her arms through the straps on her dress. I was both relieved and disappointed. "It must have been hard out there. Ash didn't tell me much after you fell asleep. He told me that Tannyn died of the same sickness Gray has, and he said that you and Merit got separated. But nothing beyond that."

I wrapped the blanket over my shoulders. Outside the wind beat against the hut. The roof shook. Bits of pebbles and dust battered the outside of Ransom's home until it blended into an almost relaxing constant white noise.

"What happened out there, Ransom?"

I looked away from Ransom's wife. I didn't know the answer to that question. I only knew what Ash told me and what I could infer from that.

"Um ... Merit ... there was an armory..."

"A what?" Aurora asked.

"This room with weapons all over the walls. I got locked inside ... somehow. And there were these people chasing us." I tried to piece together the events as I told them. "I was stabbed. I ... I thought I was going to bleed to death. I thought that was it. I thought I would never see home again." I said only the things that I knew were true for both Ransom and me.

"My body was beaten. I was stabbed. I couldn't walk. And Ash ... he ... he saved me." Aurora had a look of terror on her face. A look of worry, like if the universe had tilted just the slightest bit differently, then her husband would not have come home. But in a way, the universe did tilt, and her husband didn't come home. Not all of him. "Ash let me out of the armory. These things ... these people chased us until we made it out."

"Were they human?" Aurora asked.

"I don't really know. Probably," I guessed. "But they didn't sound like it. They didn't move like it. It was like a pack of hungry lions were after us."

"Lions? What do you mean?"

"Oh ... uh ..." I searched for another word, but I suddenly questioned every word I thought to use. *What else would be unfamiliar to her? What else might give away that I am not who she thinks I am?* "Animals. Like wild animals."

"Oh my," Aurora whispered, looking away and trying to picture these hybrid humans.

Knowing how stories grew and spread through this village, I said, "It's not like it sounds. They were people. Like you and me, just angry. Hungry. Maybe a bit crazy."

"They don't sound like you and me," Aurora said, standing from the floor. She brought more wood over to the fire, stoking the embers until flames crept around the new logs. Gray rolled over onto his side, hugging the blankets against his chest.

"He looks like he's doing better," I said, changing the subject to something more positive.

"Yes, he does." Aurora sat next to her son and patted him on the head. "How did you know those medicines would help?" For the first time Aurora's demeanor changed from curious to questioning. She could dismiss the odd use of words or the fact that I didn't accept her advances, but she couldn't shake the fact that I knew exactly what medicines would work.

"I didn't know. Not really," I answered somewhat truthfully. "When we made it out of that place, I didn't have much hope of surviving. Not in my condition. I was bleeding to death." I pulled the blanket away from my body, revealing the gauze circling my torso. It was red and soaked through with dried blood.

"Oh my!" Aurora gasped. "Ash said you were hurt, but he didn't say how badly. I didn't want to undress your wound after you fell asleep. You looked so peaceful."

"It was much worse a few days ago. Once we were out, Ash showed me all of the medicines that he had discovered underground. I examined each. That vial gave me a feeling. Something in me told me that it would help. So, I put it in my body, just like I did for Gray."

"I could slap you for being so careless! I didn't send you out there to test these medicines on yourself! What if it killed you?"

"Then I would be dead either way." The wound was closed at this point, but the nanobots did little for the pain. Dried blood stuck and scabbed over the pink flesh on my stomach. "It worked. That's all that matters. And it looks like it worked on Gray too."

"Still, that is no excuse. That doesn't forgive the risk you took. I couldn't afford to lose you both."

"That isn't something you or I have any control over. That I know for sure."

Aurora stood over me. "Get some rest." She said and leaned down to cup my face in her hands. She kissed me on the mouth, lingering her lips against mine. Her lips tasted sweet, like she had just bitten into a fresh mango. I tried not to worry if I kissed her like she was used to. I simply enjoyed the moment of peace. In that moment, I thought of Vesa. "You're gonna need it. By sun up you are gonna have a crowd of folks here that want to know every detail of what you guys found out there."

CHAPTER 12

5280
NEW ALCATRAZ

The next morning, I sat crouched outside of Ransom's home, and watched the sun creep over the horizon of New Alcatraz. It was almost beautiful. It was becoming easier to see how the people here liked this. To them this was home, not a prison. To them they were descendants of the best and brightest that my society had to offer.

I held a handmade mug up to my lips, and let the warm steam waft into my face. Aurora called it tea, but it tasted more like grass boiled in water to me. My overstimulated taste buds were used to the chemicals in food from my own time, to flavors that were created in a lab out of things I couldn't pronounce, trace amounts of arsenic, lead, DEHP, BPA, PVC, and whatever else happened to slip into our food that they didn't tell us about. Maybe hot grass-flavored water wasn't so bad for a change.

A light snow fell around me. *Where did this snow come from?* Of all the times my father had visited this place throughout history, he had never mentioned snow. It appeared New Alcatraz would always be a place of extremes. There was no moderate landscape. No moderate weather. Only harshness on either end of the spectrum.

I sipped my grass water and watched people scurry about in a morning routine that would put some of Wayfield's most efficient factories to shame. The hunters of the village came home in the early morning with their trophies and handed them to the butcher, who sharpened his knives and carved the animals into manageable chunks. Members of each family came to the butcher to trade their wares for chunks of whatever animal the hunters brought in that day.

When the butcher finished, he passed the pelts onto another villager who tanned the hides at a tannery situated on the outskirts of the village. Even though the tannery was far away, the smell of carrion still filled the air. They dried the hides in the sun, then soaked them in water and beat them to remove the remaining fat and flesh from the hide. They soaked the cleaned hides again in some mixture that smelled like salt and urine, then dried them once more. The tannery passed the finished hides off to others who cut them into smaller pieces.

Groups of women sat and sewed the hides into water skins, boots, pants, bags, blankets, and whatever else they could think of. At the center of the village a few other men dug deep holes into the earth with makeshift tools. They collected the orange clay, molding it into cubes that they carried over to a crew of builders working on a new hut, like the one I'd slept in last night.

All around, people worked together. As far as I could tell there was no leader. No elected official, board of governors, or association that organized everything. Everyone just worked. Maybe I caught them on a remarkably good day, but either way it was impressive. It was the early stages of a society, when people had no choice but to work together. They didn't have the privilege of rebellion and war. But those would come soon enough. They always did.

Throughout the night and early morning, Gray looked better and better. He didn't wake up, but he looked more comfortable as he slept. He stopped sweating, and a touch of color returned to his face. Aurora even fell asleep on the floor next to Gray's bed. She could barely keep her eyes open.

"It's okay. You can rest now," I'd told her as her head nodded down towards her chest and her eyes pulled shut. She had her son back, and she believed she had her husband back. I still didn't have the nerve to explain the reality of the situation to her. I needed Ash to be there. I didn't know how a primitive society would react to the news.

Would there be a witch hunt? Would they perform some archaic bloodletting ritual to drain whatever evil inhabited Ransom's body? Drowning? Burning at a stake? I didn't know, but I knew human nature. I knew what ignorant people used to do when they met something they didn't understand. I had to tell her. I had to tell all of them, but I had to do it in a way that protected me. I had to be careful.

"Glad you made it back, Ransom," a man said as he walked by me with a load of orange clay bricks in his arms. I nodded and cupped my mug. The warmth burned my hands in a good way. The heat spread out through my body.

In the distance, I saw a familiar, hulking silhouette walk towards me. Ash's large body was noticeable from almost twenty meters away. Even though there were plenty of nanobots for him to take, even after I had given Gray a dose, he still refused. So he still walked with a limp.

"Keep 'em for someone else," he'd told me. "I'll live." Ash had told me what he had done for Ransom and Merit back in Buckley. He'd told me how many of those people he had fought. I didn't know how he managed to stay standing, much less walk back to his village. I had given him painkillers to get him through the night, but I told him it was only temporary. "A good night's sleep, and I will be ready for a new day," he'd said and swallowed the pills in one gulp.

Now he was up and walking towards me, while I had only managed to get out of bed and get one step outside of my hut. The wind blew Ash's long beard around his face. He looked like a Viking calmly walking into battle, until he knew he was close enough for me to see him. Then he smiled wide and waved. Every bit of intimidation fell away from him, and he looked almost giddy. Maybe because for a moment he thought I was really Ransom. Or maybe he liked being the only one who knew who I really was.

A woman and young boy walked behind him.

"Hello," he said loudly over the snowy wind. I stood to greet him, and my bones cracked.

"Good morning," I said.

"Yes," Ash paused and looked around awkwardly. "I suppose it is a good morning."

Motioning to the woman and boy who walked up just behind him, Ash said, "Alys and Zeke wanted to welcome you back."

"Good morning," I repeated. His wife looked at me, scrunching her brow together.

"Uh, Ransom was just talking about what a good morning it is," Ash interjected.

Looking around the village, Alys said, "It looks just like any other morning." His wife stepped forward and handed me a thick knitted wool scarf.

"Well we are so glad you made it back," she said in a quiet voice. She looked away just as she spoke. "I ... I'm sorry about Merit."

"I'm glad to be back," I answered, fooling one more person. "I owe it all to Ash. He saved my life." I said, hoping that Ransom would have said something similar. "He is a good man."

Smiling, Alys looked the large man in the eyes. "Yes, he is a wonderful man." Ash smiled and wrapped an oversized hand around her body, pulling her into him.

"Is Gray better?" Ash's son, Zeke, blurted out.

"I think so," I answered. "He is still resting, but he seems better."

"I made this for him." The boy held out some sort of trinket made from twigs and twine.

"Thank you. I am sure he will appreciate this very much."

"Okay, honey, I've gotta talk to Ransom now. I'll come find you at mid-day." Ash leaned over and kissed his wife.

"It was good to see you Ransom," Alys said to me. She placed her arm around their son and walked back through the village.

"Nice family," I said.

Watching them walk away, smiling, Ash said, "Yeah. They are. They really are. They make me feel lucky. Proud to be alive."

"It doesn't seem too bad here," I said, looking around the village as a gentle breeze brushed my new hair over my face. "Reminds me a little of where I grew up."

"C'mon. Back where you're from, you have those medicines, and food whenever you want it, right?" Ash chuckled.

"Convenience comes at a price," I said and sipped my tea.

"What do you mean?"

"I don't know…" I thought of a way to explain things to Ash. To explain that every new piece of technology brought a new rule or regulation. A new agency. And that every convenience gave something to us, but it also took something away as well. Sometimes it took our privacy. Other times it took away our ability to do something for ourselves. Or it eliminated human interaction. "It's hard to explain, but what you have here"—I pointed out at the villagers working together, trading, conversing face to face— "our conveniences wipe all of that out."

"Yeah, you mean the *work*? You guys don't have to work. Poor you." Ash laughed.

"Oh no, we still work. Work seems to never go away. But we don't interact. It's lonely where I'm from…" I thought back to my cramped underground apartment and how deep down I was so glad that Vesa came to my door that one evening. Until then, I hadn't realized just how lonely I really was.

"Seems to me it's you who let yourselves be lonely. Some things can't be taken away from you. They have to be given up."

"Maybe you're right," I said. "I'm just saying that sometimes you can take for granted what you have. And what you have here is pretty nice. You're pretty lucky."

"I think Ransom would agree with you on that. But Merit didn't think things were good enough. Now, I don't know what he would think." Ash lowered his head. "I hope he's alive," he said, but quickly changed his mind. "Maybe he's better off dead than with those people underground. How could those people have our same ancestors? You said yourself, the people who came here from your time were great men."

Shaking my head, I said, "Not every group of people is completely good or completely bad. Hell, one *person* can't be all good or all bad. Unfortunately, every society has good guys and bad guys."

"But who wants to be bad?" Ash asked. "Who would *want* to be that way?"

"Some people don't know any other way."

The two of us stood in silence for some time. The breeze blew snow in small spirals, pushing and pulling the harsh smells back and forth from the tannery a kilometer away.

Ash finally broke the silence. "I see Aurora made you some of her famous tea?"

I nodded and took a sip to show that I really did like it.

"You don't think it tastes like dirt?"

"Dirt?" I said and tried to act surprised. "Nah, I wouldn't say that."

"Well, don't tell Aurora, but I always thought it tasted like dirt," Ash whispered.

"Don't worry, your secrets safe with me, Ash."

"Ransom likes it." A large smile grew over Ash's face at the thought of his friend. "At least he says he does. I always figured he just didn't want to hurt her feelings," he said.

Ash came and stood next to me, towering over me. We leaned against the wall of Ransom's home.

"Yeah, it is pretty nice here," Ash said to himself, tilting his head back to watch the clouds drift through the blue sky.

Leaning into me, he whispered, "So, did you tell her yet?" I shook my head and looked around to see who else was nearby. "I couldn't keep that kind of secret in for that long," Ash said. I shot him a look. "No, no, no," he said and held his hands up. "I said nothing. I just mean if I were you."

"I didn't know if she'd believe me," I said, keeping my voice low. "She's happy now. I can tell. Gray is getting better."

"That's great!"

"Yeah," I said, but I didn't share his surprise. I had little doubt the nanobots would work. The thought of Gray improving left a sinking feeling inside me. I surely didn't wish Gray ill, but I would be content if he stayed asleep for at least a few more days. I could muddle through pretending I was married to Aurora, but I had no idea how to pretend to be Gray's father. That was beyond anything I had experienced before. No frame of reference.

"That's why I didn't tell her. She deserves some peace in her life. Plus, I need you there when I tell her."

"Really?"

"Really," I said. "You know her. You can help keep her calm. You can help me convince her."

"Sure," he said.

"Really? That was easy."

"Ransom is like family to me. So are Aurora and Gray. Ransom would want me there for them too." He laid a hulking hand on my shoulder. "Plus, I don't mind helping a friend. But you better say something soon, cuz everyone around here is going to want us to explain what happened out there. They want answers, like what happened to Tannyn and Merit. People are already talking about going back there."

"Back!" I shook my head. "Why would they want to go back there? Why would they want to live down there, in the dark?"

"You keep talking like that and *I* may even start thinking you really are Ransom," Ash said and smiled.

"You're right. We need to tell them what it's like down there. We have to tell them about whoever else lived down there that tried to kill you guys," I said. "But we need to talk to Aurora."

"Talk to me about what?" Aurora said.

CHAPTER 13

2075
DENVER, COLORADO

"Cooper! Cooper! It's me, it's Vesa"

She let go of her brother only to look at his face. Under a scruffy beard that was unkempt even for a prisoner, his cheeks were sunken and his eyes were surrounded by dark circles. His skin had a pale yellowish complexion that resembled the pages of an antiqued book.

"Are you okay?" she asked. Cooper stared through her and looked at the cement wall of the holding cell.

"Coop," Vesa said and snapped her fingers several times in his face. "Coop." Cooper shook his head slightly, snapping out of whatever dream state he was in. His eyes changed from glazed to focused and he turned to look Vesa in the eyes.

"Vesa?" he asked in a whisper, like his own voice was unfamiliar to him. He scrunched his face and furrowed his brow. "Vesa?" he repeated. Vesa gasped and smiled to reveal almost every tooth in her mouth. She threw her arms around her brother once again.

"Yes, it's me Cooper." She pressed a hand into his dirty hair, pushing his head down to her shoulder. His body felt frail against hers, like an old man.

"Is it really you?" Cooper asked and slowly moved his hands to hug his sister. With each bit of contact he made with her body, his eyes seemed to focus a bit more on his sister. "It's you! It's really you."

The brother and sister embraced for what seemed like forever. They held each other and cried for the five years lost between the two of them. They cried for the missed experiences and the years they could never get back. Their bodies shook with each sob, leaning against each other. The fluorescent lights overhead buzzed and flickered.

"How?" was all Cooper could say after a long stretch of wordless crying. Vesa pulled herself away from Cooper and wiped away any tears that lingered on her face. "H-h-how are you here?" Cooper's face dropped and his eyes grew wide. "Did they catch you t-t-too?" The stutter was new to Vesa. Likely the result of his treatment by the Ministry, a learned response. Fear of finishing his sentence. Fear of saying the wrong thing.

"No … well kind of," Vesa said. "There's so much you don't know." She looked down and tried to think of where to begin. "How have they treated you?" she asked instead of diving into the grim details of Powell's *plan*. She knew how unlikely it was that the Ministry would release the two of them. She didn't need Cooper to tell her.

Cooper hesitated. "They … haven't spoken to me in … I don't know … how long have I been here?"

"Five years," Vesa answered.

"Five years!" Cooper repeated. "Five years," he said quietly to himself looking down and running his hands over his face as if he could feel how he'd aged in five years. His eyes switched back to glazed and unfocused, staring at the blank wall behind Vesa. His eyes lingered for several long seconds until he blinked rapidly. "I didn't realize … time in here you know, it's kind of hard."

"Have they hurt you?" Vesa asked, knowing the answer, just not the details.

"Early on, when they — when they — first caught me, right after the-the-the thing with Whitman in the parking garage," Cooper said and Vesa nodded. Her body tensed at the thought of Cooper talking too much about switching Whitman with an imposter android. She knew they were being filmed, and she needed to keep as much information to herself as possible. Anything she knew that they didn't was a point to negotiate from. "Early on, they beat me," Cooper said and swallowed deeply when he said the word 'beat,' like it meant more than it sounded.

"They beat me up pretty bad. Broke my nose and a couple ribs. My wrist." Cooper held his left hand in the air. "I think my brain swelled or something cuz they kept me in the m-m-medical w-w-w-ward for a couple weeks. In a coma." Vesa wasn't surprised by how the Ministry treated her brother, but hearing him recount the abuse made her burn inside. Her heart pounded, and she balled her hands into fists. "They wanted to know what I was doing with the Whitman android and who I worked for." Cooper ran his hand through his long, matted hair, contorting his face as he tried to remember what else they asked of him.

"What did you tell them?" Vesa asked.

"Nothing," Cooper said. "Eventually they st-st-stopped asking, and sometime after that they moved me to another cell. They only came by once a day to drop off my meal. Every few days they threw a bucket of cold water on me to clean me off."

"They never asked you anything else?" Vesa asked, and Cooper shook his head.

"I think I would have preferred if they did. I went must have gone y-y-years without hearing another person's voice." Cooper stared off into the distance and nervously chewed on his bottom lip, another habit Vesa had never seen in him before.

"They found me shortly after they got you," Vesa said. Cooper jerked his head to look at his sister.

"They've had you this long too?" he asked.

"No." Vesa shook her head. "They wanted me to help them."

"Help them?" Cooper said.

"They said if I cooperated I would get you back. I agreed," Vesa said.

"Vesa!" Cooper said, backing away from his sister and gripping his head with both hands. His eyes shifted, glancing around the otherwise bare cell as if to anticipate another attack or surprise. "Did Whitman agree? What about Finn?"

Vesa sighed. "I … I told them you died."

"Died?" Cooper shouted. "They think I'm dead?"

"I'm sorry," Vesa pleaded. "But I had to. If I said you were captured, they would get suspicious. They know I would do anything for you, to keep you safe. They would have kept me in the dark with everything. I would never have had any information to trade for you."

"And they would have been right to." Cooper scoffed. "You ac-actually wanted to collect information for these people?"

"Do you know what they would have done to you if I *didn't* agree to help them? You think they just decided to stop beating you after a couple weeks? It was because I agreed to help them. We wouldn't be talking right now if I hadn't agreed."

"Vesa…" Cooper said, still shaking his head. "You can't trust these people. They will *never* let me go, and now they will never let *you* go. That's how they are."

"You sound just like Powell," Vesa said.

"Powell?" Cooper asked. "Who's that?"

"Nothing. It's nobody. Just someone who distrusts the Ministry as much as you."

"Well, he's right. What did they want you to do?"

"They wanted me to get them the mind transfer device once it was complete."

"Oh my god!" Cooper threw his skinny arms in the air. "Tell me you didn't, Vesa."

"I didn't," Vesa said and Cooper breathed a deep sigh. "I couldn't, cuz we never got it working."

"Couldn't get it working," Cooper said.

"It took time after you were caught. You knew the most about the project, so that set us back."

"But five years? We were so close before. It takes more than a minor setback to lose five years," Cooper said.

"I'd say losing you was more than a minor setback," Vesa said, pacing the room. She didn't mind having this fight in front of the Ministry's cameras. Her story was the device didn't exist, and she was going to stick to it.

"I don't know if I should be relieved that you guys don't have a completed device to hand over to the Ministry, or if I should be pissed off that you guys weren't able to finish what I started."

"Finn had some ideas that just didn't pan out how he hoped. That derailed the project for about eighteen months."

"Finn … he should just stick to hacking cell phones and remotely turning people's thermostats off." Cooper shook his head in disbelief.

"Hey, he tried his best!" Vesa said.

"When we found him, he was barely a hacker. He knew just enough to screw with people's home automation. He was happy just flickering people's lights on and off from across the street. Five years. Five years. Five fucking years." He said.

"You should be happy we never got the thing to work. If we did, then the Ministry would have it," Vesa said, hoping the Ministry believed her words. Hoping that they never found it buried in the air vent of their own facility, right under their noses.

"Cuz of you!" he said.

"Look!" Vesa said, finally reaching a point beyond the back-and-forth bickering. "They would have kept beating you if not for me. They would have done god-knows-what-else to you, shock therapy, pull your fingernails out, sleep deprivation, starvation, or whatever else you and I are too naïve or not sadistic enough to imagine. They would have done it. You wouldn't have made it five years."

Cooper shot his sister a look of contempt and opened his mouth to rebut her assumption.

"I know you," Vesa continued. "You wouldn't have made it *one* year if I didn't make a deal with them. Nothing against you. I wouldn't have survived either!"

Rolling his eyes, Cooper said, "Well, w-w-we all know that if *you* can't do something then I *surely* couldn't, right?"

"That's not what I—look, face it, I saved your life!" Vesa sat back in her chair and stared at Cooper.

"I know," Cooper said, and slowly nodded, avoiding eye contact with his sister. Finally, a familiar habit. "Thank you," he said softly, squeezing his eyes shut and trapping any tear that may have accumulated. "Thank you," he repeated and hugged his sister.

Vesa wrapped her arms around her brother. "It's gonna be okay," Vesa said, in Cooper's ear. "We have a plan."

CHAPTER 14

5280
NEW ALCATRAZ

"It's about what happened in the vault," I said. The three of us stood in Ransom's home. "It's about Ransom."

"Ransom?" Aurora squinted. "You mean *you*?"

"Yes and no," I said. I looked at Ash for help. "It's ... uh—"

"The stuff down there," Ash interjected. "Aurora, it was amazing. The things down there, it was unlike anything I could have imagined from the stories. None of us could have imagined. There—there were things like these weapons we brought back." Ash pointed at the black rifles sitting on the compacted dirt floor. "And the medicines. Just the structure itself was amazing. The walls were flat. No dips or divots. I mean flat. The floor was so solid that it felt strange under my feet."

"I don't need to hear about how flat the walls were. What are you trying to say?" Aurora said, spinning her hand to coax more information out of us.

Pointing at the bag that housed the mind transfer device, I said, "There's this device. It's advanced technology. *Really* advanced. More advanced than anything else down there."

"So what is it? What does it do?" she asked. I rubbed the back of my neck and tried to string together words she could understand.

"How can I put this?" I asked myself. "A person has an essence, you see. It's part of them that makes them different from everyone else. It is something that holds their memories, their attitude, their mind. It's what makes you '*you*.'" I thought back to the time Vesa had tried to explain this device to me. These were her words leaving my mouth. Ash looked confused, but Aurora didn't seem flustered at all.

"What? Like our soul?" she said.

"Exactly!" I said. It wasn't the word I would have used, but I was thankful she had an answer at all. I should have assumed that the one thing that carried across civilizations was the mystical idea of a soul. "This device, it can take that part of you and move it." I motioned my hand around my head and then moved my hand away, like I just pulled a cobweb from my face and dropped the invisible strings on the floor away from me.

"Move it how? Where?" Aurora sat down at the foot of Gray's bed and placed her hand on his back. By now the boy slept peacefully. No more writhing in pain.

Rubbing Ransom's dirt-covered hand across my face, I said, "*How?* I don't really know. But I do know it can move your mind, your soul, to another place. Another time. Another … person." I let the last word ease out of my mouth. Aurora looked at me and then turned towards Ash, her eyes wide, pleading for more information. Ash simply nodded and confirmed what I told her.

"Another person? What does this have to do with me? What does it have to do with you? Ransom, you're scaring me."

"Your husband used this device when he was underground," I said, kneeling down to look Aurora in the eye. "I used the device also." I said.

"Yeah, my husband, *YOU*, used the device, and…?" Aurora asked.

"I am not your husband. Ransom used this device three days ago.

I used this device a very very long time ago, and somehow my mind ended up in Ransom's body."

Aurora squinted and backed away from Ash and me.

"It's true," Ash said and placed his hand on Aurora's shoulder. She quickly jerked her body away from Ash.

"What are you saying?" She moved to the other end of the room, her back against the wall. "You are my husband! Ransom! You…" I just shook my head.

"No, I am not. My name is Powell."

"Ash." Aurora ignored me and took several steps towards him. "Why is he doing this? This isn't funny. Does he think that since Gray is getting better it's okay for him to joke around?"

"It's not a joke," Ash said. He couldn't hold Aurora's gaze for long. Even a man his size was scared of an angry woman. "I found him," Ash said, pointing at me. "*Powell*, down there. He was lost. Confused. I thought Ransom had hit his head at first. I thought maybe he was just stunned. But he hasn't snapped out of it for days now."

"So what? Maybe something did happen. Maybe this is Ransom, and he *will* snap out of it." Aurora looked back and forth between us.

"No," Ash said. "The stuff he knew, Ransom wouldn't know." This was why I needed Ash here. I needed someone to corroborate my story. Back me up. "He knew the way out of the underground vault. He knew how to use these guns. Ransom didn't know that. Powell knew about these medicines. This isn't Ransom."

Aurora covered her face with both hands and moaned.

Continuing on and trying to find some positive side to our situation, Ash said, "In a way, we are lucky this happened. It made it possible to save Gray."

Aurora leaned against the wall of the hut and slid down until her knees bent up towards her chest.

"Once you get to know him, Powell is a good man," Ash said,

pointing at me.

"Stop calling him that!" Aurora yelled, no longer caring if she woke Gray or not. "What about Merit? Maybe he knows what happened to you." I looked at Ash for guidance on the subject of Merit.

"We don't know what happened to Merit," Ash said.

"I doubt he is alive," I said, wondering why I decided to chime in with that horrible prediction.

"I hate to say it, but Pow—uh, he is probably right," Ash said as Aurora scowled at even the first syllable of my name. "If you saw those people down there, you wouldn't have much hope of seeing Merit again." Aurora sobbed and covered her face with her hands. Ash and I made eye contact. "I'll leave you two alone for a little. But I will be right outside if you need me."

I locked my eyes on Ash, pleading with him to stay. Nodding at me, he stepped out into the cold, leaving me alone with Ransom's sick son and crying wife. I had inherited a domestic nightmare.

After letting some time go by, I said, "I know I look like him, but I am someone else. I am from a different time."

Aurora looked up at me and said, "If you are joking, or if you are making this up, I will kill you. If there is any bit of Ransom in you, this is your final chance to tell me the truth."

"This is the truth," I said softly. "Ransom is somewhere else."

"What about Gray? What do we tell him when he wakes up? If he wakes up."

"He'll wake up. I am confident. That stuff I injected him with, I know what it can do. Just give it time."

"He won't understand any of this, Rans—what did you say your name was?"

"Powell."

"He won't understand any of this. He needs a father. I need a husband. The village needs Ransom. Is he still inside of there somewhere?" Aurora pointed at my head. "Is there some way to get him back? Can this device reverse whatever happened to you?"

"I don't know. I'm still trying to wrap my head around all of this too. You have to understand; this device would confuse most everyone from my own time. It's not as if this is common. This device is the only one of its kind, and I was the first to use it. So nothing is for certain. There is no guarantee I will ever be able to reverse what happened."

Aurora exhaled so forcefully I imagined there was no air left inside of her lungs.

"So that's it then?" I watched as Aurora plowed through the stages of grief. She moved on from denial right into anger. "I am supposed to just take *you* as my new husband? Some person who I know nothing about, who took over Ransom's body? I am supposed to share a home with you? A bed?" Aurora gasped and held her hand over her mouth. "Last night," she said and wrapped her arms around her body. "It was you." Aurora turned her back towards me in shame.

"It's okay," I said. "You didn't know."

"Yeah, it's okay for you! *You* knew, and you let me just sit there half naked with my hands all over you! *You*, not Ransom."

Outside, I heard Ash talking to another man. Ash's voice was calm, but the other voice was panicked and rushed.

"I couldn't tell you. Not then. It was too soon. Plus, I didn't think you would believe me if I didn't have Ash here to back up my story." For the first time since I made it back from Buckley, I felt like I was truly talking to a stranger. The air inside the hut was different from the night before, when Aurora thought I was Ransom.

"That's convenient for you, isn't it? A woman throws herself at you and it's not the right time to tell her that you aren't really her husband!" The noises continued outside.

"Aurora, it's not like we did anything. I did my best to stop you."

"That doesn't make it better," she said and shook her head. The door rattled.

"Just wait one second," Ash said from beyond the door.

"You expecting anyone?" I asked Aurora. She shook her head.

I moved towards the bag on the floor that held the guns from Buckley, but the door burst open before I could grab one of them. Cold air rushed in, and a thin, ragged man stood in the doorway. Beneath a torn shirt, his chest heaved. His face had claw marks running down it, and he held his right side like at least one of his ribs was cracked.

Aurora gasped. I moved ever so slightly towards the bag with the gun. Ash pushed his way through the door, standing between us and the beaten man.

"Merit, I told you to wait just one second. Ransom and Aurora are talking."

"Merit?" I said.

Pointing a scrawny finger in my direction, Merit said, "Don't listen to a word he says. He's lying!"

CHAPTER 15

5280
NEW ALCATRAZ

"It's not what you think," I said, holding my hand out towards Merit and moving my body between him and Aurora. An instinct to protect perhaps.

"What do you mean? What is he lying about?" Aurora asked, a glimmer of hope in her voice.

"What did he tell you?" Merit asked. He winced with every other word that left his mouth. A string of dried blood traced from inside his ear down his chin. Ice and snow clung to his patchy beard. He licked at a wide gash that tore through his lip.

"What do you mean?" Ash asked. His deep voice commanded an answer. "You don't even know what Powell was telling her."

Merit's stare bore a hole through my head. Even though he was injured, Merit's legs were tensed and ready to pounce. The one hand that wasn't cupping his cracked rib was balled into a fist.

"I don't know what happened back there, but there is something you need to hear," I tried to calm him down. "I am not Ransom. I am not your brother. I am someone else."

Merit's face changed.

"What?" he asked. "Not my brother?"

"That's what I was trying to tell you outside," Ash said. "That is what Aurora and Powell were talking about in here."

"Powell?" Merit said. By now his fist loosened.

"That's right. My name is Powell," I said and placed my hand on my chest. "Something happened down there underground, and your brother … he…" Even though I had just explained it to Aurora, I couldn't arrange the words again to make it sound believable.

"Ransom supposedly used something he found down there, some machine, and it pulled his soul out of his body. And now, somehow, Powell ended up moving into Ransom's body." Aurora said.

"It's true," Ash confirmed.

"Unless you know something else?" Aurora said hopefully. "You said he is lying, right? What do you know? What happened down there?"

Merit stood still for only a second before collapsing on the floor. He sat on his knees, and his body went limp. Every bit of energy he had conserved left him.

"So you're not Ransom?" Merit asked and looked up at me. His eyes had changed from when he first barged into the hut.

"I know it's hard to understand, but—"

"Just tell me, are you Ransom or not?" Merit said with the little bit of urgency he had left in his body.

"No," was all I could say.

Merit raised his head, and his eyes met Gray. The boy still slept in the bed.

"And Gray? Is he okay? Is he still—is he still alive?"

"He is," Aurora answered. Merit exhaled and buried his face in his hands. His shoulders slumped forwards and he let out an enormous sigh.

"Thank the gods," he said.

"But what did you mean that he is lying?" Aurora asked. "What happened to you?" Merit looked up again. His eyes darted around the room. From Gray, to Aurora, to Ash, to me, and then back to Gray.

"I was wrong, I guess," he said. "When we got separated," he said and looked at Ash. "Ransom and I ran. He tripped and hit his head."

"So he *did* hit his head!" Aurora blurted out.

"Once he got up, Ransom was just spouting nonsense. Stuff about Tannyn and the sickness. He said *I* caused the sickness to spread. Stuff I knew wasn't true. He seemed out of it and started fighting me. We were attacked and got split up. That was the last I saw of him ... I hid in a small room until they stopped searching for us. Eventually I was able to find my way out. What happened with you?" Merit asked Ash.

"I fought off the rest of those people and went off to find medicines," Ash said. "Later I heard Ransom yell down one of the long hallways. He was locked in a room with more of these useless weapons." Ash said and pointed at the rifle on the floor. "He was near death, with a stab wound in his stomach and beat to a pulp."

Merit looked at me quizzically, and took inventory of my visible injuries. Most had healed or at least appeared less severe than they were days ago.

"Your stomach? How did you survive?" he asked me.

"The medicines," I said and pointed at the bag Ash had filled with whatever he could find in the medical ward. "When Ash found me, he had already found the medicines for Gray."

Merit ran both of his hands through his hair and massaged his scalp. "I don't understand," he said.

"It'll take time," Ash said. "You were right though, about the vaults underground. Your persistence saved Gray's life. You always knew we would need to go there. Your father would be proud of you."

"No, he wouldn't." Merit lowered his head. "I wasn't right. That place is not a place any person should live. That was not the salvation

I thought it would be. It was not the place my father went looking for."

"Well, I owe you my life," Aurora said to Merit as she kneeled down and threw her arms around him. "Your nephew owes you his life as well." She squeezed, but Merit kept his arms at his side. He peered over Aurora's shoulder and looked at Gray sleeping in his bed. "That goes for you too, Ash. From the sound of it, you fought off a lot of people to give Merit and Ransom a chance to make it out, *and* you found the medicines. I am forever grateful to you both." Aurora cupped Merit's face in her hands before smiling and kissing him on the forehead.

"It was nothing," Ash said and shook his head. "Ransom would do the same for my children." Merit said nothing.

"Are you sure about all of this? What about what Merit said about Ransom hitting his head?" Aurora turned to me, still hoping this was all a mistake. A simple concussion.

"I'm positive," I said.

"Aurora, I spent three days walking in the snow with this man. The way he speaks, the things he says, the things he knows." He shook his head. "It's not Ransom. I promise."

A look of defeat washed over Aurora's face. Ash turned towards the door and gripped the handle.

"Ash," I said to stop him, "would it be okay if I stayed with you and your family tonight?" He let go of the door and turned to face us.

"I would be happy to have you as my guest, Powell. But are you prepared to inform the village of who you are? Or would you rather create a story as to why you are not staying with your own wife and child?" I looked at Aurora and then back to Ash.

"It's okay," Aurora said. "You are welcome here. Gray will want to see his father when he wakes up." Aurora placed her hand across Gray's forehead. "Merit, will you stay here tonight as well? Just until Powell and I become more comfortable with our current … situation?"

Merit shook his head quickly, seemingly snapping him out of some daydream. "Yeah, I can stay here. I need to wash up at my place and catch up on sleep today. But I can be back here by sundown."

"Here," I said and moved towards the bag that held the medicine. I rummaged my hand through the pills, bandages, capsules, and vials of nanobots. I held out three painkillers, disinfectant pads, and a roll of bandages to Merit. Merit looked down at my hand in confusion. "Swallow two of these pills now, and take the third in a couple hours if you're still in pain. Clean your wounds with this, and then wrap them in the bandages." Merit turned to look at Ash, who nodded.

"They helped me," Ash said. "Like magic. But don't chew them," Ash scrunched his face. "Too bitter." Merit slowly reached out for the medicine. I nodded like I was coaxing a wild deer to eat from my hand.

"Well, I've had enough *magic* from that underground place," Aurora said under her breath.

"This will help my chest?" Merit asked, snatching the pills away as if I were a monster or the results of a failed science experiment.

"It will dull the pain. Wrap your body tightly in cloth and try not to breathe very deep. They should heal in several weeks."

"Weeks?" Merit asked, struggling to lift his hand up to his mouth and eventually dropping two of the pain killers in his mouth.

"Thirty days or so," I said. Merit nodded, understanding the concept of days.

"Rest up," Ash said as he opened the door to leave.

"Yeah, you need rest," I told Merit.

"I wasn't talking to him," Ash said. "I was talking to you. Rest up today, because by tomorrow the village will be fresh out of firewood." Ash nodded towards a beaten axe leaning against the door frame.

CHAPTER 16

Ransom's hand bled until his entire arm was bright crimson. He held his hand to his chest, squeezing his wrist to try and stop the bleeding. The agent stood in the white room, holding Ransom's pinky and ring finger in his hand, but Ransom knew his fingers looked different than these. They were smaller and too clean.

"Now that that's out of the way, we can get to know each other better." He knelt down and tossed the two fingers at Ransom. They hit his chest and rolled down to his lap. Ransom breathed heavily, his chest thrusting up and down.

"I am Agent Saunders," the man said in a deep voice and placed his hand on his chest. "Now, I didn't want to do that, but orders are orders." He grinned. Saunders was slightly older than Ransom, with bits of gray peppered through his short beard, and hair cut close to his head. Saunders stood, paced the room, and rolled his sleeves up, exposing several faded inkings tracing over his forearms. For only a moment, Ransom forgot about the pain and wondered why a person would draw on their skin or how it was done.

"I need you to tell me why you were down in Buckley," Saunders said, his back turned to Ransom. A humming noise rattled around somewhere in the ceiling, and a cold rush of air spilled into the white room. "None of this medicine bullshit. We both know that's just some story. It's not a bad tactic." Saunders nodded in approval. "Telling yourself some story in your head over and over again until you start to believe it. Pushes the truth out of your brain." Saunders motioned his hand around his head like he was pushing some invisible thing into the side of his head.

"In the service, I had fellow soldiers who became POWs, some imprisoned in Iran. Others in Russia. Some of them tried that strategy. Tell a story over and over again." Saunders shook his head, looking blankly at the white walls and picturing his imprisoned comrades. "The only ones who made it home were the ones who stopped telling that story. If you stick to that story, it will be the last story you ever tell. I promise you that."

"It's … it's not a story," Ransom stammered, still not used to his new voice. He felt different in this body. Besides the fact that he was shot in the leg and missing two fingers, something else was different. "My son is sick. Higgs got something, or maybe Tannyn gave it to him … I don't know."

Saunders walked towards Ransom and drove his boot straight down onto Ransom's bleeding thigh, pushing blood out of his gunshot wound. Ransom's screams bounced around the small white cell. It felt as if a fire had been lit inside his leg and left to burn from the inside out.

Through gritted teeth, Saunders said, "I told you, none of this medicine bullshit." He reached down and ripped the clothes off of Ransom. Ransom looked down to see the same letters as on the other man's shirt, TDA, embroidered into his own clothing. The material was stiff and rough. Just one more thing to cause Ransom discomfort. "Take it off," Saunders demanded.

Ransom slowly sat up and pulled the uniform off his body, peeling his arms out of the sleeves, smearing blood on the inside of one. Ransom worked slowly to keep his fresh wound from brushing the inside of the rough shirt. But Saunders grew impatient and jerked the clothing, dragging the shirt across his missing fingers, sending intense shocks of pain up his arm.

A quick glance at his chest told Ransom that, like his fingers, this was not him. Smaller and less hairy than he was. A long, deep cut ran across Ransom's chest. Saunders grabbed the uniform and yanked the rest of it away from Ransom. He gripped the black knife he'd used to remove Ransom's fingers and bent down until his face was almost touching Ransom's.

Slowly, he dragged the knife across Ransom's chest, but didn't puncture the skin. The cold air washed against Ransom's half-naked body.

"My buddies from the service. The POWs. The ones that didn't talk … at least didn't talk right away … they found out the hard way about this little spot between your shoulder and your neck," Saunders said and traced his knife up until the tip rested in the triangular divot between Ransom's neck and shoulder, just next to the collar bone. "It's a bundle of nerves. Any sort of injury would cause great pain." Saunders slowly pushed the knife harder and harder into the skin until he felt it give way, and his knife sunk down into Ransom.

Ransom jerked away and screamed. It was a scream unlike Ransom had ever heard, partly because he had never experienced such pain, and partly because it was in another person's voice. Saunders held his other hand over Ransom's throat, pushing him against the cold, white wall. He drove the knife deeper and deeper into the bundle of nerves resting inside Ransom's body. Ransom let out more garbled screams, but none of them fully formed with Saunders' hand wrapped around his throat.

Blood spilled out and pooled in the small, indented space near Ransom's neck. Saunders twisted his blade, making the initial opening wider and allowing more blood out. Ransom writhed. His body shook and jerked uncontrollably. He kicked his legs, and banged his head back and forth against the hard wall just to take his mind off the pain in his neck, but nothing worked. Nothing could break his mind away from this pain. Saunders pulled his knife out and wiped the blade onto Ransom's pants.

"There's another spot just like that on the other side of your neck too," Saunders said. "But I am in no rush. And don't' worry, you won't bleed to death just from that."

He stood and backed away several steps. Ransom's body shivered both from the cold and from the pain. He blinked his eyes rapidly and puffed breaths out of his mouth, trying to manage the pain. Trying to slow his heartbeat down and slow the flow of blood from his leg, hand, and now his neck. Like he had any control over the flow of blood.

"There was this guy, this assignment I had. This was an assignment for Wayfield. Not the military. But what's the difference, right?" Saunders chuckled and pointed the tip of his knife at Ransom. "He was in the cell next door … or was that his partner … maybe it was two cells down…" Saunders stopped to ponder the details of his story, then waved his hand in the air and shook his head. "It doesn't matter. This guy wouldn't do what we wanted, and his partner was almost as stubborn. We needed them to show us how a particular piece of technology worked. Simple, right?" Saunders turned his back to Ransom and breathed in deep, his chest swelling.

He moved his head to one side and then to the other to crack the bones in his neck. "Well he didn't want to do it. He kept telling us over and over again that he didn't know how this thing worked. Sound familiar?" Saunders turned back around.

"We didn't need him to talk though. We just needed him to show us, you know, with his hands. So, to speed things up I brought a pot of glue to a boil and shoved a funnel in his mouth. It took two others to hold this man down, but we managed. I pushed the funnel deep into his throat." Saunders mimicked each movement like this person was sitting in front of him. "I wasn't sure if the funnel led to his stomach or his lungs. I'm not a doctor." Saunders laughed.

Ransom shivered more and more, as the cold wind rushed into the room in a steady stream. His teeth chattered together, vibrating his entire head. He had felt colder weather back at home, but he was usually fully dressed.

"So, I got about a half a quart of that boiling glue down before this son of a bitch goes into shock. Doctors rushed in and tried to save him." Saunders shook his head. "Poor bastard. You'd think it was the actual glue that did it, right? The boiling liquid." Saunders shook his head. "It wasn't the glue that killed him.

"The medical team studied this guy's remains. They looked at his esophagus and his organs. They found it was the *steam*. The steam built up so much that it burst his organs inside of him. Ha!" Saunders laughed. "Of course, he would have suffocated anyways, but the steam got to him first." Saunders paused and tilted his head, a wistful expression on his face.

"His partner gave us what we wanted once he saw the body. The point here is that it's not always what you think will kill you. It isn't the bleeding that will do you in. It'll be this cold air." Saunders pointed towards the ceiling.

"This thing gets cold, well below freezing. You'll throw your back out shivering long before you bleed to death. Hell, your blood will probably freeze inside your wounds before long. So, I'm gonna go get me a thick jacket and a cup of tea. While I'm gone I want you to forget all this medicine shit. These stories. I need you to tell me what your purpose was. Simple. And just remember, we have your girlfriend down the hall. If I fuck up and accidentally kill you, we just move on to her." Saunders walked toward the wall, waving his hand in some random pattern until it slid open. "Get comfortable," Saunders said and left Ransom in the freezing room alone.

CHAPTER 17

Cold air puffed out of my mouth as I swung the axe into the tree. The vibrations from the axe connecting with the tree shook through my fingers and travelled up my arms. After four or five swings, I had to pause or else my hands grew numb from the cold and the shock wave.

It was midday, and I had only chopped a single tree down, and was working on my second. I remembered these trees from my first time in New Alcatraz, but I remembered them being thin and brittle. I remembered the ashy dirt that settled underneath the trees, and the long insects that crawled through it. Back then, the trees' power came from their numbers. From afar, they looked like a wall. Up close, it was dense, but there were tight gaps to slither and climb through. I wondered if this was the forest that I had slept in on my first night in New Alcatraz, or maybe the one where I'd rescued Red from his torturous captor.

I wondered how much harder this would be if I were still in my own body. Ransom's arms were strong, but I suspected something in my mind, *my own mind*, stopped me from having the same expertise or coordination that Ransom likely had developed over years of chopping wood.

I glanced at the village and back at the forest. Throughout my short time with these people, I'd observed their way of life. I had seen how they divided the labor, and how they struggled just to survive day-to-day. *There's got to be a better way*, I thought, but couldn't precisely figure out what that *way* was.

My wounds, Ransom's wounds, had healed. A short scar had formed on my stomach, from where the psychotic cannibals had stabbed me. *Why would they stab him*, I wondered. Ash had told me these men had guns, and they knew how to use them, but they had decided to attack me up close. *They couldn't have run out of bullets. I was in a room filled with weapons. Why a knife?*

My jaw still ached, likely a remnant injury from the brawl with the cannibals. But I could chew solid food. My hands and fingers had healed enough for me to wrap them around the beaten axe that I used to fell the trees, but now, after swinging the axe for the better part of the morning, I kind of wished I was still healing. Each morning and evening I swallowed more painkillers. Between me, Ash, and Merit, we would run out soon.

Ash approached, his feet sinking deep into the snow. He grinned.

"I never thought I would see the day when Ransom looked so clueless with an axe," he said, reaching out his hand. "Here, let me help you." Ash smiled as he gripped the axe in his large hand, holding it like it was light as a pencil. "The first cut, you should go straight in, like this," he said, holding the blade of the axe straight against the tree trunk. "Then come down at an angle from above the first cut." Ash moved the axe a bit higher and angled the blade down this time. "Then your last swing should be on the other side of the trunk." He circled around the tree holding the blade against the trunk. "Three swings," he said, and handed the axe back to me with a smile.

"Simple," I said, out of breath, as I sat on the only stump I'd created the entire day.

Ash's body stood blocking most of the sun from my eyes. He shuffled, and for the first time I sensed he was nervous.

"Something on your mind?" I asked.

"Well," Ash said, trying to find a place to start. "It's Ransom ... where is he? His mind? Where are you?" Ash crouched down letting the sun shine on my face once again. He rested his arms on his knees and his shoulders somehow grew even wider.

"I don't know. I can only guess. That machine he used ... it's not exact. His mind could have disappeared, or it could still somehow be in that machine."

"You mean his mind is just sitting in that box back in his home? How can that be?" Ash said and scratched his hands in his bushy beard.

"I don't know if that's possible or how it would be possible. I don't know how my mind stayed in the machine for so long either. I used it a long time ago." I squeezed the bridge of my nose between my thumb and forefinger. "My point is, almost anything is possible. Anything. But ... but the most likely outcome would be that if I am *here*, then Ransom is where I was before all of this."

"You mean in your time?" Ash asked and smiled. "With all the tall buildings and the food you can just get in stores?"

"It's not what you think, Ash. Where I was before I used that machine, the people who were after me ... let's just say there's a reason I put my hand on that box without knowing what would happen to me."

"People were after you? Bad people?"

"To me they are bad people, but to them *I* was the bad guy. It just depends on what side you're on I suppose. They've killed people, and I've killed people. They've held people against their will, and so have I." I thought back to the agent we had tied up and left in our car outside Buckley Air Force Base. I wondered if he had died of heat exhaustion in the car. I wondered if anyone ever found the car and the body, or if it had sat there until it rusted and fell apart like the cars I saw in Buford as a child. I wondered if there was some remnant of that car and the agent's body somewhere out there in the snowy desert.

"Killed people?" Ash repeated. "You killed people?"

"How did you survive down there? After Ransom and Merit left you, what did you do? You killed people down there, didn't you?"

Ash looked down at the white snow, letting his mind travel elsewhere, reliving whatever it was that had happened to him back at Buckley.

"Those people down there, they've killed people. They stabbed me," I said and pointed at my stomach. "Who are the bad guys here?"

"They are!" Ash said and snapped out of his daydream. "They were going to eat us! They cut the arm off of one of their own, and they *laughed* about it."

"But they needed to eat, right? They think they are in the right. They think they are doing what needs to be done. Well, the same can be said about the people who were after me. They are no less vicious than the people you fought down there, and they think they are no less right." I looked up, and could tell Ash's mind was trying to process the idea.

"Is that why people came here from your time?" Ash asked. "To escape these people who thought they were right, but really weren't? Is that why the smartest people left for a better place?"

"No, that's not why," was all I could say. I shook my head and thought back to Whitman and his supposed search for his birth parents, his search for where he came from. Maybe it was better not to let Ash know why people were sent to the future, where he really came from.

"So, Ransom is with these people who think they are the good guys? And they think Ransom is a bad guy?"

"That's my best guess," I said. "And believe me when I tell you,

Ransom would be better off if his mind is just trapped in that box. These people who were after me, they think I know things they want to know. Things that if they find out, more people will die. Friends of mine will die. My family will die. I ... well I don't know what would happen to me if they get what they want."

Thoughts of my life cycle drifted in and out of my mind. And I wondered to myself what might happen if any stage of this cycle were changed or interrupted. If somehow the Ministry got enough information from my body to know who my parents were. If they killed my parents before I was conceived or just after I was born. *Would I die? Would I disappear? Would my mind leave Ransom's body empty and lifeless? Would my body die with Ransom's mind trapped inside forever?*

"But my point is, they won't stop until they get what they want. They won't believe Ransom when he tells them he doesn't know anything. They will hurt him. The things they do to him will likely drive him mad, and the chances of him surviving are very slim. If his mind ever makes it back here, it may not be the same as it was before all of this."

In the distance, a woman jogged in the snow towards us. Her legs sank down and her long skirt was soaked from the snow that clung to it and melted. She waved her hands in the air trying to get our attention. As she got closer I could finally hear she was yelling Ransom's name.

Ash stood and turned to face her. I gripped my axe and pushed on it to help my body stand upright.

"Ransom!" she yelled.

"Do I know her?" I whispered to Ash.

"That's Rika, Aurora's good friend," Ash whispered back, and he took two steps towards Rika.

"Ransom!" Rika said and slowed down as she got closer to us. "It's Gray."

"Gray?" Ash asked. "What is it?"

"He's awake. Gray's awake," Rika said and smiled, revealing dimples in both cheeks.

"He's awake!" Ash said and slapped my back so hard that I dropped my axe.

"He's awake," I repeated.

CHAPTER 18

2075
DENVER, COLORADO

Ransom shivered in a shallow pool of his own blood, hugging himself for warmth and balling his body up on the floor. The gunshot wound in his thigh still bled, as did his two severed fingers and the deep hole near his neck. The flow of blood from his leg had slowed, maybe because of the cold, or maybe because his blood now had other outlets to escape his body. He rolled around, trying to discover a warm patch in the room, but he never found any position or place that was remotely comfortable.

It was a type of cold he'd never felt before, one that didn't come from the sky. Even the breeze that pushed the chilled air around the room felt different, too constant. The blood on the floor soaked into his hair and froze in red clumps. Some of the liquid stuck in his new body's patchy beard, turning to short, pink chunks of ice.

The wall slid open, revealing Agent Saunders standing in the doorway, bundled in a thick jacket with a fur-lined hood. Fingerless gloves covered his hands. In one hand, he held a mug of some steaming liquid, and, in the other, he held a thin tablet of glass. Ransom could make out writing on the thin, clear material, but from his point of view it looked garbled.

"I have to say, I am intrigued, Powell." Saunders paused to sip whatever was in his mug. Ransom closed his eyes tightly for a brief moment and thought of the tea Aurora would make him. He swallowed deeply like he was taking a big gulp of warm liquid. His mind drifted to some place other than here.

"Let's see here." Saunders' hand was large enough to grip the transparent tablet and move the text around with only his thumb. "Born in 2036. Birthplace unknown. Raised in St. Anthony's Orphanage until the age of eighteen. Mommy didn't want you, huh?" He looked up from the tablet at Ransom. "No adoptive parents. Blah, blah, blah…" Backwards text flew by Ransoms face. "Chemical Engineering degree, University of Arizona. University of Colorado law school graduated in 2063."

"What does that mean?" Ransom asked. His question could've applied to anything Saunders had just said. He could almost taste Aurora's tea on his lips.

"Looks like you started your own law practice out of school and quickly took to breaking the law," Saunders continued, ignoring Ransom. "2065, unauthorized possession of tech components and acceptance of bribes." Saunders finally looked up from the tablet. "Bribes? Powell, you took bribes?" Saunders took another sip from his mug, the steam floating in spirals up his nostrils. "Were you throwing cases to the other side?" Saunders asked in a condescending tone, like a parent asking their child if they really did brush their teeth.

"Bribes?" Ransom repeated the foreign word. "I need to go home."

"Look, you're clearly a smart guy, so there's no need to play this idiot routine. How's the hand?" Saunders asked, abruptly changing subjects. "I see the blood on your leg froze up. See, I told you it would. Things are looking up, Powell. You may not bleed to death after all." The agent's large hand gripped the transparent tablet and scrolled through more text.

"Here's the interesting part. The part you *hoped* we wouldn't find out, but DNA doesn't lie. DNA always has a story to tell, and boy your story is fascinating! 2070, arrested for the *murder* of a federal agent, Agent Emery, and *dissection* of a corpse." Saunders looked up and wrinkled his face, trying to feign disgust.

"Murder? Dissection?" He shook his head disapprovingly. "It gets better … or worse." He sipped from his mug. "New Alcatraz!" Saunders threw his hands in the air, making sure not to slosh any of the steaming liquid from his mug. "New—fucking—Alcatraz!" Saunders shoved the glass tablet into his back pocket and walked towards Ransom.

"I need to get home!" Ransom growled, using all of his energy to put any force behind his words.

Cold breath billowed out of Ransoms mouth in sporadic intervals. His breathing was erratic. "Home? Right now, you are supposed to be in New Alcatraz—well, either dead or in New Alcatraz. That's all I have. That is where your life story ends. Or so we thought, right?" Saunders set the steaming mug on the white floor, reached down and drew his matte black knife from his pocket. Ransom flinched and pressed himself up against the chilled wall as much as he could. Saunders set his mug down on the floor and gripped Ransom's wrist with his free hand.

"There's this nurse on staff here. Smoker. Horrible habit. I mean, who smokes anymore these days?" Saunders said and laughed. "This nurse's sole job right now is to keep you alive. Not comfortable." Saunders pointed the tip of his knife at Ransom's face. Ransom flinched and turned his head. "Just … alive. We need you alive. Well, *they* need you alive. Don't kill. That is my only rule … for now. So, I do what *I* need to, and she does what *she* needs to, so we can keep doing this little dance. Tug of war with you in the middle."

Saunders pulled Ransom's arm straight and spun it around, exposing the pale underside of his forearm and bicep. "But you aren't allowed to smoke in this area. She has to go *alllllll* the way down to the housing wing to the designated smoking area." Saunders pointed over his shoulder with his black knife. "This won't take long, five minutes maybe seven. And after that, there will be nothing this nurse of yours can do for you. So, you better hope, or *pray,* if that's your sort of thing, that she is not on a smoke break right now. Cuz if she is…" He let out a deep sigh.

"I need to…" Ransom whispered. "…home…"

"It won't be my fault if you die. They can't expect me to coordinate my job with her schedule. Even you would see the absurdity in that." Ransom tried to pull his arm away, but Saunders tightened his grip, yanking Ransom forward towards him.

"One more chance," he said. "Why. Were. You. Down. There?" Saunders said, running his knife up Ransom's arm until the tip rested on the inside of his bicep. Ransom just shook in a panic.

"Please," he begged. Tears filled his eyes, and his vision blurred. "Please, I—it was my son. I-I needed med—"

"Wrong fucking answer," Saunders said and sank his knife deep down into Ransom's arm.

Saunders ripped the knife out, letting dark, thick blood stream out of the hole in spurts, pooling and puddling on the floor. Ransom clamped his hand missing two fingers over his new wound, but the blood still escaped around his hand and in between his fingers. Saunders picked up his mug just before the puddle of blood spread enough to touch it, and he slowly stood. Ransom's vision blurred, he felt like he might vomit.

Saunders walked away, waving his hand to slide the door open. "Now let's go see where that nurse is."

CHAPTER 19

5280
NEW ALCATRAZ

I entered the clay hut to find Aurora kneeling next to Gray, who was propped up sipping water from a wooden bowl. He looked at me, his eyes growing wide, and he almost spilled the water when he jerked the bowl away from his mouth.

"Dad!" the boy shouted. I tried to smile in whatever way I imagined Ransom would have, but I assumed it only came across as awkward.

"Gray," I said and took several hesitant steps forward. Ash placed his hand on my back and nudged me a bit closer. Aurora looked at me pleadingly. "You're awake," I said, and decided to portray shock instead of joy. One was more familiar to me than the other. Aurora reached a hand out, and I instinctively grabbed her, intertwining my fingers in hers. Her hand was clean and smooth inside Ransom's beaten sap-covered hand.

"How are you feeling?" I asked, placing my other hand on top of the boy's head. His blonde hair was tangled in knots from resting on the pillow for days.

"Thirsty," he said and returned to gulping water from the bowl.

"I am so glad you're better. You had us all so worried."

"You went out there?" Gray asked. "There really is something out there?" I looked at Aurora for guidance.

"He asked where the medicine came from," she said.

"There is something out there," I said softly, hesitant to admit for some reason, like this village and the lives of these people hinged on not knowing what was really out there. It was better when they refused to venture out.

The door to the hut opened, and Merit stepped in. His body halted at the sight of Gray, like a force field blocked him from walking further. His hand still gripped the door.

"Gray..." he said. He looked shocked, and happy, and scared, and confused all at the same time. Merit slowly released his grip on the door and took two steps further into the hut. Ash circled the bed and brushed his hand over Gray's head, messing up his already tangled hair. His hand covered Gray's entire head, like a pitcher gripping a baseball.

"Feel better buddy. I'll leave you guys, but let me know if you need anything."

"Thanks, Ash!" Gray said and smiled.

"Thank you," I said and looked up at Ash, pleading with him to stay.

"It'll be fine," he whispered to me and left the hut. Merit moved out of Ash's way and stepped closer to Gray's bed, keeping his eyes on me more than the boy, gauging my reaction. Aurora stood and fetched a bowl of soup for her son. Steam from the broth drifted up and curled into the air.

"I'm so hungry," Gray said.

"Be careful. It's hot," Aurora warned. I settled onto the floor next to the bed, watching my 'son' gulp soup down his throat, spilling the hot liquid out of the bowl until it dripped down the corners of his mouth.

"What was it like?" Gray asked in between gulps of soup. I looked at Aurora and then to Merit.

"It wasn't what we thought it would be," Merit answered for me. "The place wasn't natural. It wasn't … supposed to be there."

"But it *was* there," Gray said, handing the empty soup bowl back to his mother.

"It was there," I answered this time. "But Merit is right. It isn't a place that should be there. It should have never been built. It isn't a place where people should stay. It isn't how people were meant to live."

"Can I go there? Can I see it?" Gray asked.

"NO!" the three of us blurted out simultaneously. Aurora cracked a slight smile and looked at me and Merit. The three of us chuckled, and I got the impression that it wasn't common for Merit, Aurora, *and* Ransom to all agree on something.

"No one can go there," Merit said.

"You sure changed since your trip there," Aurora said to Merit.

"You didn't see what this place could do to men," Merit answered and stood, making his way to the door. "It turns men bad … or maybe it lets bad men be who they can't be up here in the open air."

I stood to see Merit out. I wished he would stay. I didn't feel comfortable in this home with just Aurora and Gray, especially with Gray awake now. Maybe I stood too quickly, or maybe my body wasn't as healed from the injuries as I thought it was. Or maybe my mind was weak and more untethered than I realized. Blackness blinked in front of me. The room I stood in swirled and changed into a bright white room.

The hut disappeared and the white room blinked in front of me. It was freezing cold, colder than it was outside in the snow. Aurora disappeared, and in her place was a single person dressed in black. He wore a thick down jacket with a fur lined hood, and stitched across his chest were the letters 'TDA.' I collapsed to the floor, but it wasn't the compacted dirt floor of the hut. It was a cold, solid, poured concrete floor.

A nurse kneeled next to me, snapping her fingers in my face.

"Hey! Hey! Stay with me!" she shouted. The man in the jacket leaned against the white wall and sipped something from a mug. Cold breath puffed out of my mouth. "Powell! Powell! I need a room prepped for prisoner four-three-two-nine" the nurse shouted into a thin strip of metal that ran from her ear to the corner of her mouth. "Prep six pints of O neg and a suture kit. Call the surgeon, I think our prisoner is dying."

CHAPTER 20

Another woman in white rushed into the cold white room, carrying a first aid kit. The room still spun. The nurse opened her medical kit and pulled out syringes and vials. Gravity pulled my body down against the floor, pushing me until I felt like I would melt into the concrete.

"Two-forty-six in cell five," the TDA agent said into an intercom on the wall. The white light in the room had no source. There were no bulbs overhead, only white concrete, like the walls and ceiling themselves emitted the burning white light. "Medic is here now," the agent said.

"Update status when possible," a voice crackled over the intercom. The nurse held up a syringe and sank it into a vial, pulling the liquid into the syringe and flicking it to release any air bubbles. I looked down at my hand, expecting to see Ransom's dirt-and-sap-covered hand, but only saw my own. Blood dripped down my arm to my fingers, finally pooling on the white cement floor. I traced it up my arm to a deep cut on the underside of my bicep, pulsing out blood with each heartbeat.

"You cut his brachial artery!" the nurse yelled. "What were you thinking?" She plunged the syringe into my thigh and pressed the plunger down. A soothing calm washed over my body. The cold went away, and I no longer felt my heart pushing blood out of the cut in my arm.

"I told him I would do it if he didn't drop the act," the TDA agent said. "I said if he asked about his stupid fake son or mentioned medicine one more time, I would cut him." The agent opened the door to the white cell, revealing a dark hallway outside. Warm air rushed into the room. My eyelids grew heavier with each blink. My body felt wet from the blood, like I was sitting in a shallow bathtub. Something about this moment reminded me of the dark pools of the Golden Dawn.

"Well, he's gonna die now!" the nurse said and looped rubber tubing around my arm, cinching it tight and tying it off.

"That's why you're here, isn't it? To keep him alive." The agent walked out of the cell and shut the door. The nurse flung her head back in an attempt to swing the few strands of hair that had fallen from her pony tail from her face. She held an item in her bloody hand, biting the one end with her mouth and pulling off a cap. She pressed one end of the pen-shaped stick with her thumb, and a blue flame shot out of the other end. She brought the flaming object down towards my arm.

"Hang in there," she said more to herself than to me. "Just tell them what they want, or else they're gonna keep doing this. There's only so much I can do."

She ran the burning pen across the deep wound on my arm, and the smell of burning flesh filled my nostrils. My head was heavy, and it crashed back down onto the cement floor. My eyes shut, and there was only darkness.

CHAPTER 21

5280
NEW ALCATRAZ

Ransom flailed around the hut, grabbing his bicep. He screamed and kicked at the air as though some invisible assailant were in the hut as well.

"Powell!" Aurora yelled and moved towards him. Merit stepped in between them, blocking Ransom's kicks. Ransom yelled, his eyes were clenched tightly shut. Merit held his legs down.

"Who's Powell, Mom?" Gray asked.

"Hey! Hey!" Merit shouted at his brother. He slapped Ransom across the face, and his brother's eyes jolted open, darting around the room and landing on Aurora.

"Aurora!" he said and crawled to her, wrapping his arms around her and squeezing tightly. Over his wife's shoulder he saw Gray sitting up in bed, his son's face frozen and confused. "Gray! You're awake! You're alive!" Ransom scurried over to his son and wrapped his arms around the boy. He pressed his face against Gray's face and kissed his head, holding his lips against Gray's matted hair.

"Ransom?" Aurora said and slowly moved closer to her husband. "Is it you?" Tears dripped down Ransom's face until his son's hair was damp. He nodded, not letting go of his son.

"I had the worst dream," he said, his words muffled. He pulled his face away from Gray's and looked his son in the eyes, holding his face in both hands.

"Dad, you were just sitting here. You knew I was awake," Gray said. Aurora rubbed her husband's back, crying softly.

"Was I?" Ransom asked and smiled. "Well then I am *still* here, aren't I?" He hugged his son again, smiling at the sound of his own voice.

"Where did you go?" Aurora asked. "How did you get here?"

"I was somewhere else. Somewhere horrible. This white room." He rubbed his bicep and looked for any sign of injury. He balled his hand into a fist, moving each finger one at a time. "I don't know where I was but they were hurting me. They thought I was someone else." He ran his hands through his hair and scrunched his face, trying to make sense of any of it.

"What do you mean, Dad?" Gray asked.

"Nothing, son. Don't worry. I just had a bad dream, that's all." Ransom turned back to his wife and walked to the other end of their home. "There was this thing I found underground. A box. It ... sent me somewhere."

"Ransom," Aurora tried to interrupt.

"It put me in someone else's body. They thought this person was a criminal or something."

"Ransom," Aurora said again, but Ransom kept talking.

"They thought I was someone called—"

"Powell," Aurora interrupted.

"How do you know that?" he asked, gripping both of Aurora's shoulders.

"He was here," Aurora said. "Powell was in *your* body. He brought the box back here with him." Aurora pointed at the bag sitting on the floor. "He tried to explain it to us but it's all so strange. It doesn't make any sense. At least not to me. Ash saved him—you—from some room—"

"Ash! He's alive?" Ransom asked and smiled.

In the excitement, the room spun until the orange clay walls of the small home blurred and Ransom's eyelids grew heavy.

"Ransom? Are you okay?" Aurora asked, and now she held onto his shoulders to keep him from falling over. She looked around the room, scanning the small home for help. "Merit? Where did Merit go?" But Merit was gone.

"Merit?" Ransom asked and stumbled backwards, bracing himself against the wall.

"Dad? Are you okay?" Gray asked from his bed. He threw the thick fur blanket off and tried to climb out of bed.

"Stay in bed, sweetie. It's okay," Aurora said and held her hand out at Gray. "Ransom. Look at me." His eyes fluttered and he bent over at the waist, steadying himself and putting his hands on his knees.

"Merit..." he said. Each word struggled to leave his mouth. "Merit. Don't trust." He fell to the ground. "Don't trust Merit."

CHAPTER 22

2075
DENVER, COLORADO

Lights shone overhead. The nurse who helped stop my bleeding stood over me, flashing a light in my eyes. My lips clung together and begged for any type of moisture. I reached over to feel where my other arm was cut, but the cold metal of handcuffs pulled my hand back. Both wrists and ankles were bound to the metal railing of a hospital bed.

"When will he be ready to go back to his cell?" a voice said somewhere off to the side. I couldn't turn my neck enough to see who spoke, but it sounded like the agent who was in the room with me before I passed out.

"He lost almost half his blood," the nurse said. "You're lucky he didn't die!" Their voices sounded far away, or like they were passing through water.

"How long before he goes back?"

"Well that depends on what is he going back to," the nurse said.

"More of the same," the other voice said.

"He needs rest. He's getting blood right now, and he needs time to heal. His organs were shutting down. His artery is repaired but still healing. It could rip open with any abrupt movement."

"Just give me a time frame," the man said, a bit more perturbed this time.

"*If* I can stay and observe him in his cell, he can go back in five hours."

"And if you can't stay in his cell with him," the man asked.

"Then I will keep him here until he is healed. Several days."

"We drew his blood. This guy's got remnants of nanobots in his system. God knows how, but he does," the agent said. "So he will be healed long before then. I will expect him back in his cell in twelve hours, *without* you there to observe."

"Remnants of nanobots aren't a cure-all. Even they have their limits," the nurse said.

"Twelve hours," the man said. "No water or food in that time. You can give him one round of fluids if it's necessary. Do not remove his restraints under any circumstances. I will be back in twelve to transport him to his cell." I heard his feet shuffle out of the room, and he closed the door.

A monitor beeped rhythmically somewhere near my head. An IV was hooked into my arm and blood slowly dripped through the twisting tube like a novelty straw a child might use.

"Where ... where am I?" I asked. I was startled by my own voice. I had just gotten used to hearing Ransom's voice. My lips cracked and spread apart with each word. I glanced down at my hands again to see the pinky and ring finger on my left hand missing. Blood soaked through a thin layer of bandage wrapped around my hand.

"Denver," the woman whispered, glancing sideways at a camera positioned in the corner of the room.

"Underground?" I asked. The nurse simply nodded and continued to watch the heart monitor next to my bed. "Under the airport?" The nurse nodded again. I rested my head deep into the pillow on the bed. Even though I hadn't been in my own body, I could tell my head hadn't rested on a soft pillow for quite some time.

"Did they bring anyone else here with me?" I asked. "A woman?" The nurse ignored my questions, again discretely glancing to her right at the camera. She disappeared for a second and came back holding a syringe.

"For the pain," she said, sticking the syringe into the base of an IV bag that was hooked to my arm. "It will help you rest."

"How … how long have I been here?" The cold liquid in the IV rushed into my arm. Whatever medicine she'd injected somehow left a metallic taste in the back of my mouth.

"Less than a day," the nurse answered.

"If … if you see me again…" I tried to speak quickly, but my mind fought against me. I knew my body needed rest. "If I act different, like I don't know what's going on … tell me Aurora is waiting at home. Tell me Gray is awake. Tell me to hold on a little longer."

CHAPTER 23

I opened my eyes to see the now familiar clay hut that Ransom called home.

"He's waking up!" Ash's booming voice announced. Aurora rushed over to me, her eyes wide.

"Ransom? Ransom?" She held my shoulders. I shook my head.

"It's just me," I said and sighed, she more disappointed than I. "How long was I out?" I sat up in bed.

"Not long," Aurora answered with a sigh. "I ran to get Ash, and you woke before I could barely catch my breath."

"Where'd you go?" Ash asked, crouched down to my level.

"Back to my time. Back to my body." I rubbed my arm where I was cut. "Was Ransom here?" Aurora nodded and her eyes watered. She stood and walked away, sniffling in the far corner. "So, I was right," I said to Ash. He nodded.

"Dad?" Gray said.

Ignoring him, I said, "We at least know Ransom is alive." A bit louder so Aurora heard me. "At least his mind is alive."

"Dad, what do you mean?" Gray said again.

"Not now sweetie," Aurora said.

"But *how* is he?" Ash asked. "How were *you*?"

I looked up at Aurora. Her eyes were still red and she wiped at her face to stop any tear that might roll down.

"Not good." I couldn't lie. There were only so many lies I could keep straight in my head. Lying to the villagers that I was Ransom. Lying to Ash that his people were descendants of great men instead of prisoners. Lying to myself that all of this might actually work out for all of us. It would be unfair to give these people false hope. "But they need *me*. They need to know what I know, and until they get that, or until they are completely sure that they never will, then they will keep me alive."

"And if they learn that you aren't you? What happens to Ransom?" Aurora asked.

"Mom, what are you guys talking about? What do you mean?"

"C'mon," Ash said and reached his enormous hand out to Gray. "I think some fresh air will do you good. Your mom and dad need to talk." He wrapped his fingers around Gray's hand and picked him up in one swift movement. Aurora nodded, her permission for Ash to take her son outside for the first time since he fell ill. I was left with Aurora and her questions. No buffer between the two of us.

"What do they need you for? Who the hell are they anyways?" Aurora threw her hands in the air.

"Do you guys have any form of government here?" I tried, but I knew it would take hours or days to lay the foundation to even begin to explain the predicament her husband and I were in.

"Have what?" Aurora asked. "Gov—what?"

"Government."

"What does this have to do with anything?" Aurora asked.

"What happens when someone does something wrong, like steals or beats someone up?" I simplified.

"Usually the people get together and discuss a proper punishment. They listen to the people involved and then vote."

"Where I'm from, we have something like that, but *much* bigger. There are people who say what is right or wrong, who tell us what we can or can't own, can or can't do. We call these things laws. And we call these people the government."

"Like what I tell Gray he can't do? So they're like parents?" Aurora said.

"Kind of, but not really. Imagine a parent that doesn't care for their child, and you'll be close to what I am talking about."

"What parent wouldn't love their child?" Aurora said to herself.

"Anyways, the government has people who enforce the laws for them. These people, most of them anyway, can do whatever they want, as long as they think it could stop one of their laws from being broken. Or to catch someone who already broke a law. They can come in your home. Take your things. They can hurt and kill people." With each sentence, Aurora's face dropped more and more. "In my case, they can lock a person up until they figure out what exactly it is that they have done ... or what they might know."

"That's why they have you?" she asked. "To find out what you've done? What *have* you done?"

I sighed. "It's complicated. If they know what I know then my family could die," I said, leaving out the part about how they might die in the past while I was a child.

"I just want my husband back! My *real* husband!"

"Believe me, I don't want to be trapped here forever. I want nothing more than to get back to my own body," I lied. If I returned to my own body, I knew I would eventually break and tell the agents what they wanted to know.

As of now, having Ransom's mind stuck in my body was the best thing for me. It was the only thing keeping the Ministry from learning about Ellis and Emery, Buford and Ashton. It was the best chance I had to stop my life ending before it actually started.

But if I take that scenario to its logical conclusion, then Ransom dies. He has no information to trade. Then what? Am I here forever? Do I die with him?

"I know things they want to know, and they are willing to do whatever it takes to get me to tell them these things, which includes hurting me. Hurting your husband."

Aurora gasped and shook her head. "Will they hurt him until he dies?" she asked, her lower lip quivering.

"Not on purpose, but there is only so much a person can take." I rubbed my bicep and felt the skin that covered my brachial artery. "The stuff I injected into Gray, my own body, the body Ransom is in right now, has the same stuff. It helps a person heal from all kinds of injuries. So, my body can probably survive more than most."

"That's good," Aurora said, trying to find some positive in all of this.

"But it doesn't stop pain. Ransom will still feel the things they do to him. Every punch or cut will feel just as it would to anyone else ... and the stuff in my body only lasts so long." I thought back to my dad whose death from radiation poisoning was only delayed by the nanobots. It eventually caught up to him. I wondered what could have been if the Ministry had given him just one more dose of nanobots. How much more time would he have had with me as a child?

"This is all so horrible," Aurora said. "How could this happen to us? Why do those places underground even exist? What good can come from them?"

"Your son is alive because of those underground vaults," I said, but quickly wondered why I felt a need to defend the horrors that people from my time created.

"And he might grow up fatherless because of these vaults!" Aurora snapped back. "What does all this mean? Is there any way this can be reversed?" she asked. By now full tears rolled down her face. "So it would do no good to try and get this information to Ransom? Like if you two switched again? You are sure your family would die?"

"If they learn what I know, my parents will die. And I will likely vanish like I was never born." Aurora jerked her face back and wrinkled her brow.

"Vanish?" she asked.

"You're just gonna have to trust me on that," I said. I sat on the bed, trying to think of some way out of this, but nothing came. There was no good solution. I began to wonder if Aurora would accept me as a substitute for Ransom, if Gray would ever look at me like a father. I would be both the cause of her heartache, and the only connection she had to her real husband.

"And this device," Aurora asked, interrupting my thoughts, "would it work again?"

I looked over at the bag that held the mind transfer device. Next to it was the bag of medicines Ash had brought back from Buckley, and the rifles I had taken from the armory.

"I assume it's still charged. The lights in this village stayed lit without wires, so there's gotta be some power floating around here," I said. I wondered if the wireless power device was an exact replica of what the TDA had stolen from the Golden Dawn, or if they had improved upon it in anyway before claiming it as their own. "But it does no good unless your husband and I can both use the device. If I use it now, my mind will likely be pulled into the machine, and my body would just go limp. We need both bodies to use the device, at the same time. If not ... it's just too uncertain."

"Can he use the device in his time? Your time, I mean?" Aurora asked. I was impressed with how well Aurora was grasping the predicament her husband and I were in. I shook my head.

"Ransom could never get back to the device in my time. The place they have him … it's impossible to break out of. And even if he did, the device is hidden in *another* underground vault that is nearly impossible to break into. Believe me, I tried." The silence in the hut was like a piercing hum that left me with nothing but my thoughts of how impossible things truly were.

Aurora paced the small hut, looking down at the floor. I could tell her mind was struggling for a solution, and that she was not one to give up on her husband easily.

"I got it!" I yelled, and stood up from the bed. Aurora, startled, jerked her head to look at me. "Ransom could never get to the device where he is. The device in his time is lost to him. So, if he can't use *that* device, then he has to use *this* device!" I pointed at the bag on the floor.

"I don't understand," Aurora said.

"Ransom can never leave where he is on his own. Not without help. So we just go get him, and we bring the device to him."

CHAPTER 24

5280
NEW ALCATRAZ

I burst through the door of the hut, sticking my head out into the cold wind. Outside, Ash was holding Gray on his shoulders while they both tried to catch snowflakes fluttering down.

"Ash!" I yelled, motioning them closer.

"What is it?" Ash asked, looking slightly concerned. "Is everything okay?"

"It's fine. Aurora is going to go see if Rika can watch Gray for a little. I need you to go find Merit and meet me back here. I think I have an idea." I smiled. Even knowing that my idea was beyond outrageous, it was still something. It was more than I had a day ago. Ash gently placed Gray on the ground and took off.

Gray stood in silence for a long time, staring out into the village and glancing back at me every few seconds. He fidgeted with his hands, picking at a loose thread sticking out of a seam on his shirt.

"You ... you're ... you're not my dad, are you?" Gray said. He sat down, pressing his small back against the exterior of the hut and squinting his eyes as he looked up at me. I slid down next to him. I thought for a long time before answering.

"No," I said, knowing this would open a door to more questions than anyone in this village, much less a young boy, could understand.

"But you look like him," Gray said, brushing snow from his face.

"Yeah, I know," I said.

"Is my dad gone?" Gray asked, seemingly unaffected, like he knew from the moment he saw me. Snow fluttered down and landed on his head.

"Not completely," I said.

"Where ... where is he?"

"He's back where I came from." I paused, trying to formulate an explanation that made sense. "Your friends and family tell stories of vaults and underground places, right?" Gray nodded. "That's where your dad went when you got sick. He went to find medicine. And in this place, he found a box that lets you trade minds with another person." Gray wrinkled his forehead. I was teetering on losing him. "Well, he turned this box on and it swapped his mind with mine. My mind went into his body, and his went into mine. So, he is back where I am from in my body, just like I am here in his body."

"Where are you from?"

"A different time. From the past."

"The *past*?" Gray asked.

"Everything that happened before this moment is the past. Yesterday is the past. Last winter is the past. I am from the past but a looooong time ago. A really long time ago."

"How long ago?"

"I am from a time before your grandfather was born, and before his grandfather's grandfather was born. And even many more winters before that. It was a time when people's homes filled this desert and reached into the sky. A time so long ago that there were millions of people just in this desert alone."

"Millions?" he echoed.

"That means a lot." A single bird flew overhead, circling the small village. Thin clouds floated through the bright blue sky causing the sun to fade in and out of view.

"Powell is a funny name," Gray said, snickering.

"How—"

"That's what Mom called you." Gray stopped smiling and looked away from me. "So, is it my fault?" Gray asked after a short silence, looking down at the snowy ground.

"No!" I said, instinctively putting my arm around the boy's shoulder. I thought back to when I'd asked my dad the exact same question in Buford when I was Gray's age. Asking if my mom's death was my fault. Gray looked back up at me, his eyes wide, his eyelashes long and fine, almost translucent. "It's not your fault."

"But he went there for me," he said quietly still tugging on the loose thread on his clothing.

"He went there for himself, Gray. He went there because he wanted to, because he loves you. I've never met your father, but I can guarantee you that, knowing how things turned out, he would do it all again too." I squeezed his shoulder one more time before letting go. The snow had stopped now, and the warm sun shone down on us, glistening off the ground.

"You knew?" I asked him. "You knew I wasn't your father?" He nodded slowly like he shouldn't have said I wasn't his father. Like he should have gone along pretending. "How?"

"I just knew. The way you and Mom talked. Dad always smiles when he looks at Mom, and he doesn't talk like you talk." Gray paused. "Do you think *your* son knows my dad is there instead of you?"

I shook my head. "I don't have a son ... or a daughter."

"Like Merit?" Gray asked.

"Yeah, like Merit." Just as the two of us mentioned his name, Merit came into view, walking next to Ash. Aurora and Rika were not far behind. I stood and brushed the snow off of me. Merit got closer, looking at me skeptically.

"Ransom?" he asked from a distance. I shook my head, but Merit didn't walk any closer.

"He's gone," I said. Ash stood between the two of us. "Let's go." I motioned towards the hut, and took two steps in that direction.

"C'mon," Ash said and tugged on Merit's clothes. "What's your problem? Powell's not gonna hurt anyone. He's a good guy. Now c'mon!" Merit moved slightly, taking one step towards me. I opened the door to the hut.

"Where'd you run off to?" Aurora asked Merit. "Ransom was back, and the next thing I know you're gone. I could have used your help."

"Sorry," was all he could say.

"Well, I don't know what's gotten into you, but next time any of us needs your help, you better not run away!" Aurora helped Gray up by his arm and said, "You go with Rika for a little. I'll come get you before supper." Gray nodded at his mother, and he and Rika trudged through the snow towards the opposite end of the village. Gray glanced over his shoulder back at me. I smiled back and waved.

The four of us shuffled into the hut. Ash threw a log onto the fire and stoked it with a charred stick.

"What happened with you?" Merit asked. "With Ransom?"

"I don't know," I said. "One second I was here, and another I was there. I guess whatever this is isn't exactly permanent. Which means we need to work fast."

"So ... what does that mean?" Merit asked. "Isn't that what you want?"

"Not like that. The people who have Ransom want to know things that I know. As long as they have my body with Ransom's mind, there's no chance they will get what they want. They will keep hurting him.

Torturing him."

"Or maybe the two of you switch back again for good. Then we have Ransom back." Merit said, pacing the small hut with his arms crossed around his chest.

"But then he dies. *Powell* dies." Ash said pointing at me.

Shaking my head, I said, "You can't count on us switching back for good, and if we switch for a short time, I don't know how long I will last before I tell them everything they want to know. Then they'll have no use for me. The most likely thing is that the people who have me end up killing my body and Ransom's mind … unless we do something." I added. I walked over to the bag and pulled out the mind transfer device. The lights indicating a full charge were still lit, but the last one flickered slightly.

"Why is that my concern? Or Ash's? Or Aurora's" Merit said.

"Well, if my body dies while Ransom is back here, there is a chance that Ransom's mind gets pulled back there. Stuck in a dead body. And it's always just as likely, more likely actually, that they kill me while Ransom is still in my body. That's not a risk I want to take."

"I'm sure it's a risk that *you* don't want to take," Merit said.

"What's gotten into you, Merit?" Ash asked, pointing the charred stick in his direction. "Ever since you made it back here, you've acted like an asshole, stomping around this village. Don't you want to hear Powell's plan? Get your brother back?"

"For all we know, Ransom is gone!" Merit yelled.

"He is not gone!" Aurora yelled back.

"We don't know how this thing works." Merit pointed down at the device then at me. "And from the sounds of it, neither does he. We need to start considering the fact that Ransom isn't coming back. Maybe we should all move on!"

Aurora gasped and gritted her teeth, stepping forward with her hand back ready to slap Merit in the face. I stepped between the two of them.

"Move on? You think Ransom would just *move on* if this were happening to you?" Ash stepped closer to Merit, his large barrel chest less than a meter away from Merit.

"I don't know," Merit said under his breath.

"Well I do know!" Merit flinched at Ash's booming voice. This was the first time I had heard Ash raise his voice. "Ransom wouldn't move on! Sheesh ... I won't move on. If Powell has a plan, I am going to hear him out." Ash turned towards me. "Go ahead."

I slid the device back into the bag, and opened the other bags. Inside were bandages and empty syringes. Painkillers and coagulants. Two pistols, one rifle, and clips filled with ammunition from the armory.

"We need to go back underground," I said.

"Not happening," Merit waved his hand in the air and made his way to the door. Even Ash looked scared. "I am not going back there just to help *you*."

"Look," Ash said. The fire crackled and spit bits of embers into the air. "I want to help you, really, but we can't go back there. Those people ... they aren't human. We're lucky we made it out once. I don't think we would be as lucky if we came across them again."

I shook my head.

"Not there," I said. "Not back to where you guys went. We need to go where I am, a place called Denver. There's another vault there. A different vault."

CHAPTER 25

"This is us," I said, pointing at an orange rock with the charred stick we used to prod the fire. Ash, Merit and I stood looking at the ground. Aurora had left to check on Gray. "Now, we walked about two and a half days from Buckley, accounting for our injuries and the fact we didn't stop much, that's about one hundred fifty kilometers".

"Kilom-e-what?" Merit asked.

"Okay, the sun rose to our left on our way home, that means we are south of Buckley and the airport." I dropped another rock on the ground and moved it with my foot until it was some distance away from the rock that represented the village. "*That* is where you went." I pointed at both Ash and Merit with my stick. "That is called Buckley Air Force Base. And that means that the airport is right ... about ... here," I said and hovered a dark black rock over my makeshift map, dropping it where I guessed the airport was. Just north of Buckley.

The black rock landed with a solid thud on the compacted dirt of the hut. "*That's* where we need to go." I looked up at Ash and Merit, who were both mesmerized and staring down at the rocks.

"And what is there?" Merit asked, sounding unsure if he really wanted an answer.

"Hopefully, it's a way to get your brother back." I didn't want to over-promise. Aurora, Gray, Ash, and Merit had been through enough already, and I needed to keep everyone's expectations low.

"This place is underground too?" Ash asked. I nodded. "How many of these places are there underground?"

"Not sure. Probably a lot," I said. "I've been there before. It's a lot like where you guys went, dark tunnels, colored lines on the floor."

"Those people," Merit said, clearly straining to classify the cannibals under Buckley as people, "are they at this other place too?"

"Nothing is for sure. But this time we have guns. We are more prepared."

"I don't like it," Merit said. "Ash if you want to go, then go, but you were lucky once. Don't count on it happening again."

"Ash?" I said and turned to the large man. He wrapped his hands around his chin and ran his hand down his long beard. He looked at me, and then turned to Merit.

"Ransom would do it for me, and he would do it for you. You two might not have been all that close, but you're family, and Ransom knows that." Merit regarded Ash with a look of defeat, like the idea of going with us and not going with us were equally terrifying. "If we find Ransom in this vault, he's gonna want to see as many familiar faces as he can. With the exclusion of seeing Powell over here living inside his own body." Ash smiled and pointed at me. Merit cracked a smile and nodded.

"Okay," he said softly.

"Okay," I said. "Grab whatever we need. I'll pack up the device, guns, and medicine. Meet me back here as soon as you can."

"What about Aurora?" Ash asked. "Should I talk to her?"

"I will," I said. "Where does Rika live?"

"Near the animals on the edge of the village. There's a short cactus just outside her door."

Merit turned towards the door, and opened it just a crack when the unnatural sound of a gun exploded outside. Two more loud *pops* cracked the air somewhere in the village closer than the first. Ash and Merit jumped at the sounds, and I rammed my shoulder against the door, slamming it shut. The high-pitched screams of women and children wove through the village.

"That sound," Ash said. A look of terror washed over his face, and Merit's face grew pale. They were the only two men in the village that knew what these sounds were besides me.

"It's them," Merit muttered. I looked over to make sure no one had stolen the guns we brought back from Buckley. They were all accounted for.

"Hold the door shut!" I ordered, crawling on the floor towards the guns. I slammed a magazine into one of the pistols, yanking the slide back and letting a round fall into the chamber. I reached out to Ash, pressing his back against the solid wood door and digging his heels into the ground in anticipation of someone trying to bash it in. He shook his head.

"Take it!" I shouted just as more gunshots rang out from another part of the village. I had counted six shots already. He took the weapon but held it cautiously between his thumb and forefinger. "You're gonna drop it that way, then you really have no control over what you shoot at." I took Ash's hand and wrapped it around the black pistol. It looked like a small toy in his large hand.

"That's the trigger," I said. "Don't pull it unless you want to kill whatever you're pointing at. When you're ready to shoot, point this end at what you want to kill and pull the trigger back. You have fifteen shots. Don't use them all." I grabbed the rifle and slung it over my back, shoving the other pistol into the waist of my pants. "Move," I ordered Ash again.

Several more shots rang out. I peeked out the crack in the door. Nothing. Just desert. One woman lay on the ground, her blood spilling out of her onto the white snow.

"Shit!"

Another shot fired somewhere to my right, in the direction of the forest. "Stay here, and shoot anyone who comes through the door that you don't know," I whispered. I crept out of the hut, keeping low to the ground. I gripped the cold rifle in my hands, turning my head slowly to try and catch any subtle noise that drifted through the air. The farm animals in the distance were frantic, stomping and running in circles. I rounded the hut, keeping the structure against my back.

Two pale men grabbed for me. I fell to the ground and scrambled away as they lunged forward, their scrawny fingers pulling their bodies through the snow. I squeezed the trigger of my rifle, spraying a stream of bullets at them, shooting blood out the back of them. The two men fell onto the snow, both coughing blood out of their slack-jawed mouths until it pooled around their airways.

The two men wore ragged clothes. Torn pants and worn-out strips of leather wrapped around their feet. Their faces were gaunt and ashy gray, like they were corpses long before I shot them. Snow fell and quickly covered the men, masking the blood that oozed out of their wounds.

A shot rang out, and a bullet streaked by my face, skimming the clay hut. I ducked just as another bullet came from the same direction. Sprinting through the snow, I fired indiscriminately back towards where the shots came from, shattering several of the wireless bulbs hanging between the huts. Snow kicked up behind me as I ran through the village, and I slid on the slick ground taking cover behind another hut.

The firing stopped. I held my breath, listening.

"Over there!" a voice shouted from some other end of the village.

With my back against the hut, I yanked the magazine out of the rifle and checked how many bullets I had left. Not many.

"Shit."

On the other side of the hut, feet crunched in the snow. I peeked around to see three men. One had a gun just like mine, and the other two held long blades. They were thin even under the thick blankets wrapped around their bodies. They walked in a crouched position, shoulders hunched forward. Their heads surveying from side to side.

I spun back behind the hut and readied myself to shoot the three men. I exhaled heavily three times and turned around the corner, following the three men with the barrel of my rifle. I breathed in deep and gently squeezed the trigger, sending a single bullet through the man with the gun. A plume of blood shot out the front of him. His arms went limp and his legs buckled, the rifle falling beside him in the snow.

The two men with knives ran in opposite directions. I tracked one with the sights of my rifle, and squeezed the trigger again. This time the bullet grazed the man's thigh, collapsing him into the snow. The thin man let out a shrill scream that sounded just like the screams I had heard coming from the dark tunnels in Buckley Air Force Base. I turned to find the third man, but he must have made it behind cover. I spun around in circles with my rifle held up, my eye peering down the sights. More men came out from behind other huts, some armed with knives, some with rifles and pistols.

"Put down the gun!" a voice shouted from behind me. I spun, keeping the rifle aimed in front of me. An older man, only slightly more nourished than the ones I had just shot, stood in the center of the village, holding a pistol to a young boy's head. The man had a strip of cloth wrapped around his throat, covering some leaking wound.

The boy he held was sixteen at most. He gripped the boy's hair and jerked the boy's head around, pushing him to the ground until he was on his knees. The other intruders crowded behind the man and pointed their rifles at me. The old man tensed his face and gripped the kid's hair even tighter. He let out a fearful cry.

I surveyed the village. Most of the villagers were locked in their homes. I couldn't run, and I had maybe six bullets left in my rifle. I would be dead long before I could reach the pistol stuffed in my waistband. The wind whipped Ransom's long hair in my face, my large hands gripped the rifle.

"Put it down! I won't ask again," the man said in a raspy voice. The blood-stained cloth moved up and down when he spoke.

"Okay. Just don't shoot the kid," I shouted across the village, loosening my grip on the rifle and letting it hang to my side.

"Throw it away. Your pistol too," the man demanded. The barrel of the man's pistol dug into the boy's scalp, until the frightened teen cried both in pain and in fear for his life. I lifted the gun over my head, tossing it to the side. I pulled the pistol out from my back and threw it to the ground. "Get on your knees," he shouted and took several steps towards me, dragging the young boy with him. I looked around for something, anything to help me.

"There's nowhere to go. You won't get away from me this time," the man shouted, only slightly quieter now that he was closer. "You're outnumbered. Out gunned. You may have learned how to use these things since last we saw you, but there's still more of us. Now get on your knees." He dragged the boy even closer to me, now only a meter of white snow sat between me and the older man with the blood-soaked rag around his throat. I knelt in the shallow layer of snow, knees pressing into the hard orange dirt.

"Good," he said. "Now that you have surrendered yourself to me, I have no need for hostages." A shot burst out of the gun pressed against the young man's head and a mist of skin, bones, and blood sprayed out the other side, misting across my face. His body fell limp and lifeless into the snowy ground.

CHAPTER 26

5280
NEW ALCATRAZ

I breathed in short gasps as I stared at what was left of the boy's body in front of me. Even with a large hole in his head, the boy still looked alive, his face frozen in his final horrified expression. The man stood in front of me holding his gun on me now.

"You son of a bitch!" I yelled.

"Ah," the man said and tensed the arm holding the gun. "Don't move or you'll be next."

"Look, I don't know what you guys want, but we mean you no harm. We can give you food—"

"No harm! No harm? What do you call this?" He pointed at the blood coating his neck. "Get up!" he yelled and motioned upwards with his pistol. I stood slowly, looking around the empty village. Everyone had run and hid, either in their homes or deep in the gray forest. Neither the man nor I knew where to go, this was not our home.

"You were the one with the sick son?" the man asked. His voice was raspy and he winced each time his mouth moved. A small line of blood leaked out from under the rag at his throat and dripped down to his chest, soaking into the neckline of his shirt. "Where is he?"

"Dead."

The man looked deep in my eyes and tilted his head.

"You are different than the last time we met," he said and took a step closer, almost eliminating the space between our faces. "Not as angry. But a little more … scared. Loss will do that to a person."

"Powell!" Ash shouted and burst out of the hut holding the gun I gave him. The man grabbed me and held my body in front of him.

"No!" I shouted. "Don't, Ash. Put the gun down." The other men pointed their guns at Ash, and the men holding the long knives held them at the ready.

"Should we shoot, Marshall?" one of the thin pale men asked the older man who held me as a human shield. Ash started to lower his weapon.

"Just put it down," I coaxed Ash. "Don't shoot him," I pleaded with Marshall. His warm breath puffing against my face. His grip was weak, and I knew I could escape his grasp if I had to, but I couldn't make him feel vulnerable or he might order the others to shoot Ash.

"Don't shoot him," Marshall said. I exhaled a long puff of breath that floated into the cold air. Ash's pistol lay at his feet, the black gun contrasting with the bright white snow. "*Stab* him." One of the men took two quick strides towards Ash and lifted his knife high over his head, plunging it deep into Ash's chest.

"Aaaarrrgggghhh!" Ash's scream echoed through the entire village. I pulled free from Marshall's grip and rushed towards Ash. Blood leaked out of the wound, soaking into his handmade burlap clothes.

"What are you doing!" I shouted.

Ash pressed his hand tightly over the bloody hole, with a clenched jaw trapped anymore screams inside his mouth. His eyes were fixed on Marshall.

"Revenge," Marshall said with a smile. "You stab me"—Marshall pointed to the wound on his neck— "we stab you. You take our guns, you take our medicines, then we will take whatever you hold dear."

"Take the guns," I said and flung the pistol that Ash had dropped in the snow at Marshall's feet. "We have some of the medicines still. Take those. Just leave this place," I begged.

Ash scooted through the snow until he could rest his back against the orange clay hut. His bloody hand left a trail in the white snow.

Behind the three men and Marshall, villagers poked their heads out of their homes to see if they could come out. Most of them quickly retreated and pulled the doors closed. Others took several cautious steps out into the village for a better view. A man and woman stumbled through the snow, kneeling at the body of the young boy. The woman buried her face into the boy's chest, sobbing, while the man hugged his wife.

"We will," Marshall said and nodded. "We will. But there still needs to be a balance, don't you think? You killed three of my men."

"Take the guns, take the bullets, take the medicines."

"What is revenge without balance?" Marshall spun around to see a handful of villagers standing outside their homes. "These two came into *my* home," Marshall yelled "This village sent people to my *home*. They stole *my* things. This one stabbed me in my throat and left me for *dead*!" Marshall spun back around to lock eyes with me. "Then we come here to retrieve our belongings, and he kills three more of my friends!"

"We only needed medicine," I said softly. "We meant no harm to you."

"We will take what is left of our weapons and our medicines," Marshall yelled on, ignoring my words. "But by my count, there is still an imbalance in our situation." Marshall walked until he was in the center of the village. "This man killed three of us!" He pointed at me. "We will ignore the numerous beatings you three administered to my people." Marshall said quieter and directed his words at Ash. "And we killed two of yours today!" Marshall pointed at the boy whose head he blew apart and then at the other body that lay in the snow. Both bodies surrounded by a puddle of tacky pink snow.

"That leaves one life still owed. Because I am fair, I will give you a choice. Choose the one that came into our home and plunged a sharp bone into my neck, *or* choose the one that is close to death already. If the sun goes down and no decision is made, we will kill each and every one of you here."

CHAPTER 27

5280
NEW ALCATRAZ

From mid-day until the sun dipped to just above the horizon, the villagers whispered, cried, and hid in their homes. After collecting all of our weapons and the medicines, Marshall and his men let the villagers walk back and forth between houses to discuss what should be done. Who should be handed over to the intruders. Some of the villagers stayed inside and refused to take part in any discussion. Others naturally thought Ash, Merit, or I should turn ourselves over since we were the ones who broke into the vault dwellers' 'home.'

Since I arrived here, I had seen how these people interacted with each other. I had seen how they worked together. One chopped wood, while another used wood to build fences and corral animals. One hunted animals, while another tanned the hides. Every person had a job, handed down through generations. And if one was able to trace its origins back far enough it was simply done out of necessity at some point.

These were the relationships that I knew could develop—had developed—even in New Alcatraz. They were natural and necessary for our survival. This village was unlike anything I had seen before, an almost utopia-like predecessor to the inevitable. But now Marshall and his men had crept above ground, out of their vault, and they sought to tear these relationships apart. The evil that I saw in people from my own time was not a recent invention, nor was it something that could stay absent for very long in a new society such as this.

Just as the relationships that naturally emerged in New Alcatraz, sadism, jealousy, dishonesty, and evil rested in all of us. That evil sat deep inside everyone, buried, waiting for the circumstances to be just wrong enough, waiting for our needs or desires to grow strong enough. Waiting until any reason to act as a decent human being was stripped away. Waiting until we realized there was no god keeping score of our behavior. And then it would emerge, burrowing through anything that got in its way.

Somewhere down the line, those circumstances came together and the evil deep inside Marshall surfaced. Maybe it was the lack of police or the lack of rules. Maybe it was the hunger that caused him to become so crazed. Or maybe it just felt more natural to him. Either way, Marshall and his men circled the village, corralling the villagers and watching the blood-red sun dip below the horizon.

"We don't have much time left," I said. "No one is going to volunteer." Ash, Rika, Merit, Aurora, Gray, and I sat huddled together over a dying fire. "Maybe I should volunteer," I said and scanned the faces of everyone.

"No," Aurora said emphatically. "You are *not* making that decision for Ransom."

"Okay," I agreed.

I glanced outside to see a deep purple sky with thin clouds stretching for as far as I could see. It would have been gorgeous, if only the setting sun didn't bring with it Marshall's deadline.

"Time's almost up!" Marshall shouted from outside.

"Fucking piece of shit," Merit whispered. "That asshole was going to *eat* us, and he acts like we shouldn't have tried to escape?"

"I'm still not entirely convinced that if we send one person out there as a sacrifice, he won't kill the rest of us." I said.

"Well then we're fucked either way," Merit said, pacing the small hut.

"Obviously we aren't sending any children," I said, summarizing the points we had already established just to make sure we didn't miss anything. "No one who is of child-bearing age or of working age. That leaves us with six elderly people. Four women and two men."

"They won't agree," Ash said, peeking under the gauze I'd wrapped over his stab wound. Before Marshall's men took the rest of the medicines, I'd dumped a packet of the coagulating powder on his stab wound and wrapped it the best I could. The nanobots were gone at this point. "I don't blame them. He hasn't even said how he plans to kill this volunteer. I'm willing to bet it will be slow and painful," Ash said.

"He'll probably just eat him alive in front of all of us," Merit said, panic setting into his voice.

"Time's up!" Marshall shouted, his voice was slightly garbled from the hole in his throat. "Looks like it's gonna be all of you!" The door to the hut opened, and one of the vault dwellers stood in the doorway, holding a rifle. His long spindly fingers were wrapped around the barrel. He nodded, ushering us all out into the cold night air. The sky was still colored, but the sun was well below the horizon. Our shadows stretched out, long and lanky, following us as if waiting to see what happened next. It would be pitch black soon, with only the few wireless bulbs left to cast their orange light over the village.

More of Marshall's men ushered everyone to the center of the village. All the inhabitants of the village crowded together, the vault dwellers jabbing the villagers' backs with the rifles, like cattle prods. Marshall stood in front of the large group.

"I gave you all a very simple task," he shouted over the snorting hogs and the bleating sheep behind him. I could tell it hurt his throat to speak so loudly. I guessed that if not for that wound, Marshall would have been the type of person to ramble and make prolonged self-righteous speeches. "Just one person. One!" He held a single finger in the air. He paced back and forth, making eye contact with each villager. Some looked away while the braver ones stared right back at him.

"You were too gutless to carry out a simple task of survival. To me and my people, it wouldn't even be a decision. It is instinctual. Animal. Find the weakest, or maybe just the one that no one really likes, and sacrifice them. It's for the good of the herd."

The cold round point of a gun barrel stuck into my back. I turned my head to see the man I had shot in the thigh earlier in the day. He smiled and bared his yellow-crusted teeth.

"In that way, we are more selfless than your group. We would sacrifice one for the rest of us. And that one person whose sacrifice we required would be happy to ensure the longevity of our clan." He paced back and forth for what seemed like forever. Marshall's shoulders were thrown back and his fingers interlocked together behind him, like a general or head TDA agent giving orders to his team. "I will give you one last chance. If anyone wants to step forward and make that sacrifice, they can. No harm will befall anyone else. I promise." Marshall held both hands over his heart and nodded slightly. Ash grunted at the promise.

Time slowed to a halt, or so it felt. And my mind was torn in two. One half wishing someone would volunteer, and the other half hoping no one was dumb enough to fall for Marshall's promise. I wondered if I died right now, if my mind would somehow travel back to my body and force Ransom out. Maybe in the split second before Ransom's body really stopped living, our minds would swap back. Aurora was right though, I had no right to volunteer Ransom's body any more than he had the right to do something like that to mine.

Marshall stopped pacing. He walked slowly towards us, eyeing each person.

"This one," he said, pointing at Aurora. The village let out a collective gasp. The man who I'd shot, grabbed Aurora by the hair and forced her forward towards Marshall. I lunged forward to grab her, but another vault dweller stepped in between us. Aurora screamed and fought as she was dragged forward, kicking and scratching so the man's wounded thigh dripped blood. But he limped on, throwing her at Marshall's feet and slamming her face into the snow.

"No," Gray yelled and ran several steps forward through the dense crowd. I pulled him back towards me and held my hand over his mouth.

"Shhhhh," I said and put my finger over my mouth. "Close your eyes and turn around," I told him. Gray's lip quivered as he slowly turned around. His face scrunched as he shut his eyes tight, as though willing them to stay closed forever.

"Is that your husband?" Marshall leaned forward and asked Aurora, pointing at me. Aurora spat in his face, but Marshall didn't even bother wiping it away. "Okay," he said, "I'll take that as a yes." Marshall held his hand out to one of his men, who shuffled forward and placed a knife with a long, tarnished blade in his hand. Marshall took the knife and threw his shoulders back, puffing his chest out. "Your husband should have volunteered," Marshall said, looking directly at me.

Gray, who had been wriggling in my grasp, turned around. I held onto his arm as he dug his feet in the snow and tried his best to pull free from me. Ash stood next to us, holding on to Gray as well.

"I'm disappointed that you think I am dumb enough to believe that your son really died." Marshall shook his head, looking at Gray and then at me. "Or are you still gonna tell me this little shit isn't your son?" Marshall pointed at Gray with his knife. "Coward *and* a liar."

Ash and I grabbed Gray by his slim shoulders, holding him back. Marshall slowly ran the knife over Aurora's neck and face, taunting her with the blade. Aurora's eyes were steady on his face. Gray cried and screamed, tears running down his face.

"No!" Gray yelled. His cries echoed over the noises of the farm animals and the gusts of wind. "Please!" he said, not to Marshall, but to me, pleading with me to let him go to his mother, if only to hug her one last time.

"You should thank me," Marshall said to Aurora. "If I were a cruel man, I would kill him before you. But what kind of man would make a mother watch her son die. I am not monster. But I can't promise I will show the same kindness to his father." The rest of the vault dwellers laughed, like a pack of hyenas.

The men with guns circled the group, and pointed their guns at the faces of random villagers, pressing the barrel hard against their heads. One villager pushed back, and the vault dweller rammed the butt of the rifle into his skull, collapsing the man into the snow.

"We have to do something," Ash whispered to me. Looking around at the group, I saw the piercing judgmental glares of the other villagers, who expected a husband to sacrifice himself to save his wife. To save the mother of his child. They must not have realized that Aurora would be the first of many to die tonight. Or maybe they did, and now they realized it was Ransom who brought these men here. It was Ransom who went underground and awakened whatever evil rested there. I returned to this village as their savior—the man who left and came back—but now they realized what followed.

Marshall's muscles tensed. His fingers gripped tighter around the knife and his bicep flexed, readying to drag the knife across Aurora's throat. A thin cut had started to grow where the tip of the knife rested.

"It's not just Aurora," Ash whispered. "Everyone's going to die.

We have to fight. We have no choice." Ash readied his body to pounce from the crowd, and I wondered how many men he could take out before they riddled him with bullets. Marshall would surely slit Aurora's throat, and in the same split-second, the vault dwellers would empty their magazines into the crowd.

It felt as if a fist had gripped my insides and, before I knew it had happened, I stepped forward, pushing Gray and Ash behind me. I shoved my way out of the crowd and stood in front of Marshall.

"Wait!" I yelled. "What if I could pay you back? What if I could get you more food, more medicine and ammunition? A lot more," I said. "What if I could get you out of this place?"

"What do you mean?" he asked. "'Out of this place'?"

"Out of New Alcatraz," I said, knowing that name meant nothing to Marshall. "To another time."

CHAPTER 28

5280
NEW ALCATRAZ

Marshall asked and tilted his head, still holding the long knife in his hand. "New Alcatraz?"

"Never mind that. I can get you food, medicine, weapons, a new place to live. All of it. But not if you harm any one of them." I pointed at the group of villagers in front of Marshall and at Aurora, the vein in her neck pulsing rapidly, a line of blood dripping down. Marshall shifted his eyes back and forth between me, the villagers, and his own men.

"You kill her or us and what does that get you?" I asked, trying to reason with the crazed man.

"Food," he said.

I tried to ignore the implications. "Then what? I'm offering you food, *and* medicines, and shelter, and weapons."

"We have shelter," he said. "If we kill all of you right now, we take your weapons, take your animals, take the clothes from your backs." Marshall threw his arms out and raised his eyebrows. "What is it that you *really* can offer me?"

"You've heard the stories," I said. "You of all people know what these vaults hold. The weapons. The medicines. You know what it's like to live without them, why else would you have come all this way? I can offer you a way to go back to before the world was like this. A way to travel to another time."

"How can I trust that you aren't lying to me?"

"Because I am from another time." Marshall looked confused. "There is a machine out there that can move you to a time where you don't have to struggle to eat. A time where you don't have to live underground. I know where this machine is because I have used it. Twice. It isn't far from here. If I am lying, then you can kill me. Come back and kill the rest of them too."

"Tell me where to go," Marshall said. His eyes darted like he couldn't wait to leave this place and time. "Where is this place?"

"I go with you. That's the deal," I said and did my best to look confident. "And I take a few others from my group to come along."

Marshall shook his head. "You are in no position to give me orders."

"You kill me or anyone else then I tell you nothing. If I take you there, I need my own people there to make sure you won't just kill me once we get there."

"And what if I just send my people out in all directions until they find this place you speak of? What is stopping us?"

"Nothing." I shook my head. "You will probably find the place I am talking about … eventually. But you won't know how to work the machinery. You won't know how to power it up, how to set the right time and place. You need someone who has used the machine before. And I am the only one."

Marshall gritted his teeth and clenched his jaw. "If we do this, we still take back our weapons and medicine."

"Sure," I said. A small price to pay to keep everyone in the village alive.

"All right. We leave tonight," Marshall stated.

I glanced over at Ash, and he nodded his head ever so slightly. "Okay, we can manage that."

"You will all be spared," Marshall shouted to the villagers, huddled together, shivering in the cold night air. "You will all be unharmed ... for now. But if this man"—Marshall pointed at me— "if he fucks with me in *any* way, if he is lying, marching me out into the cold to die, or attacks me out there"—he turned to look at me— "I will come back here and cut the throats of each and every one of you. If you have children, they will die first so you can see them bleed out."

CHAPTER 29

5280
NEW ALCATRAZ

"What did Ransom do to that guy?" I asked Ash as Aurora packed a bag for me.

"He stabbed him in the throat with a piece of bone," Ash said.

Aurora looked up and gasped. "A *bone*?" we said at the same time.

"They were going to eat us," Ash reasoned.

"There's something about him," I said.

"No shit!" Aurora said as she slammed a few pieces of meat and a thick sweater into a bag. "The guy who dragged me out into the middle of the village and was about to slit my throat … you think there's something *about* him?"

"No, I mean something else. It's like he knows me or knows I don't belong here. I don't know," I said and tried to shake the thought out of my head.

"Well he scares the shit out of me too," Ash said in his booming voice.

Merit burst into the hut with a small bag of his own.

"Hey, Merit," Ash said, but Merit's eyes were fixed on me.

"So this place, you think it really exists?"

"I know it's out there. I've been there, both in my own time and in this time. Well, not exactly *this* time, but give or take a couple hundred years."

"I don't think we should trust these people," Merit said. "What's to say they don't come back here and kill everyone anyways?"

"Well then, I suggest we all make it back here before they can do that," I said.

"We have no choice," Ash interjected. "They either kill all of us tonight or they come back and kill everyone in five or six days. At least this way we have more time."

"Plus," I said, "these people won't do anything without their leader giving the order. They are all too scared to make a move. Did you see how they all obeyed him? I know people like this. You take out the leader and the rest will scatter."

"I hope you're right," Aurora said, but she sounded doubtful. "How is this going to work? How do you expect to give that man what he wants, and still be able to bring Ransom back?" Merit's eyes darted back and forth between me and Aurora, waiting for an answer.

"I don't know," I said.

"Don't know?" Aurora shrieked.

"Well, I am trying to be honest here. What little plan I had before would have been a long shot already. Now with these guys ... I don't know. I was just trying to buy us some time."

"Maybe it's too risky," Merit said. "Maybe we should start thinking about just dealing with Marshall and his crew and abandon the plan to get Ransom back."

"Abandon Ransom!" Aurora cried. "He is your *brother*!"

"Believe me, I know that. I'm not saying this lightly. It's just that—
"

"There is nothing you can say to make me give up on my husband. If you think I'm just going to throw my hands up and let him go, you're wrong! I don't care what that asshole out there wants, and I don't care what you think you can give to him." Aurora turned to me, her eyes tearing through me. "Whatever plan you had to get Ransom back, that is all that matters. Don't bother coming back here without him."

"I may not have a choice," I said.

"Promise me!" Aurora ordered.

"Okay," was all I could say.

Turning to Merit, Aurora said, "And I don't know why you are so fucking quick to leave your brother in some other place. Leaving him to whatever it is those people are doing to him."

Ash cleared his throat, breaking the tense silence that spread throughout the small hut. "I'm going to see Alys and Zeke one last time before we leave."

"Tell her that I'll come by once these people leave," Aurora said and finished packing whatever supplies she thought I might need for the trek ahead of me. "We wives need to stick together. Even if my husband isn't really the one out there with those monsters." She threw the bag at my chest, and I wrapped my arms around it before it fell to the ground.

Ash walked out into the cold night.

Merit stood, fidgeting. "I'll go see if anyone needs anything else before we get going."

He turned and left Aurora and me alone in the hut. The fire crackled and spit ash into the air. Aurora sat down in a wooden chair, her body sinking like her legs had been waiting to sit all day.

"I'm sorry," she said with a sigh.

"For what?" I asked.

"For acting this way." She leaned back in her chair. "This isn't your fault. Well, maybe it is. What do I know? But you are trapped here just as much as Ransom is trapped there. And you are trying your best to get things back to normal … whatever normal is for you."

"I don't know what's normal anymore. If it makes you feel any better, this device isn't normal to me either. I don't understand how mine and Ransom's minds are switched." I sat down on the hard bed across from Aurora.

"Why would that make me feel any better?" she said. "That makes me feel much worse." She sighed like she was pushing out some sort of bad feeling or anger that sat deep in her lungs. "This damned sickness. It caused all of this. Higgs got it and spread it to Gray somehow. How could such a thing could cause all of this." She threw her arms towards the bag that held the mind transfer device. I wondered what would have happened to my mind had Ransom never gone to Buckley and used the device himself.

"But Gray is alive still," I said. It was the only bright spot in Aurora's life right now, the only good that she could focus on. "At least the trip to the vault underground wasn't a waste." Aurora nodded and squeezed her eyes shut, brushing away any remnants of tears. I slung the bag Aurora had packed for me over my shoulder, and then slung the bag carrying the mind transfer device over my head. "I should get going. I don't want to make Marshall and his men wait much longer." I took several steps towards the door.

"Wait," Aurora said and stood from her chair. "When you switched bodies, when Ransom was back here, he said something, something about Merit."

"What did he say?" I asked.

"Just keep an eye on him," she said. "Something is off with him ever since he made it back."

"Okay," I said. "I have to go." I turned towards the door.

"Wait!" She said. I turned back around.

She wrapped her arms around Ransom's body and squeezed, pressing her head against my chest. I slowly reached my arms around her, reciprocating the hug. Aurora looked up and held my face,

Ransom's face, in her hands. She peered in my eyes as if she was searching for some sign of Ransom, some remnant of her husband. She pulled my face down towards her, pressing her soft lips against mine and lingering there.

She pulled away slowly. "Bring him back to us, Powell. Please. Bring him back."

CHAPTER 30

2075
DENVER, COLORADO

Cooper rolled his eyes and shook his head. A key rattled on the other side of the cell door, and the door swung inwards. The young man who had escorted Vesa to the cell stood behind another man wearing what looked like some sort of military uniform, but it was embroidered with the Wayfield logo, along with several other emblems she had never seen before. Vesa stood, placing her body between the man and her brother.

"Hello, Vesa," the man said. "Cooper. My name is Carson. I was told you wished to speak to someone in charge?" His face had the rugged look of a man who had lived long enough to gain important life experiences, yet not long enough to be completely disappointed in how his life had turned out.

"Who do you work for?" Vesa asked, not budging an inch. "Wayfield? The Ministry?"

"A bit of both," Carson answered with a smile. "I'm sure you understand how complicated things can get between the two." Carson turned to the young man behind him. "Can you bring them both some water, please?"

"We don't need anything," Vesa said to the young man.

He turned back around to face the brother and sister. "Would you like anything else?" Vesa shook her head. "That'll be three waters. Make mine sparkling water." The young boy nodded and scurried away.

"I told you we didn't need water," Vesa said through clenched teeth.

Carson made his way further into the small room. "Would you like to sit?" He motioned towards the chair. Vesa shook her head and stood stoically. "Do you mind if I sit?" Carson asked.

"Go ahead."

He pulled the chair towards him and sat, keeping his back straight like he sat against a wall. He placed his hands on his lap.

"Well, here I am. Someone in charge. Now if I read everything in your file correctly, you have been part of a five-year covert operation. Is that correct?"

Looking up at his sister, Cooper said, "Covert? Five years?"

Vesa scrunched her face at the implication that she had always been working for the Ministry. "I guess," she answered, just hoping to move things along.

"The goal of which was to infiltrate a rebel group named 'The Paradox Rebellion.'"

"The what?" Vesa said and looked back at Cooper, who shrugged his shoulders. "We—they never had a name. They aren't called anything."

Carson stood and walked back towards the door, pulling it open and motioning for someone outside.

"Can you pull up the Paradox file on the screen in here?" he said to some unknown worker. He returned to the chair. The wall to Vesa's right lit up, turning into one large screen. Carson pulled a small remote out from his pocket and pointed it at the wall.

"The Paradox Rebellion," he said and flicked his hand across the remote. "A rebellion group founded around 2062. Originally formed by disgruntled employees of tech firms that went out of business once Wayfield gained a competitive edge over their rivals." Images of news stories flashed on the wall. Headlines like *Could Wayfield Industries Be Our Answer to China's Booming Industry?*, *Wayfield's Partnership with Government Only Temporary Says Lawmakers*, and *Illegal Companies Raided in New Mexico by Ministry of Science*. Pictures of abandoned factories and entire towns that were abandoned scrolled past.

"The employees of these smaller businesses blamed their failure on Wayfield's success, so naturally they wanted to do something. It started simply as a friendly competition with Wayfield. No problems with competition, it's the American way."

Vesa rolled her eyes and shot Cooper a look.

"But eventually a more extreme leadership took hold." Carson kept scrolling with his remote. Under the headline *Domestic Terror Takes Hold* were pictures of tables lined with firearms tagged and catalogued. Another headline, *Successful TDA Raids Keeps Technology Out of Extremists' Hands*, was followed by a similar picture showing a table filled with electronic parts surrounded by masked TDA agents.

"This is bullshit," Cooper said under his breath. Vesa turned from the large screen and placed her hand on Cooper's shoulder to calm him.

"Part of this group was captured in Ashton, Idaho. But we believe there are still several factions spread around the country. Groups like this cannot be allowed to thrive in our society," Carson said. "We can't let advanced technologies fall into the hands of those who either don't know how to properly use them, or, God forbid, know how to use them and plan on doing so against us." Carson turned to Cooper. "Your sister understood the importance of this task, and she agreed to help us take this group down." Cooper locked eyes with his sister. Vesa shook her head ever so slightly.

"I never said I would 'take the group down,'" Vesa said, using air quotes. "I promised that I would help the Ministry of Science get a specific piece of technology in exchange for the release of my brother. That's it. Plus, it's not like you guys gave me a choice."

Carson's slideshow continued to play out on the wall. A picture of a collapsed building flashed across the screen with the headline *Domestic Terrorist Group Uses Advanced Technology to Implode Wayfield Factory.*

"You think *we* blew up that factory?" Cooper said.

Ignoring Cooper, Carson asked, "And where is that piece of technology you were supposed to get for us?" Carson looked at both Vesa and Cooper, knowing that she did not deliver as promised. "It's not here. For all I know, it's still in the hands of those terrorists."

"It doesn't exist!" Vesa said, throwing her hands in the air. "They never built it."

Carson pointed at the large wall of propaganda that flickered by. "The way I see it, you owe us. You worked hard, I will give you that. It couldn't have been easy to live a lie for five years while working for us."

"There you go again. If I am *working* for you, then show me to my office. Maybe I'll walk down to the break room and get a cup of coffee. Or better yet, lead me to the HR department! Cuz these work conditions fucking suck."

Letting his smile fade to a flat mouth, Carson said, "Now, now, Vesa. I can't let you out until we get what we want. I have superiors I have to answer to, so the three of us need to come together and give them something worthwhile."

The young man re-entered the cell, carrying a tray with two bottles of water and one glass filled with sparkling water. Carson handed the bottles to Vesa and Cooper, then grabbed his glass and stood.

"I will leave you for a moment so you can discuss this with each other. But between the two of you, I am going to need information I can take to my supervisors. If not…" Carson shook his head and looked away. "Then it's back to the drawing board." He sipped his water, turned, and left the cell. The lock clanged.

"Back to the drawing board!" Cooper exclaimed just as the door swung closed. "Back to the drawing board! He needs to w-w-work on his threats. And what's with all these articles and the *Paradox Rebellion*? We've never had a name! And if we did, it would be better than the Paradox Rebellion!"

"Propaganda. Don't drink that," Vesa said, reaching out to take the bottle of water from Cooper.

"What? Why poison us? We're already their prisoners." Cooper ripped the cap from the bottle and chugged the entire thing.

"It's all bullshit they feed to the media," Vesa said. "Praise Wayfield, vilify us or anyone else they can't control."

"And those guns? The blown-up building?" Cooper asked.

"More bullshit. C'mon, don't act surprised," Vesa said. "That Wayfield factory *we* supposedly blew up was set to be demolished anyways. I remember that plant years ago."

Vesa paced around the small cell.

"Wayfield wanted to build an updated plant, but some environmental group created a PR nightmare for 'em. Finn and I even joined their protests just to fuck with Wayfield. It had something to do with the dust in the walls poisoning the nearby wildlife if they tore it down or some shit. So, Wayfield blew it up at night, planted some shit about a terrorist group, fed the story to the media, and problem solved. They got the factory torn down, no PR nightmare, in fact they got sympathy for being the target of a 'terrorist' attack."

"And we got the blame," Cooper finished her thought. "You gonna drink that?" he pointed at the other bottle of water.

Shaking her head, Vesa said, "They've really ramped up their efforts since you were captured. They're getting more desperate. You think those were our guns?" Vesa pointed to the screen where the photo of TDA agents surrounding a table filled with automatic weapons had been. "Whenever they need to change the course of the news or distract people from some real issue, they take their *own* weapons, put evidence tags on them, and then pose for a picture. We're the only ones that know it's bullshit, cuz we know we weren't raided! They *wish* they had caught us and taken our weapons."

"Shhhh," Cooper said, pointing around the room where he assumed were embedded cameras.

"Who gives a shit," Vesa quipped. "It's not like any of this is a secret to them."

Cooper shook his head and stared at the screen, pictures still flashing in regular intervals. "We must be getting somewhere for them to act like this. Making progress."

"And the sad thing is, this guy"—Vesa pointed at the cell door—"he probably believes it all. Not everyone here is let in on every little secret. He sees the headlines and the fabricated file on our group. He eats it all up, chases us down, orders TDA agents to shoot on sight. Whatever it takes to stop us. Then he goes home to his wife and kids thinking that he did something good for his country. A patriot."

Cooper sighed and shook his head. For the first time since they'd been reunited, he stood up. His body wavered on his legs, and his shirt swallowed his gaunt body underneath. His hip bones protruded, pushing through his skin.

"We have to get you out of here," Vesa said, at the sight of him.

"What are we going to tell him?" Cooper asked. "What was this plan of yours?" Vesa walked over to the cell door and pounded her fist on the metal. The lock clicked on the other side and the door swung open. The young man opened the door.

"Hey, no-name," Vesa said.

"Yes," he said calmly.

"Tell Carson we have more information. There's a prisoner on site being questioned. Tell Carson I know everything he knows."

CHAPTER 31

2075
DENVER, COLORADO

"That information would be much appreciated, and I would do my best to get both of you out of here if you are cooperative," Carson said, placing a small recording device on the table and switching it on. "Go ahead."

Vesa swallowed and stared at the recorder. Feeling herself getting pulled deeper and deeper into the grasp of the Ministry of Science, she hesitated. "His name is Powell. He was an attorney with the ARC until he was arrested for murdering a Federal Time Anomaly Agent in Phoenix. He was sent to New Alcatraz, but escaped a short time later." She stopped and looked up at Carson, expecting a reaction.

"Go on," was all he said.

"In the future, he used the same time machine housed here in Denver to get back to his present time. Apparently, it was still functional." Once more, Vesa paused and waited for some reaction from Carson.

"I appreciate the effort," Carson said, "but we pretty much know all of this already. We ran his prints through the system and found out who he was, and where he was supposed to be. After that, it was just a matter of deduction to figure out how he made it out of New Alcatraz. I sure hope you have something else to tell us?" Carson settled into his chair, crossed his arms, and waited for Vesa to reveal something he didn't know yet.

"His blood. His DNA," Vesa blurted out. "It's not normal. He has something inside of him. He has the DNA of someone else."

"Someone else?" Carson asked.

"He has his *own* DNA, but there is other DNA in his body ... from another person." Vesa worked hard to get the last part of her sentence out. She knew this was what Powell had told her to do, but she still felt like it was a betrayal.

"And this is important because?" Carson asked, leaning back and settling into his chair. The recording device sat in the middle of the table, taunting Vesa. Cataloging every bit of her betrayal.

"The DNA in Powell is James Wayfield's DNA."

"Vesa!" Cooper hissed.

"James Wayfield?" Carson echoed. "Why would this prisoner have Wayfield's DNA? Mr. Wayfield died long ago."

"Project Blue Brain," Vesa answered.

"Even if I were to acknowledge the existence of a Project Blue Brain, I could not talk about it with you," Carson responded.

Vesa shook her head. "You don't need to discuss anything with me. Just listen. The participants of Blue Brain, like James Wayfield, stored their DNA in androids. *Decommissioned* androids that, I would bet dollars to donuts, are stored about one hundred feet right below us."

"I couldn't confirm or deny such a thing," Carson said.

"But this DNA. Look," she said., "somehow James Wayfield's DNA was put in some android down there." She pointed straight down to the floor. "I don't know which one," Vesa lied. "And Powell discovered this. So, he injected himself with the DNA. Now, if James

Wayfield stands any chance of ever being resurrected once you guys figure out the technology to do such a thing, or whatever the plan is, then you need that prisoner, Powell … alive." Vesa sat on the edge of her chair tapping her foot on the ground. Her knee bounced and bobbed her elbow, which was resting on her knee, up and down.

She looked back at Cooper, who stood behind her, gripping the back of her chair tighter and tighter with each bit of information she divulged. He shook his head, releasing his grip on the chair, and paced the room. Vesa knew her brother well, better than anyone else, and she knew what he was thinking. He was thinking that Wayfield's DNA was inside Whitman. He didn't know this Powell, but just the mention that they had James Wayfield's DNA, or admitting they knew about Project Blue Brain, made him more than uneasy. Vesa could feel his tension inside the small cell.

Vesa turned to face Carson. "Go ahead, test it out. Run it through whatever centrifuge or fancy machine you guys have here and run the DNA against all of the participants of Project Blue Brain. It's the truth."

"I will look into that," Carson said, nodding his head. Vesa knew this was as close as he would come to admitting Project Blue Brain existed. Vesa could see him working things out in his head, not working out how to salvage Wayfield's DNA, but how to shift blame or take credit for this discovery. Vesa knew he was already two or three steps ahead of testing the DNA.

She knew that right now Carson was wondering who was in charge of storing the DNA and who had put that person in charge, mentally scanning some human resources chart that mapped out who was superior to whom in this mess of an organization, deciding how to proceed and whom to tell about the misplaced DNA.

"So, is that enough?" Vesa asked. "Enough to get us out of here?"

Carson smiled, and, for a moment, Vesa thought maybe he would actually try to get her and Cooper released. Maybe he really just saw this as a trade of information for freedom. No tricks or double-crosses. Vesa knew organizations like the Ministry of Science and Wayfield Industries needed people like Carson. People that were insulated, removed from the actual torture of prisoners. The Ministry needed people who truly believed in their cause, and thought it was noble. People who would obey just because.

"I am afraid I will need more to bring to my superiors. They have asked for specific information."

"What information?" Vesa asked, scared of what they might ask.

"They want the location of your base of operations. Where did you work out of?" Carson stared at Vesa, unblinking, expecting an answer. She swallowed, pushing a lump down her throat. Cooper shook his head.

"Vesa…" he said.

Vesa looked at her brother. Everything in her screamed not to answer the question. She knew what that meant. She knew there was no way she could warn the people back at the motel. She knew they would die or be captured. But she was here now. Her only option was to cooperate.

"Gray Mountain, Arizona," Vesa said, the words barely audible as she pushed them from her mouth.

"Vesa!" Cooper yelled.

She looked away from her brother. "There's an old motel on highway 89."

"Dammit, Vesa!" Cooper yelled.

"It used to be called the Anasazi Motel."

"Great!" Carson said. "I'll see what I can do. In the meantime, I must take you back to your cell, Vesa, and we'll get your brother cleaned up."

Carson stood and knocked on the door. The young man who had brought them water opened it.

"Take Vesa back to her cell. Then come get Cooper and take him to the housing wing to get showered and shaved. Get him whatever he needs. Food, water, whatever. He turned back to Vesa, still smiling. "This will show my superiors some goodwill, but it still isn't the device they were promised."

When Carson was gone, Vesa turned and hugged Cooper, but he kept his arms stiff at his side. "I'm sorry," she whispered.

"You just killed all of them," Cooper said. "In one hour, you gave them what I have been withholding for five years."

Ignoring her brother and letting him go, Vesa said, "We will get out of here."

"If we don't, this was all for nothing."

"I haven't told them everything yet," Vesa whispered. "There's still more they don't know about Powell. About his parents."

CHAPTER 32

After Ransom returned to Powell's body, he slept. But there was nothing but darkness. He never made it back home or saw his family again. Now he lay balled up on the cold white floor of his cell. His arm was sore, he could barely lift it above his waist. The stumps on his hand where fingers used to be throbbed. *Powell's fingers,* he corrected himself. The ends were now crudely stitched, just enough to stop the bleeding. The same was done to the hole near his neck. The nurse had injected Ransom with something and then sewed the wound closed. He still limped, and winced in pain whenever he put weight on the leg with the gunshot wound.

What did Powell do to deserve this? Ransom wondered. *If this is how these people treat others, maybe it is a good thing not to fit in here. Not to be liked. Maybe it's good to be an outsider to this group.* Ransom's mind wandered to his wellbeing, or the wellbeing of the body he was in. *How much longer will this last? How long can they do this to a person before they kill them? Maybe if I died I could go back to my body. Back home.*

The nurse entered, wearing a thick fur coat, and approached Ransom with a long needle.

"Hold still," she said, her voice soothing. "My name is Evelyn." She knelt down in front of Ransom. Her breath floated out of her mouth and mixed with the frosted air that left Ransom. She reached out and gently turned Ransom's arm over, exposing the pale soft skin on the underside. "This won't hurt," she promised and slid the needled in.

Ransom flinched slightly at the abrupt sting, but then realized she meant no harm to him. He stared the nurse in the eyes, watching her watch the needle as the syringe filled with Powell's blood.

"They know about your blood," she whispered. "At least they know what your friend told them. They want to test this."

Ransom looked in her eyes and shook his head. "I'm not Powell," he told her. "They don't believe me." Ransom shifted on the floor, wincing at the slight movement. "My name is Ransom and I need to get home. I need to get back to my family."

Ransom blinked and wished he could go back to sleep, maybe sleep forever.

"Maybe it was a dream," he mumbled to himself. "Maybe I never actually went there." He breathed deep and exhaled a puff of air. "What happened to me before?" Ransom asked.

"You passed out."

"Can you make me pass out again? For longer?" Ransom looked Evelyn in her eyes. "Can you make me pass out for good?"

"I—I can't do that. That's not really what I do here." Evelyn pulled the needle out of Ransom's arm and placed a cotton ball on the small puncture. She bent Ransom's arm back, trapping the cotton ball in the crook of his elbow. She put a cap over the needle and stowed the syringe in a pocket of her thick coat.

"Keep pressure on that," she told Ransom. She smiled and rubbed her hands on her arms for warmth. "Earlier in the trauma room, you told me that if you seemed different to tell you something. You said to tell you that Aurora is waiting for you, and that Gray is alive. You told me to tell you to hold on for just a bit longer."

Ransom gasped and smiled at the mention of his family. *Maybe it wasn't a dream.* He was brought back to that brief moment in his hut. His arms wrapped around Aurora. Gray awake. Smiling. Alive.

Returning his gaze back to Evelyn and leaving that moment in his home, Ransom said, "I have to get back there. I have to get back home. My family needs me."

"I've seen this before ... the hallucinations. But if it's real to you, then hold onto it. Family gives you something to fight for," the nurse whispered.

"Let me leave," Ransom said, without knowing where he even was. "Please ... I don't know anything."

"It doesn't matter if you know anything or not. All that matters is they *think* you know something. They won't stop. I do my best, but there's only so much a person can take."

Ransom straightened his arm and pulled the cotton ball away from his arm. A small drop of blood leaked out of the vein and then slowly formed into a frozen red ball.

"How long have I been here?" Ransom asked, his voice quiet but not on purpose. He had no energy left in him. His body, Powell's body, wanted a way out.

"One day," Evelyn answered. "Most don't make it three." She looked into Ransom's eyes, her voice soft but entreating. If you have what they want, give it to them. You can't fight this."

A kind smile grew on Evelyn's face. She stood and walked out of the cell, leaving Ransom on the floor. His teeth chattered together and his body shook, exacerbating the aching in his wounds. *Two days,* Ransom thought. *Two days and this could be over. Maybe then I will be home again.*

CHAPTER 33

Our feet crunched in the snow as we left the village behind us. I turned around to see the dark-haired man who Ash believed to be Marshall's son pointing his rifle at my back. Behind him the wireless bulbs tied to thick twine that crisscrossed the dirt pathways of the village twinkled through the thin sheets of blowing snow. Marshall walked in front of the group, setting the pace. He didn't carry a gun, or anything else for that matter.

"What's going to happen to us?" Merit asked me in a whisper.

"I don't know," I whispered back.

"But you have a plan, right?" Merit asked.

"I did before they showed up." Ash glanced over at us, clearly hearing my words of doubt. "Now ... I don't really know."

The man with dark hair and pale skin prodded my back with his gun. "Shut up," he said.

"How do you know about this place?" Marshall asked from up ahead. I reached into my bag to retrieve the thick woven sweater Aurora had packed for me. The sweater was warm around my body. It had a familiar feel to it, like an old bed I'd slept in a long time ago. I clasped the wooden buttons through the small leather loops sewn into the wool.

"I've been there," I answered.

"When? How?" Marshall asked. "How did you discover this place? Why have you never gone back?"

"It's a long story," I said.

"But you know it is there?" A vault dweller asked from behind.

"It's there," I reassured him.

"And the things you say are there? Food? Water? You know they are there as well?" Marshall asked. I thought back to the last time I was in the underground vault in Denver. I thought of the water bottles that were shot and destroyed, spilling out and soaking into the dry concrete floor. I thought of the dehydrated food in the Mylar bags that Hamilton and I had eaten most of, and what was left was exposed to the outside air. I thought of the explosions that had shot through the walls and floor of the underground vault, and I wondered if the entire place had collapsed shortly after I'd used the time movement device underground for the last time.

"Yeah," I said. "It's all there. I promise."

We walked through the night and watched the sun rise over the snow-dusted desert. As it crept into the sky, the nocturnal snowstorm faded away, like some cosmic agreement was made long ago and it couldn't share the same sky with the sun. My body was used to the cold by now, and by mid-day the weather almost seemed pleasant. By nightfall, I guessed we would be just south of what was left of Colorado Springs.

Marshall walked hunched over, his arms hanging at his sides and feet dragging in the snow. Every once in a while, he held an open palm against the bloody rag wrapped around his throat. A reminder of his last encounter with Ransom. With me.

As time moved on, so did we. Walking kilometer after kilometer, stopping only to start a fire and melt snow for water. All of us were tired. Marshall, the man Ash believed to be Marshall's son, or Baker as the others called him, and the other two vault dwellers following at a safe distance should anyone try to run, they were all tired. Their pace slowed, their endurance waning. The men no longer held their rifles at us, they now hung at their sides, the slings pulling them down.

Merit, Ash, and I walked slowly too. Ash kept one large hand pressed against his chest where he had been stabbed, breathing shallow breaths so as not to reopen the wound that had been mostly sealed shut by the powdered coagulant. Merit held his side, still cradling his cracked rib. The mind transfer device buried in my bag pulled me down.

With the disappearance of the sun came the chilled winds and snowstorms of the night. The wind whipped so vigorously that keeping a fire alive was nearly impossible. The seven of us sat and shivered in the snow, our captors huddled together for warmth. Ash, Merit, and I did the same. Merit's teeth chattered so loudly that I heard them over the howling winds.

"I think I would rather it be hot," I said, "how it was last time I was here. D-d-d-does it ever stop sn-sn-snowing here?" I asked. Ash nodded, but I couldn't tell if it was voluntary or not.

"It-it does," he said. "But stays l-l-like this most of the t-t-time." We never slept. Our bodies getting little rest and our minds staying alert and aware. Exhausting our brains for the day to come.

Marshall was the oldest of our group, and the elements were wearing on him. A bristly stubble grew over his face, and his bald head was red from the constant sun beating down on him. A small patch of skin was peeling away on the very top of his head. His body wasn't used to the sun or other elements.

Marshall stopped and looked to his left and right, placing his hand over his eyes to block the sun. "We are near our home," he said to no one in particular. He looked up to check the position of the sun in the sky and looked at the shadow cast by a lone cactus nearby. "That way." He pointed to his right and squinted. "This place, where is it?" he asked me.

"North of your home," I said.

"North?" he asked.

"That way," I said and pointed in the direction of Denver. "A few more hours that way."

"Good," he said. "Give me a weapon." He reached his hand out to his son. Baker handed him a pistol, and it weighed down Marshall's hand. He stuffed it into the waist of his pants and exhaled loudly. "Let's keep going," he said.

CHAPTER 34

The wheels of the SUV skidded on the loose rubble in front of the old motel. Oil, brake fluid, and gasoline dripped out from under the car, soaking into the dry orange dirt below. The car door opened, and Doc tumbled out onto the ground. He gripped his six-shooter tightly in his hand as blood dripped down to coat the wooden handle.

Doc stood, forcing his body to move towards the dilapidated motel, dragging his feet and kicking up dust behind him. He pulled his body to the front office and leaned against the splintered door. He kicked on the door with the sole of his boot, wincing with each movement.

"Haley!" Doc yelled. "It's me! Open the door!" Doc slammed his boot against the door again, almost kicking it in this time. The door swung open, and a thin woman in overalls with a bandana tied around her wrist stood in the doorway. Doc spun around and fell into the woman, dropping his pistol on the brown carpet floor.

"Jesus!" she shouted. "What happened?"

"Things didn't go according to plan," Doc growled.

"Here. Lie down." Haley led Doc to a musty couch in the old lobby, most likely a remnant from when the motel was operational years ago. Doc crashed down, and a puff of dust drifted up from the plaid cushions. "Where are you injured?" Haley asked while she pulled at Doc's counterfeit TDA uniform and unlaced his military boots.

"Shoulder," Doc said through gritted teeth. The dark uniform masked the large circle of blood that had oozed out of a gunshot wound just below Doc's collar bone where his arm met his chest.

"I'll get Finn," Haley said and ran off down the stairs leading to the room with weaponry and blueprints hanging on the walls. Doc picked up where Haley left off and slowly peeled his shirt from his body. Blood was smeared over his chest and dripped down his stomach, soaking into the waist of his pants.

He managed to get his uninjured arm out of the sleeve and worked on pulling the rest of his shirt off. The wound pulsed and pushed blood out of the dark red hole with each heartbeat. The skin around the gunshot wound was bruised a dark purple.

"Fuck," Doc muttered as he saw his wound for the first time since fleeing the base. He was lucky to have just the one gunshot wound, he thought to himself. He was lucky to be alive.

"What the hell?" Finn said as he and Haley ran into the room. He slid and kneeled down next to Doc. "Are you hit anywhere else?" Doc just shook his head. "You gotta sit up," Finn said as he brushed his sun-bleached blonde hair out of his face. Doc struggled to sit up, moaning with each movement. Finn helped him, supporting his back. He pulled the TDA uniform around and slid the remaining sleeve off of Doc's arm. "No exit wound," Finn said, and Doc moaned at the news. "We're gonna have to dig it—"

"Just leave it in," Doc growled. "It can't do any more harm than it already has. You'll fuck things up more by digging around in there."

"Sure, if it's a *normal* bullet," Finn said. "You know they use tracking bullets."

164

"And lace some with radioactive materials," Haley chimed in.

"Okay. Okay." Doc rolled his eyes and grunted in disapproval. "Do we at least have anything for the pain?" Finn looked at Haley and she shook her head rapidly. "Whiskey?" Doc asked.

"Go," Finn ordered Haley. "Bring me the first aid kit!" He turned back to Doc. "Vesa?" Doc shook his head and breathed shallow breaths. "Whitman?" Finn asked.

"Gone," Doc answered as Haley returned with a bottle of whiskey, a first aid kit, a pair of forceps, and a roll of gauze.

"Here," she said handing the whiskey to Doc and the other supplies to Finn. Doc poured whiskey down his throat until it spilled out the sides of his mouth. He pulled the bottle away from his mouth and coughed, wincing with each violent jolt. The alcohol flowed through him and warmed his body as he slumped down into the dusty sofa, resting the bottle of whiskey between his legs.

"Gimme that," Finn said, taking the bottle away from Doc and pouring the alcohol onto the gunshot wound.

"Fuck!" Doc screamed and twisted his body out of the stream of whiskey.

"Hold still," Finn ordered. "Hold him down." He motioned to Haley. "I'm not gonna be delicate," he told Doc. "The slower I go, the longer it's gonna take. I'm just gonna go in and rip that thing out. Okay?"

Doc nodded.

Finn dug the forceps into the open wound, triggering every nerve in Doc's chest. He screamed and howled at the sharp shooting pain. His hands balled into fists, gripping the stained fabric of the dirty sofa. The cold metal forceps dug into Doc, like a large burrowing worm or insect. Finn spread the tool open, stretching Doc's skin. He clasped the metal slug inside Doc. In one swift motion, he yanked the bullet out, ripping the gunshot wound open a bit more.

Doc blinked, his head was dizzy from the pain and alcohol.

"Lie back down," Finn said. "I got it." He held the bullet out to Haley who reluctantly held her hand out. Finn released the bullet, dropping it into Haley's hand. "Take that downstairs and have it analyzed. If it's a tracker, destroy it."

Doc's eyes pulled shut and darkness overtook him.

"Hey," Finn said and snapped his fingers in Doc's face. Doc slowly opened his eyes, and winced at the sudden pain. He wished that Finn had let him sleep just a bit longer. "Hey," Finn snapped his fingers again. "Doc! Wake up!"

"How long was I out?"

"An hour, maybe," Finn said.

Doc gently sat up. "What do you want?" He was still shirtless, but his wound was bandaged and his chest had been wiped clean of tacky blood. He lowered his legs off the stained sofa and rolled his head back and forth to stretch his neck.

"We need to know what happened," Finn said. "Where is everyone else?" Haley stood behind him, and another man, Franklin, sat in a chair off to the side.

Doc breathed in as deep as he could until his chest stung and kept him from breathing any deeper. He ran his hand through his greasy hair.

"Where's my gun?" he asked, though it was more of a demand. Franklin reached out, holding the barrel of Doc's beaten pistol. Doc slowly reached out with his good arm and grasped the wooden handle, pushing the cylinder out, checking if it was loaded. "Bullets," he grunted.

Haley walked behind the counter to retrieve a handful of bullets and held them out to Doc, who dropped the brass rounds in his lap and pushed them, one by one, into his gun, until it was fully loaded. He pressed the cylinder back into the pistol and slid the gun into his holster.

"We made it to Buckley," Doc said quietly. "They caught on though. I don't know how," Doc said, cutting Finn's question off. "Powell went with two men, one military and another from Wayfield, and left us with some guards." Doc shook his head. "Next thing I know, Powell comes back around the corner with a knife wound across his chest, looking like some sort of stumbling zombie."

"I knew there was something up with that guy!" Finn said and stood up beginning to pace back and forth. "From the moment he came here with Vesa. I knew it."

"Relax," Doc said. "It wasn't anything he did. It was a stupid plan from the start."

"Yeah, it was *his* plan!" Finn said.

"And we agreed to go along with it," Doc countered.

"So, then what?" Haley interjected, trying to get the story back on track. Her overalls were stained with oil and dirt, and the bandana that had been wrapped around her wrist was now used to tie her hair out of her face.

"Then we ran down the tunnels deeper into Buckley." Doc ran his fingers up his chest until they met the bandaged area around his shoulder. Slowly, he edged his fingers near the wound and pressed, testing the sensitivity.

"You went deeper into Buckley? Why not just turn around?" Finn said.

"That wasn't the plan," Doc said, still pressing around the gunshot wound.

"Ha! The plan," Finn muttered under his breath.

"Yeah, *THE* plan. Powell's plan, our plan, whatever the fuck you want to call it. The plan was to charge the mind transfer device, and to do that we had to go deeper into Buckley. Their wireless power source only reached so far out. The closer we got the stronger the charge.

Without a charge that thing is just a hunk of metal."

"A hunk of metal that took us years to build!" Finn shot back.

"So the device?" Franklin asked and pushed his glasses back up his nose. "Where is the device now?"

Doc shook his head. He knew none of them would like his answer. He breathed in as deep as his chest wound would allow before streaks of pain stretched through his pectorals. "I don't know." He sighed, letting the breath out and relieving any pain he felt from breathing in.

"You don't know!" Finn shouted. "You don't know?"

Franklin hung his head. Haley stared in disbelief. This had been their life for the last five years.

"This is Ashton all over again." Franklin sighed. "They're always one fucking step ahead of us. They got the time movement device from us. Now they very well could have the mind transfer device."

"Vesa and Powell took the device to get closer to the wireless charger inside Buckley. Whitman and I stayed behind to fight off any guards that came after us, to buy them time. Once they left us, I don't know what happened to them."

"And Whitman?" Haley asked. "You stayed with him?"

"I stayed with his body," Doc answered. "He plugged himself into the security system or some shit. To help distract the guards, and keep them away from Vesa and Powell."

"Wait, he plugged straight into the system?" Franklin asked, his eyes glazing over with awe.

"Is that bad?" Finn asked.

"I ... don't really know," Franklin said, pushing his rolled sleeves even higher up his arms. "It could mean Whitman's consciousness is somehow still inside Buckley, he might be able to continue to monitor their communications, or maybe, if all of the Ministry's bases are connected, Whitman could have traveled to some other part of the country ... or..."

"Or...?" Finn prodded.

"Or the Ministry of Science was able to trap or isolate his mind, meaning they could hack Whitman's brain and extract information from it."

"So, they have Whitman's *body*, might have Whitman's *mind*, and they likely have Vesa, which means they likely have the mind transfer device. Tell me again how we are better off than we were before," Finn said.

"I'm still here." Doc smirked and stood from the couch, testing the steadiness of his legs.

"We need a plan," Finn said. "A *new* plan."

"For what?" Haley asked as she inspected the bandages around Doc's shoulder.

"To get the device back," Finn said throwing his hands up in the air.

"It's gone," Doc said, brushing Haley aside and making his way to the rooms behind the front office. "There's nothing we can do. Even if we thought we could get into Buckley before, we definitely can't now. I'm sure they'll be increasing security as we speak. We can't intercept the device while it's being transported, cuz we don't know if they're transporting it or where. We don't know if they have it. We don't know a damn thing. It could be smashed to a million pieces or be riddled with bullets!"

"It took us five years to build that thing," Franklin said as he ripped his glasses from his face. This was a rare outburst from the otherwise reserved bookworm.

"C'mon, guys! I know you all put a lot of work into this thing. So did Whitman and Vesa. Hell, Cooper *died* trying to make that device a reality. But we aren't on the offensive anymore. We don't have Whitman, and that means no more cure for Dark Time, no more Wayfield DNA. We lost the smartest man we had five years ago—no offense, Finn, but you know Cooper was the brains behind the early research." Finn opened his mouth but decided not to argue the point.

"We lost Vesa and Powell, who both know the location of this motel. And if Franklin is right, then they might even have Whitman's brain, which means access to everything he knew. *Everything.* Given enough time ... how much time, Franklin?"

Franklin was mumbling numbers to himself, tapping his fingers against the wooden front desk. "Maybe a day or two to isolate Whitman's consciousness inside their system, then a few more to extract the information."

"That means we have four days at the *most*, and that's only *if* Vesa and Powell don't crack before they hack Whitman's brain and give this place up."

"Vesa won't give this place up. No way," Finn said.

"The point is, we can't sit here and start from scratch on a new device. We need to pack up and get the hell out of here. We need to go somewhere that neither Vesa or Whitman knew about."

"You can leave, Doc," Finn said, flinging his hand in the air. "I'm gonna do whatever I want to do."

"No!" Doc thundered. The sudden noise made Haley jump. Until now Doc had been calm, but now a sudden strength was in his voice. "We all leave, now! If anyone stays here, then you are putting those who do leave at risk, cuz I'll bet my bottom dollar they are coming here. They are coming here with guns, and armor, and bombs. They are coming here with snipers that they will post up on the mountain ridge with their high-powered scopes. Cuz you're right, Franklin, this *is* Ashton all over again. We know what happened there. They kicked in the door and shot anything that moved. Indiscriminate, like they were spraying napalm. Two men in Ashton survived. *Two.*"

Finn crossed his arms, his jaw clenched. Franklin looked off, likely still contemplating what would come of Whitman's mind.

"But they weren't let go. They were both sent to New Alcatraz! Might as well have died right then and there. Oh, I guarantee you they were questioned and beat within an inch of their lives before they were shipped off to die. And I don't trust any of us, myself included, to not crack and give them more information. If you stay, you put the rest of us at risk. Plain and simple. So pack your shit! We leave by sundown."

Doc paused, but no one moved. They were either stubborn or frozen by fear. Fear of the government or fear of Doc's sudden outburst, he couldn't tell.

"Go…" Doc said, more gently, and waved his hands in the air, like he was ushering a group of children out the door. "Go, let's go,"

At that moment, the window at the front of the office exploded, spraying shards of glass around the small room. A bullet shattered into the wall next to Haley, scattering bits of plaster over the floor. Another bullet ripped through the door, grazing Doc's chest, and burning a streak near his rib cage.

"Go!" Doc yelled. "Go, go, go, go!"

They ran for cover. Doc pulled his pistol from his holster, and kicked in the door that led downstairs to the makeshift armory.

CHAPTER 35

2075
GRAY MOUNTAIN, ARIZONA

Bullets flew through the walls and windows of the old motel, tearing down what little strength the rotting structure had remaining. Dust, plaster, wood, and glass puffed up, bursting through the air in clouds. The explosion of bullets drowned out all other sounds, like rapid firecrackers blowing up in a never-ending deafening string. Barely audible over the gunfire, Doc shouted, "Let's go!"

Even to himself, his voice sounded far away and underwater. To everyone else it was a soundless gesture. Doc, barefoot, jumped down the stairs two at a time. Haley, Finn, and Franklin followed. Once below the main buildings, the noise of the gunfire was muffled somewhat, but it still rattled through the foundation of the building.

Doc's side bled from the bullet that had grazed his ribs. It was a slow trickle, and the skin looked like he was branded instead of shot. The four of them found themselves in the small room with maps and blueprints hanging on the walls. All of the research their group had on the Ministry of Science, Wayfield Industries, Project Oracle, Project Blue Brain, and Dark Time hung on the walls or sat in filing cabinets. At the back was a wall of weaponry.

Pointing at the maps and blueprints of the various government installations hanging on the walls, Doc shouted, "Rip those down!" Franklin jumped into action and pulled at the hanging documents. Colored thumbtacks and android schematics sat balled up on the stained carpet. "Now burn them!" Doc shouted at Franklin. "We will hold them off, so you can destroy everything down here."

Franklin nodded and kept tearing things down. He ripped open the drawers of a filing cabinet and threw the contents onto the floor.

Doc ran to the wall of guns and pulled them down, tossing Haley a pistol with a long barrel and an extended magazine. Finn caught a long automatic rifle and swung it around his shoulder, and in one swift motion, caught a second pistol and stuffed it in his waistband. Doc holstered his six-shooter pistol and grabbed a heavy sniper rifle with an extended barrel and long scope.

Nodding to the back of the motel where the garage opened up to the desert, Doc yelled, "You two go out the back to the garage and keep anyone from coming in. I'm going back up there."

"Be careful!" Finn shouted over the rapid gunfire tearing through the other rooms of the old motel. Doc nodded and lunged up the stairs. Haley and Finn made their way to the back of the garage.

Keeping well below the windows, Doc re-entered the front office, crawling behind the front desk. Glass from the windows crunched under his knees and hands, shards digging into his palms and bare feet. He moved briskly so as not to keep one hand or knee pressed into the glass for any longer than necessary. Still shirtless, Doc rested his bare back against the wooden front desk, and pulled the slide back on his sniper rifle. A long bullet fell into the chamber, and Doc shifted the scope ever so slightly. By now the gunmen outside had moved on to shooting up other parts of the motel. Doc heard the distinct sound of bullets ripping through his SUV outside.

Doc turned around, propping his gun on the counter and peering through the scope. On the ridge, exactly where he said they would be, were agents of some sort. They were too far away for him to make out the initials on their uniforms. TDA, TAA, CIA—it didn't matter, they were agents nonetheless. Doc lined them up in his sights, thinking of what order to shoot. He mapped out the movements he would have to make, knowing that as soon as he fired one shot, the agents would turn to locate him.

Doc breathed in deep, and as he exhaled he squeezed the trigger of his rifle, sending a bullet towards the first agent posted on the mountain ridge. He pulled the slide back, inviting another bullet into the chamber, and, without watching where his first bullet went, he pointed his gun at another agent and squeezed the trigger again. This time, he saw the bullet hit its target. The second agent's chest exploded and he fell over into the orange desert dirt.

Doc pulled the slide back a third time, but before firing, he ducked and crawled to a different location in the front office, narrowly missing a stream of bullets that ripped through the front desk. He pressed his back against one of the walls, just below a window. Doc's cut hands stung as he gripped the sniper rifle. Blood oozed between his hands and the gun, forcing him to concentrate so as not to let it slip from his grasp.

The agents turned their gunfire elsewhere. Doc leaned out the broken window and rested his rifle on the sill. He fired one round towards the ridge and quickly loaded another bullet, firing it at a different agent. Both rounds made contact, killing two more agents instantly.

Doc saw a line of armed agents with small submachine guns slowly approaching the front of the motel. His position was made, and it was a death sentence to stay any longer. Doc ducked down and threw the sniper rifle on the floor. Crawling on his belly, he made his way back down the stairs as more bullets tore apart the motel front office.

Panels of drywall fell to the ground, the frames of the windows pulled away from the exterior walls, and the light fixtures sparked and fell from the ceiling. Doc crawled and stumbled down the stairs to find Franklin dousing all of the documents in gasoline.

"Match?" Franklin asked, and in one swift motion Doc reached in his pants pocket and tossed Franklin a silver lighter.

"Hurry," Doc said without stopping. "They'll be coming down those stairs any minute."

Doc approached the large machine gun that sat on a tripod in the corner of the small room. He unlocked the wheels on the tripod and pushed it out the door, towards the garage in the back of the motel. Franklin tossed the lit lighter onto the pile of maps and blueprints. The papers burst into a bright orange flame that almost reached the ceiling.

"Let's go!" Doc shouted.

Franklin kicked the table and chairs into the fire, blocking the stairs to the main office. He turned and grabbed a pistol from the wall of weapons, and followed behind Doc.

In the garage, Finn and Haley were ducked behind a car in the garage, sporadically firing bullets into the desert. Men in black dotted the horizon, none of them fazed by the bullets. Doc locked the wheels of the tripod in place, and fed the long string of bullets into the side of the gun. He gripped the sides, bracing for the massive recoil of the weapon, and pulled the trigger. A string of oversized bullets fired out into the orange desert, bursting up clouds of hot sand.

Doc's body shook and vibrated, but he managed to readjust his aim without taking his hand off the trigger until his bullets made contact with the line of agents approaching the motel. From left to right, they fell over and flew backwards at the sudden force of the bullets, tiny specks of red puffing out of their backs. Some tried to run, but the desert provided no cover.

Doc pried his fingers from the gun, and shook his arms out to try and stop the continuing vibrations from running up his body. More agents rounded the corners and scurried through the large bay doors of the garage. Doc grabbed Franklin and pulled him behind the car just as the agents' bullets pierced the walls behind them.

"Hide behind the wheel wells," Doc ordered the other three. He pressed his back against the thick tire of the vehicle and stared down the hall that led back to what used to be their armory. Flames spread through the room, eating through years of hard work and research. The heat reached Doc's face. The fire spread, melting the old brown carpet that covered the floor of the musty room.

Whatever bullets remained in the armory burst and exploded in the heat. Now the sound of gunfire surrounded them, in front and behind. Finn edged his way around the vehicle and shot several precise rounds towards one of the agents. The agent screamed as a bullet tore through his thigh, but he was able to fire back. More agents fired indiscriminately, drilling holes through the doors and windows of the large vehicle, ripping it apart just as they had done with the old motel.

"Argghhh!" Franklin yelled from behind Doc. He spun around to see Franklin holding his side, blood oozing out onto the dirty garage floor. He lifted his hand only briefly to examine his wound, and blood rushed from his stomach.

"Shit!"

"Just stay there," Doc ordered. "Don't move." Doc crawled to the front of the vehicle and rolled on the floor until he reached a bank of heavy metal tool carts. Bullets bounced off the metal on the other side, and Doc reached his hand around the side firing a single bullet towards an agent. The bullet zipped through the man's skull, and he fell over in a lump of lifeless flesh.

The fire billowed out from the room and made its way towards the garage, engulfing a barrel of gasoline in the corner. Crouching behind cover and watching the barrel burn bright orange in the flames, Doc mumbled to himself, "Shit."

The barrel exploded and threw shards of metal through the air, scalding and slashing through anything they touched. The burning gasoline spilled out over the cement floor and ran into other barrels and oily rags until the entire garage was enveloped in flames. A burning scrap of metal flew through the air, landing in Haley's throat.

"Fuck!" Finn shouted. He cradled Haley's head in his lap but quickly realized there was nothing he could do for her. He pulled the gun from her hands and fired whatever ammunition remained towards the wall of agents who still persisted, even in the face of the blazing fire. The slide locked up on the pistol as Finn fired the last bullet. He threw the gun at one of the agents and swung the long rifle around from his back.

Doc fired several more bullets from behind the tool cabinets, missing one agent and grazing another in the neck. The agent dropped his gun and pressed both hands over his neck. He fell to the floor and bled out in a matter of seconds. A second explosion rocked the foundation of the garage, throwing shrapnel in every direction. Doc choked on the thick smoke billowing from the fire and drifting up to the tall ceiling. Out of bullets, Doc holstered his six-shooter.

"Finn!" he shouted. Finn sat frozen, staring at Franklins body sprawled out on the floor. "Finn!" Doc shouted again, snapping Finn out of it. Finn looked over, his eyes watering and bloodshot from the ash and smoke. His left arm was covered in blood. "Gun!" Doc shouted and held out his hand. Finn reached out and pried Franklin's fingers off of the gun he once held.

"Here!" Finn shouted over the deafening staccato sound of the agents' gunfire and the crackling of the blazing fire. A bullet tore through Doc's hand as he reached up to catch the gun.

He screamed and yanked his hand back down behind the cover of the metal cabinet. He tried to grip the gun with his left hand, but knew he wouldn't be as accurate.

A third explosion ripped through the garage, and part of the metal ceiling caved in, crushing several of the agents. The falling sheets of metal pushed the hot air around the garage, blowing ash into Doc's eyes. He peered over his cover and saw only a few agents still standing. He took out two of the three agents before his gun ran out of ammunition. He threw the gun at the last agent, striking him in the chest.

The agent stumbled only slightly. He held his long rifle at Doc. The flames burned tall around both men, one dressed in black military gear. Doc was still shirtless with the bandage wrapped around his original gunshot wound. The agent steadied his aim just as a bullet flew through his chest.

Doc breathed heavily, and turned to see Finn holding his gun. The growing fire spit hot embers around the room. The rest of the metal ceiling groaned and bowed toward Doc and Finn. They ran out into the hot desert just as the flames overtook the last remnants of the garage and what remained of the ceiling caved in.

Finn coughed and gagged on the wave of ash that puffed out of the garage. Doc bent over, bracing his hands on his knees. Finn looked over at Doc. Blood flowed down his arm, and Doc could now see that Finn was shot through his bicep. His face was littered with cuts and soot. Tears had carved wavy lines through the ash down Finn's face. "Franklin ... Haley..." he said.

Doc assessed his own injuries. His original wound from Buckley had split open and bled through the bandage, the cut on his side still bled slightly, and his pinky finger was gone.

"Shit," Doc said, wincing and holding his hand up to his face. Another explosion shook through the collapsed garage as the fire engulfed the final flammable barrel buried under the old building.

"How did they get here so fast?" Finn asked. "I thought there would be more time."

Doc shrugged. "Someone gave us up. There's no way they could have hacked Whitman's brain this quickly."

"Powell," Finn said and shook his head.

"I suppose so," Doc agreed. "I just didn't peg him as someone who would give up so easily. I had more faith in him."

The two turned to walk around to the front of the motel. They rounded the old structure to see that the fire had spread through the office and into the rooms. Flames billowed out of the broken windows, and smoke drifted into the blue sky.

"Freeze!" An agent came around the other side of the old motel. His rifle was trained on the two unarmed men. "Get on the ground!"

CHAPTER 36

5280
NEW ALCATRAZ

Through the falling snow, I heard Marshall's son shout, "Over here! I think I found it!" Baker waved his hands in the air, his black rifle hanging at his side. The two other vault dwellers huddled around Baker. One was tall and thinner than the others I had seen back at the village. His arms stretched down the side of him, and, even after years of practice, he still seemed to move in an awkward rhythm. The other man was the one I shot in the thigh. He limped in the snow, and every so often I caught him scowling at me.

"Move," Marshall ordered and pointed his pistol in my direction. I complied and walked over to Baker and the other men, who stood in front of a broken metal door. The door was ajar and detached at the top two hinges. Snow and dirt spilled in, covering the long staircase that led down into darkness.

"Is this it?" Baker asked. I nodded and looked over at Ash and Merit. Merit's face was as white as the snow on the ground. Ash tried to look tough, but underneath his thick beard was the face of a worried man.

"You go first," Marshall ordered me, nudging my back with his gun. My feet slipped on the snow-covered steps, but the deeper I went the more grip I found. I walked the same path that I had walked five years ago … or two hundred years ago. My father, Red, Hamilton, and I had traveled down these same steps and this same hallway, only now the hall was caved in and crumbling. Entire walls had fallen inwards and crumbled across the floor, and snow drifted into the hall from above, where the desert floor had opened up. Small slivers of light shone through above our heads, but around us was mostly darkness.

"What happened here?" Merit asked.

"Last I was here, there was an explosion in the medical wing. Or maybe just an earthquake or something."

Merit looked down at the colored lines on the floor. Some of them went to the same places as in Buckley, like the white line that led to the armory, the green line that led to housing, and the blue line that led to the medical wing. But some were different, like the red line leading to the maintenance area or the yellow line that traced its way deep into the facility to the deployment center.

"I can't do this," Merit said at the sight of the familiar painted lines. He shook his head and turned back towards the staircase.

"Ah-ah," Marshall said and pointed his gun at Merit. "We all stay together."

"I'll wait outside. You guys go ahead," Merit told Marshall.

"So you can sneak up and jump us from behind?" Baker blurted out. His pale face was like the moon hanging in a dark night sky. "Or so you can make your way to the armory and loop back around here? No. You come with us."

"Merit," I said and widened my eyes, coaxing him to continue instead of causing any unneeded trouble.

"You don't know what's down there," Merit said and pointed down the long black hall. "You say you've been here before, hundreds of years ago or some shit! But you don't know what's here *now*. And I am not going for you, or him, *or* my brother!"

Baker pointed his rifle at Merit. The man I'd shot raised his gun as well. Baker's blue eyes pierced through Merit "You are coming with us. There is no discussion."

The tall lanky vault dweller who never spoke simply walked up to Merit and towered over him, clenching a long blade in his hands. Merit looked at me and Ash for some sort of help, but I just shrugged and continued to walk deeper into the underground base.

"So where to?" Marshall yelled up the hallway to me. "Housing?" He pointed down at the cluster of painted lines on the floor. I wondered how a man who grew up underground at Buckley surrounded by cannibals his entire life knew how to read the word 'housing.' Maybe his ancestors had retained some sense of a normal life before they devolved into cannibals. Maybe they had provided an education to their children.

"No." I shook my head. "Housing is just a long hall of cells with beds. Last I was here, there was food and water near the maintenance area. We follow the red line."

In the never-ending darkness, our feet knocked into chunks of cement that had fallen from the cracked walls or ceiling. Rusted rebar jutted out from where the cement used to be, the metal rods bent and twisted inside the gray cement. Every few paces I scrapped against a twisted length of rebar.

We approached a section of the hallway that was completely caved in, except for a small crevice that we crawled through. It took both Merit and me to pull Ash's large body through the small opening. Ash's chest was still bandaged from the stabbing back at the village. For the most part, Ash did a good job masking his pain, but this tight squeeze was too much for even him to hide his pain. The red line veered away from the others, towards the bank of offices I remembered from last time I was here.

Crushed cubicles lined the large room. Wires hung from the ceiling, some ripped so that the orange copper inside was exposed, while others were still tucked in their metal conduits. We had traveled down, well below the earth's surface, and now, towering over our heads two or three stories up were holes in the ceiling that let in slivers of light. Snow drifted down to mix with the cement dust in the air. The gray and white particles spun and floated together, fading in and out of the rays of light peeking through the cracked ceiling.

"Wait here," I said. "I'll get the lights on."

"Don't try anything," Marshall ordered. He pulled Ash towards him and pushed the barrel of his pistol into Ash's back.

"Just wait here," I repeated, and walked away. The bank of electrical boxes was twenty paces ahead of me. Last time I was here, my dad and Red had been the ones to get the power back on, while I had stayed behind and ate with Hamilton.

The metal boxes filled with circuitry and wires stretched to my left and right for as far as I could see. Unlike before, the metal boxes were dented and caved in from falling cement, and wires hung from several of them.

I walked along the line of boxes until I found a large lever with the words 'MAIN POWER' spray-painted under it. The lever was already in the on position.

"Shit," I mumbled. I pulled the lever down and then pushed it up again, hoping that something would happen.

"What's taking so long?" Marshall yelled out.

"This place isn't exactly in the best shape," I yelled back into the darkness. I squinted my eyes at the other breaker boxes. Most were labeled with strings of letters and numbers that made no sense to me. I walked down to the other end, and found one box with two levers, one labeled 'EMERGENCY POWER' in the 'off' position.

I flipped the large lever for the emergency power, and a low hum echoed through the breaker boxes. Sparks flew out from the wires that connected each box, and the red emergency lights overhead faded in and out as the power struggled to make it through the entire facility. I smiled at the sudden life breathing into the facility, but it was short lived. The lights dimmed to the point of almost going out. The sparks jumping out of the exposed wires died out until the wires just glowed a faint orange. The hum from the circuits quieted. I sighed and shuffled through the darkness back to Marshall and the others.

"What happened?" Marshall growled.

"I don't know," I answered. "It's an old place. But the food and water are over there somewhere." I pointed in the direction of the break room and kitchen area, though I knew the water was gone. The prisoners who had followed Ellis, Red, Hamilton, and me down here hundreds of years ago had fired countless bullets into the glass bottles.

"I didn't come here for water!" Marshall yelled, and I felt his gun jab into my ribs. Even in the darkness, I felt his body next to me, breathing and wheezing air out of the hole in his throat. "I came here for what you promised—a way out. I came here to leave this place, like you told me I could." With each word, the gun pressed harder and harder into my body. "If you can't power up this device, then I have no use for you. I have no use for any of you." I felt Marshall's breath spill over my skin. "And I have no reason to let anyone back at your village live."

With his final threat, the hum from underneath the floor returned. The noise spread through the bank of breaker boxes, and the broken hanging wires over our heads sizzled. The humming grew louder and louder, and the sparks burst out and showered down around our heads, lighting the air around us with an orange glow.

I thought back to the last time I was here, threatened by the other prisoners. Just like Marshall, they had been ready to kill us. Back then, it was a blackout that had provided me the precious seconds I'd needed to escape.

But darkness was what these vault-dwellers were used to, what they were born in, what they lived in. I couldn't count on the darkness to provide me with any help. But maybe the light…

The lights blinked and eventually stayed on, but the wires still popped and burst with orange sparks. Everyone looked around as the underground base was revealed. The maintenance area, cubicles, and the office break room illuminated. Ash, Merit, Baker, and the other vault dwellers stared with their mouths hung open. The only people who weren't looking around were the people who were not intrigued by any of it. Me and Marshall.

I stared at Marshall and he stared back at me, like he didn't care about any of the things down here. This was the perfect time for me to make a move, to try and subdue him, and he knew that.

The lights now burned overhead, flickering and casting harsh shadows over our faces.

I pivoted to move out of the way of Marshall's gun just as he fired off a shot. It rang through the maintenance area and burrowed in cement somewhere in the distance.

I grabbed his wrist and drove my knee into his groin. Marshall let out a loud burst of air. I ripped the gun out of his hand and flung him to the ground.

"Run!" I shouted at Ash and Merit.

"Get him!" Marshall yelled from behind me, squeezing his words out of his contracting lungs.

I jumped over chunks of cement and turned down the long hall just as a string of bullets bounced around me. Our feet pounded on the cement floor. Ahead of us was darkness. The electricity crawled through the base, lighting up the hall just as we ran down it. We were in a race to outrun Marshall and his men, but we also were outrunning the emergency lights.

We ran and stumbled over the cracked floor and broken walls. Merit fell over a block of cement. His face crashed against the floor, and bright red blood immediately poured from his face. Ash scooped him up without stopping and pulled him until Merit was able to get his feet underneath him.

"The yellow line!" I yelled, as more bullets sparked around us. "Follow the yellow line." I'd barely got the words out when I felt the familiar scalding burn of a bullet rip through my shoulder. The bullet exited the front of my body and drilled into a cement wall.

I screamed out and stumbled, but regained my footing quickly enough to keep my distance from Marshall and his men. I fired two shots blindly down the tunnel, hoping the vault dwellers would take cover and give us a chance to put more distance between us. Suddenly the floor under our feet angled downwards, and the three of us fell onto a jagged concrete slide.

Our bodies slid uncontrollably into pure darkness, hitting chunks of cement and scraping against pieces of rebar jutting out from the ground. One piece of floor would end, and, after a short drop, the three of us landed against the hard ground covered in sharp rocks. Our bodies bounced from one ramp to another, and I heard Ash and Merit let out bursts of air combined with groans each time we landed on a new piece of sloped ground. Far below us, I saw lights.

We headed towards the flat ground at an extreme speed, and I knew for sure that if we did nothing to slow our descent, we would surely break several bones on our final fall to the floor. Thick wires traced below us over the flat ground.

"Grab the wires!" I shouted as we approached the final drop. I was the first to slide off the angled cement. I reached out, and my body flew through the air into a web of wires. I flailed my arms until I grasped a bundle. The exposed metal cut through my hand as I slid down towards the flat ground. I had no choice but to hold on tightly. Once I was far enough down, I let go and crashed into the ground.

Ash flew in right behind me, and fell squarely into my body, slamming against the gunshot wound in my shoulder. Merit dropped down from the ramp overhead. He grabbed frantically at the wires above us, but didn't make contact with any of them. His arms swung and missed.

The sound of Merit's body meeting the cement floor was like the sound of a baseball bat making contact with a ball. Ash crawled over to him and flipped him onto his back.

"He's out," Ash said in a panic. I made my way to Merit's body and felt for a pulse.

"He's alive," I said, and Ash sighed deeply. I scanned his body to assess his injuries. His left leg was bent at the shin, and the bone bulged out. Blood matted his hair and ran down his face, mixing with the blood from what appeared to be a broken nose. A long gash ran down Ash's back from some piece of cement or rebar that must have cut into him on the way down. His hands were cut from the wires just as mine were. I looked back up the ramped cement floor, squinting my eyes to barely make out our four pursuers. They stopped before falling onto the cement slide. One of the vault dwellers readied his rifle.

"We need to move!" I shouted. "Help me get him," We pulled Merit's unconscious body down the hall. Gunshots ricocheted off the ground where we'd just been.

"You're hurt," Ash said and pointed at my shoulder. Now that we were somewhat safer, the shock began to wear off and pain rushed through me. My shoulder pulsed and burned, as blood leaked down my arm and soaked into my thick sweater.

"We need to get help," Ash said as he looked at his own injuries. "We need medicine." We searched the ground. We knew what line we were looking for, but it was nowhere to be found. The only line on the floor was the bright yellow line leading to the deployment center.

CHAPTER 37

Ransom shivered in a tight ball on the white floor of his cell. *Two days*, he thought. *Two days and this will be over. This body I am in will give in.*

He tried to let his mind drift away, to go to a time other than this. He thought back to playing hide and seek in the dense forest with Gray. Whenever Ransom found him, Gray's laugh would echo through the forest, and Gray would run through the trees, kicking clumps of snow behind his feet. He thought back to the times he would slowly walk through the village with Aurora, holding her hand as the snow fell around them. He remembered the slight shadows cast by the dim bulbs hanging in the village. He remembered how beautiful his wife was, how soft her hands were.

The door to his cell slid open and Ransom jerked his head up to see Agent Saunders step inside. Behind him was a man Ransom had only seen glimpses of while they had transported him. Sheldon, the man who'd demanded his hand be mutilated, like for like. Both men were wrapped in thick jackets with fur-lined hoods, gloves, and scarves. Saunders lugged a shiny metal bucket at his side that sloshed with water.

"Look, Powell," Sheldon said, the words seeping through his grinding teeth. "There is something special about you. Something you are *clearly* hiding."

Saunders moved closer to Ransom and placed the bucket on the floor. Ransom peeked in and saw a thin film of ice had formed over the surface of the water.

"We took your blood. Your girlfriend down the hall"—Sheldon motioned somewhere off to his right— "she gave you up. She told us what you really are." He took several deliberate steps towards Ransom and nudged the bucket with his foot, splashing some of the water out towards Ransom. "She told us about James Wayfield and his DNA. At first, we didn't believe it. We thought it was some stalling tactic."

Sheldon knelt down to face Ransom.

"But we took your blood. We ran it through a centrifuge." Ransom squinted his eyes at that last word. "We found four things in your blood." Sheldon held up four fingers on his good hand and then glanced down at Ransom's sutured hand with a smile. "Your DNA. That was a given. Number two, slight remnants of nanobots, likely left over from your travels to and from New Alcatraz. Serum four-three-eight-one, or, as you and your little group may call it, the cure for Dark Time. Sheldon fluttered his fingers in the air. "Too bad we destroyed your time displacement device in Ashton. One without the other... Well, that's just pointless, isn't it?"

Sheldon pushed the bucket of water closer to Ransom.

"The fourth item on your genetic inventory was more DNA. Not *your* DNA though. Our scientists ran it through a database and it matched. It matched James Wayfield. Your girlfriend wasn't lying, apparently. And as you must imagine, a whole new set of questions ran through our minds." Without looking away, Sheldon reached behind him and Agent Saunders handed him a long ladle.

"More questions mean we need more answers. More than you've given us up to this point." Sheldon dunked the ladle into the water, first tapping it on the thin ice on the surface to break through. He pulled a ladle full of ice-cold water and poured it back into the bucket. Ransom shivered and his body tensed.

"How did you get Wayfield's DNA?" Sheldon asked with a crooked smile. "How did you learn of Project Blue Brain?" Ransom stayed silent. He knew they wouldn't help save his son. He knew they didn't care about any misunderstanding. These people were worse than the ones he'd tried to evade in Buckley. Those people were crazed, but Ransom understood their motives. Hunger. It was simple. But these people's goals, if they even had any beyond wanting to torture him, were a mystery to Ransom.

How could we have come from this? Ransom asked himself.

"Did someone who works here give you access to the database downstairs?" Sheldon asked. "Are there more of you? More people with others' DNA? Stolen DNA?" Ransom shook his head, but quickly thought better of saying anymore. "Okay," Sheldon said, lifting the metal bucket and emptying the entire container of ice water over Ransom's head.

CHAPTER 38

5280
NEW ALCATRAZ

Ransom gasped, sucking in the damp air underneath the collapsed airport.

"Arrgghh!" He screamed and ran his hands over his face as if to wipe away his wet hair. "Stop it!" He gasped rapidly, collapsing to the ground.

"Powell!" Ash yelled. "Powell! What's wrong?" He kneeled down next to Ransom, who breathed short shallow breaths through his nose and pulled his eyes open wide. He patted his dry clothing in a panic, then focused on his hands, wiggling each of his fingers. He finally locked eyes with Ash.

"Ash?" Ransom said and wrapped his arms around his friend, fighting through any pain that emanated from his injured chest.

"Ransom?" Ash asked, holding his friend tightly.

Ransom pulled away and wiped tears from his face. A large smile stretched over his face. "I'm here. I'm back."

"You're back!" Ash yelled and wrapped his hulking arms around Ransom once more. The two men hugged and laughed with nothing but emptiness around them. They embraced for so long that blood from

Ransom's gunshot wound spread out from his arm and shoulder, and soaked into Ash's patchwork clothing. "Are you here for good?" Ash finally asked.

"I don't know." Ransom had a frightened look on his face. "I don't think I will make it much longer in that place. You don't know what they've done to me. These people ... they're monsters! They cut my fingers off!"

"They what?"

"They stabbed me, beat me. This fucking guy cut my arm." Ransom pointed at the underside of his bicep. "I almost died. They have this lady whose entire job is to keep me alive so they can keep hurting me."

"Powell told me these people were bad, but he didn't say anything like this."

"Powell!" Ransom said. "What do they want from him? What can I tell them? If I tell them, it will stop."

"I don't know," Ash said. "He says those people will kill you once they get what they want. He says that right now it is best for both of you if you stay in each other's bodies. It's safer that way."

Looking at his hands and massaging his pinky and ring finger, Ransom said, "I bet he fucking says that. What do you really know about this guy? He may know those monsters are going to kill me and plans to stay in my body forever."

"It's not like that. Powell wants to switch back. He has a plan, but it isn't going to be easy."

Inspecting the rest of his old body, Ransom asked, "A plan? What's the plan?"

"I don't know exactly."

"Well, maybe you should find out, Ash! You can't just trust this guy. In the last few days, we've both seen that people are fucked up. Everyone we've met since we left our home has been violent and crazed. Maybe our home isn't normal. Maybe people don't work and live together peacefully. You have to consider that Powell deserves what is happening to his body. How do you know he hasn't lied to you?"

"You're right," Ash said, looking down at the floor. "But ... I trust him. I have to trust him. We can't become people who assume the worst about people. That attitude will eat away at you. It will corrode our village."

Ransom's hand finally made its way up to his shoulder. "Ahhhh!" He inhaled and winced, noticing his shot arm for the first time. Blood stuck to his hand as he pulled it away from the damp tacky cloth. "What happened to me? Where are we? Are we back there?" He jerked his head around and readied his body to fight or flee.

"No," Ash answered and placed a hand on Ransom's good shoulder. "Not *there*, but somewhere else." For the first time Ransom noticed several cuts on Ash's face and hands.

"What happened to you?" he asked.

"We fell," Ash answered and pointed back at the gaping hole that stretched up through the mesh of exposed wires and rebar. "You and I made it, but Merit's knocked out. Pretty sure his leg is broken."

"Merit!" Ransom said through clenched teeth. He stood. His body was noticeably stronger than the one he just inhabited, but even still, Ransom knew he was weak. He stumbled and tripped, falling on top of his brother. "You piece of shit!" Ransom yelled, trying to punch the unconscious Merit in the face but wincing with each weak blow. Ash grabbed his arm and pulled him off.

"Ransom!" Ash yelled, keeping his body between the two brothers. "What's gotten into you?"

"He poisoned him!" Ransom's voice echoed around them.

"What? Poisoned?"

"He poisoned Gray." Ransom held his eyes shut for a brief

moment. It had felt like an eternity since he'd held his son and his wife. Like decades had passed since he last heard their voices. Ash scrunched his face.

"He what?" Ash asked and looked back at Merit.

"He poisoned Gray." He and Tannyn found whatever it was that infected our village. They found the source, and they gave it to Gray. They almost killed my son! And Merit stabbed me when I found out. He left me for dead."

"Wait. Wait. Wait." Ash shook his head. "Why would they do that? Tannyn was a jerk, but not a killer. And Merit … he's … he's your brother."

"They wanted to find the underground vault. They knew the village would only let us go if I was behind it, so they gave me no choice. They forced me to go looking for medicine. It was their plan all along." Ransom looked away from Merit and stared Ash in the eyes. "Tannyn didn't die from the sickness. I strangled him in the snow when I found out. And I beat Merit when I found out he was involved too. I threatened to bring him home and expose what he did to the rest of the village. I told him I would kill him once everyone knew what he and Tannyn did."

"So he stabbed you," Ash said quietly, looking back at Merit like he was a stranger. Like instead of a human on the ground there was something else. "He told us you two got separated down there."

"Separated! Is that what he told you? He left me to die. He looked me in the eyes, stabbed me, and shut the door! Now move! He has to pay for what he did," Ransom said. He took one more step and pressed his body into Ash. Maybe out of instinct to protect a friend, or maybe out of some small bit of hope that Ransom was wrong, Ash held him back from his brother. He wrapped his strong arms around Ransom's body, squeezing his wounded shoulder.

"Let me go!" Ransom yelled, shaking his head and squirming to get loose.

"There's more going on here, Ransom. There are other things happening right now. Listen to me! There are worse people down here than Merit. We have to stick together!"

Ash tried to hold Ransom back, but he broke free and ran up to Merit with his fist pulled back. All of the anger towards his brother swelled in his fist, as did the rage he felt towards his torturers in another time. Ransom felt disdain for a society that would allow such behaviors, and part of him hated himself for coming from such people. Once he was within reach, Ransom drove his fist into Merit's head and then dropped his entire body onto Merit.

"Ransom! Stop!" Ash said, but Ransom wrapped his hands around his brother's throat, squeezing until he was sure Merit couldn't breathe, until Merit's face turned red and purple. "Stop!" Ash yelled again, and curled his hand into a fist.

"I'm warning you, Ransom. Stop!"

But Ransom still pressed his hands onto Merit's throat. "Stop!" Ash ordered once more before reeling his arm back and punching Ransom in the back of the head. Ransom's body went limp and slumped over his unconscious brother, his hands still loosely wrapped around Merit's throat.

CHAPTER 39

2075
DENVER, COLORADO

I jolted awake in the white room, soaking wet and numb. My lungs contracted and I involuntarily gasped for breath. My heart beat rapidly as it struggled to push blood through my shrinking blood vessels. Water dripped down my face, and my clothes were soaked through. An empty bucket sat on the floor. Sheldon and the other agent stood just inside the freezing cell.

I tried to wrap my arms around my body for warmth, but I could not control my limbs. They hung around me like they belonged to someone else. In a way, they did. I fell over, my face pressing against the standing water on the floor and crunching through a thin layer of ice.

"I am growing very tired of your games, Powell," Sheldon said as he pulled his thick jacket tight around him. Cold air puffed out of his mouth with each word. "If you don't tell us how you came about the cure for Dark Time, serum four-three-eight-one, or Wayfield's DNA, then we will have to move on to your friend, Vesa."

"V-V-V-Ves-Vesa?" I stammered. My teeth chattered together.

"Yes, she is just down the hall. She was very happy to be reunited with her brother and has been helpful so far. Quite willing to help us actually. She gave up your group at that run-down motel in Arizona."

"Motel..." I managed to get out.

"It was destroyed during the raid. Two dead. Two detained. That's two more people on their way here to be questioned. Soon we won't even need you."

The agent behind Sheldon smirked at the idea of being unleashed, allowed to do whatever he wanted to. Whereas, before I thought Ransom and I were better off in each other's bodies, I now thought of how Ransom and I both were better off in his body. No one was better off in my body. I wondered if there was a way that we could coexist.

"Vesa told us about you and Wayfield's DNA." Sheldon motioned to the other agent, who stepped forward.

Slowly, he stepped down on the hand missing two fingers. Pain shot up my arm.

Small drips of blood seeped out of the fresh sutures where my fingers once were. The agent, Saunders it said on his uniform, pulled his fist back and drove it hard into my face, slamming the other side of my head into the cold cement.

My brain felt like a tiny ball rattling around inside my skull, bouncing off the walls and slamming into every nerve ending. Saunders landed two more punches to my face, each time pushing my head more and more into the ground. I knew my skull would give way much quicker than the frozen white cement.

Blood pooled in my mouth until it was too much to hold in or swallow. It leaked out the corner of my lips and spread out around my face. My body shook almost to the point of convulsing. I already felt my face begin to swell. Steam drifted up from the puddle of blood and dissipated into the frigid air around me.

Saunders turned his attention to my torso and drove his heavy steel toed work boot into my stomach and rib cage, pushing out what little air I could retain in my lungs out. I tried to tense my muscles in anticipation of each kick, but my body was frozen. Blood crawled back down my airway until I gagged and coughed it up, splattering and spraying into the air with each kick Saunders landed.

"Okay," Sheldon said and placed a hand on Saunders' shoulder. "Take a break." He turned his attention to me. "You have twelve more hours. Twelve hours and then we move on to Vesa."

"But in twelve hours you *will* die. We will get a cleaning crew in here. Mop the floor, move the body, and then march Vesa into the same cell. Maybe we will use the same interrogation techniques on Vesa. At least at first. But we'll try some new stuff too. Maybe I'll give Saunders a bit more privacy with her. You know, turn off the cameras." Sheldon knelt down and marveled at my mutilated hand. He looked at his own bandaged hand, and I wondered if he took this much pleasure in torturing every prisoner that came through here, or if he particularly hated me for chopping his fingers off.

Sheldon pulled the glove off of his one good hand, and reached towards my bad hand. He pinched one of the sutures on the part of my hand that used to hold my ring finger. He slowly tugged and pulled on the suture until the dried blood flaked away and my skin pulled upwards. I screamed out as he pulled and pulled until the suture ripped out of my hand.

My breathing was still out of control. My lungs still acted independently of my desire to slow my breathing. My body shook and shivered and I coughed blood onto the floor. Sheldon gripped another suture and pulled. A slow stream of blood crawled out from my knuckle and dripped towards my wrist. My eyes fluttered and rolled to the back of my head. The room blinked from white to gray. At one moment, Sheldon knelt in front of me. In the next, I saw Ash. And for a moment, I felt both Ransom's injuries and mine.

CHAPTER 40

5280
NEW ALCATRAZ

I pried my fingers from Merit's throat to reach the back of my head. A large lump stuck out.

"Who are you?" Ash's voice boomed from behind me. I spun around on the floor to find Ash clenching his fist.

"Powell." I grunted and held both of my hands against my head, applying pressure to either stop the bleeding or stop the pain. "What the fuck happened?"

Ash sighed loudly. "I don't know," he said and shook his head. "Ransom was here, and he was *pissed*."

"I don't blame him," I mumbled.

"No, he was pissed at his brother. He says that Merit poisoned Gray."

"Wait, wait, wait," I said. "What are you talking about?"

"It can't be true!" Ash said. "But why would Ransom make it up? None of this makes sense. Ransom said that Merit and Tannyn *poisoned* Gray so that Ransom would agree to go out searching for the underground vault."

"Shit," I said quietly and rubbed my eyes. I looked at Merit's body.

"That's why he's seemed skeptical of me ever since he came back, like he didn't want to be around me. Is he alive?"

"I think so," Ash said and slumped onto the hard floor. He shook his head and stared at nothing. "What am I doing?" he said to himself. "What are *we* doing? I just want things to go back to normal. Back before the sickness, before we found those cannibals, before Ransom and you switched bodies. I just want to go back." Ash hung his head.

"I know the feeling," I said, still rubbing my head. "Believe me, I want things to go back to normal just as much as you."

Ash asked, "How do I know that?"

"What?"

"How do I know you want things to go back? How do I know you don't want to stay in Ransom's body? I don't even know what we're doing. I'm just following you around blindly!" Ash took a large step towards me.

"Ash…" I held my hand out to try and calm him or stop him from getting too close. "I know things are strange and it's hard to understand it all. But you have to know I'm working to get things better. Better for Ransom. And better for me."

"Prove it," Ash demanded. "What is the plan? How do you plan on getting Ransom's mind back here for good?"

"We don't have time. Those men" — I pointed up from where we fell — "they are looking for a safe way to climb down here. They have guns! We have nothing. We can't stop so I can give you a lesson on how all of this works and what I plan to do!"

Ash looked back and forth at me and the large hole in the ceiling. No doubt, he was working out what he was willing to risk for proof of my plan. How much time he was willing to waste.

Sensing Ash was on the fence, I continued, "If I wasn't looking out for you, why would I have helped Gray, or shown you what medicines to take? Why would I have struck a deal with those cannibals that put *my* life in danger if I wanted to stay in this body forever? Look, you want things to go back to how they were. We all do. But we are dealing with things that I barely understand myself. Switching minds between two bodies ... thousands of years apart! That's not normal! I can't explain all of this to you. But I will try my hardest to get things back to normal. I promise. Are you with me?"

Slowly, Ash nodded and unclenched his fist. I stepped towards him and stuck my hand out.

Looking at my hand, Ash asked, "What?"

"Shake my hand," I said.

"Shake? What?" Ash squinted.

Grabbing his hand, I said, "Here. Take my hand." I gripped Ash's large hand in mine and shook it up and down. Ash tentatively went along, growing more comfortable in the motion with each second. "This is shaking hands," I said. "Where I am from that's what two friends do when they make a promise to each other."

A small smile grew on Ash's face. He let go of my hand. His large shoulders curved over his body. "So what do we do now?"

"Nothing's changed." I looked around the floor at the colored lines. "The yellow line," I said and pointed at the line with the words 'Deployment Center' written on it. "We have to get there before Marshall and his crew catch up to us."

"Is that how we can get Ransom back?" Ash asked.

"Yes and no," I said. "We can't just go get him. Where he is ... well I don't even know where he is. Not exactly. The cell he's in is guarded, and hidden somewhere in the facility. This facility" I pointed at the ground. "He is in this facility but in *my* time. This is only the second time I have been here, in this place. We need to find the machine in the deployment center."

"So this machine can get us to where Ransom is? To Ransom's time?" Ash asked. Maybe he did understand more of this than I gave him credit for.

"Yeah, but we can't go there. Not yet."

"Why not? Let's just go get him!" Ash said, determined to rescue his friend.

"Like I said, I don't know exactly where he is in this facility. It's a big place."

Ash threw his hands in the air. "So what can we do about that?"

"Before we go find Ransom, we need to get help. We need more people. People who know their way around this place. People who lived here. People who worked here."

CHAPTER 41

Our feet fell on the yellow line. In the last couple hundred years since I'd walked this line, the ground had split and torn it into small slivers separated by cracks. Merit had woken up, too disoriented and injured to walk on his own. Too dazed to talk coherently to Ash about what Ransom had told him. I'd tied off his wound as best I could to stop the bleeding. Ash didn't offer to carry him, so I wrapped my arm around him and bore half of his body weight.

Merit spoke very little and Ash said even less to him. Once Merit woke, Ash simply said, "There is no forgiveness for what you have done." Although he seemed angry, there was a sadness in how Ash spoke to Merit, like Merit's actions forever changed things and Ash already grieved for the way things used to be. After that Ash didn't speak for a long time. He just wandered ahead of us, randomly shaking his head in disapproval. We stumbled along the cracked yellow line, occasionally tripping. Merit would wince and the bone sticking out of his leg would push against the inside of his pant leg.

"How could you?" Ash asked under his breath, clearly unable to hold back his questions any longer. "He is your nephew." Ash looked back at Merit.

"It was Tannyn's idea," Merit said, wincing and grunting with each movement. "I didn't even know until it happened, till it was already too late. I had no choice but to go along with it. I was no different than Ransom. I had no choice."

"Save it," Ash growled. "It's easy to blame Tannyn when he's *dead*."

"You know me, Ash. You don't *really* think I would do this ... at least not like you think. Yeah, I always thought we should go looking for these places. Yes, once I knew Tannyn poisoned Gray, I knew Ransom would go looking for medicine."

"And you never thought to tell him that you knew how Gray got sick? You just played dumb the whole time?"

"What good would it have done? It wouldn't have changed anything. We still would have gone looking for medicine."

Turning to look Merit in the face, Ash said, "No, it would have changed something. It would have changed this." Ash waved his finger back and forth between himself and Merit. "If you had told your brother what you knew, we wouldn't be having this conversation. I wouldn't be pissed at you, and your brother wouldn't want to *kill* you. If you came clean, then we wouldn't think you had anything to hide. That's what it would have changed." Ash turned back around and continued down the long tunnel.

"You know, Ransom always said you were obsessed with finding these underground vaults. Obsessed with finishing what your dad started. Following in his footsteps. He said you pictured these wondrous places with shiny machines and bright lights." Ash laughed. "You must have been so disappointed when you saw that place. Dark and dusty. Filled with fucking crazy people. That's what you ruined your life for. What you ruined Ransom's life for. It makes sense that you always wanted to find these vaults. You have more in common with the people living underground than with any of us."

"I'm sorry," Merit whispered. His breathing was shallow, and I wondered if he'd broken a few ribs on the way down, too. Blood dripped down his forehead from some crack or cut. Even more blood was caked around his face from his broken nose, and it ran down his chest. "Have you seen them at all since we ran?" Merit asked me.

"No," I said. "They have to find another way down. That might take them a while." I struggled to hold Merit up, and we re-positioned often.

"What if they just slide down after us?"

"If they did that then they would have been right behind us."

"Maybe they just left. Maybe they took whatever water or food was in that room we were in and went home." Merit winced with every other word and cradled his chest with his hand. Ash pulled back his shirt to look at his stab wound. It appeared to have pulled open again.

"Marshall doesn't seem like the type to just turn around and go home." By now my entire right arm was covered in blood from my shot shoulder, and I left a trail of it behind me, like breadcrumbs should Marshall and his men ever make it down here. "Plus, there is no food or water in that room. I lied."

"Lied?" Merit asked.

"Yeah, something you are clearly familiar with," Ash said from ahead.

"Last time I was here we drank most of the water and ate the food. Whatever was left got shot up and destroyed," I said.

"Shot up?" Merit asked.

"Yeah, with guns, those weapons you found down in Buckley. Someone shot at all the food and water. It's destroyed. Unusable. So the only thing left of value down here is this machine, and revenge I guess."

Ash's feet pounded on the hard cement, sending booming echoes throughout the hall. We came upon an area where the tunnel was totally collapsed. The walls and ceiling had fallen inward, leaving only a small triangular hole for us to climb through.

"Who's first?" I asked, but no one volunteered. I shrugged.

"I won't fit through *that*," Ash said.

"You go first," Merit said to me. "Then Ash. That way you can help pull him through. I'll go last, since it looks like this could cave in at any moment."

"Okay," I said. Ash didn't argue with the order. I leaned Merit against the pile of gray rubble, and he balanced on his one good leg.

I slid the bag containing the mind transfer device through the small opening, and climbed in head first. The slabs of cement rubbed and pushed against my wounded shoulder. It burned inside where the bullet had ripped through muscle. Pain shot through my arm and down the entire side of my body. I bit my lip to hold back any cries of pain, so as not to alert Marshall and his men, so all that came out were muffled groans. More large chunks of cement pressed their jagged edges into my back.

With my good arm, I reached through the hole and pulled myself through, wiggling my body until I spilled out on the other side, all while trying not to shift the precarious mass of cement. Once through, I pulled the patchwork clothing away from my shoulder. The cloth stuck against my wound, peeling my skin with it. My shoulder looked black like it was burnt more than bruised.

I surveyed the hall on the other side of the debris. Crushed containment units filled with android parts lined the side of the hall. This was the hall I had found myself in hundreds of years ago, where I had found Whitman's remains, the cure for Dark Time, and Wayfield's DNA.

Glass from the storage units was scattered everywhere. Even if I wanted to find Whitman's parts, I wouldn't know where to go. Metal plates, actuator motors, computer chips, and bundles of wires were all piled on top of one another. Some of the cases were completely buried underneath a collapsed wall.

"I'm coming through," Ash called out from the other side.

"Okay. Just get your shoulders through, and I will pull your arms."

"Just don't let this collapse on me."

Ash reached and stretched out his arms, grunting and pulling himself through the small opening. The pile of debris shifted slightly and bits of dust crumbled down, falling in Ash's face. His forearms made it through, and I grabbed his hands. My right arm was no good, so I didn't even try to use it. Ash wrapped his huge hands around my left forearm as I pulled him through. He groaned as the cement slabs seemed to close around him, until his left shoulder broke through the hole. After that, it was a matter of pushing and pulling his body.

At last Ash slid through, and the force of his sudden release sent us both sprawling. We sat on top of the cement shards, both of us breathing heavily, wincing with each breath.

Merit pulled himself into the small opening. The rocks crumbled and shifted as Merit crawled through using his elbows. Some muffled noises came through the small opening, like the vault was yawning or moaning.

"Did you say something?" I asked to Merit who was halfway through by now. Merit just shook his head and kept inching forward. His face contorted in pain as his leg dragged across the sharp rocks. More noises drifted through the cement barricade. "Wait. Wait." I held a hand up and cocked my head. Merit stopped moving, likely happy for the break. More noises. Maybe words. "There. That. Did you hear that?"

Then there was a sound clearer than the others. Merit's face dropped and his eyes widened. "It's them," he whispered and continued dragging himself through the opening, now faster. Ignoring his injuries.

"There they are," was the first actual series of words I made out through the pile of cement.

"Hurry!" I yelled to Merit. His face was pale and sweaty, contorted in panic as he scratched and pulled his slim body through the hole. He winced and cried out each time his broken leg brushed against a hard surface. I looked around to make sure the entire hallway was blocked off, to make sure Marshall and his men couldn't somehow get to us another way. We rushed to grip Merit's arms, yanking him through to the other side.

The sound of bullets pinging around the collapsed cement rang through the tunnel, leaving my ears ringing. A mist of cement puffed around the small hole Merit just crawled through. Ash threw Merit's arm over his shoulder and hoisted him up.

"Go!" Marshall's voice rang out on the other side of the cement. The men's feet pounded on the ground. Ash took off in front of me, not even glancing at the advanced technology, dragging Merit with him.

I tried to run swiftly towards the deployment center, while still surveying the area. I needed to find more vials of nanobots, or else no one would survive traveling through time without receiving a large measure of radiation. My feet crunched on the floor. I heard one of the men grunting thirty paces or so behind me as he crawled through the tiny opening.

I glanced back to see the man I shot back at the village making his way through the crumbled wall. He pushed a rifle ahead of him until it clattered on the floor. As I turned back and continued down the hall, I saw a glimmer of something buried in the crushed containment compartments. Something familiar. I continued hobbling forward, looking back to see the first vault dweller spill out of the hole onto the floor. His hand gripping the rifle on the ground.

I spun my head, surveying the ground as I ran. I started to see more and more vial shaped objects on the floor, but I didn't know if I should stop to grab them or keep running from Marshall's men. Die now or die later. No good options.

Risking getting shot, I stopped at the next vial I saw on the ground. I scooped it up and shoved it in my bag. Nearby, I saw two more vials of nanobots lying next to a syringe, and I grabbed them too.

"Shit!" Ash yelled from up ahead. "Dead end!"

I jerked my head up to see a single door carved into the wall. Ash reached the door first and drove his shoulder into it, bursting it open. He fell inside, and dropped Merit on the floor.

"Get your ass over here!" Ash yelled at me. I ran my hands through the old android parts, feeling for more vials. I found three more and shoved them in my bag. A bullet zipped next to me, scattering the android debris. Then another bullet. And another.

"Hurry!" Ash was yelling and waving his hands, motioning me to move forward. I stood and stumbled toward the door as more and more bullets shot around the large tunnel.

"Get them!" Marshall shrieked from down the long tunnel just as a burst of bullets sprayed around me. A familiar burning sensation ignited deep inside of me, and more bullets flew past, bouncing off the cement surrounding the deployment center.

I stumbled forward and crashed onto the ground, my kneecap making contact with the hard cement. My body slid face-first through the doorway. Merit pulled me all the way into the deployment center, and Ash slammed the door as more bullets ricocheted off the wall outside.

I rolled onto my back to assess my wounds. Blood poured out of my stomach where the bullet had exited my body, Ransom's body. I crawled and leaned against the wall between us and Marshall's men.

Ash pressed his body up against the door, flinching with each bullet that slammed into the other side.

"Can those things get through the door?" Ash asked over the loud barrage of bullets drilling into the metal door.

"Probably not," I said through gritted teeth as I watched blood ooze out of my stomach. "If they know what's good for them they'll stop shooting soon. They only have so much ammo."

At that moment, the bullets stopped, replaced by the sound of the men's fists and feet pounding against the door. Ash pressed against it as it rattled. Sitting on the floor, I leaned my back against the door.

"Can you make it over here?" I asked Merit. He nodded and pulled himself on the floor towards the door. "You need to find something to lean against the door," I said to Ash. Merit sat next to me, the banging from the other side vibrated through both of our bodies. "Or maybe you can find a screwdriver or crowbar to wedge underneath it." Ash gave me a puzzled look. "Never mind, just find something heavy."

Ash disappeared into a corner of the deployment center and returned rolling a barrel filled with some liquid. Ash stood it on its end and pushed it against the door.

"Okay, now stay here," I told Merit, like he had much of a choice. I pushed myself up to my feet, holding my hand over the wound on my stomach. The pain was unlike anything I had felt before. It was like the stab wound I woke up with in Buckley, but worse. It burned and sizzled inside me, all while feeling like my intestines were being twisted in a knot.

The large stage surrounded by pistons was still intact. The thick cables that converged on the time machine were still here. I limped over to the control panel and flipped the main power switch to the entire room. Floodlights lit up the room like it was mid-day out in the desert. On the control panel was a tool box with a screwdriver inside.

"Here," I said. Each word and breath was a struggle. My vision was beginning to blur and my head grew heavy on my neck. I tossed the screwdriver towards the door. "Wedge that as far as you can under the door. It should help."

The tool bounced just out of Merit's reach. He dragged himself to pick up the foreign tool and then dragged his body back over to the door. He seemed panicked, like he was left with no good options. He couldn't leave, but if we were successful he would be forced to face his brother. For now, I couldn't worry about their fractured family life. I just needed my body back.

The banging from the other side of the door continued, but now it was steadier. More orchestrated, like they were all kicking or ramming the door at once. Ash's large body bounced back ever so slightly with each hit from the other side.

"What are you doing?" Ash yelled over the loud banging.

With my bloody hand, I entered the date and location I wanted to travel to. The numbers and dials blurred in and out, making it a slight guessing game as to where I was actually traveling to. My breathing was shallow, and the room around me started to spin. The pounding on the door was now accompanied by screams from outside. The noises mixed into a strange rhythmic chanting. The pistons around the stage began moving up and down, adding to the noises coming from the other side of the door.

On the wall opposite the control panel was a cabinet with the retrieval devices that my father had used during his time in Project Oracle, the devices designed to pull you back to your own time through the wormhole. This was the first time I had used one. It was the first time I planned on returning to the time I was leaving.

I limped over to the large stage, holding my hand against my stomach. The pistons were moving up and down and gaining speed. Air churned around the stage, blowing my hair around my face. It hurt to stand, so I sat down on. Visions of when I was first sent to New Alcatraz rushed through my head, and visions of when I returned home followed.

"What are you doing?" Ash shouted, straining against the metal door. Merit sat with his back against it, trying to relieve Ash of his duty, but his slim frame barely added any weight against the door.

"I'm going to get help. I won't be gone long. Just hold that door closed until I get back. You can't let them in," I said, barely loud enough to be heard over the churning pistons and the banging on the door. "I'll be back in no time."

"Back?" Ash yelled. "Back from where? Where are you going?"

"Home," I said, and the underground vault disappeared.

CHAPTER 42

I opened my eyes to find the forest in front of me. The trees swayed, and the silent breeze that blew against my face was in stark contrast to the banging and shouting of Marshall's men back in New Alcatraz. The wind rustled through the leaves and tall grass, creating a soothing, constant white noise. The quick tappings of a woodpecker drifted from some far-off tree.

I couldn't help but feel as though I had been here before. Not just here in Buford, but here, in this exact time, in this exact spot. In this exact body. The feeling of *déjà vu* washed over me, like the sudden realization that you left something behind while on vacation, like the feeling somehow came out of nowhere. Under the soft sound of the wind, I heard voices. I stumbled forward.

"How did you hear about this place?" a female voice asked. The voice, like this spot in the forest, was also familiar, as was the question she asked.

It was my father's voice that replied. "What? Buford? Someone in New Alcatraz mentioned it. I don't know why. It was like he wanted me to come here for some reason. Or he knew this is where I would go."

His voice was hoarser than I remembered.

I made my way through the clearing in the forest, and stood outside the trading post, listening to a conversation I'd heard before. This was the conversation I had heard the first time my mind had left my body at the Golden Dawn headquarters.

"But it's perfect, right?" my dad said, as I stood and dripped blood onto the dry leaves under my feet. *How is this possible?* I wondered. *How could my mind move into a future that hasn't happened yet?*

I stepped toward the trading post, and pain shot through my body. I couldn't tell if it originated from the gunshot wound in my shoulder or the one in my stomach. I was pushing the limits of the single vial of nanobots I'd injected into Ransom's body days ago.

"Ellis, you know I can't stay here. They'll test me for whatever Dark Time I have in my body. It won't take a genius to know what I was up to if they find I was gone for *nine* months. I'll be arrested and questioned, and then they'll come for you."

"And they'll come for our *child*. You paint a wonderful picture, but it can't happen. And I worry about you here all by yourself. Everyone needs someone. Even you."

I peeked through the dirty window of the trading post. Emery placed a hand on Ellis' arm. He looked down at the floor and clenched his jaw.

"We have no choice," my father said. "You're pregnant now. You can't go *back*."

"But I can't stay here," my mother said.

"At least staying here gives our child a chance in this world. *This* world." Ellis pointed to the ground. "Not that one. Not that time. If you give birth to a child in 2070, who knows what they'll have to live through." Ellis walked away from Emery and picked up a rusted hammer and nails.

"We will figure out how to make it all work. You. Me. The baby. The TAA. We will figure it out. For now, we're together. And no one is looking for us … yet."

Blood streamed down my throbbing arm, dripping from my fingers. My eyelids clamped down, heavy as lead. I saw two of everything in front of me. Two doors, and two rusted doorknobs. Just as I had done before, the last time I was here, I swiped at one knob with my good arm, but there was nothing to grab. I tried the knob next to the phantom one, and felt the solid rusted metal in my hand. I closed my eyes, twisted the knob, and pushed the door open.

Emery jumped back at the sight of me, and let out a startled scream. I raised my bloody hand in the air towards her, my eyes more closed than opened. My dad still gripped the hammer in his hand. He reached his arm around Emery and pulled her back behind him.

"It's me," I managed to say, but in Ransom's voice and in Ransom's body. I knew this made no sense.

I fell to my knees. Everything went dark. It could have been ten minutes or eight hours, I had no way of knowing.

I peeled my eyes open and breathed in deep. The smell of smoke from the wood-burning stove mixed with the scent of the prairie air outside. The day's last rays of sunlight reached into the window, reflecting off the bare shelves that lined the walls. I was home.

I tried to stand, but my legs were too weak. I slid back onto the wood floor with a soft thud. My dad turned around to face me.

"He's waking up," he said quietly. "What are we supposed to do?"

My mom shook her head. I stuck my hand under my tattered clothing and felt the skin underneath. The gunshot wound on my arm throbbed.

"What if the Ministry sent him?" Dad asked. My mom mumbled something I couldn't hear.

"Who sent you, huh?" he asked forcefully. "TDA? The Ministry? Wayfield?" He walked closer and pulled his fist back. I shrank into the corner and protected my wounded shoulder.

"Ellis!" my mom shouted. "He's already injured. I don't think you need to hurt him anymore."

My dad backed off and kneeled down, his face close to mine. The V-shaped scar traced over his eye, still bloody and scabbed from when I had hit him during our time in New Alcatraz. To him that was only days ago.

"If they sent him here," my mom said in a calmer tone, "then they know where we are. Or at least they know *when* we are, and the general area we're in. It's only a matter of time. We might as well accept that. Plus, look at him. Since when have you seen an agent dressed like *that*?" Ellis sighed.

The sun dipped below the horizon until the cabin was dark. The flames from the stove flickered, and the light bounced off the walls. Crickets chirped outside. My lips were dry and cracked, my tongue large inside my mouth.

I watched my father as he stared back at me in confusion. Behind him, past the stove and the three rows of empty shelves, I saw a half-built crib, and my mom standing over it. She wasn't showing yet, but she still held her belly, cradling the unborn child inside of her like she could protect him in case I decided to attack her and my dad. My arm and stomach bled into my clothing until a small puddle formed on the floor.

"We should clean his wounds. He can't hurt us in this condition," she said.

My dad didn't agree, but he didn't stop my mom from approaching. She knelt down and pulled the thick woven sweater off of me to reveal a large circle of blood around my chest and another down by my stomach.

"Get me a rag," my mom ordered my dad. I'd never got to see them interact before, but I always imagined she would have been the one to order him around. "We've got to stop the bleeding."

The pain increased and blurred my vision. The sight of the blood made my wounds hurt more and I couldn't make a fist with my hand. My dad returned with a cloth and reluctantly handed it to my mom. Last time I was here, when my mom pressed the rag on my wound, my mind was ripped back to the Golden Dawn headquarters. But this time I stayed here. I stayed in Buford. My mind had nowhere else to go.

CHAPTER 43

Emery dabbed the damp cloth on my shoulder, wiping the blood away to reveal deep purple bruising around a dark black hole. Each time she wiped away some of the blood, more trickled out.

"He's shot," she said and looked back at Ellis. "Who shot you?" I just shook my head. There was no way to explain this.

"Ellis," I managed to say in Ransom's gruff voice. My dad jerked his head around and glared. He took three large steps towards me and knelt down.

"How do you know my name?" he shouted loud enough that it echoed outside the trading post. I slowly reached into my pocket, and both Emery and Ellis took a cautious step backwards.

"It's okay," I said in my strained voice. I pulled out the vials of nanobots from the disassembled androids back in Denver. The plastic vials were able to make the trip through time.

"How did you get these?" Ellis asked. I held out one of the vials and a syringe, and nodded for him to take it. "What time are you from?"

"Inject me," I wheezed. My lungs shrank inside my chest. "I can't

... last much ... longer." Ellis reached for the vial and syringe and gripped them in his hand.

"Why should I?" he asked. "If you have these, then that means you've been to one of the underground bases. That means you probably work for the Ministry."

"Your scar," I said and pointed at the V-shaped scar over his eye. "I know how ... you got that." Ellis cocked his head to the side and squinted his eyes. I struggled with each breath. "In New ... Alcatraz." Ransom's voice had changed to something that I knew was uncharacteristic of him. He was dying. Even more than he was when I first jumped into his body under Buckley.

I swallowed and fought to keep my eyes open. "Powell ... he—he hit you over the head."

"How do you know that?" Ellis asked. "Did he send you here? Is he still alive in New Alcatraz?"

"The nanobots," I said. "I'm bleeding to death. T ... trust me." Ellis looked at Emery for permission. She nodded and motioned for him to inject me. Ellis drew the nanobots into the syringe, and plunged it deep into my bicep, pushing the plunger down and injecting the warm nanoscale robots into my body.

"There," he said. "Now tell me what's going on." I settled against the wooden wall and let the nanobots crawl through Ransom's body and repair my wounds.

"I *am* Powell," I said. Ellis scrunched his face, and Emery sat down on the floor, crossing her legs, like a schoolgirl ready for a lesson.

"No." He shook his head. "I don't care how long Powell spent in New Alcatraz after I left, there's no way he could look so different. Maybe he could grow his hair out, but your face ... and your body ... no." I let him speak to give the nanobots more time to start the healing process. Emery sat back.

"I left New Alcatraz after you and Red left," I told him. "I ... I killed the other prisoners. Found more nanobots. I travelled back to my present. 2070. For five years I lived in hiding." I skipped over what happened when I went back to the year 2070. The part where I killed Emery.

"I met a group of people, people like your group in Ashton," I continued, looking at my mom. Her eyes widened at the mention of Ashton, and she leaned forward towards me.

"How do you know about Ashton?"

"Ellis," I said and pointed at my dad.

Still dismissing my explanation, Ellis said, "I told Powell my story when we were in New Alcatraz. Maybe Powell told this guy about it too."

"I *am* Powell," I insisted, needing them to believe me. I took a deep breath. "This other group, they were based in Gray Mountain, Arizona at an old motel."

Emery jerked her head around to look at Ellis.

"We did have a group there working on some pretty high-level tech," she whispered to Ellis, but still loud enough for me to hear.

"*Very* high level," I continued. "They built a device that lets people transfer their minds to another person. Take over their body." I leaned even more against the crumbling wooden wall of the trading post. The throbbing had weakened to a small pulse in my body, and the cuts on my face and hands didn't sting anymore.

"Holy shit," Emery said. "So you took over this guy's body?"

"Yes," I said and nodded. "His name is Ransom."

"Ransom?" Emery asked. "What kind of name is that?"

"I don't know. He's from the future, the far future, sometime long after the Ministry established New Alcatraz."

"How did you end up in the future? Why did you switch minds with this guy of all people?" Emery asked.

"I wasn't in the future when I used the device. I was in the year

2075. Somehow my mind traveled through time … or maybe my mind sat in that machine for three thousand years until Ransom used it himself." I trailed off, still trying to figure out the logistics of how the device worked.

Shaking those pointless thoughts away, I continued, "But *he* used it. Ransom used it in his own time, and I ended up back in New Alcatraz, probably some two hundred years after you and I were there." I looked at Ellis, who clearly still didn't like when I mentioned that he and I had spent time together. He saw me as an unfamiliar, dying, disheveled man from the distant future.

Emery stood to retrieve a canteen of water. She held one hand gently under my chin and lifted my head back while pouring the water slowly down my throat. It tasted clean and fresh, like it was the purest water ever collected. Maybe since this was the first time *this* body had tasted water that wasn't from New Alcatraz, it registered as fresher than it really was.

Emery placed the canteen on the ground and continued to blot the blood away from my two gunshot wounds. By now, the pain was less than before, and Emery could press the rag against my chest without my body instinctively pulling away.

"Let's say I believe you," Ellis said and stood, turning his back to me and Emery. "Let's say you are Powell—"

"I am Powell," I interrupted. "How else would I know about you and Red? How would I know about that scar, or even this place? I was the one who told you to come here."

"Is he telling the truth, Ellis?" Emery turned to look at him. "You told me someone from New Alcatraz told you about this place. Was it Powell?"

Ellis nodded reluctantly. I knew my dad was logical. I knew he would come around.

"Okay, you're Powell," Ellis said and threw his hands in the air.

"What are you doing here? And why would you use that device if you didn't have another body you wanted to switch with? Why is your mind inside this other person?"

I could see the look in my father's eyes. It was the same look he'd had when I'd told him I was arrested for murdering a female Time Anomaly Agent. It was the look of his own mind running through every possible scenario. He tensed his lips.

"That is a bit more complicated," I said. "I did it to protect the both of you … you're my parents."

CHAPTER 44

2036
BUFORD, WYOMING

"Parents?" Ellis said and scoffed. "Parents?" He looked at Emery for confirmation that this sounded as crazy as it was. Emery simply stared at me, holding my gaze. "How are we your parents? Powell's parents? Powell was the same age as me. Maybe even older!" Ellis said.

"But we are here now," Emery said without looking away from me. Her voice was soft, but sure. "We are in the past. The past to us. The past to him."

"You're pregnant now, right?" I said. My shoulder hurt less and less until I was able to actually raise my arm. Ellis stepped forward at the mention of their baby, like he didn't even want to tell a stranger that Emery was pregnant. "Pregnant with me. You're going to give birth here, then you'll go back to your own time. 2070. And you will stay here and raise me."

Ellis stood perfectly still, like moving even slightly could result in something terrible.

"You ... Dad ... you raised me." I swallowed a lump deep inside my throat. For so long, I thought I had to make sure everything happened as it already did. But now it didn't matter. There was nothing that could change anything. "Your child, me—not this body, but the *real* me—I will walk from here to Ashton. I will grow up in an orphanage. I will live life. Most would call it a typical life. But eventually I will be arrested and sent to New Alcatraz, which is where we will meet ... or where we already met. But believe me, it's true. You are my father, and you are my mother."

Ellis turned away from me and clutched his head, like he wanted to pull his thoughts out, look at them, and rearrange them in some order that made sense.

"When did you know?" he asked with his back still turned from me. "It was the scar, wasn't it?"

"You're right. From the moment I saw you. From the moment I saw that scar over your eye." I smiled at the memory of the first time I saw my dad in New Alcatraz. I recalled the first time I was able to hug him since he'd died twenty years before. That moment made what I went through in New Alcatraz worth it. All of it.

"So the whole time..." Ellis' voice trailed off. After a short pause, he said, "When we were together in New Alcatraz, you knew the entire time ... that ... I'm your ... dad?"

"I'm sorry. I didn't know what to do. What to say. I thought that if I said anything or did anything that it would change something for you or me. I couldn't risk that."

Ellis turned to look at me. "You sacrificed yourself so that Red and I could escape." His eyes wavered with tears.

"I couldn't let anything happen to you. If you didn't make it back here, then I would never have been born. None of this would have happened. I ... I didn't know what would happen to me. Disappear. Die. I just knew you had to make it here. To Buford."

The bewilderment returned to my father's eyes.

"The murder," Ellis blurted out. "You were in New Alcatraz for murder!" He looked at Emery. I knew this would come up once I told them who I was. Once Ellis remembered that the man he spent time with in New Alcatraz, had been charged with murdering Time Anomaly Agent Emery.

"Murder?" Emery asked. "Who did you kill?"

"I…" I didn't know how to answer. I looked into my mother's eyes and thought back to that night in Phoenix. The night she demanded I take her life. Take her organs and hide them from the Ministry. I thought back to the clarity my mother had. I thought back to how she hadn't been surprised at all, in fact she had been expecting someone to be in that abandoned warehouse.

Her eyes grew wide as the pieces of the puzzle rearranged in her head.

"He was framed," Ellis blurted out, saving me from whatever jumbled explanation I could come up with. "Whatever it was, he was framed." Ellis' eyes pierced through me, pleading with me. As though I *wanted* to tell my mom I murdered her.

"Why are you here? *How* are you here?" Emery asked.

"New Alcatraz." I tried to think of where to start. Like most of my life, this too was a convoluted mess. "Hundreds of years after we left"—I nodded towards Ellis—"they kept sending people there, and they must have sent women, cuz they had children. They found a way to survive there."

"They're surviving there?" Ellis asked quietly.

"The vaults the Ministry built, they became these legendary places. But no one wanted to go looking for them. They were scared. But Ransom"—I pointed at myself—"his son got sick. He and a group of people went looking for medicine, and they found Buckley Air Force Base. Things went badly there. They found a group of people down there, who were … hungry."

"You mean—" Emery said.

"Yes." I nodded, cutting her off so as not to go into the grim details of the vault dwellers' diet. "Something happened down there, something with these people, and something with Ransom and his brother." I shook my head to rattle the thoughts loose. I couldn't worry about Ransom's family squabbles now. "Ransom was injured and probably going to die. After I used the device in 2075, someone hid it in the air vent under Buckley. Well, apparently, no one found it … until Ransom. He found the mind transfer device, and he used it."

"How did you switch with him? How did the device get from you to Buckley?" Emery asked.

I sighed a deep breath out of my lungs. It was so much to explain.

"The group at Gray Mountain—"

"The ones who invented this machine?" Emery asked.

"Yeah. They needed to charge the device, and the only place we could do that was in Buckley."

"You broke *into* Buckley?" Ellis said sternly.

"Yeah," I said quietly, ashamed, because it had been my plan, and it was my fault it fell apart. Whatever happened to Whitman, Doc, and Vesa was on me.

"What were you guys thinking?" Ellis said. By now it was completely dark outside. The stars blinked in the clear sky, and the gentle breeze that had lasted through the day was replaced by nothing but stillness.

"It's not that secure," Emery said, coming to my rescue. "I've been to Buckley, and it's pretty tame. Not like Denver."

"Well, obviously it was more secure than they thought," Ellis said.

"It was," I agreed. "We got cornered in their armory. I had no choice but to use the device and have my mind removed from my body. I couldn't let them know what I knew."

"What you knew?" Emery asked.

"Yeah, that I broke out of New Alcatraz, that I knew of others who escaped also." I looked over at my father. "And that I knew where they were. When they were. Who they were with."

"So you and this Ransom guy switched minds? You know this for sure?" Ellis asked me.

"Yeah. I've switched back a couple of times. Back to my own body. They have him. The Ministry has *me*, and they want to know what I know. Badly."

"Shit," Emery mumbled. "I can only imagine what they're doing."

"It's not pretty," I said and felt my hand where, on my own body, my two fingers were missing. "That's why I am here. I don't have much time. My real body can't last much longer. I need to get it out of there. I need to give Ransom back his own body. He has a family of his own. A kid of his own. I can't just stay in New Alcatraz forever."

"Maybe that's the best solution," Ellis said. "Maybe that is the *only* solution."

"No." I shook my head. "If I keep switching back without any noticeable pattern, there's no telling when I may switch back for good. And then I would be in their custody. My mind. My body. I have to get Ransom out of there, and switch our minds back."

I pressed my bloody palm on the wood floor and tried to stand on my shaky legs. "I need to get inside the vault underneath the Denver Airport. I need to find Ransom, and I need your help to do it." I looked at them, gauging their reactions.

"No," Ellis said and shook his head, turning his back to both me and Emery. "You can't go there, Emery. You're pregnant!"

Emery stood and placed her hand on Ellis' back. "It's our son either way. Either inside my womb, or grown up, he's our son. We have to help him."

"Both of you have been down there way more than I have. You know where things are, where they keep prisoners, plus you're still technically a Time Anomaly Agent. I need you both."

"I do still have my uniform here," Emery said. "We'll do it."

Ellis never agreed, but he stopped resisting.

After patching my wounds as best as she could, my mom changed into her TAA uniform, and the three of us left our old home. Ellis poured water on the fire in the stove, and latched the door shut to keep any animals out, hopeful that he would return. We trekked the short distance through the long grass and the tall trees to the three sticks I'd set out to mark the spot where the wormhole waited for us.

"There," I said and pointed at the sticks. I reached in my pocket and pulled out the retrieval device. The three of us huddled close together, wrapping our arms around one another.

"Ready?" I asked. My mom and dad nodded. I breathed in one deep breath of the Buford air, holding it in my lungs. Then I pressed my thumb on the button and shut my eyes tight.

Under our feet the ground changed from dirt to cement. The darkness around us changed from natural darkness with specks of starlight to man-made darkness with the haze of red emergency lights. I exhaled my breath from home. Ash was still leaning his hulking body against the door while Marshall's men pounded on the other side.

"He's back!" Merit shouted and pointed at us.

"Good, cuz I can't hold this much longer!" Ash shouted.

CHAPTER 45

Ellis, Emery, and I, leapt off the platform. When my feet landed on the ground a shockwave of pain vibrated through my body. There were too many injuries on my body for the nanobots to fix immediately.

The men on the other side of the door had managed to break the handle off. Now, nothing held the door in place except Merit, Ash, a screwdriver, and a couple barrels.

"Help him hold that door!" I commanded my father.

"Mom, er, Emery," I said, "come with me." I limped over to the control panel, reaching into my pocket to count how many vials of nanobots I had left.

"Who's on the other side of that door?" Emery asked. "And who are these two men?" She pointed at Merit and Ash.

"Ransom's brother, Merit," I said, pointing. "The large guy is Ash. A friend."

"Of Ransom's or a friend of yours?" Emery asked.

"Both," I said. "They agreed to come here and help me." I said as I began dialing in the coordinates for the year 2075.

"And on the other side of that door?" Emery asked again, not letting me avoid the question.

"It's the people from Buckley Air Force Base." I motioned to Emery to help me drag another barrel in front of the door.

"The hungry ones?" Emery asked.

I nodded.

"What do they want?" Emery shouted over the banging on the other side of the door. We positioned the barrel against the rattling door as best we could.

"Food. Water. Maybe ammunition."

"What do they want with you?" Emery asked, but the look on her face told me she didn't really want to know. Maybe she had reached her limit of bad news for the moment.

"They want Ransom dead. They probably want all of us dead. For food. For revenge. Shit, maybe just for fun. We can't let them through here, and we can't let them leave New Alcatraz."

"So what's the plan?" she asked. "Travel to 2075 and rescue ... *you*?"

"Basically. Once we get back here, we use the mind transfer device." I pointed at the bag.

She looked at Ellis, who was standing next to Ash, their backs pressed up against the door. She clenched her jaw. "Okay." Her voice was reluctant. "It's too dangerous to change the location we arrive at in Denver at all. So we have to land exactly in the deployment center. Once there, there will be two Ministry officials on duty—scientists, unarmed. Plus, one guard, armed. We neutralize the guard first, then stop the scientists from sounding the alarm."

"I have a gun," I said and pointed at the pistol I had taken from Marshall.

"No," Emery said and shook her head. "It's metal. Too much metal. If we had something smaller, like a knife, that would probably work, but not that gun."

"So what do we do? How do we take out the guard?" I asked.

"What's the plan here?" Ellis yelled, his body bouncing with each hit on the door from the other side. Emery held her hand up to her chin and then squeezed the bridge of her nose. She jerked her head to look behind her and then took off somewhere on the other side of the enormous room.

"We're working on it!" I yelled back, as I returned to the control panel to double check my coordinates.

Merit handed Ellis a crowbar and he wedged it between the cement floor and the door. "There." He was out of breath from holding the door closed. "That should hold them for a while. Just keep an eye on the door." Along with the screwdriver and crowbar jammed under the door, they had propped up some sort of metal bar against it. The top of the door still rattled with each pounding fist or foot from the other side, but the bottom of the door was locked tightly in place.

"Where's Emery?" Ellis asked in a slight panic.

"Here." Emery returned, holding a glass container with a clear liquid inside.

"What are you doing with that!" Ellis scolded Emery. "You want to blow us up? Or burn our skin off?"

"No, not *our* skin," Emery said with a slight grin. Turning to me, she said, "This is pure liquid sodium, used to cool the nuclear reactor of the time movement device."

"Isn't this thing electrical?" I asked. "What does it need the nuclear reactor for?"

"It *is* electrical, but it needs a ton of power to create the initial wormhole. That's where the nuclear reactor comes in," Ellis explained, still looking at Emery holding the liquid sodium. "This is stupid. I thought *you* had a plan." He pointed at me.

Once they were sure the door would hold without them, Ash and Merit approached the three of us. Ash was cautious, and Merit even more so. He stayed several steps away from my mother and father, leaning on one foot.

"Ash. Merit. This is Emery and Ellis, my par—uh, my friends."

"Hi," Ash said in his low grumbling voice, his chest still leaking blood from his stab wound. A large red circle grew across his chest. Merit simply held a hand in the air to wave hello. He flinched with each booming noise that came from the other side of the door.

"They are here to help us get Ransom back."

"Okay, let's get going then," Ash said and approached the large stage of the time movement device.

"I'm not going near that thing," Merit protested.

"C'mon!" Ash said angrily. "I don't have time for your shit, Merit! What are you afraid of?"

"I don't know what that thing does. Where I will go."

"You will go where your brother is. Maybe that's what you are afraid of," Ash shouted. His voice boomed over the banging from the other side of the door.

"What's that supposed to mean?" Merit asked, raising his voice too.

"You know what it means."

"Enough!" I shouted over both of them. "Enough! You can't go anyway, Merit. Someone needs to stay here and make sure that door stays shut." I turned to Ash who still stood in the center of the large stage. "And you, I need you to come with us and help Ransom come along. I don't know what state he will be in when we find him, and seeing his own body standing in front of him might not be that comforting. He needs to see someone he knows. Someone he trusts."

Ash nodded, grunted, and crossed his large arms over his chest.

"Now this sodium, what will it do?" I asked my mom.

"It reacts with the air, making sodium hydroxide."

"Sodium hydroxide..." I tried to think back to my schooling in chemical engineering. "That's—"

"Lye," my father finished. "It's lye. And it will burn through skin on contact. That's not to mention the hydrogen gas and explosion that will occur when that sodium mixes with the water vapor in the air. It's too dangerous."

"It will explode, yes," Emery admitted. "That's the point, but the explosion will be contained as long as there is no other fuel source."

"And if they just so happen to be in the middle of using the time machine on their end?" Ellis asked. "If we time it while they are creating a wormhole? Then what?"

"Then the whole place comes down on top of us. But the Ministry won't be using the device on their end."

"You willing to take that chance?" Ellis asked.

"Yes. And they never keep a wormhole opened for very long. It's not standard protocol. It's all we've got.

"Wait," I interrupted, still fast forwarding through my chemical engineering courses. "Isn't sodium metal?"

"Liquid metal. Not solid. It can make it through with us." Emery was quick to answer, like she had thought of this many times before.

"Okay." I shrugged. "We have to give it a shot." I looked at Ellis.

"This won't work," Ellis said to me.

"Go start it up," Emery instructed Ellis and nodded towards the control panel. I was right. Emery was the one who bossed my father around. Deep down, my dad was a pushover.

Ellis ran to the control panel and pressed the button to send us to the time I had typed in earlier. He ran back as the pistons started humming and moving up and down. The air rushed around the four of us. My vision blurred.

Ash stood with crossed arms, trying to make his body as small as possible. Emery and Ellis stood together, she holding the glass ball filled with liquid sodium in one hand and Ellis' hand in the other. I stood there with my two gunshot wounds, cracked skull, busted kneecap, scrapes, bruises, and cuts, and I thought that this body was probably in much better shape than I would find my own body in.

"Don't let them get through!" I shouted to Merit over the sound of the circulating wind. Merit didn't offer a response.

CHAPTER 46

2075
DENVER, COLORADO

"What the fuck!" the guard shouted, reaching for his sidearm.

Emery launched the glass globe filled with liquid sodium towards him. The scientists stood by the control panel, frozen in shock and fear. My parents ran off the side of the stage while the liquid sodium was still in the air. I grabbed Ash by the arm and pulled him with us.

The glass shattered, splashing the sodium in all directions, and covering the armed guard. He tried to wipe the liquid off his arms and face, but it was too late. The chemical reaction was instant. The liquid sodium reacted with the air, the lye corroding and burning into the guard's skin.

"Go!" Ellis shouted, as Ash and I stood staring at the guard as his skin bubbled and turned bright red. He screamed and flailed his arms, still trying to wipe off the corrosive substance. "The scientists!" my father shouted again.

Ash and I snapped into action and rushed the two scientists, grabbing them and knocking them both unconscious.

"Get down!" Ellis shouted from across the cavernous room. Just as Ash and I ducked behind the control center, an explosion rocked through the room, like one of the many flashbangs the TDA had thrown at me over the last few years. A burst of white light and heat erupted, the guard being the epicenter of the explosion.

"We're clear," Emery said and emerged from her hiding place. Ash and I stood hesitantly, Ash covering his ears. The smell of chemicals and fire wafted throughout the deployment center.

Ellis scooped the guard's gun from off the floor and tucked it into his pants. The guard's body sat slumped against the wall, his skin burnt and scabbed over from the lye and the secondary explosion of the sodium mixing with the humidity in the air.

"Where now?" I asked.

"Up," Emery said and looked at the elevator. "My guess is they will keep prisoners in the living quarters."

Ellis tapped the button on the wall to summon the elevator. Ash looked around in amazement at the undamaged deployment center.

"Amazing," he said with his head tilted upwards. "It looks so … nice."

"Trust me, it's not," Ellis said as he tapped the elevator button again and again. "What they do in here, what you will see for yourself, it isn't *nice*. It's the furthest thing from nice." The elevator doors pulled open, and the three of us stepped in, leaving Ash in the deployment center.

"Let's go," I said and waved Ash into the elevator. He looked inside to find nothing but a box. "It's okay. Trust me."

He stepped inside and the elevator sank down ever so slightly. Ash gasped at the movement.

"The floor, it's moving," he said and bounced up and down. My father pressed the 'up' button until the doors to the elevator closed and we rocketed upwards. Ash reached his large arms out to brace himself against the wall. The air rushed around the outside of the elevator.

"What's happening?" Ash asked.

"We're going up," I tried to explain. "It'll be over soon."

"Get ready," Emery said. "There will be two guards outside the elevator, and they probably aren't expecting someone to come up."

"I'll take the one on the right," Ellis said, pulling the pistol out from his waistband.

"I got the left," Emery said and nodded at my father.

The doors slid open to reveal the familiar long tunnels of the Denver Airport. Before the guards could react, Ellis and Emery jumped out and wrestled them to the ground. Ellis smacked the guard on the right with the butt of his gun, knocking him out instantly. Emery wrapped her arm around the other guard's neck and squeezed until his body went limp, and then she stripped him of the rifle slung around his body. Ellis tossed his pistol to me and kept the other rifle for himself.

"Now what?" I asked, looking at Emery for guidance.

"This way." She nodded down the tunnel, and the four of us made our way towards the living quarters, our feet pounding on the gray cement. Ellis and Emery lead the way at a quick pace. Ash helped me walk down the hall. The nanobots were still working inside me. Something about this place was different than it was in the future. It was more frightening. More deadly and sinister.

In New Alcatraz, this place was just a place. But now, in the present, it was a portal to a prison. It was a prison itself. It was a black site for secret torture programs. *It is the people here that make it what it is,* I thought. *It is the people who gave this vault its meaning and evil connotation. Without us, it would have been nothing.*

"Here," Ellis whispered and waved his hands at us as we approached a fork in the tunnel. He pointed down a long hall. It was the hall that the two of us had traveled down together thousands of years in the future. The hall with the pixelated screen, broadcasting scenery from around the globe.

We walked softly. Just as my father had described it when he recounted his time in Project Oracle, the pixelated wall showed a picture of the Inca city of Machu Picchu. The stone structures contrasted against the green grass and the bright blue sky. Ash stepped towards the wall cautiously and brushed his large hand across the screen.

"What is this?" he asked, reaching out as if he would actually brush his hand through the white clouds. His hand fell flat against the screen.

"It's a picture," I whispered.

"A pick sure?" Ash tried to repeat the word to me. "It's beautiful."

As we walked, we peered in each cell to our right. Ellis ran his hand along the glass walls lining each of the cells.

"They won't keep a prisoner like you here," Ellis said, second guessing his first instinct. "You will be in the secure wing up ahead."

"Hey!" a voice came from behind us.

I spun around with my pistol aimed down the hall. Ellis and Emery held their rifles pressed against their shoulders.

A young man in a lab coat stood with his hands raised. "Don't shoot," he pleaded.

I trained my pistol on his chest, and Ellis walked up to him with his rifle still aimed. He circled the young man and patted him down, feeling his waist and under his arms.

"The prisoner," Ellis said. "Take us to the prisoner."

"Which one?"

"The one they brought from Buckley," I said.

"Okay," he said. "Okay. Just don't shoot." The man started walking with his hands still raised above his head.

"Put your fucking hands down," Ellis said. "Just act like you're giving us a tour or something. Normal."

"Nothing about this is normal," Emery said.

"It's just up here," the young man said, and pointed a few meters down the hall. "She's just up here."

"She?" I asked. "She?"

"Yes, just up here."

A few more steps and we stopped at the cell to our right. There, inside the same cell where Ellis had spent time in, was Vesa.

CHAPTER 47

2075
DENVER, COLORADO

"Vesa!" I said, dropping my pistol and pressing my palms against the glass. "Vesa!"

She stood and squinted at the strange group of people standing in front of her. I waved my hands around the transparent wall, trying to trip whatever mechanism there was to open the cell door.

"Open the door," I ordered the Wayfield employee.

The employee approached the cell and tapped in several seemingly random spots on the glass until the door opened and a rush of air fell out of the pressurized cell. I ran to Vesa and wrapped my arms around her.

"Vesa! You're okay!"

Vesa pushed away from me with a look of both disgust and confusion.

"Woah, woah, woah," she said, backing away. She tilted her head to look behind me, examining Ash, then Emery, then Ellis. "Who the fuck are you guys and how do you know me?"

"Powell!" I said and patted my hands against my chest. "It's Powell!"

Vesa shook her head rapidly, like she was trying to shake an image out of her mind.

"Powell?" she asked quietly. "Powell?"

"Yes. It's me." I stepped closer to her. She still didn't touch me, but she didn't retreat further into her cell. "I'm in Ransom's body, but it's me. From the future." Vesa scrunched her face, clearly not believing me completely.

"How'd we meet?" Vesa tested me.

"You came to my apartment. I let you in. We escaped together. The Golden Dawn. Buckley. It's me!"

"Powell!" Vesa leapt forward, wrapping her arms and legs around me, squeezing until even the nanobots inside me couldn't mask the pain from my gunshot wounds. My body gave way and we both collapsed to the ground. She ended up on top of me, our faces nearly touching. I winced. "You're hurt!" she said and let go of me.

"I injected myself with nanobots. The bleeding stopped a while ago."

"Oh my god! I can't believe you're here! How did—? What happened—? Who are these people?" Her partial questions came rapidly. Although she deserved an answer, I, my body, didn't have time. I knew Ransom could only hold on so much longer.

Pushing up from the ground, I said, "I'll explain later. But we have to go."

Ellis paced back and forth inside the cell, looking at every square inch, no doubt remembering his time there. By now the pixelated wall had changed to show the white sand deserts of Alamogordo, New Mexico.

"Is that snow?" Ash asked of no one in particular.

My mother stood just outside the cell, her rifle trained on the timid Wayfield employee. She took no chances, but I got the feeling this young man would help us if we just asked politely.

"No," Emery said to Ash. "It's sand."

"White sand…" Ash said to himself.

"Which way?" I asked my father.

"Wait! My brother," Vesa blurted out. "Cooper. He's here. We have to get him. And Doc and Finn. They're all here. I saw them bring them in. Down the hall somewhere."

"Your brother. He's here?" She continued to nod. "And Doc, they got to him too?" Vesa nodded, but it was a less enthusiastic nod. Something about the subject made her feel ashamed. I turned to look at the young Wayfield employee. Without asking, he motioned down the hall at the other cells.

"Let's go!" I said with a renewed vigor that I hadn't had since I came up with the failed plan to break into Buckley. The young man cautiously led us down the long hall. The landscape of some coastal volcano leaking molten lava into the ocean on our left.

"It's just up here. The prisoners they just brought in."

First, we saw Doc sitting on the edge of a messy bed, shirtless and bleeding, holding his hand.

"Doc!" Vesa said and tapped on the glass. Doc stood abruptly and reached his hand to his waist to grab for a gun, but he found nothing. His eyes widened and bulged out of his face.

"Vesa?" Doc said, his voice muffled behind the wall of glass. He smiled wide. "What the…?"

"Open the door," I ordered the Wayfield employee once again, and, with little hesitation, he waved his hands in front of the glass to open the cell door. Doc barged out of the cell before it could open completely.

"What's going on?" He said. He gripped Vesa's shoulders to look her in her eyes, checking to make sure it really was her, before hugging her and sighing. "I thought you were dead. Back at Buckley … I thought you and Powell … well, I didn't know what happened to you."

"I'm here," Vesa said, her cheek pressed against Doc. "I thought *you* were dead."

"Just about," Doc said and let go of Vesa. He held his hand up. A black and red hole was drilled through his palm, dripping blood. He winced at the slight movements it took to hold his hand up.

"Get Finn," Vesa ordered the Wayfield employee and pointed at the next cell over. By now Finn had seen the commotion. He stood at the glass wall, trying to peer around to see who was in the hall. The Wayfield employee opened his cell, and he leapt through the door, tackling the young man to the ground.

"You son of a bitch!" he yelled. Finn glanced up, his fist raised in the air over the young man's face, frozen. "Vesa?" he said quietly. He looked around the hall at each of us. "Who? What?" Finn looked back at the employee, whose face was locked in wide-eyed fear, staring at Finn's tight fist and waiting for it to land square on his nose.

"Finn," Vesa said and smiled. It was a smile different than when she saw Doc. She'd given him the same smile when she was reunited with Finn in Arizona, when she first brought me to the beaten down motel. It was a smile that twisted my guts and left a brief empty feeling in my stomach.

Finn let the young man go and stood, his fist still clenched at his side. He wrapped his arms around Vesa and squeezed, lifting her off the ground.

"Powell," Ellis said, trying to snap me back to the original plan. "What are we doing? We came here for *you*, not these people."

"Powell?" Finn said and dropped Vesa back to the ground. "What do you want with that traitor?" Finn stepped towards Ellis, and Ellis took a step towards Finn.

"*This* is Powell," Vesa said to Finn and pointed at me, at Ransom's body. "And what do you mean 'traitor'?"

"What do you mean this is Powell?" Finn said. "Powell gave up our location. The motel. He told the Ministry where we were. How do you think *we* got here? They found us. They *killed* Franklin and Haley."

"They what?" Vesa asked, her eyes pulled down to the floor and her head tilted. "Franklin? Haley?" Vesa took two slow steps and leaned against the fake scenery. "They're dead?"

"I haven't told the Ministry anything."

"You're not Powell," Doc stepped in, holding his good hand over a long laceration across his stomach.

Holding my hands out to stop or slow Doc's progression towards me, I said, "I am. I am. I used the machine. Back in Buckley. I used the machine and my mind somehow transferred to someone else. To someone who lived in another time."

Finally breaking his hypnotic gaze at the scenic view on the screen, Ash stepped towards Doc.

"Back up," Ash ordered Doc and Finn. Ash's body towered over them both.

Looking Ash up and down, Doc said, "I don't take orders from anyone, and especially not some oversized hobo, so *you* back up."

"My *body* is here, but my mind isn't. So there is no way I could have told them about the motel. There's no way I could have told them anything. That's exactly why I used the machine."

Doc tilted his head. "It worked?"

"Sort of," I said.

"So how did they find out about the motel?" Doc wondered.

"*I* told them," Vesa blurted out, her head still tilted down at the ground. When she looked up, her eyes red and her teeth were clenched.

"You what?" He said loudly.

"I had no choice."

Doc took a step towards her, his voice gritty. "No choice! You sure don't look like you've been tortured. Franklin was shot in the gut and bled to death in the garage!"

"I'm sorry," Vesa said quietly, like she knew it was pointless.

"You know what happened to Haley?" Doc yelled, ignoring her. "A chunk of burning metal tore through her goddamned throat." Doc walked closer and closer to Vesa until she was pinned between him and the artificial nature scene.

"Doc, wait," Finn said and gripped him by the shoulder.

"No!" Doc yelled back at Finn. "You were ready to write off Powell when you thought *he* was the traitor, but just because you have a schoolboy crush on her you think she gets a pass!"

"You gotta keep your voices down," Ellis said.

"I don't even know who the fuck you are!" A look washed over Doc's face that I had never seen on him before. Other times, his anger was something that he could channel, but now it seemed to spill over everything.

"She doesn't get a *pass*. Just give her a chance to talk," Finn said to Doc.

"I can't believe you fucking told them. Them! The same people who killed your brother. Why, Vesa? Why?" Doc placed his hand against the fake image of the volcano that Vesa leaned against, smearing blood against the bright blue ocean.

"Cooper," Vesa said, almost a whisper. "They've had Cooper this whole time." Doc jerked his head around to meet Finn's shocked expression. "Cooper was the reason I did all of it."

CHAPTER 48

Vesa looked the same as she did in the Golden Dawn headquarters, when Quinn, had held her at gun point and used her as a human shield. She looked like her mind had left her, or maybe she wished that it could leave her. She stared through everyone and everything in her path.

"I volunteered for her to turn me in," I said. "I told her to let me use that device and then hand over my body to the Ministry. I thought that would be enough for them to give her back her brother."

"Cooper's alive?" Finn said.

Doc stared at Vesa and gritted his teeth. He balled his good hand into a fist and pressed his bad hand hard against the scenic screen.

"I thought that my body would be enough to please the Ministry. I had escaped New Alcatraz, and, if my prediction was right, I had the cure for Dark Time and Wayfield's DNA in my blood."

Grabbing Doc's shoulders and turning him away from Vesa, I met his gaze, trying to snap him out of whatever trance he was in.

"We need to get you, Finn, Cooper, and my body out of here. We need … I need, and a lot of other people need me to switch back into my own body. I have a plan, but we need to move. We need to go now!"

"Does your plan involve bringing back Franklin or Haley? What about Whitman? Do we get him back? Or the years of research that we burned up at the motel? Do we get that back!" Doc spat. I saw a fierceness in his eyes that I'd also only seen back at the Golden Dawn headquarters. It was the same look he'd had in his eyes before he pulled the trigger of his gun, shooting a bullet through Vesa's ear and killing Quinn.

"We *can* save each other. I can get you out of here. I can save you, Finn, Vesa, Cooper, and a lot of other people who count on whoever's body I am stuck in right now. But we need to get moving, and I need you with me. I need your help. I need you."

Doc's eyes finally relaxed, and I hoped he was considering that this was not the time or place to hash things out with Vesa. I hoped he was coming around. But he said nothing. He only turned away from us. I thought that maybe simply not escalating things further with Vesa was the most I could expect of him for now.

"What's the plan?" Doc asked after a few beats of silence.

"They used to work here, and they helped us break in." I pointed at my mom and dad. "They think, they are keeping my body deeper in this facility and this man is going to lead us there. Right?" I looked at the young employee. Ellis held his gun on the young man and he nodded rapidly. "We rescue my body and then we get out of here, using the time machine down below."

"So you want us to go deeper into a second government facility and then travel to another time?" Doc scoffed.

"Can we just go?" I asked. "I'll explain the rest on the way."

Doc looked at Finn, who shrugged like he could go either way. "Okay," Doc said. "But I'm not going because I have much faith in your ability to put together a successful plan. But we are safer in larger numbers. Lead the way."

Turning to the Wayfield employee and motioning down the hall, I said, "Go."

Continuing forward, I said, "Once we travel to another time, the Ministry of Science won't be a problem anymore. We will all be able to travel to whatever time and place we want."

"What time," Finn asked as we walked at a brisk pace.

"The future. Maybe around 5200."

"5200! Why so far?" Doc asked.

"It's where this man is from." I pointed at myself. "And him." I pointed at Ash.

"But you don't know the exact year. How do we get there?" Doc asked, almost ready to turn around.

"I have the retrieval device. The wormhole is staying open and this device will pull us back to that time."

"Well it seems your plan is more coherent than I expected." Doc said.

"There are guards around this corner," the Wayfield employee said. His face was pale and his eyes fluttered around. "About fifteen meters down the hall is the cell holding her brother. Two guards. And if we round this corner they will know you are here."

I never thought we would get out of here without a commotion. I'm surprised nothing's happened yet. I turned to my mom and dad. "We need to take these guards out before they get a shot off. Can you both hit one of the guards on your first shot?"

Emery nodded and readied her rifle. Ellis shook his head and gripped the rifle. "I don't know. I'm a good shot, but if someone here wants to take over the duty, then I am willing to step aside."

I looked at Doc. I had seen how accurate his shots were in the past. I saw him skim Vesa's ear, missing her face by a centimeter, and still shooting Quinn in the head.

"Doc?"

"Sorry," he said and held up his bad hand. "I think my shooting days are over. At least in this hand. My left hand is good, maybe as good as your right, but nowhere as good as *my* right." I turned back to Ellis.

"I'm too injured to shoot with any precision," I said.

"I'll do it," Vesa said and reached out for a weapon. "No time to draw straws here." Ellis handed Vesa his rifle, and she moved into position next to Emery. After a quick glance and nod at each other, the two women turned and disappeared around the corner. We waited only a split second before the first shot rang out through the hall, quickly followed by a second.

"Clear," Emery said.

The rest of us followed around the corner. Vesa ran to the guard and pulled his security card from his belt. She swiped the card in a panel next to the door and ripped it open.

"Cooper!"

I ran and collected the firearms from both guards, tucking my pistol in the back of my pants and slinging one of the rifles over my shoulder. I turned and held the second rifle out to Ash.

"No," he said. Not defiantly, just as if he were saying 'no thanks' to a second helping of food. "I'm no good with those things."

"Finn," I said.

He lingered in the back of our growing pack of rebels, preventing the young Wayfield employee from running off, but it seemed the young man had no interest in escaping. Finn met my gaze and nodded. He said nothing, simply made his way around Ellis and Ash, and gripped the black rifle in his hands. He slung the gun over his bleeding shoulder and hung it to his side.

Cooper and Vesa emerged from the cell. Vesa's brother looked unhealthy, like a homeless man or someone lost at sea. His skin was pale and had the complexion of melted wax. He wasn't tortured to the extent that my body likely was at the moment, but the Ministry clearly hadn't been kind to him either.

"Coop!" Finn charged towards Vesa and her brother. The two embraced for an extended time. "We thought you were dead!" Finn said, his face still pressed against Cooper's shoulder.

"I know," Cooper said and let go of Finn. "Sorry."

"It wasn't *your* fault," Doc said and took a step towards Cooper, but he kept his eyes locked on Vesa, who just lowered her head and let out a sigh. "I'm just glad you're okay." Doc stuck his good hand out towards Cooper, who took it.

The group now consisted of the most conspicuous people ever to walk the halls of this vault. Ash and I wore stitched patchwork clothing soaked with blood and melted snow. Our faces were scraped. I had a half-healed gunshot wound in the stomach. Ash had his bandaged stab wound from back at the village.

Finn wore a tank top and shorts. His face was covered in red dust and streaked with sweat. Doc was shirtless. His stomach bled from a long burn or cut, his shoulder was wrapped in blood-soaked gauze, and his hand had a bullet-sized hole through it. My mother wore a black TAA uniform, but among this group she stood out the most.

In no time, the guards would be on us, summoned by the sound of gunfire. They would flood this hall with the full force of however many agencies worked down here.

"We've gotta keep this reunion short," I said. My voice boomed through the cement hall. "Where are they keeping me?" I turned and asked the Wayfield employee. He looked at me, scrunching his face, confused by my phrasing. "Where are they keeping the prisoner? The one they brought in with her?" I pointed at Vesa, who had her arm wrapped around Cooper, like he could disappear at any moment.

"He's down there," he said, pointing down the hall and shaking his head. "You'll never get him out though. It's too guarded."

"We have no choice, kid." I looked away from him and met the eyes of each person in our group. "I'm going down there. No matter what, I am going there. I won't force any of you to come." I scanned the group. Cooper, who I had never seen before looked dazed, and Finn, who I barely knew, looked anxious. "That way"—I pointed where we came from—"will take you back to the deployment center. There are no guards that way. It's safe."

I saw Ash's chest heaving up and down. Vesa stared at me, not budging either way. Half of her surely wanted to run for safety, wanted to keep her brother alive and well. I guess the other half knew she owed this to me, to my body.

Pointing at the young Wayfield employee, I said, "He may be right. Maybe it's impossible, but our chances are better together. Together, we stand a chance against whoever is down there. We do this and we get Ransom back. We get him back to his family." I looked at Ash, who nodded and stepped forward next to me.

Holding his hand out to shake mine, he said, "We made a promise. I won't leave. I won't leave Ransom. I won't leave you." I shook Ash's hand and looked at the rest of the group.

Ellis was ready to pounce and take a bullet for Emery should the need arise. Emery held one hand over her stomach, knowing that she would never see her son grow up.

"If we do this, then your son can live. *I* will survive, and the Ministry will never find out about you." I nodded at my dad. "They won't know we escaped from that future prison. They won't come looking for you."

Turning to Finn and Doc, I said, "If you come with us, then you'll get the opportunity to pay these fuckers back for what they did to your friends. Franklin and Haley. Whitman." I stared in Doc's eyes. They burned with an intensity, like he was filled with anger and just needed a horde of masked and armored agents to take it out on. He nodded at me.

"Count us in," Doc said, speaking for Finn, who looked over at Doc but didn't protest.

"Let's go get your body back," Vesa said.

"Let's go get Ransom," Ash said in his low grumbling voice as he clenched both of his enormous fists.

I lead the assembled group of rebels farther and farther down the hall. The walls stared at me and taunted me. The darkness that was both in front of and behind me was like an open mouth laughing at my belief that we could actually do this.

Nothing had ever gone right in this place. I shouldn't have assumed anything would change this time.

"Let's go," I whispered to myself.

CHAPTER 49

2015
DENVER, COLORADO

"What's your name?" I asked the Wayfield employee.

"I already tried that." Vesa said.

"Clay," the young man said.

"Hey!" Vesa shot Clay a look of disapproval. "I asked you like four or five times, and you refused. Then *he* asks once and 'Hi I'm Clay.'"

"That was before all this," Clay said. Our group snuck and moved slowly down the hall. There was nothing for what seemed like a kilometer. No doors. No cells. Not even a colored line on the floor.

"What? The guns? Or the seven other people who came to my rescue?" Vesa asked.

"Either. Both," Clay said softly. I could tell his nervous demeanor was nothing new. He didn't need a large group with guns to make him unsure of himself.

"Clay," I said, "what should we expect up ahead? You said there were a lot of agents up there. What can you tell us?"

"Nothing, really." Clay shuffled his feet. "They don't let me in this wing. I've only been at this post for a month. So they only let me transport lower-risk prisoners, and pass messages back and forth that they don't want to type in an email. Sometimes I just get people coffee." Something told me that this was not the glamorous career with the Ministry of Science that Clay had hoped for. Maybe he had believed he would really be working on advanced technology or protecting the citizens from themselves by collecting tech from them.

"Well, someone has to get the coffee," Doc said.

"There are worse things they could make you do," Emery said.

"What did you do before?" Vesa asked and glanced behind us every few steps.

"Engineer," Clay said unenthusiastically. "Private sector."

"I didn't know any private engineering jobs still existed," Vesa said.

"They don't," Clay said. "This wasn't exactly official."

I nodded my head. "I see."

By now, the nanobots had stopped the bleeding from my stomach. My clothing still felt cold and wet against my skin, but I was pretty sure I wouldn't bleed to death. I still limped with each step, and the pain from my injuries shot through my body.

"You were conscripted." Clay nodded. "I know the feeling. It's no fun. Thanks for helping us."

This was the first time Clay looked up and looked me in the eyes.

"It's no problem. Just … if the time comes, make it look like I didn't cooperate. Make it look like you hate me just as much as you hate the rest of these people."

"I won't let them know you helped us. When the time comes, I will treat you like shit. You've got my word." I said and smiled.

Clay cracked a slight smile, but quickly straightened his mouth. "The guy you're looking for … the one in the cell…" Clay shook his head. "I don't know much, but I've heard people talking. I doubt he'll be alive by now."

"What did he say?" Ash slowed down and walked next to me and our willing prisoner. "Ransom is dead?"

"We don't know that," I told Ash. "We don't know anything yet. Let's just get to where they're keeping him and take it from there. Trust me, I want him to be alive more than anyone else."

"It's just up there," Clay whispered. "Around the next corner. There's a security checkpoint. There's no way through ... at least not quietly."

"Vesa. Finn," I whispered. "Ellis. Emery. Be precise. We don't have any ammo after this. I'd guess there are twenty-five rounds in each rifle, and probably twelve rounds in my pistol. Make every shot count. We'll stay behind the four of you." Doc, Ash, and Cooper all nodded in agreement. "Grab a weapon if you can. Extra ammo. Anything. Ash." I stared at my new friend. At Ransom's oldest and best friend. "You stay close to me. While they hold everyone back, you and I are going to find Ransom. I'll need you there to help me get him out. I doubt he'll be in any shape to walk out on his own."

Ash nodded and gripped my shoulder.

"Let's go," I said and motioned for Doc, Ellis, Emery, and Finn to round the corner.

CHAPTER 50

Emery fired two rapid shots down the hall. Vesa was next. Finn and Ellis weren't far behind, all of them shooting short bursts of bullets in the direction of the security checkpoint. I darted around the corner behind them. The three agents at the end of the hall reached for their firearms, but fell and stumbled as the streams of bullets ripped through them.

One agent crawled behind a glass barrier where a series of monitors and buttons were.

"Intruders in sector ten! Two agents down," he coughed into his radio. The agent pulled himself up far enough to reach a red button on the wall behind the glass barrier, sounding an alarm that rang throughout the facility. It screeched and howled, echoing through the halls and inside my eardrums.

Finn ran up to the last agent and fired a single shot into his chest. The rest of us, the ones who were either injured, limping, bleeding, burnt, shot, or simply without a weapon, stayed back. We only approached once all of the agents were down.

"Here," Finn said and snatched the guns from the dead agent. One of the agents dressed in black armor groaned and moved ever so slightly when Finn retrieved his weapon. Finn rammed the butt of his rifle into the man's face, cracking the faceplate over his chin and mouth. The agent stopped moving. Finn tossed pistols to Vesa and Ash.

"No," Ash protested again. "I can't." He held the gun timidly, not gripping the handle, but holding the barrel.

"Here," Doc said. His voice was weak, drowning beneath the noise of the siren, and he winced as he reached his left hand out. "I can try with my other hand." He wrapped his hand around the pistol and felt the weight of it. "Just no one stand in front of me," Doc said and cracked a smile. He knelt down, squeezing the handle of the gun between his thigh and calf, pulling the slide back with his left hand. "Son of a bitch didn't even have a round in the chamber!"

"Let's move," Vesa shouted over the loud siren. She shot the handle of the door on the other side of the checkpoint.

I pulled the Kevlar vest off one of the agents and handed it to my mom.

"Here," I said. "Just in case." She nodded and threw the vest over her. "Dad, Ash," I said and handed two more vests to them.

"It won't fit," Ash said. Both of us looked at his barrel chest. "You take it."

"Hand it over." Doc reached out, his gun stuffed in his waistband. "If I'm gonna risk my life to get your body back, I at least deserve a little protection. I've been shot enough today." I helped guide Doc's injured hand through the opening in the vest and strapped it around his body.

Up ahead, Vesa and Finn were already in another firefight with more agents. Streams of bullets bounced off the hard gray walls. Beyond the security checkpoint was a circular room with doors spaced around the edge. Some doors looked like they led to more halls, while others were of solid metal with only a strip of glass to peer in. Cells.

"Get cover!" Ellis shouted and pushed me behind a bank of computers. Several agents with rifles flooded in from some other wing of the facility and fired indiscriminately around the room, taking no precautions to keep from shooting the Wayfield employees scurrying around the room and ducking for cover. One armor-clad agent shot a bullet that ripped through a woman in a white Wayfield lab coat, spraying dark blood from her chest. She fell next to me, and her mouth hung open, gasping for air. Doc crouched behind a mobile medical cart, pushing it around the room to various vantage points. He made each shot count, never missing his targets, even with his left hand.

"We'll hold them off!" Vesa yelled. "You get Ransom!"

Time slowed. Sparks flew from bullets crashing into computers and the overhead lights. The sound of bullets firing filled the room until it blended into a constant static. I saw Clay cowering just outside the door, hiding by the three dead agents back at the security checkpoint.

Ash tried his best to shrink his large body behind the circular counter in the middle of the room. He flinched every time a bullet landed anywhere near him. Finn sprayed a stream of bullets directly into the doorway from which the agents poured, killing several before they could cross the threshold. Their bodies piled on the floor and slowed the agents behind.

"Go!" Vesa yelled at me.

But where? I thought. The room was like a clock with doors at each point where a number should be. If the door we entered was six o'clock, then the door where the agents came from was twelve. The five doors to my right looked like cells, with little or no glass to see through them. The five doors on my left were mostly glass doors that led to more long white hallways. I shuffled to my right and examined the first cell I came upon.

"I can't open it!" I shouted back to Vesa. "I need a card."

"Stay there!" Vesa shouted over the gunfire.

Finn had posted himself by the door where the agents came from and fired bursts of bullets down the hall. Several agents were posted behind cover in the hallway, and they returned fire. The bullets dinged against the door frame and zipped past Finn, burying into the cement wall at the other end of the round room.

Vesa shuffled around the circular counter, keeping her body low until she was crouched at Finn's waist just outside of the doorway.

"Cover me," Vesa said to Finn. Finn nodded and fired a string of bullets down the hall. The agents ducked behind cover, and Vesa reached out, dragging one of the dead agents into the safety of the room we had secured. She ran her hands over the corpse's clothes until she came across a security card. "Got it!" she yelled and shuffled her way back to me.

An agent burst through the door at nine o'clock and pounced on top of Vesa. She fell to the floor, her face skidding across the cement. The agent drew the pistol holstered on his hip, but Vesa flipped onto her back and grabbed the agent's wrists. The two wrestled until Ash toppled the armored agent and drove his large fists into the agent's face. He tried to steady his gun and aim at Ash, but his body shook and went limp each time Ash landed a punch. The agent's armored mask had flown off by now and blood was streaming from his nose. Now I knew how Ash had managed to survive the attack by Marshall's men underneath Buckley.

A second agent in full riot gear flew through the door with a baton pulled back ready to crack Ash on the head. Doc fired a shot at the agent, but missed. He corrected his aim and fired again, this time hitting the agent square in the chest. Then Doc pointed his pistol at the agent who Ash was wrestling with, shooting him in the head. The agent's body went limp and Ash jumped off of him in shock.

"Whoa," Ash said and looked to see where the bullet came from. "I had him."

"Were you gonna beat him to death?" Doc asked. Ash shook his head. "Then you didn't *have* him," Doc said. "No middle ground here."

The gray cement was now splattered with dark blood that ran down to soak into the ground. Vesa slid the key card across the floor to me. I picked it up and swiped it on the first door. A light turned green and the door swung open. Inside the cell was nothing but bright white lights. No person. No me.

"We need to hurry!" Finn shouted from the other end of the room. "I've got this door covered, but more agents will be coming, and I don't know which door they'll be coming from!"

Pointing at the doors that led down other hallways, Vesa said, "I got this one! Can you two cover another door?" Ellis and Emery nodded and each posted themselves next to another door. Finn was posted at the twelve o'clock position, Vesa at eleven, Ellis at ten, and Emery at nine. All of the doors on the other side of the room were cells. Cooper kept his frail body hidden behind the circular desk in the center of the large room, and Ash knelt next to me.

"I'm out of bullets," Doc said and dropped his pistol on the ground.

"Here," Finn said and pulled another pistol from the holster of one of the many dead agents, tossing the gun across the room to Doc. "I'm almost out too." He slammed the half-empty magazine back into the rifle, yanking the slide to check if a bullet was in the chamber.

At each door, I swiped the security card and the door swung open, revealing an empty white room. A burst of chilled air rushed out of each cell, pushing against my face and reminding me of New Alcatraz. Not the scalding furnace that I had experienced with my father, but the unrelenting icy snow globe that housed the small village where Ransom's family awaited his return. Not my return. His. With each empty cell and each burst of cold wind, any hope that my body and Ransom's mind were here diminished.

Maybe they moved him. Maybe he's dead. I'm dead. Maybe they had already found a way to erase me from existence and my body simply vanished, like I long suspected it would if the Ministry ever interrupted whatever delicate time loop I created for myself.

I reached the last cell. The last door with no way to see in or out. It was just a solid metal door, locked tight and sealed shut. I swiped the card and gripped my cold fingers around the thick door, pulling it open.

Another white room. More light seemed to come from nowhere and everywhere at the same time. Frozen air rushed and blew Ransom's hair against my face, whipping around like I was in the middle of a snowstorm. Inside was a person. Shirtless. Beaten. Pale. His hand was black and red with fingers missing. On the white cement floor was a circle of dried and coagulated blood, most of it had already soaked into the floor.

"Ash! Get over here!" He crawled and stayed low, even though there were no agents coming at us, at least not at the moment.

"Who is it?" Ash asked. He wrapped his large arms around his body at the sudden change in temperature as he stood next to me in the doorway.

"It's me," I said.

CHAPTER 51

2075
DENVER, COLORADO

"Is he alive?" Ash asked. He was the first to step into the cell.

"I don't know." I was worried to know the answer.

"Holy shit," Vesa said, pushing her way between Ash and me. "What did they do to you?"

"Nothing good," I said.

Vesa rolled my body over. The first thing I noticed was my face. It was broken and swollen on the left side. My lip was split. My eye was swollen shut. Vesa gripped my hand.

"What the fuck?" she muttered. "They cut your fingers off! Those fuckers! They barely sewed this shut!"

"They did this … to Ransom?" Ash asked, shaking his head.

"Technically, I guess so," I answered, but I didn't really know the answer. Ransom *felt* what they did, but it was my body. If we ever switched back into our own bodies, then I would have to live with what these people did.

"But … why? Who would do this?"

"The same people who would lock up Vesa's brother for five years," Doc said as he made his way into the ice-cold room. "Or the same people who would attack our home and kill Franklin and Haley. Take Finn and me prisoner. The same people who would make so many things illegal that it becomes impossible to not break the law." Doc bent down next to Vesa and placed his bloody hand on her back. It was the first time I saw the two act like I remembered them, like a man who had lost his real sister and a woman who had lost her real brother, and then found each other. Siblings not by blood, but by circumstance. "The same people who would round up prisoners and ship them into the future to die in some future wasteland like New Alcatraz," Doc said. "That's who would do this."

"Prison?" Ash said to himself and then looked at me.

"Let's get moving," I said, avoiding the question.

"Powell?" I heard my dad's voice behind me, but he wasn't looking at me. He was looking at the limp body crumpled up on the white cement floor. "Oh my god!" he said and stepped forward. "Let me help." Ellis knelt down and helped Vesa, Ash, and Doc lift my dying body from the ground.

They carried me like pallbearers at a funeral. Ash lifted my two feet. My father and Vesa each grabbed a shoulder, and Doc tried his best to help with only one good hand. My arms dangled down in unnatural positions. My chest barely lifted with each shallow breath I drew.

We made our way out of the cold cell. Finn guarded the halls. Cooper stood behind him, still in a daze. The fog of five years in prison clouded his head.

"Is that him?" Emery asked.

"It's him," Ellis said softly and looked down at my beaten face as they shuffled my body through the large round room. "It's Powell."

"It's *him*?" she asked me and placed her hand on her own stomach.

"It's your son."

I walked over to one of the bodies on the floor, ripped its Kevlar jacket off, and wrapped it around myself. I took the pistol that sat in the hip holster and pulled off the long rifle slung over the dead agent's shoulder. I knew by the weight of the pistol that it was fully loaded. I checked the magazine of the rifle to make sure it too was loaded.

"Doc," I called out and waved him over to one end of the room as the others made their way back to the security checkpoint. "You know how to get back to the cells you were in?" I asked him, almost in a whisper. Doc nodded. "Okay, once you get there, you need to get to the *deployment center*. Follow the yellow line."

"Why? Where are you going?"

"I'll be right behind you, but I need you to make sure my body and Emery make it back to the deployment center. If nothing else, *they* need to survive. I know you enough to know you can get these people back there … even with only one good hand."

"Let's go!" Vesa said from the other room. Clay was gone, presumably having run to safety.

"That man." I pointed at my dying body.

"You mean *you*?" Doc said.

"No. The person who is trapped inside my body. He deserves to live. He has a wife and child. He didn't ask to get wrapped up in our shit." I handed Doc the retrieval device that would pull them back through the wormhole to the future. "His fight is not with the Ministry. He just wants a simple life with his family." Doc nodded understandingly, like he knew how appealing a simple life would be, but that none of us would ever have the opportunity for a simple life. Helping Ransom was probably the closest any of us would ever come to experiencing such simplicity.

"That woman," I said and pointed at my mom, "She is carrying a baby. She is carrying *me* as a child."

"You're about as far from simple as I've ever seen," Doc muttered.

"If anything happens to her … I can't afford to find out. Protect her."

"I sure as shit don't understand what you're into, but I will see that they both make it to the deployment center. You have my word." Doc stuck his one good hand out and shook mine. He pulled me in for a brief hug, a gesture I didn't think Doc made very often.

Vesa, Ash, and my dad approached us. "What's going on? Let's go!" Vesa said and motioned back to the long gray hallway we came from.

"I'm not going with you," I said.

"What?" Vesa and Ash said simultaneously.

"But Ransom…" Ash said.

"I'll be right behind you. There's just something I need to do here."

"What? What is so important that you would risk getting caught *again*?" Vesa asked.

"If I'm right, there is something down here that could give me my life back. It could give me my family back." I looked at my dad, who was clearly still grappling with the idea that the man he escaped New Alcatraz with was his son, and now that same person was nearly dead just a meter away.

"I will make it," I assured all of them. "I will meet you at the deployment center."

"I'm going with you," my father said and stepped forward. "If you're right, then Powell … my son … you gave me the chance to be with Emery, to live. I can't let you go alone." I didn't argue with my father. I knew it would do no good. I had seen how determined he could be. Ellis walked away and pulled Emery off to the side. I saw them speak briefly, and Emery nodded. The two embraced and clung to each other. Something they were both used to by now. Saying goodbye without knowing when the next hello would come.

"Don't do this," Vesa pleaded with me. Her eyes red. Her jaw clenched. "Don't leave."

"I will find you. I promise. I will be right behind you guys. Right now, I need you and Doc to get everyone else to the deployment center. There's no time to argue."

When I could see she was about to do just that, I reached out and hugged her for what seemed like forever. Her body felt natural against mine.

She gripped my patchwork clothes that were sewn by Ransom's wife and buried her head into my chest. I wondered if Aurora would have been upset to see her husband embracing another woman. I didn't care. I pulled away and looked her in the eyes. "Come back," Vesa said, and once again I thought of Aurora and her same demand to me.

"I will," I whispered. "Let's go," I said to my dad.

We turned and stepped over the pile of dead agents who blocked the doorway and made our way towards the heart of the vault.

CHAPTER 52

"You weren't lying about all this. Swapping bodies and all," my father said as we crept through the tunnels of the Denver Airport. These were the tunnels that weren't marked. It was the hidden and off-limits part of an underground vault whose very existence was denied by the Ministry of Science. What I looked for might prove to be just as illusive.

"I mean, I didn't think you were outright lying, Powell." This was the first time my dad had called me by my actual name since I had found him in Buford.

"I just thought maybe you were crazy. Some sort of psychosis from traveling through time. Or maybe the Ministry really did send you to find me and Emery. But seeing Powell's body in that cell. *Your* body." Ellis stopped and grabbed my shoulder, turning me to face him. "I shouldn't have doubted you. I never thought I would get the chance to thank you for what you did for me. You held those men off so that Red and I could escape."

To him, my sacrifice in New Alcatraz, had happened maybe a week ago. But to me, it had happened five years ago, and since then I had traveled back to my present. 2070. Now I stood in front of my father, whose mind was likely much younger than mine.

"Now you understand, though?" I asked. "You understand why you surviving was more important than me surviving? If you died back then…" I shook my head. "I needed you and Mom to meet in 2036. In Buford."

"I just wish you had told me who you were. Who you really were. I wish I knew my son was the one making the sacrifice for me."

"Well, you know now," I said and gripped his shoulder.

The lights in the hall were blinding compared to the dimly lit halls in the rest of the vault. We approached an intersection. Ellis held his hand out to stop me from walking any further. The sound of pounding boots came from around one of the corners. We waited.

The first armored agent sprinted from the right, but Ellis fired a single bullet to his neck, dropping the agent in an instant.

"Shots fired!" another agent screamed from around the corner. Before the warning could register, I leaned around the corner and fired a stream of bullets down the hall. My rifle kicked hard into my shoulder, pushing my body back. I readjusted my aim to keep the stream of bullets from veering away from the agents. The men in black slumped to the floor, some dead instantly while others coughed and choked on blood.

"Reinforcements inbound," a voice crackled over a radio.

"Where to?" Ellis asked. His eyes darted around, looking down each corridor, waiting for more agents.

"If that's where they're coming from, then that's probably where they are keeping what I need. Grab the bullets." I pulled as many magazines from the dead bodies as I could carry without weighing myself down too much. Ellis pulled a rifle from one of the agents and tucked his pistol into the waistband of his pants.

We ran down the hall, ready to meet whatever threat or force came at us. I forgot about all of my other injuries. The pain from my head, gunshots, cuts, bruises, and twisted limbs all went away with each step. Maybe it was the nanobots, or maybe it was the adrenaline flowing through me. My feet clapped against the white ground. The lights overhead hummed and buzzed. More agents appeared ahead of us.

We fired shots in their direction without stopping. We didn't break stride as we took out another group of agents sent to murder us. They ran at us with the same attitude as we had. Kill or be killed. Maybe they knew what they were doing, knew the type of government they were protecting. But maybe they didn't. Maybe they had been told that they were the protectors of our safety and freedom so many times that they actually believed it. Either way, they saw my father and me as the enemy. We were the terrorists. The criminals. The murderers. Maybe they weren't wrong.

Maybe I had allowed myself to become what they are. Maybe I told myself that my goals were more important than theirs, but really, we were two sides of the same coin, finding some way to excuse our actions. The evil and ill will that seeped out of all of us had to be excused or explained away somehow, or else most of us wouldn't be able to live with ourselves.

"If you don't know where we are going," my dad said in between short bursts of breath, "do you at least know what we are looking for?"

"Yeah, something they took from me. My blood."

CHAPTER 53

Every few steps, Ellis turned around, keeping an eye behind us. His steps were light. "Behind!" Ellis shouted and spun. The loud popping of bullets echoed behind me down the hall, and I felt the bullets whiz past both of us. Ellis crouched against the wall. We had no cover here. I fired indiscriminately.

"Get behind me!" Ellis said, gripping my clothes and slamming me against the wall. He shot precise rounds at individual agents while I continued to fire wildly. "Aaarrggghh!" He fell against me. Blood splattered against me, and I cradled him against my body as he continued firing at the agents who had snuck up behind us.

I stood, gripping Ellis' shirt collar and dragged him down the hall and away from the approaching agents. I peddled backwards, gun in one hand and Ellis in the other. He stayed on the ground, sliding down the hall. Ellis' left arm bled through his clothing. We kept shooting until the last agent had collapsed in a black pile of armor and guns.

"Can you walk?" I asked, jerking my head back and forth, checking each direction.

"Yeah." Ellis grunted and stood. We never stopped walking, but

Ellis checked his arm and winced at the sight of his blood. "Went straight through," he said and ripped his sleeve open to take a closer look.

"In front!" I yelled. Two agents exited a door that sat at the end of the hallway. "Get down!"

I dropped to the floor, pressing my stomach flat against the ground just as more bullets flew overhead. I fired back. Their bodies shook as the bullets ripped through them and drove into the door behind them.

"You hit?" I asked my father, keeping my eyes on the door.

"No," Ellis said.

I scurried to my feet and pulled my father towards the door at the end of the hall. We jumped over the two dead agents, and I slammed my shoulder hard into the metal door, flinging it open.

Beyond the door was a lab. Microscopes and centrifuges littered the long black lab tables, and cold storage containers lined the back wall. A woman in white cowered in the back corner, her hands covering her head.

"Don't worry," I said softly. "We aren't here to hurt you." I walked cautiously towards the woman. She spun, pressing her back against the wall and readying her fists for a fight. It was the nurse who had taken care of me, of Ransom, when I was injured. The one whose sole job it was to keep me alive. "It's me," I said and then quickly remembered I was in a different body than last time I saw her. "I mean ... I'm with the man you helped. The prisoner."

The nurse's fists and teeth were clenched, and her eyes darted between me and Ellis. She looked at us, our guns. I let go of my rifle, letting it hang at my side, and I held my hands out.

"Remember? The prisoner. You told him to just give them what they wanted. Tell them what they wanted. You were looking out for him." I slowly crouched down to her level. The nurse's fists began to open and her breathing slowed just a bit. "You helped him. I don't want to hurt you." The nurse nodded rapidly, though she shot a glance at Ellis every so often.

"I need you to help me. They took something from the prisoner. They drew his blood." The nurse nodded and glanced to another corner of the lab. "Do you know what they did with the blood?"

"Yes," the nurse finally said, but the word barely made it past her lips. "Yes," she repeated, this time with a bit more force.

"Good. Where did they take it?" I glanced over my shoulder at the place where the nurse looked. "Is it back there?"

"Yes. They separated his blood."

I walked towards the back corner of the lab, where a refrigerator sat. The front door was solid glass, and a blue light glowed around the inside edge. The rubber seal around the door let out a soft suction noise when I opened it, and a cold burst of air brushed against my face.

"We need to hurry," Ellis said. He leaned against the wall, tying a strip of cloth around his arm to slow the bleeding. Once he was done, Ellis let go of his rifle and switched to his smaller, and more manageable, pistol.

I scanned the shelves of the refrigerator. Vials of blood, nanobots and other serums filled each shelf. All of them placed perfectly symmetrical and labeled in alphanumeric order. I scanned until I saw what I was looking for, the serum that Sheldon had spoken of while he tortured us. Serum 4381. The cure for Dark Time. I slipped the vial into my pocket along with several vials of nanobots.

"Thank you." I turned back towards the nurse. "For everything."

"Freeze!" someone instructed from the door that led back to the halls. I turned to find the large man who had tortured us, Agent Saunders, holding a pistol to my father's temple. "Drop your weapons. Throw 'em over there." He pointed to the other side of the lab.

Ellis dropped his pistol and then slid the rifle off his shoulder. He kicked them across the floor. I placed both of my guns on the lab table in front of me and slid them away. "What the fuck are you guys doing?" Saunders asked and smiled. "I mean really, what are you doing? And what the fuck kind of clothes are you wearing?" He nodded at me and my thick woven clothing. Blood had soaked through large portions, but by now the nanobots had scabbed over the wounds and the bleeding had stopped.

"I got 'em," Saunders said, touching some small device planted in his ear. "Lab two. Understood."

Saunders returned his attention to Ellis and me. "Where are the prisoners?" he asked, flexing his large tattooed forearm that gripped the pistol pointed at Ellis' head. Neither of us spoke. "Where?" he repeated.

"We don't—" my father started to speak. To lie. But I knew this man. I knew what he was capable of.

"The deployment center," I blurted out. I didn't know if he would keep us alive if I told him, but I knew what would happen if I didn't. I knew my father would die in front of me and I would follow him in a matter of seconds.

"You motherfuckers," Saunders said, reaching up to his ear to relay the message. "The prisoners are heading to the deplo—"

Ellis kicked out behind him driving Agent Saunders' knee backwards. He dropped to the ground, screaming and took Ellis down with him. I ran and pounced on him, wrapping my arm around his thick neck. He grabbed me and flung me against a wall with little effort. He knelt and winced at the pain of his leg, but kept moving. He drove a fist into Ellis' face, spilling blood all over the ground.

I crawled back to him and tried to kick him in the ribs, but the agent caught my foot and twisted my ankle until I was forced back to the ground. Saunders stood, placing most of his weight on his good foot. He fired a single shot at my chest just as Ellis jumped on him. The bullet drove into my Kevlar vest. Ellis clamped his teeth down on

Saunders' ear and yanked his head violently. Saunders screamed, and the flesh connecting his ear to his head spread and ripped apart.

Ellis pummeled his fist into Saunders' temple over and over until the bones in his hand must have cracked or broke. Saunders kneeled once again and held a hand over his bleeding head where his ear used to be. Now, it sat on the floor in a bloody splatter. I kneed Saunders in the face, and the crack of his nose rang through the room. I reached for a gun, either mine or Ellis' or Saunders', which was now lying on the floor next to his ear.

Ellis wrapped his arm around Saunders' throat, blood flowing from his broken nose and missing ear.

"Sit up!" I yelled at Saunders. Ellis slowly released his grip. "Sit the fuck up!" I lightly felt the pocket that held Serum 4381. The vial was still intact. "You tortured me within an inch of my life!" I yelled.

"I don't fucking know you." Saunders muttered and wiped the dark blood running from his nose into his mouth.

"No, you know me." Ellis grabbed his rifle and pointed it at Saunders' back. "Take his knife," I told my father and nodded down at the knife strapped to Saunders' thigh. "Get on your knees," I said and took one step closer to him.

He didn't move. Once Ellis pulled the knife from its holster, he kicked Saunders' until he rose to his knees.

"I didn't torture you," Saunders said again. Less like begging and more stating a fact, like he was annoyed by his predicament.

"From the looks of my body, you cut my fingers off, beat me, stabbed me, and tried to bleed me to death." I reached out for Ellis to hand me the knife, but kept my gun trained on Saunders' face.

"I didn't do that to *you*," Saunders said and spat a glob of blood onto the floor. "That was that piece of shit New Alcatraz prisoner that wouldn't shut up about his fucking sick kid."

"You're right. You didn't do that to only me. You did it to a man who was innocent. Even by your standards." I grabbed Saunders' hair, pulling back his head. He looked up at me, confused but not scared. "And whatever I do to you won't even come close to punishing you for what you've done in your life. For the people you've tortured, beaten, killed." I gripped his hair until I felt clumps of it coming loose in my hands. Saunders groaned, but his expression didn't change.

"Powell," my father said and placed a hand on my shoulder. "We need to move," His tone was neither passing judgment nor encouraging me. He was a father letting his child follow their own path, and learn of the consequences on their own.

"I do what I am ordered to do," Saunders said. I turned back to him.

"You say that like it's some sort of blanket excuse, like it absolves you of any wrongdoing just because your boss is a fucking psycho. You're just lucky that I don't have the time to do to you what you did to me. Just remember, this is mercy. You just better hope that nurse tries just as hard to keep you alive as she did for me." With that, I wedged the knife into his armpit, and twisted the blade towards his bicep. I jerked the knife back, slicing through the soft flesh on the underside of his arm and cutting through the brachial artery.

Saunders gasped and gripped his large hand over the fresh wound. His eyes fluttered and he fell face-first into the floor.

"Let's go," I said.

As a parting gift, I kicked Saunders hard in the back. He slumped over, slick with his own blood. His mouth hung open but no sound came out. His eyes drifted shut.

CHAPTER 54

We ran through the halls, retracing our frantic steps from before, passing the groups of agents who had ambushed us in the halls. Ellis' rifle dangled at his side and his pistol was stuck in his waistband. His good hand clamped around the gunshot wound in his other arm.

"You okay?" I asked in between short puffs of breath. Our feet thudded on the ground in a fast, rhythmic pace.

"I think," he said and pulled his hand away from the wound ever so slightly to get the briefest look at the injury. "I can't hold a gun in that hand."

"Just hang on. We can get you help once we're back in New Alcatraz. We can use the nanobots."

"New Alcatraz!" Ellis said. "Why would we go back there?"

"That's where Ransom is from. We need to switch bodies."

"Your body didn't look like it would last long," Ellis said. His pace started to slow and the rifle looked like a heavy weight pulling him down to the floor.

"Here," I said and reached out. "Give me your rifle. I can carry it." Ellis handed over the weapon with no protest, wincing as he pulled it over his body.

"Like I said, nanobots. We just need to make it back there and hope no one else gets severely injured and needs more nanobots than we have."

We approached a corner and slowed down. We pressed our bodies against the wall and crept forward. I peeked around the corner for a split second and saw a blur of agents.

"Shit," I whispered. Ellis slid down the wall to the floor.

"How many?" he asked, pulling his pistol from his waistband.

"Ten … maybe twenty."

Ellis quietly pulled the magazine out of his pistol. "I got about six here." He slid the magazine back into the gun.

"Here," I said and handed him my pistol. "Take my bullets. We have a full clip between the two of us."

I sat next to my dad, both of us out of breath, our chests heaving up and down. I took the bullets from both rifles and combined them into one clip as well.

"Think he's dead?" Ellis asked.

"Who? Saunders? Don't know." I shook my head. "But I do know he isn't going to be in any condition to sneak up behind us."

"Powell, if I knew you were my son when we were in New Alcatraz, I would have never left—"

"But you didn't know," I interrupted. "I knew, but I still didn't even believe it. It took everything in me to not say anything. I didn't know what would happen. If it would change things. Alter things. I just felt like I had to let things play out as they always had before. You get out, meet Mom, raise me in Buford, and…"

"And what?" my dad asked. "What happens after your mom goes back and leaves us in Buford?"

"You raised me."

"And me? What happened with me?" Ellis asked like he knew it was nothing good.

"You ... you die ... eventually."

"When?"

"I don't know how much to say. How much is too much to know." I peered around the corner to see the agents loading guns, readying themselves for battle.

"What does it matter? You've changed things already. *This* never happened before. You never came to Buford and took your mom and dad back to the year 2075. It's altered. Forever."

"I was twelve," I said. My mind drifted back to my time in Buford when my dad grew sick. His complexion changing, his hair falling out in clumps. "I think it was radiation."

"From traveling through time?" my dad asked. I nodded. "But they ... they gave me the nanobots every time I travelled."

"Not enough. You had enough in your system to stave off the poison for over a decade, but it overtook the nanobots ... eventually."

"Shit," Ellis said quietly and looked down at the floor, rubbing his arm where the Ministry had injected him with doses of the nanobots. I kept an ear trained to the agents around the corner, listening for any sound to indicate that they were approaching. But they stayed stationary. They knew where we were coming from, and they knew we had to pass through that hall.

"Don't worry, though. I have more nanobots. I have some here." I held out the vials I had taken from the lab down the hall. "And I have more back in New Alcatraz."

"But what does that get me? Another year?" Ellis said.

"Yes," I whispered and gripped Ellis' good shoulder. "Maybe another decade, maybe more. Neither of us know how long these nanobots will keep working inside you. Maybe you can beat the radiation completely. You never know. Like you said, I've changed things. How things go from here, who knows. But we need to go. We need to get through this blockade." I nodded at the corner.

"Okay," Ellis said. He gripped the pistol as best he could and slowly stood.

"Make every shot count," I said.

My first stream of bullets took down two agents. As I ducked back around the corner to take cover, a seemingly endless wall of bullets flew past my face.

Ellis ducked low and reached his hand around the corner. He fired two shots and pulled his hand back. "We are never getting back to the deployment center," Ellis said. His eyes were wide.

The wall of bullets diminished just long enough for me to reach my rifle around the corner and fire four shots. One bullet flew into the chest of an agent. He fell back and toppled onto another agent. There were three more sprawled on the floor. Their bodies were limp, and only one of them was still moving, his hand against his chest.

I pressed my back to the cold gray cement and looked at my father. He was checking how many bullets he had left. "Six," he said. His clothing was matted to his arm. His face was growing pale, except for dark circles around his eyes. He shook his head hopelessly at the futility of our fight and twisted his head around to make sure no agents were coming from other directions.

"Stay here," I said, and as soon as there was a break in the stream of bullets, I dove across the hall and took cover around the corner opposite Ellis. The agents fired just as my legs cleared the hallway. Their bullets zipped down the corridor, flying into an endless stretch of tunnel.

I reached my rifle around the corner fired blindly. I heard two distinct screams of pain and the groans that come after the initial burning pain of a gunshot wound. By my count there must have been six or seven dead or injured agents, leaving maybe ten alive and well. The only advantage we had over the wall of agents blocking our path to the deployment center was that we had cover. They were out in the open with nothing but their body armor to protect them.

I glanced over at my father. His pistol sat on the floor next to him, the slide pulled back and locked in position. Empty. He looked at me for guidance. The look in his eyes was one of pleading. Pleading for me to get him back to Emery. Back to Buford.

The firing stopped, and the noise was replaced by the muffled voice of an agent "You are trapped! Surrender."

I pulled the magazine from my rifle. I had maybe five bullets left. With twice as many agents as bullets, I had no plan. Kill an agent and take their gun. *But how, without getting shot by another agent first?*

"You're outnumbered. Come out now and—"

A single loud shot burst through the hall. Several more gunshots rang out, but the bullets didn't fly past us down the hallway like the hundreds of others. These bullets made contact with the soft flesh and clothing of the agents down the hall. Screams of pain and shock filled the air.

"You there?" I heard Vesa's voice. "You okay?" I peeked around the corner to see her standing behind the wall of guards, with a rifle propped against her shoulder, still peering through the sights of the weapon. She was ready to fire at anything that came around the corner that wasn't me or Ellis.

"Vesa?" I asked, but I knew it was her. She stood behind the pile of dead agents.

"Are you injured?" she asked as I slowly made my way around the corner. I looked at Ellis and waved him out from his cover.

"Not me, but Ellis is shot."

"The others are at the deployment center. We need to go." Vesa checked behind her and then looked to her left and right, still holding the rifle ready to fire. Her body was tense and alert. I pulled the magazine out of one of the dead agent's guns and slammed it into my rifle, shoving a backup in my pocket. I reached out and held my father by his shoulders, but was mindful of his injured arm.

"Are you okay? Can you make it?"

Ellis nodded, his eyes fluttering slightly.

"Lead the way," I told Vesa.

She turned and jogged down the hall, towards the deployment center. Our fingers over the triggers of our rifles, ready to fire.

CHAPTER 55

"Why'd you come back?" I asked Vesa as we ran towards the deployment center. "Why'd you risk it?"

"Risk?" Vesa echoed. As usual, I was more out of breath than she was. "I couldn't take you dying. Not making it back. Not after all this. What we've been through. I couldn't stand seeing how it ends without you there. It wouldn't seem right. Plus, you needed me," Vesa said and smirked, slightly crooked.

It seemed like an eternity since the last time I'd seen that smirk, but in reality, it was only a few days. Like my mind had rested in that machine for thousands of years before it went inside Ransom's body, only I didn't realize it. Maybe my mind had floated in some blackness, like the pools at the Golden Dawn headquarters. Maybe it really had been much longer since I had seen Vesa.

Ellis was slower than us. He winced each time his foot landed on the hard ground, sending waves of pain through his body. For the first time, I wondered if the bullet had skimmed an artery. I slowed down to let him catch up.

"You need a break?" I asked.

"No, keep going."

By now, we had made it out of the more secure area of the underground vault, and were back where the colored lines were painted on the floor. The yellow line stretched down the hall until we came upon an elevator, the same elevator I had stood in five years ago when I was sent to New Alcatraz. I could almost hear my shackles clanking together as I shuffled down this hall in my orange jumpsuit. Memories of my first trip down this hall blinked through my mind. On that day, it felt like the end of me, like this was where the final frame of my life would take place.

Two agents were slumped on the floor. Vesa pressed the button to call the elevator then turned to face the long hall behind us. She held her gun steady, ready to fire. I helped my dad lean against the wall, positioning him so he was shielded by me and Vesa.

"Thank you," I said to her as we pointed our rifles into the long darkness.

"I owed you," she said, breaking her concentration to look at me for a second. "You took me in when you didn't even know who I was. You gave me a place to hide when those agents were chasing me. I owed you. Plus, we have so much catching up to do."

"A lot has happened in the last few days, huh?" I said.

"Yeah." She smiled at me. This time it wasn't a smirk. It was a genuine smile. Her eyes burned into me, like she could see the real me inside of Ransom's body somehow. Like she had always seen the real me.

The elevator beeped and the doors slid open. I helped my father inside while Vesa kept her rifle pointed down the hall. The doors closed, and I pressed the button, launching the elevator down to the deployment center.

The wind rushed around the elevator as it sped down. Vesa let go of her rifle and shook her hands, like they had been glued to her weapon, and she was relieved to have them back. The elevator slowed and jerked to a stop. The doors pulled open to reveal the large time movement device.

"It's us!" Vesa yelled, her voice floating in all directions. Doc and Finn appeared from behind two of the large pillars surrounding the stage in the center of the room. Cooper stood behind the control panel.

"Mom!" I shouted into the darkness. I couldn't see her. I looked back to Ellis, who summoned the energy to move quickly and glance around the room as well. We swiveled our heads around. "Emery!" I shouted again.

"Here!" her voice echoed to my left. She and Ash were kneeling behind a stack of barrels next to my beaten body with Ransom's mind inside. They had found a stretcher and placed my body on it. I lay there like a corpse. She ran to Ellis. "What happened?" She reached out to his arm, but Ellis winced and pulled away.

"I was shot," he answered. "It went through."

"Why is there so much blood?" Emery asked and then turned to me.

"I don't know," I told her. "It may have nicked an artery, but I'm really not sure."

"We have to get him help," Emery demanded.

"It's okay," Ellis said, almost a whisper.

"I have nanobots and a syringe back where we came from. For all of you." I said the last part louder. "We can help anyone who is injured once we get out of here."

"Well, I'm sure as shit not gonna stay here," Doc said, standing in the center of the time movement device.

"Everyone get in the middle of the stage," I said and motioned like I was herding sheep into a pen. "Leave the guns."

"No," Doc said.

"No metal," I said.

"No metal? Is my zipper gonna burn my dick off or something?" Doc mumbled, only half joking.

"Small amounts are acceptable," Emery said. "But no guns. Definitely no bullets. One of those things goes off inside a wormhole and both ends could collapse. It wouldn't be pretty."

Doc pulled his rifle over his head and slid it on the floor, away from the stage. Finn did the same. Vesa and I dropped our rifles before climbing on. Ash lifted my body from the stretcher and carried me, careful not to be too rough. Ransom's mind was the only thing familiar to him in this place. He'd been silent since we'd arrived here, unsure of the environment and customs. Now he handled my body like it was part of his family.

"Get close to the center," I told them and reached out to Doc for the retrieval device. I pulled everyone close together until we were all pressed against each other, like we were posing for a family photo. I wrapped my arm around Vesa and gripped her body tight. I saw Ash hesitantly stand, surrounded by people he didn't know. He held my dying body in a bear hug from behind.

"You good, Ash?" I asked, looking in his wide eyes. He nodded rapidly, like he just wanted to answer me so he could get back home. "We're close," I said. "Almost there."

"Thanks," Ash said. "Let's get back."

"Everyone ready?" I asked loudly, with the retrieval device held tight in my hand, my thumb hovered over the button. "Ready?" I asked Vesa quietly. She nodded.

"Let's go to the future," she said.

"One, two, three," I said and pressed the button, pulling us back through the wormhole to the future.

CHAPTER 56

The pistons on the large machine in the center of the floor still pumped slowly up and down, several minutes after Ash and Powell had left Merit alone in the deployment center. Marshall and his men were outside, still banging on the door. The barrels and the other things that the three of them had pushed against the door rattled with each blow.

"Put your weight into it!" Marshall yelled at the younger vault dwellers. His voice was forceful even through the metal door. "Not like that, you piece of shit!" Marshall yelled again after another failed collision with the door.

Merit sat on the floor. His chest heaved up and down, and his leg throbbed. With each hit form the other side, the door budged a little more, pushing the barrels and Merit more and more. The hinges rattled. *This won't hold much longer*, he thought.

He wondered how he would ever make it out of this place alive, or if he even deserved to. *Ash knows*, he thought. *Ransom knows. And this other man, Powell, he knows too.* The three of them knew the worst of Merit.

They knew that the contaminated sheep's pelt was forced onto Ransom's son. A catalyst. An invisible hand that would push Ransom and others out to find a cure.

Now, Merit sat on the cold hard floor of his second underground vault of the week. A smaller group of crazed cannibals banging outside the door. This time, instead of human flesh, they sought weapons and medicine. But soon their attention would turn to food, and the weapons gained here would be used to reach that end. To them, Merit was nothing but a piece of flesh. His only value was to be food.

"At the same time!" Marshall yelled. "Hit the fucking door at the same time!" With each word, his voice grew closer and closer to the bizarre screeching scream made by the rest of the cannibals under Buckley Air Force Base. Each push of the door sent shock waves through Merit. He could no longer feel the toes on his broken leg, and he imagined no feeling was better than pain.

I can't go back with them, Merit thought. He found himself in the same dilemma he was in at Buckley. After all these events, stabbing his brother, escaping the vault, trekking through the cold desert and making it home, finding that he did not kill his nephew after all, and that his brother's body had been taken over by some person from another time, the attack on his village, and the second trek to another underground vault ... Merit simply found himself back in the same predicament. To dig deeper or give up. To cover bad deeds with more bad deeds or face whatever consequences awaited him. But inside of him was a drive to survive. *What kind of life will I have, if any, back at the village. I will be treated like one of the men who lived underground. Evil. And maybe I should be. Maybe Ash was right and I have more in common with the vault dwellers than those back home.*

Now, the pistons on the time device had stopped. Except for the banging and Marshall screaming orders, there was no noise in the room. There was no one in the room besides Merit. His body was cut and bleeding. His leg was swollen and red.

There was something in him that simply wanted to see where his life would go. He wanted to see how time would play out. And to do that he had to survive. For his entire life, it seemed there was a mystery out there. Some unanswered question or void that his father had set out to solve. Something still burned inside of him to solve the mystery that his dad couldn't. Find the place that his dad couldn't.

One thing is for certain, he thought. *I will not see how time plays out if I go home with Ransom. Back there is nothing but shame and punishment. Death. Maybe my best hope, my only hope, is to find a new life. A new home.*

He had to decide how to proceed quickly. This door between him and Marshall was his only bargaining chip. If they open it on their own, which they surely would very soon, then it would be over. But if he opened it, then he would be helpful … useful beyond a simple piece of flesh.

"Okay!" Merit finally screamed, surprised by his own voice. His words pierced the metal door and cut through the screams coming from the other side. "Okay, goddammit! I'll let you in!" Merit's chest moved up and down in excitement. He didn't know what would happen. His life was suddenly not as predictable as it was before all of this. His choices and decisions carried more weight than before.

The banging stopped.

"If I open the door, do you promise you'll let me go?" Merit heard soft whispers on the other side of the door.

"Yes," Marshall said after a brief moment. His voice had returned to a normal pitch. "Yes, we will let you go. Just open the door."

"Hang on," Merit said. He pushed himself up from the floor, hobbling on his one good leg. He pushed his slim body against the barrels, nudging them bit by bit until they were away from the door. Sweat dripped down his face, coating his lips with a salty taste.

"Hurry up!" Marshall ordered from the other side of the door.

Merit was betting that his odds were better with these people than with Ransom, Ash, and the rest of his village. But it was not a bet he was all that confident in. His leg gave out and he fell to the floor. Pain streaked up his leg and pulsed in his head. Marshall pushed on the door and peered through doorway.

"Where are the others?" Marshall asked through the door. "Did they leave you behind?"

"Kind of." Merit grunted as he pushed the last large barrel from the doorway. "I don't mean you any harm. I just want to leave here alive. You promise you won't harm me?"

"Yes," Marshall said again. "Do you promise this is not a trap? How do I know the others aren't inside and ready to shoot us?"

"You don't know, but I'm telling you they are not here. They will be back ... I think. What will you do with them?" Merit asked.

There was a silence. "Does that concern you?" Marshall asked.

Merit thought briefly. He didn't want to jeopardize the fragile deal he'd just struck with Marshall. "Will you let them leave here and go back to the village?"

"I highly doubt that," Marshall answered. Merit pulled the door open.

CHAPTER 57

5280
NEW ALCATRAZ

I pulled my eyelids closed, unsure of what would happen to us. If we would make it, or if the wormhole would collapse onto itself and create a massive explosion, bringing down the underground vault in both timelines. I didn't know. And I assumed that no one *really* knew.

Vesa's body was still pressed tightly up against mine. Her cheek against my neck, my arm around her waist. I pried my thumb from the retrieval device and looked around. Ash still held my real body against his chest. My dad leaned into my mom, his bloody arm pressed against her and his blood soaking into her clothes.

We were there. The future. The deployment center had aged several thousand years in the blink of an eye. The cement was cracked, exposing thick wires buried deep in the walls. The floor, and even the center of the time movement device, was covered in dust.

"My, my."

Marshall's voice.

I glanced around.

"What a large group," his voice said, not coming from one place but from everywhere, circling around us.

I jerked my head around to find him. I saw the open door and the barrels pushed off to the side.

"Merit!" I whispered to myself through gritted teeth.

"Where did you come from?" Marshall asked and walked out from behind the control panel. His son and the other two men stood from a crouched position. Marshall's son held Merit by the arm, his gun pressed into Merit's side. Marshall shuffled his feet through the thin film of dust on the ground, tilting his head as he watched us. There was a gun in his hand and he had the bag with the mind transfer device slung around his body.

"Another time," I said, keeping my answer vague. "I can get you there. Get you to a place where there is food, shelter, people." I talked softly.

"You," Marshall said and looked at Vesa. "Who are you?" He took a step closer.

"If you touch her," I said and pushed Vesa behind me, "if you hurt any of us, you get nothing."

"Then you die."

"And you're stuck here, in the biting cold or the blinding heat depending on the time of year. You will die locked away underground."

Laughing, Marshall said, "I've told you before. I have lived my entire life underground. Your promises of more people and a more bearable environment don't intrigue me ... much. Growing up, I saw more people than I ever wanted to. Enough that they started to lose their meaning. Lose their essence."

Marshall motioned for all of us to step off the time movement device. We moved together, like we were one organism.

"That's what I suspect happened here before us. The early men. The settlers. They lost themselves. The problem with a group of people losing what makes them human is that they do things they normally wouldn't." Marshall looked back at Merit.

The other two vault dwellers stepped forward, pointing their guns, and motioned for us to stand against the wall. Marshall stood close to me. I pressed my back against the wall. Vesa stood next to me and interlocked her fingers in mine. Her hand was soft and cool. Next to her were my mother and father. They too held hands, and my mom helped my dad stand. His face was pale, and by now I knew his brachial artery was hit. Depending on how badly it was cut, he didn't have much time. Ash stood next to my parents holding my body up. He locked eyes with Merit and shook his head in disapproval. Finn and Doc stood at the end of the line, flanking Cooper and helping him stand.

"When people go mad like that, two things can happen," Marshall continued. "You either kill each other in a bloody mess, with the last survivor simply tearing his hair out in some crazed fit, or they harness that energy. Point the psychopaths in a direction. Lead them." He moved slowly down the line, looking each person in the eye. He paused at Vesa and brushed his hand against her cheek.

"You don't look too good," Marshall said to Ellis, whose eyes were sunken. "You see, I was a born leader. And I have led many groups. Occasionally, someone comes along and promises me something. Food. Women. Children. Or something that is meant to amaze me. Something I have never seen before—What the fuck is this?" Marshall pointed at my body in Ash's arms. "You carrying around a corpse?" Marshall asked Ash.

Ash was frozen. His head pressed against the back wall, as far away from Marshall as he could get.

"This guy is dead!"

"No, he is *not*," Ash said forcefully, but his voice was barely a whisper.

"If he isn't already then he's pretty damn close. Drop him. Let him go." Ash shook his head and gripped my limp body tighter. "Let him go," Marshall repeated and pointed his gun at Ash. Marshall lowered the gun slightly and pointed it at my beaten and bruised face. Vesa squeezed my hand, Ransom's hand, and looked up at me.

Ash loosened his grip on my body and lowered it to the floor, cradling my bloody head and gently resting it on the cold cement. He peered into Marshall's eyes, and for a moment I thought he might try to tackle him or at least swing at him. But a glance at the gun-toting vault dwellers behind Marshall stayed his hand.

Marshall knelt by my body and took inventory of my injuries. My missing fingers, stab wounds, broken nose, swollen eye, cracked-open skull, tacky blood coagulated in my hair. My skin was a pale blue, whether from the frozen conditions of the cell or because it was already dead, I didn't know.

"There is nothing that amazes me anymore. Nothing that you can offer me that would make me want to leave this place. This is my home. These are my people. I am like their god. They won't do anything unless I tell them to. What's better than that? Why leave that?"

Marshall made his way down the line and looked at Finn. He looked him up and down, felt his arms, and grabbed his face in his hand. Finn shook his head, but Marshall held on tight, squeezing his cheeks together.

"No, I think I will stay here. So that means I don't need you. I don't need whatever it is you're offering me. The way I see it, you still owe me one body. One death." He looked back at me. "Everything needs a counterweight." Marshall moved down and stared at Doc. Looked his body up and down, Marshall said, "Hmmmm. No meat on your bones." Marshall backed away from Doc. "I've had people like you before. Not worth the trouble."

Doc's eyes darted around the room, taking note of each of the vault dwellers' reactions. "What the fuck?" he whispered.

Marshall clenched his jaw and wrapped his skinny fingers around Doc's throat. His face began to turn red, his eyes bulging as he tried to pry Marshall's wrist away.

Marshall looked at me, squeezing harder around Doc's throat. "You don't get to choose this time. I already know you can't make the hard decisions."

Finn stepped forward, but the lanky vault dweller jerked his gun at Finn. Vesa gripped my hand tighter and tighter, then took a step forward. I pulled her back towards the wall.

"No," I told her and shook my head. Her eyes pierced me as she silently pleaded with me to do something or let her do something. "No," was all I could say.

"But," Vesa said. I moved my eyes to our left, towards the other vault dwellers with guns. Marshall pushed Doc against the wall and lifted his pistol into Doc's field of view.

"Wherever you came from, you will never make it back," Marshall growled. The words squeezed through his tight lips and clenched teeth.

Finally, Marshall let go of Doc's throat and backed away. Doc gasped for air and rubbed his neck.

Marshall pointed his gun at Doc's face, gripping the handle, and placed his finger on the trigger.

CHAPTER 58

Blood splashed against Doc's face, dripping and crawling down the gray cement wall behind him.

Where Marshall's head used to be was now a bloody mess. Exposed bone and strips of skin dangled where his eyes and nose had been. His body fell to its knees briefly before slumping on the floor.

"Freeze!" an agent shouted through his black mask. There were four of them on the large platform in the middle of the deployment center. They gripped weapons resembling the rifles they used back in Denver. In the present. But these were white. Plastic and able to travel through time.

One of Marshall's men fired at the agents and ran for cover. Doc grabbed the weapon out of Marshall's limp hand and ducked behind a cement column, wiping blood off his face. One agent fell backwards, his head exploding and splattering blood over another agent.

The rest of us scattered. Bullets bounced all around, spraying dust and fragments of cement into the air. We barely had time to reach cover before the firefight was over. All the agents were dead. We crawled out from behind barrels and columns that reached up into the darkness above.

"Anyone hit?" Doc yelled out. He gripped the pistol in his one good hand and cautiously shuffled around the perimeter of the room. "Drop it!" he shouted. A vault dweller stood near the bodies of the two others that were with him. He gritted his teeth and gripped his rifle. "Drop the fucking gun," Doc ordered again.

With no further discussion or warning, no more time to let the man contemplate, Doc fired a single bullet into his chest, toppling him in a pile with his dead friends. Vesa ran over to Marshall's body and jerked open the bag that held the mind transfer device.

"Holy shit," she whispered. "It's still charged. I can't believe it." She turned her head to look at me, and then glanced around the room. "Where's your body?"

I scanned the room. Finally, my eyes landed on Ash's hulking form slumped over my own. A large bullet hole sat in the middle of Ash's back.

"Ash!" I ran to him, sliding to my knees. Vesa joined me and we rolled him over. My body, my real body, was uninjured, or at least not injured any more than it already was before the gunfire. Ransom opened his eyes slightly. "Ash. Talk to me." I shook his shoulders and pried his eyelids opened. "Ash!" I shouted. I leaned down to listen to his chest. Ransom groaned and rolled his head from side to side. I started chest compressions, pushing my entire body weight onto Ash. It was like I was pushing on a solid stone statue.

"What ... Where?" Ransom mumbled and managed to lift his hand to his face.

"The bag!" I shouted. "Nanobots. Bring them here." Vesa dug her arms into the bag and fished out a syringe and a vial of nanobots. She plunged the needle into the vial and drew the nanobots into the syringe.

"Here," she said. I stopped my chest compressions to grab the syringe of nanobots. Ransom mumbled softly, cradling his cracked ribs. I jabbed the syringe into Ash's thigh and pressed the plunger down. Ash didn't flinch. I dropped the syringe and continued my attempt to revive him, ignoring the burn of exhaustion spreading through my body.

"I think he is gone," Vesa whispered. I continued pushing on Ash's chest, breathing into his mouth until I was out of breath.

"No," I said. "Just give the nanobots time to work." Sweat pooled on my forehead and dripped down my face.

"Who are *you*?" Doc asked. "Who is this guy?" he shouted across the large deployment center. I looked over my shoulder to see Merit's thin body standing in the darkness.

Vesa felt for a pulse on Ash, but found nothing. "Powell, I am sorry."

"No! The nanobots," I said in between labored breaths.

Emery came and placed a hand on my back. "They aren't a cure-all. Some things you just can't come back from." Blood spread through Ash's clothes, soaking through until my hands pressed into the bloody cloth.

"There's nothing you can do," Vesa said.

I slowly stopped chest compressions and pulled my hands away, now covered in Ash's blood. My arms were tired. My wrists hurt. I looked down at Ash and saw a man with no life left in him.

"What the fuck did you do, Merit?" I asked quietly. I hung my head down and Ransom's long hair dangled in my face. Merit stood still and said nothing. "What the fuck did you do?" I screamed. My words bounced around the large stage in the center of the room.

I scooped a pistol off the ground nearby and charged toward Merit. I gripped the weapon and pulled the chamber back to make sure it was fully loaded.

"Why?" I asked. "Why are you so intent on killing your brother?"

Merit shook his head in denial. "You opened that door. That's what you did, didn't you?" I took a step closer, and he took a step back. "You were too coward to face your brother yourself, so you let them in, hoping they would do the dirty work for you."

Merit hobbled backwards into the wall. He pressed his head flat against the cold cement.

"Whatever you had with your brother, that was your business. You two can deal with each other once I am gone." I pressed the barrel of the pistol hard into Merit's stomach. "But you let them in here." I nodded towards the dead vault dwellers on the floor. "*Ash* is my *friend*!" I said and rammed the gun deeper into Merit's gut until it likely pressed his organs against his spine. "He *saved* me. He saved you down in Buckley when you were too weak to fight for yourself. And you let them come in here. For what?"

Merit stared back at me. His pupils opened large to let in any bit of light in that was in the dark deployment center. He clenched his jaw and pressed his lips together to try and hold back any words.

"You don't understand," Merit whispered. "You *couldn't* understand. You come from a different place. A different time. A time when people just accept that places like this exist. You come from a place where you don't have to fight to survive."

"You don't know a goddamn thing about where I come from!" I growled through clenched teeth.

"I am sorry to all of you!" he said loudly to the rest of the group. "I am sorry, but I couldn't let Ransom wake up. I couldn't give him a chance to come for me. To kill me." Merit looked at me, and his eyes were red and watery. His cheeks were sunken in. "If I was right, I would have been able to get just a fraction of what you all have in your time. Food. Water. Comfort. Shelter. If I was right, I would have saved lives in the long run. I would have found what my father went looking for. I would have found…" Merit dropped his head, pushing his chin into his chest. He let out a deep sigh and looked down at the gun that was still pressed into his stomach.

"But you *weren't* right," I told him. "You went to Buckley and found none of those things. You found something else we have in our time. People corrupted by power. That's what you found in Buckley. That's probably what your father found there too. You led those people right back to the very village you were trying to save. You keep digging yourself deeper and deeper. You would do anything, including killing your own fucking brother, just so no one else would discover just how wrong you were."

I pushed my pistol hard into his stomach one last time before backing away.

"I'm not going to kill you. Your fate should be decided by your brother. He should be the one to decide if you die or if you live to face the people back at your home." I clenched my jaw and fought the urge to shoot Merit for what he did. But I knew what he did to his brother. I knew he had poisoned Ransom's son, left Ransom for dead, and now caused the death of Ransom's friend. I had no right to take Merit's punishment away from Ransom.

"Am I awake?" I whispered to Vesa, turning and pointing at my body sprawled out on the floor.

"Barely," Vesa said.

I stuffed my pistol into my waistband and smacked Ransom across the face. I held my ear near my own mouth, my real mouth, to see if Ransom was still breathing. He was.

"Wake up!" I shouted at him. I shook his body and noticed that he opened his eyes slightly.

"How about the nanobots?" Vesa answered and dug around in the bag.

"No," I said. "Give some to my dad first. I should have some remnant of nanobots in myself from years ago. Get the mind transfer device." Vesa handed a vial of nanobots to Emery and then reached in the bag, pulling out the briefcase-sized object.

It was this device that was supposed to be the catalyst of victory for Vesa and her group. It was supposed to allow them to take over the bodies of those in power, so they could create some sort of change from the inside out. But instead it simply prevented the Ministry of Science from ever learning exactly where I came from. Who I came from. I looked over at my parents. Emery injected Ellis with the nanobots.

I sat down next to my body and moved the device into my lap. The indented handprint on the device was dirty and smeared with dried blood from when Ransom last used it. "Once I do this, put his hand on the device." Vesa nodded.

Then she leaned forward and kissed me. Her fingers wrapped around my head and through my hair. I wished I was in my real body for this. Her lips lingered a moment, soft and warm. Too soon, she pulled back and opened her eyes.

"In case you don't wake up," she said, and smiled.

I smiled back.

Taking my final breath in Ransom's body, I held my hand over the mind transfer device. The box seemed to pull my hand down, like gravity was stronger around it. My hand settled into the indented print, eyes fluttering as the room grew into a bright white, and then there was nothing.

CHAPTER 59

5280
NEW ALCATRAZ

"What now?" Doc asked. He still held his gun on Merit, but he turned his head so he could see what was happening. Merit hung his head down, his hands running over his patchy beard. They were still stained a permanent orange color from digging through the mud of New Alcatraz. His nails were worn down and brittle.

"Is he out?" Doc said loudly. Vesa didn't reply. She was too busy tending to Ransom's limp body. Powell's mind was now lost somewhere inside the machine, floating in an empty black pool. For a brief moment, Vesa thought of the peacefulness that might come with such a place.

"He's out!" Vesa shouted back to Doc, snapping out of her daydream. The others looked around the room. Finn gripped his rifle and swiveled his head around, like a gun turret patrolling a military installation. Cooper stood still, his arms at his sides, and his hand barely holding the pistol that Finn had given him earlier. The three dead agents were still slumped in the center of the deployment center in one big black mound of clothing and armor.

"How are you doing?" Emery whispered to Ellis. They both still held their hands tight against Ellis' arm, trying their best to stem the flow of blood. By now Ellis' entire arm was red, as were Emery's hands. Ellis' face was white, and he shivered slightly.

"I've been better," he said.

"We'll be fine." Emery smiled. "You've got a home to build for me. What will you do first? Get the water flowing? Re-wire the place?"

Ellis smiled back at her. "I think patching the holes in the walls comes first," he said. Emery chuckled. "And then maybe finish building the crib." Her smile faded.

"You know I can't stay," she said. "I have to go back or else they'll come looking for me."

"How will they find you? How will they know where you are? *When* you are?"

"They'll know. They always know. And I can't lead them to you … or the baby." Emery looked over at Powell's body on the floor. It was alive, but not well. Whatever mind rested inside of that body was struggling to hold on. Emery watched Vesa bring the mind transfer device over to Powell.

"Do you really think that's him?" Emery asked Ellis. "Is that really our son?"

"I don't know," Ellis answered. "That's Powell. That's the man who helped me escape New Alcatraz. I know that for sure. But … our son?" Ellis shook his head in confusion.

"I think it's him," Emery said, still watching Vesa prepare Powell's body for whatever would come next. "It's him." She smiled and then looked down at her stomach. "Somewhere. Some time. In another life or something, I went back to the year 2070. I left Buford. Left the both of you there to live out your days. Safe. Together. That's the only way he could be here right now. If I stayed, then he would have been dead long ago."

"And what about you?" Ellis asked. He moved his hand over

Emery's, gripped around his arm. "What happens to you? How will you protect yourself?"

Vesa was whispering to Ransom now, wiping his hand clean before she placed it on the mind transfer device.

"I just will," Emery said and looked back at Ellis. "I just will."

"And if you don't? I can't let you go."

"You know that's the only way."

Ellis closed his eyes and squeezed them tight. "I just wish there was another way. A way we could all stay together," Ellis said.

"Me too," Emery said. The two leaned in together, keeping their hands wrapped around Ellis' gunshot wound.

In the distance, Vesa pressed the hand of Powell's body against the mind transfer device. Ransom's eyes jolted open and he gasped for air. He raised his hand up to his bicep, where his torturer had cut his brachial artery.

Vesa stared down at Powell. There was nothing. She leaned in and laid her hands on his chest, feeling for a heartbeat or the rise and fall of his chest. She looked for any physical sign of life even though that was not what she cared about most. She needed Powell's mind. His spirit. She needed to know that by barging into his apartment when they first met, she didn't damn him to an eternity of darkness, where his mind floated on endless waves of nothing.

"Powell, please," she whispered close to his ear. "Please be in there." Her soft words drifted from her mouth, more an apology than a plea.

Beneath her fingertips, she felt a change in the rhythm of Powell's heartbeat. She felt something else too. Something she couldn't put into words, except that it was like the feeling of seeing someone and feeling deep down that you have met before. Powell's eyes opened onto Vesa's deep green gaze.

"Did it work?" Powell said in a raspy voice. "Am I me?"

CHAPTER 60

5280
NEW ALCATRAZ

"How do you feel?" It seemed Vesa looked at me differently now that I was back in my own body. She looked at me with relief and longing, whereas before she looked at Ransom like someone would look at the ball on a roulette wheel after they placed their life savings on a single number.

"Like shit," I said. My own voice, my real voice, startled me. I reached my hand to my throat and rubbed my neck. I tried to prop myself up on my elbows, but a sharp pain shot through my arm and my shoulders.

"Your arm," Vesa said and helped lower me back down to the floor. "There's a wound underneath your bicep. It looks fresh. Cauterized. And it looks like you were stabbed near your collarbone too. You need to take it easy."

"Ransom?" My voice was gruff, and my lips were dry and cracked.

"He's awake. He's doing better than you are, but he's still kind of out of it. He comes in and out of consciousness."

"My parents?" I asked and turned my head around as much as I could.

"Parents?" Vesa asked.

"Ellis and Emery."

"They're your parents? But your parents ... you said..."

"They were dead when I first met you," I grumbled. "But they were alive in the past." I tried a second time to prop myself up on my elbows. This time it worked, and I could sit up. Vesa wrapped her arms around me to support whatever weight I couldn't hold on my own. "They've been here before. They knew their way around this facility. It's all I could come up with."

I turned to see Ransom propped against one of the towering gray columns that supported the ceiling of the deployment center, however high up that ceiling was.

"Get everyone together. Bring them here. We have to keep moving." I kept my breathing shallow to prevent my lungs from pushing my ribs out. Vesa left my side to gather the others. Doc stood in the distance with his gun still pointed at a defeated Merit.

"Powell?" I heard my father's voice to my side. Ellis walked towards me, his hand still clamped around his shot arm. Emery walked beside him. "Is it you?" Ellis asked.

I nodded slightly, the only bit of movement my body could stand.

"Are you okay?" I asked them, concerned about my father's gunshot wound.

"I think I'll make it," Ellis said. Emery smiled and looked at him. "I never got to thank you, Powell. The *real* you," Ellis said and knelt to look me in the eyes. "What you did in New Alcatraz back then, sacrificing yourself so that I could escape."

"I made it out after all, though," I said in a gruff whisper.

"But you didn't know you would." Ellis placed a hand on my shoulder. I remembered how his hands had always seemed so large to me as a child. They were large now, but still nimble.

"I knew I would make it out in one form or another," I said and nodded at Emery's stomach. "The years before New Alcatraz were much more important than any that would come after. I knew if you made it back, then I would be able to see you again, in Buford." Ellis squeezed my arm and pressed his eyes closed. "You were a good father," I told Ellis.

I remembered him teaching me how to hunt and forage for food. He taught me the basics of electrical systems, starting me down the path of becoming an engineer. I remembered the story he told me about my mom, how she died during childbirth. But that was a lie. She had to leave us so the Ministry of Science wouldn't find me or Ellis back in Buford. Then I remembered my father dying.

I remembered how he deteriorated. His hair fell out and his skin turned an ashy gray color. He slept more and more until he finally died quietly in his sleep. I remembered having to bury him. As a child, I'd just wished that we had more time together. Maybe a week. Maybe a year. Just more time.

More time…

"More time," I said to myself and for the first time since I had switched into my own body my voice had some force behind it. "Emery, can you grab that bag over there?" I pointed at the bag containing the medicines.

Emery jogged over to the bag and brought it back. I winced at the pain lancing through my body. Forgetting that my hand was missing two fingers, I tried to grip the bag with my bad hand. With my good hand, I reached in and fished out a handful of syringes.

"Nanobots?" Ellis asked.

"Dad, you die too soon."

"He dies?" Emery asked. "When? How?"

"When I am twelve years old."

"Twelve?" Emery gasped. She turned her gaze on Ellis. "Did you know about this?"

Nodding, Ellis said, "He told me just a little bit ago."

"What do you do? How do you survive?" Emery asked me.

"Dad sends me to an orphanage in Ashton," I answered.

"Ashton?" Ellis said and looked over at Emery. Emery smiled at the thought of Ashton. It was the place my mother and father had officially met for the first time. It was the base their rebel group operated. Where they had built a time movement device. Where Dad was arrested. "How did you get there?" Emery asked me.

"Walked."

"Walked!" Emery said

"That's not the point. The point is none of that needs to happen." I smiled at the thought of saving my father again. Or at least giving him more time. "He dies from radiation poisoning. All of the jumps through time catch up to him." I held out the syringes of nanobots. Ellis and Emery looked down at the thick gray liquid swilling about inside.

"I already gave him some," Emery said.

"Take more," I said and pushed the vials of nanobots at Emery.

"What about everyone else?" Ellis asked. "Everyone here needs a dose."

"There's enough to go around."

"How long will this keep me alive?" Ellis asked, reaching his good arm out to the syringes."

"I don't think anyone really knows. But it will be longer than you had when I was a child."

"I don't know what to say," Ellis stammered and held the syringes tightly in his hand.

"Dad," I said, "you staying alive will help me too." I looked over at my mom. "At least some version of me. Whatever version of me you are carrying right now. That version will benefit from these nanobots. He'll have more time with you than I did."

Emery nodded and placed her hand on Ellis' back. "Go ahead," she told him. "Listen to your son." She smiled and grasped my hand in hers. We huddled together as a family, in the only moment I had ever spent with both my mother and father at the same time.

CHAPTER 61

Vesa approached me and my parents slowly, trying her best not to interrupt whatever family discussion was taking place. "Ransom is waking up now. He's asking a lot of questions. I think you need to talk to him. He doesn't know any of us."

"He doesn't know me either," I said.

"Well, he knows you more than any of us." Vesa stepped towards me and braced my body, ducking under my arm. My mom supported me from the other side so only the slightest weight was placed on my legs.

A sharp explosion rang out across the room. Vesa let go of me and stepped away. She gripped her pistol in both hands, training it on the time movement device.

Five TAA agents stood in the middle of the large stage, holding white plastic rifles. Finn shot a bullet straight through the chest of one agent, spraying blood out of his black uniform. Two other agents stumbled over the bodies of their fallen comrades.

Doc spun and fired three rounds at the four men. Rapid gunshots rang out inside the cavernous deployment center, and the agents' boots pounded on the ground as they ran for cover. Finn, Vesa, and Doc all peered around from rapidly-sought cover and fired single precise rounds at the three remaining agents.

"By order of the Time Anomaly Agency," one of the agents shouted through his black armored face mask, "put your weapons down!"

Doc reached his one good hand around a large cement column and fired at the guard yelling for our surrender. I spun my head around the room to see my mom and dad huddled behind the time movement device's control panel.

Ducking to avoid Doc's bullet, the agent said, "You are charged with the illegal use of a time movement device!" His back was pressed tightly against a column on the other side of the room. From my position, I saw that his thigh was bleeding and he was trying to tie something around his leg to stop it. "If you surrender now, you will not be harmed!" The slightest bit of pain crept into his voice as he cinched his tourniquet tighter.

I crawled on my stomach towards a stack of large drums. Once behind cover, I glanced around the room. Doc fired in the guard's direction, distracting him while Finn crouched low and approached from the side.

Ransom sat on the ground with his back against one side of the time movement device. Underneath the thick beard, I saw a white face, like he had just awoken from a horrible nightmare. His chest heaved up and down with great speed, and he wrapped his arms around his body, like he was trying to keep his body from going anywhere else.

"If you do not surrender," the guard continued, "more guards will arrive. We have tapped into your wormhole and we are holding it open on our end. There is nothing you can do. You are trapped!" Towards the back of the deployment center, another agent darted out from cover and slid behind a column, making his way closer to Doc. Vesa fired towards the guard, but he was too quick. Her bullet pinged against some solid surface deep in the dark corner of the deployment center.

Vesa ducked back behind her cover just as the third agent fired in her direction. The bullets chipped away chunks of the cement column Vesa hid behind. One second slower, and she would be dead.

With the agent's position exposed, Finn fired. Two bullets sank into the agent's chest and neck. He choked and gurgled on his own blood as it pooled inside his throat, collapsing to the floor with a loud thud. The injured agent fired three rounds in Finn's direction.

Now Vesa and Doc emerged from cover, both firing shots at the already-injured agent. With him down, Vesa moved quickly towards Finn's location. Doc crouched low and made a beeline for the agent, alternating his aim between the two men. The agent that yelled for our surrender was cornered on each side. He pushed his body against the cement column, like he hoped to simply be absorbed by the hard surface. Like if he pushed hard enough, the two objects could become one. But he could not merge with the cement column, and a stream of bullets entered his body.

Bright flashes burst from the darkness as the last agent fired whatever remaining bullets he had. I ducked my head as the bullets bounced around the deployment center, and then abruptly stopped.

The smell of gunpowder filled the air, and cement dust drifted in and out of the streams of light.

"Anyone hurt?" Doc yelled out. His voice sounded far away, like he was shouting down at us in a deep canyon. I turned first to find my parents, still huddled together behind the control panel.

"I'm good!" Finn shouted from the darkness. He emerged from a distant corner, the slide on his gun pulled back and locked in place. "I'm out of bullets though. A little longer and we would have been sitting ducks."

Vesa was already making her way towards me. "That was close," she said and shook her head. "Can they do that? Hold a wormhole open like that? Was he telling the truth?"

"It's possible," Emery said. "Either side can hold the wormhole open, it's just that usually no one on the other end knows it's there. And even if they did, they wouldn't have the available technology to hold it open."

"So, we opened a wormhole in the only place where the Ministry could tell it was there *and* hold it open?" Vesa rolled her eyes.

I made it to my feet, but my legs were weak. My muscles were sore, like Ransom had stayed tense for the entire time he was in my body.

"We had no choice," I said. "It's where you were. It's where Ransom was." I stepped slowly towards Ransom, who was still huddled on the floor with his back pressed against the large stage of the time movement device. I braced myself against the stage and slowly lowered myself to the floor. He was a man I hardly knew, but our lives were intertwined. Our minds were interconnected.

"Are you okay?" I asked him. Ransom looked at me. His eyes drifted up and down, taking in every feature of the body he had inhabited for days. His eyes lingered on my maimed hand, and he balled his own hand into a fist as if to make sure his fingers were still in place.

"I … I don't know," he managed. His voice was familiar, but it was different as well. He inflected his voice differently. He spoke softer than I did while in his body.

"Your wife and son," I said, and Ransom's eyes widened, "they're safe. Gray is alive."

"I saw them … I think. Did I see them?" I nodded and tried to tell myself that the brief moment of captivity I had endured when I jumped back into my own body gave Ransom a brief respite. My own body mapped out the torture Ransom's mind had endured during our switch. My fingers, the holes where Agent Saunders plunged his knife deep into my collarbone, and the burnt black scar under my arm where they had cut my brachial artery, almost bleeding me to death, were all I had to remind me that the torture occurred. But Ransom had the memories.

"I'm sorry," I told him. "I'm sorry you had to go through what you went through." Ransom looked at the floor and shook his head. His jaw clenched and he swallowed like he had been holding in a large mouthful of bitter medicine forever. "You didn't deserve that."

"No one deserved that," Ransom said. "What kind of place do you come from? What kind of people are you?"

I had nothing to say. Nothing I could say. No excuses or explanations. He was right. What had become of us? "I'm sorry this happened to you."

"I just want to go home," Ransom said. His voice gruff. "See Aurora. Hug Gray. Ash can help me get home. Our fight isn't with these people." He ran his dirty fingers through his hair. His large hands reminded me of my fathers after a long day of working outside in Buford.

"Ransom." I tilted my head to make eye contact with him. His eyes were empty, not focusing on any one thing. "There's something I need to tell you ... Ash..." My eyes watered.

"No," Ransom whispered. Under the beard, I could see his skin turn red. A tear puddled in his eye before running down his cheek, streaking through the layer of dirt that covered his face. "No," he whispered again, this time even softer. His voice caught deep in his throat.

"I'm sorry," I told him. "He's gone."

Ransom shook his head and looked around the room. His eyes fell on Ash's body, a large figure spread out on his back, all life drained from him. Ransom scurried towards the body and lay across Ash, sobbing and repeating the single word—no. I stood as fast as my injuries allowed and made my way to him.

"He came here for you," I said and placed my arm around Ransom's shoulder. I knew so much about him, but had never spoken to him. We shared a bond that no one else in the universe had shared. We were able to truly experience the life of another. "He came here to get you back. To save you. He never hesitated or questioned. He saved you, saved me, down in Buckley. In the armory."

Ransom sat up and wiped the tears from his face. "How did this happen?" he pointed at the gunshot wound on Ash's chest.

"He was shot."

"Shot?" Ransom wrinkled his brow at the word.

"With a gun. The weapons you saw down in Buckley."

"Who did it?" he asked, looking around at the strangers filling the deployment center. Ready to pounce on anyone else that could have been responsible.

"It's hard to say. It was likely the man you knew as Marshall. Or at least one of his men. The men you encountered underground."

"Where are they? Where did they go?" Anger seeped into his bones and beat through his body.

"Dead," I answered. "They were all shot too. They were locked out of this room while we came to rescue you. The door was barricaded, but when we got back, they were here. They had gotten in."

"How?" Ransom asked. "How did they get in?"

I breathed deep and sighed loudly. I knew this moment would come. The moment when Ransom remembered what his own brother had done. Poisoned his son. Left Ransom for dead. And now he was the one who had let in Ash's murderers.

"Merit." Ransom's eyes changed. They pierced me.

"Merit," Ransom mumbled and pressed his lips tightly together.

He stood quickly and scanned the room. I tried my best to stand, to stop Ransom from charging at his brother.

"Wait!" I pleaded with him. Even in normal health, I could not have stopped Ransom from getting to his brother. "Ransom, wait." I held my hand out.

But he had already spotted him, across the deployment center. Doc had returned to his post, holding his gun on Merit. Ransom marched towards his brother, fists clenched, chest puffed out. I watched as Ransom stepped towards Merit. I watched a body that, just moments before, had acted differently. Acted like me. But now he was filled with the stresses of torture. The maddening lack of information of how his wife and son were doing. Now I saw this body inhabited with the days of journeying to Buckley, the betrayal by his own brother, the memory of facing his own mortality as he was locked in the armory underneath Buckley Air Force Base.

"Ransom, no," Merit stammered and held his hands in front of his face. "No Ransom. Wait."

Doc moved away and lowered his gun, stepping away from whatever conflict the two men had.

Ransom pulled his arm back and drove his fist into Merit's face with a loud smack. The sound echoed through the room as we watched Ransom follow up his first blow with another and another, until Merit dropped to the ground. Blood streamed from Merit's mouth and nose, and his screams of pain turned to gargled choking sounds.

Vesa looked at me like it was my job to step in. Maybe she was right. I was the only one left who remotely knew these two. I stepped towards Ransom and hesitantly placed a hand on his shoulder.

"Ransom," I said. "Stop." I motioned to Doc for help and the two of us pulled Ransom back. "Enough," I said as we dragged him farther and farther away from his bloodied brother.

"I will fucking kill you, Merit! These people won't be around forever!"

"Listen to me!" I shouted in Ransom's face. "You need to think this through. Listen. You kill him and then what?" I asked.

"Then I go home to my wife and son," Ransom said.

"And you're left with whatever hatred you have for him. It'll be stuck in you. Trapped forever. And this anger you have for your brother will just eat away inside you like acid."

"What's acid?" Ransom mumbled.

"Never mind," I said. "Being angry at Merit is like grabbing a hot coal to throw at him. You are the one who gets burned."

"He needs to pay for what he did," Ransom said, jaw clenched.

"He will," I said. "He is."

Vesa stood over Merit's body. He was unconscious, and blood oozed from his nose, mouth, and left eye. "He is out." Vesa said to no one in particular.

"Ransom, look at me." He still stared at Merit's limp body. "Hey!" I said and snapped my fingers in his face. "Look. Everyone needs to get out of here. You need to leave and the rest of us need to find a way home. After that, you can do whatever you want with your brother. But the longer we wait around, the more likely it is that more agents with guns will come here."

Ransom didn't respond. His hands were cut. His knuckles covered in blood, both his own and Merit's. His chest heaved up and down, and his eyes stayed locked on his brother.

"Watch him," I said to Doc. "More agents are going to come through that wormhole and we can't hang around for that." I turned to my mom. "Please tell me we can redirect the wormhole even if they are holding it open on the other side?"

CHAPTER 62

"It's tricky," Emery said. "They're using a lot of energy on their end to hold this wormhole open." She looked at Ellis. Both of them worked in this field. But neither of them had built the device. They weren't the team that worked out the formulas. They only *used* the device, and knew just enough to not collapse space-time on itself. "It's..." Emery trailed off.

"We don't know," Ellis interrupted. "You can try to dial in another time, but we can't say what will happen. You may go to that time. You may go straight back to the year 2075 and materialize right in front of a group of armed federal agents."

"Or maybe," my mom interjected, "maybe the wormhole they're holding open gets redirected to wherever you open the new one."

"Or maybe this entire place evaporates to nothing." Doc stepped forward, leaving Merit's beaten and unconscious body on the floor. Ransom had walked off, pacing around the time movement device. Like he was getting himself used to his own body again. How it walked. How it breathed. How his eyes blinked and his heart beat. "Maybe it implodes and we're all lost in some non-existent state." Doc looked at his allies from the old motel.

I'd had time to adjust since Doc and I last saw each other. I'd had time to recuperate. I'd travelled to New Alcatraz and spent days there. Resting. Eating. But to Doc, he'd broken into Buckley Air Force Base *yesterday*. He'd lost Whitman maybe half a day ago. He'd survived the TAA's ambush at the old motel only hours ago. He was shot and beaten. Suffering from several losses. His mind wasn't in a place to accept anything complex.

"We have no choice," Vesa said to him. "We can't stay here. First, they sent four agents. They killed one of us." Vesa pointed at Ash's hulking dead body on the ground. "They didn't bring us back. They didn't even come back themselves. So they sent five agents. Now *they're* dead." Vesa now pointed all around the deployment center.

It was filled with bodies. Ash was dead. Merit was almost dead. The bodies of nine agents filled with bullet holes were scattered in the dark corners of the cavernous room. Marshall, whose head and face were blown apart by the agents' bullets, sat crumpled on the ground. His men lay dead in the distance. Over a dozen bodies in total.

For so long, the Ministry's underground vaults reminded me of large graves, dug out only to house things that no longer had a use. Now, with the bodies lying limp and bleeding on the floor, this vault finally served its purpose.

"How many agents will they send next? They could be here any minute!" Vesa continued, her plea echoing around the room. "We have to leave this place. This time. We have to go." She turned to look at me.

"Everyone has to leave here," I agreed. "You have to go back to Buford." I turned to my parents. By now, the color had returned to my dad's face.

"And you?" she asked. "Will you come?"

I shook my head. "No. No, I can't go with you. I don't know how that would change things. How it would change how your son grows up. Plus, it would be too weird, seeing me as a baby. Seeing me grow up. Too much could go wrong there." I smiled at the thought of me and my father in Buford.

"Vesa," I said, "can you help me to the control panel?" Vesa came and scooped her body under my arm, supporting my weight.

"Let me help you," my mom said. She wrapped her arm around the other side of me, and the three of us walked slowly to the control panel. My dad followed.

"Mom," I said and turned to look her in the eyes, "do you know why I came to New Alcatraz in the first place? What I was accused of doing?"

"Murder," she said. The two women leaned me against the control panel. Finn and Doc kept their weapons trained on the large stage.

"That's not important now," my father interrupted.

"It's important," I said to my dad. "Her sacrifice. For both of us."

"No!" my father said sternly. "She doesn't need to hear this!" Ellis looked at me like he did back when I first met him in New Alcatraz, back before he knew who I was, and who he was to me. His harsh tone reminded me of his drive to escape this place and return to Emery. It reminded me that he would do anything to protect her. "You don't get to decide this," he said and shook his head.

"It's okay," Emery said and stepped between us. "I know what has to be done. I know what Powell has to do. What he already has done. And when the time comes, I will be happy to do what is necessary.

Emery blinked quickly, fighting back tears. She wrapped her arms around me and squeezed my broken body. I thought back to the time we first met in Phoenix. We stood in the middle of the abandoned warehouse on the outskirts of town.

Now we stood in the middle of another abandoned place. My face pressing against her shoulder. My cut face sticking to her clothes and leaving traces of my blood.

"Sorry," I said and wiped at her shoulder. "My blood ... it's on your clothes."

Emery smiled. "It's okay," she said. "I don't mind."

"My blood..." I said to myself. "My blood." I had nearly forgotten. "Doc! Can you bring me that bag?"

Doc scooped the bag up from the ground and brought it to me.

"Maybe things can be different this time," I said and dug through the bag, brushing aside medicines and syringes filled with nanobots. There at the bottom was the vial marked 'Serum 4381.' "What if the Ministry couldn't know how long you stayed in the past. How long you stayed in Buford?"

"Then I could stay for as long as I wanted ... to a point. I couldn't come back looking like an old lady."

"But you could come and go as you pleased. Back and forth without them knowing."

"Powell, you're talking about Dark Time. There's no cure. We worked on it in Ashton, but they raided the orphanage. We failed."

"*You* failed," I said. "*They* didn't." I pointed at Vesa and Doc. "Their group finished what you started. They found a cure. Whitman." I looked at Vesa. Her eyes darted back and forth, running through the events of the last few years and the last few days.

"Whitman!" she said. A smile grew across her face.

"They found a cure for Dark Time, and they stored it in an android named Whitman. Whitman was stored *here,* underneath the Denver Airport."

"And?" Ellis said.

"And before I escaped New Alcatraz five years ago, I injected myself with his serum. I needed the nanobots to protect me from the radiation."

"So that means..." Emery trailed off, looking at the vial in my hand. "Your blood contains the cure for Dark Time?"

CHAPTER 63

"Take it," I said to my mom. "Take it with you. Find them." I pointed to Vesa, Doc, Cooper, and Finn. "They can help duplicate it. Make more doses."

"And each time I come back from Buford?" Emery said with a smile.

"The Ministry will never know how long you were gone. You can come and go as you please. Spend time with Dad and me," I said, matching my mom's smile, but quickly letting it fade. "Well ... spend time with your son. Not *me*. But you know what I mean."

"It's you," Emery said and wrapped her hand around my face. "To me it will be you. You're my son."

My life, the other version of our life, was the only one I would ever know, but at least some version of me would benefit.

I ran my bloody hands over the control panel and dialed in the year 2036. The latitude and longitude for Buford.

"Hurry," I said. "Before anyone else comes through here." I pushed the final button to start the time movement device. Finn dragged the last of the dead agents from the stage. The pistons started to crank up and down, pushing gusts of air around the dark room and blowing our hair in our faces.

"Thank you," my mom said. She brushed her hand across my face. "You're a good man." She smiled and walked towards the stage, leaving me and Ellis alone by the control panel.

"Come with us, Powell," my father said. "I let you send me away from this place once already. I can't let you do it again." Ellis held his arm against his body. The scar over his eye from when I hit him with a rock during our first encounter in New Alcatraz had barely healed.

"When I was a kid, you told me that time isn't a straight line. It twists around on itself and sometimes ties itself into a knot. Well, I think I am at the center of that knot right now. My life has been settled, but not for you. Not for Mom. And not for your son." The pistons pumped at full speed. "You better get moving." I motioned at the stage.

"What will happen to you?"

"I don't know," I answered. "But isn't that half the fun?" We both smiled at each other, then he wrapped his arms around me.

"I'm gonna miss you, son."

"Me too, Dad. Me too."

We let go of each other. My dad jogged to the stage and climbed the steps. He stood next to my mom and grabbed her hand in his. I smiled and waved as the air rushed around us and my parents blinked in and out of sight. Even though I knew they wouldn't hear me over the noise of the machine, I told them I loved them. And then they vanished forever.

CHAPTER 64

I stared at the empty stage. As the pistons slowed to a halt, the idea that I would never see my mother or father again sunk deep into my stomach. My body wavered back and forth, and I fought back tears in my eyes.

Placing her hand on my shoulder, Vesa asked, "Do you think they made it?"

"What do you mean?" I asked but kept my eyes focused on the stage. This device had become so many things to me over a short amount of time. First, it was my executioner, condemning me to a death in New Alcatraz. Later it became my savior, giving me a chance to escape prison and stop the murder that sent me down this path. Just hours ago, this time movement device was my portal to break my friends out of prison. It was my only way to get my body back, to get Ransom his life back. Now, it was a force that separated me from the only family I had ever known. I wiped away the tears that had puddled in my eyes.

"Do you think they made it to 2036?" Vesa asked. "Or do you think they ended up in 2075, where the Time Anomaly Agents are waiting?"

Shaking my head, shaking any thought that I had sent them right to the same people I had just escaped from, I said, "I'll never know."

"I'm sorry," Vesa said and wrapped her arms around me. "What you did … it was nice. To give them a chance at a better life." She let go of me and kissed me on the cheek. "I think I liked Ransom's face better." She smiled. "Rugged is one thing, but what you've got here it's … too much."

I tried my best to contort my face into a smile. "At least *my* face will heal. Yours is permanent."

"Oooooo. Ouch. That hurts Powell. Hey, since when did you become such a philosopher?"

"What?" I asked.

"Yeah, that stuff you told Ransom. 'Anger is like holding a burning coal…'" Vesa wrinkled her brow.

"Oh, that," I said. "Buddha."

"I didn't think you were religious."

"I'm not, but if I had to choose one…"

Vesa smiled and turned back to the rest of the group. "We need to go. We can't stay here any longer." She walked towards the control panel. "Cooper. Doc. Finn. Get on the stage."

The three men cautiously walked up the steps to the center of the stage. The floors and walls of the deployment center were cracked. This place wouldn't last much longer.

"Wait!" I said, hobbling towards the bag I had brought with me. I fished around inside and withdrew a handful of vials filled with nanobots. "Nanobots!" I said. "For the radiation." I pulled my body towards the stage, and the three men stepped down to meet me halfway. I handed them all a vial and a syringe. "Draw in as much as you can. You'll have taken three jumps in time, so you need as much protection as you can get."

"What if I take too much?" Doc asked. Finn jabbed his syringe into his arm without question.

"Too much?" Finn said. "Is there such a thing? Would you rather die of radiation poisoning?"

"Finn's right," Vesa said. "It can't be worse than the alternative." I handed a syringe to Vesa. She pulled the gray liquid in the syringe and injected herself in her arm. Doc looked at the thick liquid and squinted his eyes, like he was trying to find something hidden inside. Cooper injected himself.

"Well, if anything happens to me, I'm coming after you first," Doc said with a grin and jammed the large needle into his arm.

"No, you won't," I said.

"Huh?"

"You won't come after me. I'm not going. At least not where you're going."

"What?" Vesa asked. "You have to come. What else are you going to do? Where else would you go?"

"Right here," I answered. "Just a few thousand years in the past. I can't let those agents keep coming here. I can't let Ransom's village get invaded by agents. For the first time, we have an open door right to the heart of the Ministry. We can take them out ... at least some of them. Plus, you just injected yourself with the last dose of nanobots." Vesa's face dropped.

"Take them out?" Doc said. "I like the sound of that. Let us help you."

"No," I said. "I'll use the time movement device to go back to 2075. Ambush them."

"Ambush them?" Vesa scoffed. "There's going to be dozens of agents in that room. You'll take out two or three, *if* you're lucky."

"No." I pointed behind the time movement device. "Just over there, not *here*, but in the year 2075, is a drum of liquid sodium. Highly explosive. One shot to that and normally it would just cause an average-sized explosion, but … well, if they *are* holding a wormhole open on their end, there will be a disruption so large that, I imagine, the entire place will collapse on itself. No more deployment center. No more time movement device. No more underground vault. And no more androids housed underground."

"No androids?" Vesa said. "As in no more vessels for the Ministry officials to house their genetic makeup in? No more Project Blue Brain?"

"No shit?" Doc said.

"Yup," I said.

"What about the gun?" he asked. "It's metal."

"Not theirs." I pointed at the white rifles the TAA agents from the future had brought with them.

"That's pretty gutsy of you." Doc slapped my back, his hand pushing a wave of pain through my beaten body. "Sorry." Doc reached in his pocket, and pulled out a hand-rolled cigarette. He lit the end, and through clenched lips, he said, "I'm damned proud to have met you, Powell. I gotta admit, I was kind of skeptical of you when you showed up at the motel with Vesa." Doc's eyes closed ever so briefly at the mention of the old motel. I imagined his mind drifted back to the firefight there earlier and the deaths of his friends. "But now, I'm glad she dragged your ass there. Good luck to you. I hope you take out as many of those fuckers as you can."

Doc stuck his hand out, the hand with the hole in the middle. I reached out and shook it with my hand that was missing two fingers. He took a long drag of his cigarette. As he turned around to walk towards the time movement device a puff of smoke wafted around his head.

"But—" Vesa started, then she stopped. She knew it was the best chance to finally deal a fatal blow to the Ministry of Science. To Wayfield Industries. To the Technology Development and Time

Anomaly Agencies. "Doc's wrong. I shouldn't have barged into your apartment that night. You didn't ask for any of this."

"You coming to my place that night was the best thing that happened to me. You brought me to Buckley, back to my parents. You made it possible for me to give my parents a chance at a better life. A chance for me to have a better life."

"Hey!" Finn yelled from the stage, still gripping an old-fashioned metal rifle in his hands. "Are we going or what?"

"Just a second," Vesa yelled back. "And you better leave *that* rifle behind unless you want it growing through your stomach back in 2075." Finn wrinkled his brow and dropped the rifle on the hard ground away from the large stage. Doc chuckled, still holding his cigarette in his lips.

"I want you to do something for me," I said to Vesa.

"Anything," she said and ran her hand down my body until it met my hand. She gripped it softly and brought it towards her.

"I want you to find me," I said. "When you get back to 2075."

"You?" Vesa asked.

"Powell. Not me. If everything went as planned, I just sent my parents back to Buford. To the year 2036. My mom is going to give birth to a son. I want you to find him." Vesa's eyes watered and she tightened her grip around my hand. "Check in on him. Make sure his life turned out okay. Tell him what I did. How he got where he is. Tell him that for everything that begins something else must end. That nothing is created without something else being destroyed. Tell him life is for the living."

Wrapping her arms around me and pressing her head into my shoulder, Vesa said, "I will. I promise."

We stood in the middle of the cavernous deployment center for what seemed like forever. Everything around us disappeared. The time movement device and control panel. The bodies, both alive and dead.

The cement fell away, and I imagined we were standing in an open field. The prairies of Wyoming. I could almost feel the wind blow against our bodies.

"I am going to miss you," she whispered, still hugging me. I felt her heart beat against my chest and her breath drift over my neck.

"Me too," I said. I pulled back from her and motioned my head towards the large platform where Finn, Cooper, and Doc waited. "It'll be alright," I said. "You need to go."

With tears puddling in her eyes, Vesa nodded slightly and walked towards the stage. I dialed in the year 2075 and the location of the old motel. By now, all the agents would have left, and it was likely burned down. But it was a safe place to send them.

The pistons churned up and down, picking up speed and pushing air around the large room. Vesa stood between her real brother and Doc, wiping tears from her face. Doc, in a sign of forgiveness, slung his arm around Vesa and pulled her into him. This was how I'd remember them. Smiling and waving. Safe. The pistons reached their fastest speed and then they were gone.

CHAPTER 65

"Ransom!" I said loudly, swallowing a large lump down my throat, staring at the spot where Vesa was just moments ago. "How are you feeling?" I asked him.

Walking out of the darkness, Ransom came into view and said, "Feeling? I don't really know." He ran his hands through his hair and patted his body. "It's … strange."

"I know," I said. "But are you hurt? Can you walk back to your village?"

Bending his knees to test their readiness, he said, "I think."

"Okay, well you should—"

More agents appeared on the large stage, arriving from the year 2075. But this time, they gave no orders. They opened fire. I counted five of them before raising the pistol in my hand and firing all of my bullets in their direction. At the same time, I ducked behind the control panel. Their bullets pinged around in the dark.

"Get down!" I yelled at Ransom.

Merit still lay down half-awake, slumped against the wall behind the control panel. Two agents fell to their knees as my stream of sporadic bullets passed through them.

"Fuck," I mumbled to myself, as I felt a familiar thick liquid running under my clothes and dripping down, pooling in my lap. It was my stomach. At least one bullet hole. My head spun and my vision blurred.

The deafening sound of gunfire subsided. I had to find a gun and return fire before the agents scattered, and took cover throughout the deployment center. One of Marshall's vault-dwelling minions lay near Merit's body, a rifle was buried under him.

I crawled, fighting through the pain, and moved the man's body off the rifle. Pulling the slide back and dropping a round into the chamber, I spun my body around, my back pressed against the hard cement wall, and pulled the trigger. Large-caliber rounds flew towards the stage, sinking into the bodies of the agents as they fled in all directions. Some of them fell down, lifeless before they hit the floor. Others stumbled as the bullets ripped through their legs. One agent screamed and wrapped his hand around his neck just before collapsing in a puddle of his own blood.

I quickly expended all of the bullets in the rifle. One agent crept out from his cover, rifle pointed at me. I crawled out from behind the control panel, blood streaking behind my body, leaving a crimson trail on the gray cement. By now, I felt the blood leaking out of my mouth. One more agent came from the darkness, pushing Ransom in front of him. He pointed his white plastic rifle at Ransom's back.

"Where are the others?" the agent asked through his face mask.

"Gone," was all I could say.

"By order of the Ministry of Science and the Time Anomaly Agency, I hereby charge you both with crimes against humanity." Ransom held his face still, a resigned expression etched into the lines.

"Humanity." I scoffed, blood splashing out of my mouth. "You think what you do is humane?" I managed to sit up and press my hand hard against my gunshot.

"We have been given the authority to carry out your punishment on the spot. Death."

"I really wanted to see what happened," I said.

As I swallowed a mouthful of blood, a large shot rang out and the agent behind Ransom stumbled backwards, falling to the ground. I ducked and lay flat on the floor just as a second shot rang through the large facility. The other agent's body sat limp on the floor. As fast as my body would allow, I turned around to see Merit holding a pistol.

Emerging from cover, Ransom said, "Merit! How did you know how to use that thing?"

Pointing the barrel of the gun in my direction, Merit said, "He showed me."

"Put the gun down, Merit," I said. My voice was growing weaker by the minute. My head felt light.

"I didn't mean any of this to happen," he said to Ransom. "You have to believe me. I didn't know what Tannyn did until after it was done. I never meant to hurt Gray. But we *needed* to find this place. If nothing else, to learn that there is nothing of value out here. At least to know what dangers are out here. To prepare ourselves. Protect ourselves."

"I'm not having this conversation with you again, Merit." Ransom stepped forward, ignoring the pistol in his brother's hand.

"You and Dad both left the village to preserve what you had. What you *still* have. A family. I'm not going to hurt you. I was stupid. Crazed. I panicked and stabbed you. I'm sorry." Merit's face was swollen from Ransom's beating. The swollen lumps barely moved as he talked, and his words came out garbled and malformed. "Go back to Aurora. To Gray." He dropped the pistol on the floor.

"I can go back, but I don't think I can ever truly return. Not after what I've seen. What I've been through..." He shook his head, looking off as if he was picturing the events of the last few days. "Fuck." He let out a deep sigh. "I saw people who were evil. Pure evil. Look at him." Ransom pointed to me. "That is what they did to me. What I had to endure. All while wondering how my wife and son were. Not knowing if they were alive. Sick. And those people who did this made *these* people"—he pointed to Marshall and his men lying dead on the ground—"look kindhearted by comparison. Let's just say it put things in perspective."

Ransom stepped forwards and kicked the pistol to the side. It slid into the darkness on the outskirts of the deployment center. "I have to learn to deal with what was done to me ... by everyone. You, them. And killing you won't do anything for that ... or so I'm told." Ransom looked at me.

"I can't ... *we* can't ... let ourselves become like these people. It's not acceptable." Ransom looked away. "And I can't do what I have done to you, not again. As much as I want to beat you senseless, it's not right. And I can't just decide to kill you." The last part was a struggle for Ransom. His lips tensed as he spoke, but he meant it. I knew he meant it. After living with his friends and family, I knew Ransom was honest. He meant what he said.

Ransom walked over to Ash's body and knelt beside him. Sighing, he said, "I'm sorry, Ash." He shook his head, trying to make sense of everything. "You were a good friend. A good person." Ransom placed his hand on Ash's chest. "I'm going to miss you, brother." Ransom reached around Ash's thick neck and untied a necklace made of twine and a single colorful stone that was buried inside his shirt. He gripped it tight and stuffed it into his pocket.

Peeling my hand away from my stomach and watching the blood steadily flow down my body, I said, "Ransom, I don't want to rush you, but you gotta get outta here. You can't be here when this place does whatever it's gonna do once I go back to my time. And I don't have much time myself."

Ransom turned to me. "I don't know you." He said it like he should, like we had been through so much together but he had never learned anything about me. "But thank you for what you did. For me. For Gray. I wish I could repay you." He stepped closer to me and reached his hand out, helping me stand.

"Go get me one of those guns," I said, pointing at one of the white plastic rifles the Time Anomaly Agents had brought through the wormhole. "The white one." Ransom hustled over to a pile of dead agents and peeled one of the rifles from some pair of limp hands.

"Okay, now help me over to the control panel," I said. Ransom scooped his body under my arm and hoisted me almost completely off the ground. I leaned my bloody hands on the panel of buttons in front of me, wondering if I would be able to crawl back to the stage. I could barely stand.

"What are you going to do?" Ransom asked.

"I'm going to kill the people who tortured us. If I don't do anything, they will keep coming here. They will find you, your village. I'm going to make it so they can never come here. So they never go anywhere looking for me." I swallowed a mouthful of blood. The metallic taste almost numbed my mouth.

"You are a good man, Ransom," I said, trying to think of something more meaningful to say. Trying to think of some frame of reference that we both could understand. "I know what it is like growing up without a parent." I coughed blood into my hands and wiped it on my sleeve. "But, like your dad, it was for my own good."

Looking past Ransom to Merit, who stood behind his brother, I said, "And I know what it's like to dig yourself deeper and deeper into a hole trying to make a bad plan somehow turn good." Merit blinked, but only one eyelid moved. His other eye was swollen shut, and all of his weight was on his one unbroken leg. "I've been betrayed by friends.

I've been lied to, but sometimes you have to look at the motives behind the betrayal. Sometimes a horrible situation may reveal itself to be something wonderful, given enough time."

Ransom nodded, then looked back at Merit. "Let's go."

Shaking his head, Merit said to me, "Can I go with you?"

"What?" Ransom asked.

"I don't know what those people did to you ... to him. But someone, someone from our time, from our home, needs to do something about it. To punish them. And to make sure they don't come looking for us. I want to help."

Ransom didn't say anything. He just stood and clenched his jaw.

"You can barely walk," Merit said to me.

"Neither can you," I said.

"Maybe together ... you need help getting to that thing." He pointed at the stage. "You need someone else who can shoot a gun. Plus ... I'll just slow you down getting back home," he told Ransom. "You've got a family."

"You're part of it," Ransom said, stepping towards his brother.

"You know what I mean. Aurora. Gray. The village needs you. They look up to you. They all need you to make it back. And from the sounds of what is about to happen here, you need to be able to get out of here fast, not dragging me behind you."

"He's right," I said.

Ransom clenched his fists. His chest moved up and down as he took long, deep breaths. "Okay," he said. "I just wish—"

"I wish a lot of things would have been different too," Merit interrupted. "But this is the life we had. We can't change anything that has happened. Not between us. Not with Dad. Almost anything can be forgiven. All the rest, we just have to live with. Both of us."

Ransom gave a solemn nod and walked towards the door leading out of the deployment center.

When he reached it, he turned around and said, "I love you, Merit. And I was wrong for keeping everyone stuck in our tiny village. You were right that we needed to know what was out there. Now we know."

"That's nice to say, but you don't really believe that," Merit said.

"Not all of it," Ransom said. "But I do love you, brother. I won't tell anyone about Gray."

"Tell them I died saving you. Died protecting the village." Merit's face contorted into what I could only guess was a grin.

"Don't push it." Ransom forced a smile, something that I knew didn't happen often. "I will tell them it was a good death." With that, Ransom walked out the door and raced to the surface, to the frozen deserts of New Alcatraz.

CHAPTER 66

"Merit," I said, my voice was weak, fading with each word. I dialed in the year and location on the control panel. "I'm not going to bother trying to convince you to leave. Cuz I need you."

Nodding, Merit said, "What do you need me to do?"

"Grab another gun, one of the white ones." My head bobbed back and forth, swiveling like a plate spinning on the stick of some street performer. I pounded my fist on the final button, and the pistons at the four corners of the large stage started moving once again. Merit returned, holding a white rifle in his hands.

"You sure you know how to use that?"

"Yeah, pull back on this thing," he said, hovering his finger over the trigger. "Simple."

"Yeah, simple," I said, thinking that such a simple physical act was anything but simple when you were shooting at someone. "Help me to the stage." I nodded my heavy head towards the time movement device. Merit ducked under my arm. Together, we dragged our beaten and broken bodies to the center of this man-made cavern.

The wind kicked up around the stage, tossing tiny bits of cement through the air. Once on the stage, Merit and I collapsed in a pile. Both of us groaning, fighting against our bodies that screamed for us to stop. Begging for us to rest and let our wounds heal. But there was no getting better this time. There was no healing or recovering.

Ever since I was sentenced to New Alcatraz, I wondered what fate had in store for me. And for years since, I'd thought there was no fate. I thought I was stuck in a cycle that some other version of myself had set in motion some infinite number of lives ago. I thought my only choice was to continue on that predetermined path, charging towards whatever destined end was in store. Or else I would disappear. Vanish without ever having truly existed.

But now, I knew that was wrong. I'd found a way to change things. To improve things. A way to stop those that kept me on that path for so many lifetimes.

"When we get there," I said over the humming pistons, "there will be a tank, a large container right there." I pointed to where the tank of liquid sodium would be. It was where my mom got it from in this time for us to use as a weapon in the year 2075. But now that same tank, separated by thousands of years, would become a weapon once more, only this time it would be a deadlier weapon.

This time, the liquid sodium would not only explode, it would react with the energy the Ministry was using to hold their wormhole open. The link they hoped to use to harm us would end up destroying them.

"Shoot that tank!" I shouted over the loud pistons. "Don't shoot at the people, and don't worry about anything else. Just shoot that tank!" Between the two of us, one of our bullets would hit the sodium. I hoped.

"Will it hurt?" Merit asked. "When we go to a different time?" His eyes were wide and his knuckles were white, gripping the rifle.

"No," I said. "It will be over before you know it."

I pushed myself up from off the floor and stood as best I could. I surveyed the drab gray surroundings. I couldn't stop my mind from drifting to the first time I stood on this very stage. A guard had unshackled me and scurried away from the stage, like he was feeding me to some hungry lion. I gave myself four days to live in New Alcatraz, if I was lucky. But I underestimated myself.

This revenge wasn't just for me. Not just for my mom and dad. It was for their friends who died in the raid on Ashton, like Dr. Adler, or my dad's friend, Beckett, who died here in New Alcatraz, beaten and burned by some other prisoner. I could get back at the Ministry of Science and Wayfield Industries for creating a society that would accept this place as just and necessary. For making a society where the lawmakers were the true criminals, and the ones who broke the law, sometimes, were the heroes. I could get revenge for Vesa and Cooper. For Whitman.

The gray-dark deployment center flickered away, and the bright white lights of the newer deployment center of 2075 came into view. I gripped my gun tightly.

"Get ready!" I said to Merit. With each blink of my eyes the deployment center alternated between dilapidated and new, until the bright new deployment center remained and the old, gray, cracked cement of the future was gone forever.

Around the stage were scientists and agents. They circled together, apparently strategizing their next move, deciding how long to wait before sending another wave of faceless agents to kill us. By the control panel were scientists in lab coats, frantically dialing in coordinates and typing commands into a computer, working to keep the wormhole open.

The agents turned their heads in our direction. All of them held the plastic white rifles that could safely travel through time. Merit's mouth hung open. His eyes were wide. This was what he wanted to find. This was what he wanted his dad to find. A place that was alive and of some use to him. He wanted to find bright lights and safety, but instead he found collapsing vaults and cannibals. I knew that he was wishing that everyone from his village could see what he saw.

"The tank!" I yelled.

The deployment center was filled with rapid gunshots. Some mine. Some Merit's. But most of them came from the dozens of agents who filled the room.

The first bullet that hit me was in the shoulder. It pulled my body to the side. Wincing, I readjusted my aim for the tank. Another bullet ripped through my leg, another flew through my back and came out my chest. Through blurred vision, I saw Merit's body jerk as he was hit by the agents' barrage of bullets. But he still stood. He still fired, trying to hit the tank. Trying to take out everyone in this room. Trying to take out everyone in this entire facility. For a moment, I pictured Ransom climbing out of the vault in the future, clawing his way to the surface, and leaving the spot that would likely be a giant sinkhole if we succeeded.

Eventually, my body couldn't stand anymore. I fell to my knees just as a fourth bullet grazed my side, tearing open the skin. Even more than before, the taste of blood flooded into my mouth. I coughed and choked. By now, Merit lay flat on the stage of the deployment center. Unable to hold myself up any longer, I too collapsed face-first into the ground.

The firing diminished. "Hold your fire!" I heard one agent scream. "Jesus fucking Christ! Do you want to bring this whole place down?"

I inched my body forward towards the edge of the stage, making my way to Merit. Blood leaked out of the corner of his mouth. He blinked his eyes slowly. The agents approached. Their boots pounded on the steps to the stage.

"I'm sorry," I said to Merit. I couldn't offer anything else to him.

As I inched closer, the large tank of liquid sodium came into view. It was just off the stage, waiting for me.

"It's beautiful, isn't it?" Merit said, smiling, blood coating his teeth.

"Yes. Yes, it is," I answered, pulling the trigger of my gun, firing a single round at the tank.

Everything turned bright white, and then there was nothing.

CHAPTER 67

2052
BUFORD, WY

The old trading post stood, watching over the three inhabitants of the forgotten town. The sun hovered above the horizon, as if taking in one last look before disappearing for the night. The wind pushed against the trees, swaying a little in the air, leaves rustling and branches snapping. The sounds echoed across the prairie. The smell of burning embers wafted from the wood-burning stove inside the trading post.

"Dinner will be ready in about an hour," Emery said.

She had grown to love the domesticity here in Buford, a welcomed break from her other life in another time. The trading post had become more than just a trading post. Ellis had added to it over the years, and when Powell was old enough to help him, they expanded the structure, building actual bedrooms.

"A teenager can't just live in one room with his parents," Ellis had said when Powell turned thirteen. "You need your own place, where you can think and read without any distractions." Powell didn't complain. He enjoyed building and working with his dad. They always seemed to find projects around Buford that they could tackle together. Now, they sat down around a table they built from scratch.

"So, where have they been sending you?" Ellis asked Emery. He gripped his wife's hand from across the table. Her hands were soft and clean. No ring on her finger to symbolize her marriage. She couldn't let anyone know at her job that she was married. She had to play a role while in the future.

"Well," she said with a smile, "it's more like where am I sending them." She squeezed Ellis' hand. "They promoted me to SES."

"Senior Executive Service?" Ellis marveled.

"Wow, Mom! Congrats!" Powell exclaimed from some corner of their home, wiring an overhead light with old wires he'd scavenged from another part of Buford.

"Yeah, after all these years, they're still talking about how I infiltrated that 'rebel' group in Ashton." Emery rolled her eyes.

"You can thank me for that, you know," Ellis said.

"I know, I know. How could I forget?" The two leaned forward and kissed each other across the table. "So now that I have more freedom to use the time movement device, I can probably come back here more often."

"Not just every three months?" Ellis asked.

"Probably more like every month. Plus, I tell the other agents what times to travel to, which *criminals* to go after." Emery used air quotes when she said the word 'criminals.' "And … I have easier access to these." Emery pulled out two vials of nanobots from her pocket.

"Ugh." Ellis grunted. "I haven't felt sick in a year."

"Yeah, but it's best to be safe. Don't you think?" Emery said, placing the vials on the table in front of Ellis.

"I just hate the feeling of these things when I inject myself."

"Don't be a baby, Dad," Powell said as he walked to the table and sat down. Powell's hair hung down his forehead and rested behind his ear. Like his dad's, his hands showed signs of building and harvesting. He joined the two of them at the dinner table.

"Plus, if I can inject myself after each trip with these things," Emery said, "*and* inject myself with the Dark Time serum, then you can suck it up and suffer through a few more tiny injections." Emery reached across the table and pinched Ellis' cheek like a baby.

Swatting her hand away and rising from the table, Ellis said, "Okay, fine. I'll go get the syringe."

"How have you been, Powell?" Emery asked.

"Fine," Powell said.

"So talkative." Emery brushed her hand on Powell's head, messing up his already matted hair.

"C'mon Mom!" Powell pushed her hand away and tried to fix his hair.

"Oh yeah, that's so much better," Emery joked. She watched her son, looking for some sort of recognition, hoping that maybe something inside of him was a remnant of someone else. But it wasn't. He was just an ordinary boy. *Maybe that's for the best,* she thought. Normal. Ordinary. Maybe that was better than something more complex.

"After dinner, you wanna see what I've been working on?" Powell asked, pointing at some heap of metal and wires.

"Oh, you gotta see it," Ellis said as he returned to the table rubbing the crook of his elbow. "It's impressive." He wrapped his arm around his son and pulled him close.

"Sure," Emery said, smiling and watching her husband and son. "I would love that."

CHAPTER 68

Ransom wiped sweat from his brow. The bright sun burned through the wispy clouds overhead. He slung a pack full of timber over his back and made his way home, crunching orange sand under his feet. It hadn't snowed in a long time. At first, the change in temperature was welcomed by most people in their village, but now, most dreamed of the days of snow and biting winds.

Ransom trudged through the desert, making his way past the huts and animal pens in the village. He walked by a two-story home, the first of its kind. He nodded at other villagers as he passed them, all of them hard at work.

"I got you!" Gray yelled as he rounded the corner of a hut. He held a long branch in his hand, one end pressed into his shoulder and the other end pointing towards another boy. They made loud explosion noises with their mouths, and the other boy fell to the ground, rolling around and clutching his stomach. Gray still pointed his rifle-shaped branch at his friend.

"Hey!" Ransom said, stepping between Gray and the other boy. "Stop that." He grabbed the branches from both boys. "We talked about this, Gray." Ransom knelt down to look his son in the eyes. "You don't play like that."

"I know, Dad," Gray said and looked away. "But we were just—"

"Ah," Ransom interrupted. "I don't want to hear it." Ransom stuffed the branches in his pack with the rest of the timber he chopped down in the forest.

"Okay," Gray said, defeated. "I'm sorry."

"Alright," Ransom said, patting his son on the back. "Now go play." He stood as Gray and the other boy ran off, weaving through the maze of huts in the village. Ransom shook his head, and wondered how much last year's events had really changed everyone. His son. His wife. Himself.

He reached his own home and opened the door. Aurora greeted him with a kiss.

"How was it today?" she asked.

"Hot," Ransom said.

"Hot!" Aurora said, trying to get the word out before Ransom did. "You don't say. Hot. Such a surprise." She smiled and rubbed his back. "Well, drink some water."

Ransom set the wood and his axe down at the door, and sat on his bed. A black rifle was stashed under the bed, the only physical reminder of what had happened here a year ago.

"I caught Gray playing guns in the street," he said in between gulps of warm water.

"We talked to him about that," Aurora said, and shrugged.

Ransom nodded his head at the pile of wood by the door. "They had those branches, shooting at each other." Aurora shook her head and stepped towards Ransom, holding her pregnant belly.

"I hope it's a girl," Ransom said, pulling her closer and resting his head gently on her stomach. "I think a girl would listen to us more."

"Ha! If my mother were here I'm pretty sure she would change your mind about that theory," Aurora said and wrapped her hands around Ransom's head. The two sat silently for a moment, holding each other.

"As long as it's healthy," Ransom whispered, and the two slowly let go of each other. Ransom poured a cup of water, and Aurora reached for a makeshift broom sitting in the corner of the hut.

"You really should get rid of that thing," she said, pointing at the rifle under the bed.

"I don't like it here anymore than you do, but what if they come back? What if we need it?"

"I don't care," Aurora said and sat next to Ransom on the bed. "We got along just fine without it before. We will survive without it now."

"Things are different now," Ransom said. "Things have changed. We can't ignore what's out there. *Who's* out there." He lowered his head and stared at the floor. "We have to be ready if they come again. Our village is growing. Our *family* is growing. More is at stake."

"Their leader died. He's buried out in that large sinkhole in the desert that somehow just appeared out of nowhere … you still never explained how that even happened."

"There's nothing to explain. I don't even know how it happened. It's something Powell and Merit did after I left. Something they did in another time I suppose. But that's what I mean. A year ago, we didn't know about these guns or the vaults. There were none of these machines or even other people. There's more to worry about now."

"One vault is buried and the others lost their leader. The rest of them probably don't even know how to get here," Aurora said and placed her hand on Ransom's leg.

"Leader or no leader, those people are dangerous. It's just a matter of time until they come here. Sometimes I think we should go out and get them first."

"Do you hear yourself?" Aurora said and stood from the bed.

"Now who do you sound like?"

"I know. I know," Ransom said. "I'm sorry. I won't mention it again."

Kneeling down and facing Ransom, Aurora said, "That's the fourth time you've said something like that. Something about going back out there, and it's becoming more and more frequent. I get that you went through a lot. More than I will ever know. But you can't let it change you."

She placed her hand under Ransom's chin and raised his head to face her. Looking in his eyes, she said, "I need you here, Ransom. Gray needs you. Our baby needs you."

"Our daughter?" Ransom smiled.

Grinning, Aurora said, "Sure. But you have to promise me this is the end of it. You won't mention going out there again. Okay?"

A long silence filled the room. Ransom swallowed. He thought about his dad. About his brother. He wondered if they were right all along. He wondered if it was human nature to want to discover the unknown. If the violence he experienced last year was something that would have happened eventually anyway. Fighting, anger, hatred, jealousy, greed. Were these things that would have infected their village sooner or later, even if those men from Buckley hadn't followed him home? Was it pointless to try and go fight them, to try and end those things? Would they just find their way back into his home one way or another? He shook his head rapidly to try and shake those thoughts away.

"I promise," he said, cupping his hands around Aurora's face. "I'm here for you. Here." He pointed at the ground. "I'm never leaving you. I promise." He nudged the black rifle with his heel, pushing it further under the bed. Further out of reach.

CHAPTER 69

"So, then, what is death?" the professor asked, his hands clasped behind him as he paced back and forth.

"Organ failure," a young woman said from the middle of the large auditorium. "No heartbeat. No brainwaves."

"Okay, Miss Edwards has started the ball rolling, but what other forms of death are there? This being a course in robotics and artificial intelligence, try to focus your answers to forms of death that might apply to all people. Humans and android alike."

"Professor Powell?" a man sitting in the back said, raising his hand.

Pointing at the student whose hand was raised, the professor said, "Yes, Mister Lucas."

"In the case of androids, it could be defined as a loss of usefulness."

The student awaited Powell's response. His fingers hovered over his keyboard, poised to type out the answer for later regurgitation.

"Yes, that is one way to define the soul. And Mr. Lucas, can you tell me whose theory of death that is? The loss of usefulness?" The professor paused, but the man had no response. "Anyone?" Silence.

"Aristotle," the professor announced. "He believed that the soul existed when someone reached their potential. In our case, humans, that would be their ability to reason." Powell pointed to his head. "Once a person loses the ability to reason, then Aristotle would say they were dead. That they had lost their soul. Now, we don't know what Aristotle would have thought about androids. So, it is hard to say whether he would have believed that they even have a soul."

"Some atheists give death a fancy name—eternal oblivion." Powell typed the term on his laptop, so the word appeared in large print on the white board behind him. "The idea is based on the belief that there is no afterlife, and that death is defined as the moment when a person simply is no longer self-aware. Perhaps permanently unconscious."

"So, wouldn't that be the proper definition of death for androids?" a third student asked.

"Maybe ... maybe," Powell answered and looked off as if he didn't have any more of an answer than anyone else in the class. "There is another form of death that may apply though. Informational Theoretic Death." Powell let the term sink into the students' brains. He typed the term out, plastering it up in large font on the board.

"This form of death is when the brain is scrambled or distorted so much that it doesn't retain the same properties it did before. It's distorted to the point that there is no recovery. Like an android's hard drive being reformatted. Or a human who suffers some brain trauma, causing their memories to disappear, forcing them to re-learn everything."

"People who subscribe to this theory of death would say a person is dead if their personality, their hopes and dreams, have been destroyed. Or if their past experiences—or at least the memories of those experiences—have disappeared beyond any sort of recovery."

Powell paused to let the students' racing fingers finish typing.

"This definition of death is particularly important to companies that are still perfecting cryogenics, those still hopeful that we could survive, our brains ... our souls, could survive outside our bodies."

Looking at his watch and shutting his laptop, Powell said, "That's all for today. I will post your next assignment on the campus intranet this evening, and I'll see you next week."

Each student gathered their belongings at once, causing the room to rustle and buzz. Separate groups of students broke into conversations, picking up right where they'd left off the moment class began. They flooded into the aisles and walked up the stairs towards the exit. Everyone except one person. A woman clutching the strap of a bag slung over her shoulder. She took each step with excitement and hesitation. Confident and unsure all at once.

Finally reaching the bottom step and approaching Powell, she said, "What do you believe?"

Powell looked up, immediately captured by her green eyes. The woman smiled, slightly crooked. And there was a sense that she was holding back, trying not to smile too big. An attempt to temper her excitement. "Eternal oblivion?" she asked. "Seems pretty ... permanent." She took several steps closer. Her jeans tucked into boots that were laced up to the middle of her shin.

Something inside of Powell seemed to stir. Perhaps he was suffering from *jamais vu*, a sense that a moment is familiar yet unfamiliar. A sense of recognition, yet one knows they have never truly experienced this ... at least not yet.

"What about Buddhists?" She said.

"I'm sorry, I haven't seen you in class before. Did you just transfer?" Powell asked. The woman sensed he was trying to explain the feeling that stirred inside of him.

"I'm just sampling some of the courses here. Considering enrolling."

"Okay, then, Miss..."

"Vesa," she answered. "Just Vesa."

"Okay, Vesa. Buddhists?" Powell asked.

"Yeah, I've always been partial to their teachings out of any of the major religions. I mean if I *had* to choose…"

"Well, they don't believe in anything as permanent as eternal oblivion."

"Yeah, exactly!" Vesa said and laughed. It was a gentle laugh, subdued with a slight hint of nervousness. "In fact, they believe that everything is always in flux. Nothing is permanent."

"Yup, always changing," Powell said, still shoving his belongings into his bag while trying to shake the feeling that he had been here before. That he had met this person before.

An awkward silence fell between them. Powell, *this* Powell, wore glasses, and his sleeves were rolled up to his elbows. Unlike the Powell Vesa knew, this Powell had a scar on his right forearm, and she wondered what the story behind it was. Some adventure or something more mundane. They were different versions of the same person, only this time he'd had different experiences than any version that came before him. He was new. One of a kind. Not just some repeated person with no choice but to follow what was set out for him.

"So … what can I do for you?" he asked. "Or did you just want to discuss Buddhism?"

This was a face Vesa had seen only days ago. Her wounds from the week before had barely healed. She wondered what Powell thought of her, cuts and scrapes on her arms, makeup covering bruises. Her time in Buckley Air Force Base was still on her mind, its aches still in her muscles. In the days following her return, news of the Denver Airport collapsing into an enormous sinkhole was everywhere.

"Vesa?" Powell said.

Shaking her head and snapping herself out of her daydream, Vesa said, "Sorry … it's just … the lecture…"

Powell nodded. "Yes, if you want to discuss it further my office hours should be posted on the student site."

"No," Vesa said. "It's just ... what made you want to teach about life and death? About the soul?"

This made Powell pause. No one had ever asked him this before. "I don't know," he said. "It's just something that's always interested me. Even as a child. Like my curiosity of the subject was just in my brain the whole time, waiting to reveal itself. You ever had anything like that?"

"No..." Vesa smiled. "I can't say that I have, Powell. Would you want to grab a coffee or something to discuss this more? Plus, I'd really like to catch up." Vesa smirked, knowing that this would intrigue Powell, even this version of him.

"I'm sorry?" Powell said. "I don't think we've ever met."

"Well, technically *we* haven't," Vesa said. "But I know you. I knew you." Vesa's eyes pierced through Powell. She knew the curiosity that lived inside of him, any version of him, and that he would agree.

"Okay," Powell said hesitantly. "There's a place on campus." He pointed randomly in the direction of the cafeteria. "But ... I still..."

"Don't worry, Powell." Vesa wrapped her arm around him and ushered him up the auditorium stairs and out into the mid-day heat. "I'll explain everything. Hopefully, just as well as when you first explained it to me."

A message from the author:

I truly hope you enjoyed reading New Alcatraz: Loss Paradox and the New Alcatraz Series. Please reach out to me on Facebook if you want to discuss the series or just want updates on other books I will be releasing. If you have a print version of this book, feel free to pass it on to anyone you think might enjoy the New Alcatraz series. Books are meant to be read, not collect dust on a shelf. Happy reading.

Grant Pies

Made in the USA
Columbia, SC
28 December 2017